D1117492

Paul Charles

was born and raised in the Northern Ireland countryside. He now lives and works in Camden Town, where he divides his time between writing and working in the music industry. The next Paul Charles novel will be the Beatles-themed, *The First Of The True Believers*, with the sixth Christy Kennedy mystery, *I've Heard The Banshees Sing*, following close behind.

First Published in Great Britain in 2001 by
The Do-Not Press Limited
16 The Woodlands
London SE13 6TY

Casebound edition: ISBN 1 899 344 70 5
C-format paperback: ISBN 1 899344 71 3

British Library Cataloguing in Publication Data. A catalogue
record for this book is available from the British Library.

1   3   5   7   9   10   8   6   4   2

Printed and bound in Great Britain by
The Guernsey Press Co Ltd.

The Hissing of the Silent Lonely Room

The fifth Detective Inspector Christy Kennedy Mystery

Paul Charles

For words on words, big thanks to Catherine, Jim and Ciara. For energy and support, thanks to Edwin and Richard. For in the beginning (without whom) thanks to Andy and Cora. For being my best friend and much, much more, thanks to Catherine.

Prologue

TOMORROW WOULD be better.

She promised herself that tomorrow would be better. The children would behave like she dreamed children should behave. No devilment, cute as it was. They'd eat the food she wanted them to, when she asked them to. They wouldn't play with their food and make a mess at the table in her small kitchen. She wouldn't have to shoo them off into the equally small living room, only to find they'd soon be making a mess in there as well.

They weren't all that bad, really. They could be loveable and cute when they wanted to be, even if 'when they wanted to be' always seemed to coincide with when she was telling a visitor how naughty Jens and Holmer were. Then they'd just act as good as gold and the visitor would be thinking, and sometimes even saying, 'Are you sure you're all right on your own?'

Tomorrow would be better because he might come back. He was always saying that they were meant to be together; that they would end up together. The novelty would soon wear off with Droopy Drawers and he'd be back and they'd be a family again. Tomorrow would be better, easier if they were a family again. For heaven's sake, how could a father behave like that? Even apart from the infidelity, she had to admit that she was somewhat disappointed in him as the father of her children. As a father he had responsibilities: morally, legally, emotionally, every way you could think of, and all of them ending in 'ly'. Hell, even her father... She decided that she didn't even want to dwell on thoughts of her father. That was just too painful.

Tomorrow would be better. Some of her songs (works in progress) would resolve themselves; her downstairs neighbour would continue to be as pleasant as he had been recently and maybe her friends would stop wanting too much from her. Tomorrow would be better and the maisonette wouldn't feel so cramped. The smallness of the maisonette really galled her. She was supposed to bring up two children in it, while he lived in their cottage. Her money, her hard-earned money, had paid for the beautiful cottage in the Cotswolds. They'd named it Axis together. *Axis* had been the name of her most successful – both critically and financially – album and it had been his idea to name the cottage after it. Yes, his idea to use *her* title. It was unbearable to think about that now. *Their* cottage, and he was there, in *their* bed, with *her* now.

Tomorrow she would not have these thoughts – thoughts like how firm Droopy Drawers' young body was. Well, it would be, wouldn't it? She was *only* twenty-three years old. Yes, twenty-three. She hadn't had two difficult pregnancies within eighteen months. Everyone knew it was only a matter of time before the infatuation wore off. He was a better catch on paper than he was in bed. She'd found that out to her cost. Sex wasn't everything, but it was something. Something she could happily do without if it meant eventually getting him back, if it meant the children having their father back and if it meant all the bad thoughts she was having would disappear.

Tomorrow would definitely be better, but only if she could manage to get a good night's sleep. She wound herself up so tight these days, it took at least three barbiturates to send her into blissful, painless, trouble-free slumber. He'd found out about the best pills for her. He'd said she needed something to help her unwind so that her sleep would be rewarding and would recharge her batteries.

Yes, tomorrow would be better. The storm blowing outside her window would dispel all the bad clouds. The windows were rattling incessantly in their frames. She hoped they would stop, at least until the pills kicked in and she fell under. She thought she heard her front door open but it was probably just the wind rattling. The storm seemed to be dying down, but she was sure she could hear floorboards creaking. She was wondering about how safe the trees on her beloved Primrose Hill would be against the wild winds when her 'mother's little helpers' at last began to take effect. Now, securely in her blood stream, they were working their magic, transporting her on the fast track to tomorrow.

There was something she needed to do before she surrendered to the drug, something vitally important. She summoned all her physical and mental resources, rose giddily from her bed and made her way through the maze in the general direction of the kitchen. She bumped into several objects on the way. She could hear things fall around her and the sound slowing down, echoing on and on until the sound of another fallen object overtook it. The echoes all seemed to roll into one as she stumbled onwards. She knew she needed to complete her task. If she succeeded, tomorrow could be the beginning of a better time.

Chapter 1

DETECTIVE INSPECTOR Christy Kennedy was prowling up and down the hallway like a bear with a thorn in his paw. Bear-like, he used the back of his hand to knock on the door of the ground-floor flat. There was a sickly-sweet smell wafting around the hallway, even though the hall door was wide open and the cold winter wind was blowing through. The wind could send a shiver down your spine; chill you to your very bone, but it didn't seem able to remove the smell of gas from the house.

The house of death.

'The next-door neighbour, Mrs Mason, says he's still indoors, sir,' Detective Sergeant James Irvine began. 'She says he's regular as clockwork. Says he, Edward Higgins, wakes up at seven-thirty, turns on the radio, Radio Four. She claims she can hear it clearly through their adjoining wall. He leaves the house at eight; goes up to Primrose Hill; buys a copy of the *Telegraph* and picks up a cappuccino and a toasted poppy-seed bagel on the way back. He returns home, reads his paper, drinks his cappuccino, eats his bagel and continues to listen to the radio until ten, at which time…'

'Okay, okay, I get the picture, sergeant,' Kennedy cut in. He was being uncharacteristically short with his trusted bagman, but having seen the scene upstairs, well… he just 'wasn't himself', as his mother might have put it. 'If he's in here let's make a racket until he hears us,' Kennedy said, proceeding to bang on the door with his fist and kick it on every third beat.

Perhaps he was trying to use the noise to dispel the scene he'd witnessed twenty minutes earlier, when he'd walked into the first floor maisonette.

An incident had been reported at 123 Fitzroy Road, literally a two-minute walk from Primrose Hill. Just before 8.00am, the children's nanny, Judy Dillon, had been about to let herself into the first and second-floor maisonette, when she smelled gas. She immediately called the police on her mobile phone. Four minutes later a patrol car pulled up, followed within seconds by a gas company van. The gasman immediately turned off the supply to the entire house. The children's nanny led the police into the flat, automatically opening the first door on the left. As soon as she had looked into the kitchen she screamed like a banshee and immediately collapsed with an almighty thud on to the floor.

Her employer, Esther Bluewood, lay on the kitchen floor.

The first constable on the scene, PC Allaway, felt Esther's throat for a pulse. He evaluated no signs of life and granted the gasman access to the property. The gasman appeared very cool under the circumstances, tugging on a pair of polythene gloves, turning off the gas supply to the cooker before opening all the windows in the flat. Meanwhile, Constable Allaway called in the incident to North Bridge House and about three minutes later the back-up team, including Irvine, began to arrive at the scene.

By the time Kennedy arrived, ten minutes after Irvine, the team was so busy, silently going about their business, they'd failed to notice two children standing outside the kitchen door, staring at their mother's body. Kennedy knew he would never forget the scene for as long as he lived. The boy stood to the right. He wore white pyjama bottoms and a Wallace & Gromit sweatshirt. His long, curly, blonde hair was dishevelled from his recent adventures in dreamland. He was holding, very tightly it appeared, the hand of his sister. She also had a head of blonde, curly hair, was about two-thirds the height of her brother, and dressed in a pair of Winnie the Pooh pyjamas. She was holding her scruffy teddy by its arm. The well-loved and battle-bruised bear was dangling in the air, as lifeless as the body of the woman on the kitchen floor.

As Kennedy climbed the darkened stairwell, the sadness of the silhouette of the two children and the teddy bear hit him with such power that he was momentarily overwhelmed. Images of wasted lives, happy families, laughter-filled rooms, unfulfilled dreams, and broken promises filled his head. He felt his eyes well up and he had to fight back the tears.

Kennedy took a second to compose himself before he proceeded up the stairs, placing a gentle hand on to each of the children's backs. As they turned towards each other and looked over their shoulders at the new presence, the detective said, 'Let's go and find a room of our own.'

The wee girl asked, 'What's wrong with our Mummy?'

The boy asked, 'Why is she sleeping on the floor?'

Kennedy gently broke their clasped hands apart. He had to use a little force, as the boy didn't seem to want to let go of his sister's hand. Kennedy took each of the recently freed little hands and led them up the hallway and away from the death scene. As he did, he nodded to WDC Anne Coles to follow him.

They discovered that the living room too was packed with SoC ('Scene of Crime') investigators. Kennedy noticed a door that seemed to lead to another flat. He took the children through it and up the stairs that led straight to the children's bedroom. The wee girl and boy simultaneously broke free from the detective and sat together on the nearest bed. The boy put his arm around his sister's shoulder and the wee girl hung on to her teddy as if her life depended on it.

She smiled at Kennedy.

Kennedy tried to smile back. He found himself trying to compose what he imagined would look like a smile but because he was so self-conscious of the exercise he felt the grin on his face probably looked hideous.

The boy looked more warily at the policeman.

'Is Mummy sleeping now because she cries at night?' the wee girl asked plaintively.

'No, no,' the boy answered, wiping the sleep from his eyes, 'I told you: she cries because Daddy has found a new Mummy.'

Chapter 2

KENNEDY WAS still banging on the door of the flat downstairs as these thoughts swam around his head. It would have been easy to force the door. But he was mindful that it was someone's private property, someone would have to clear up the mess, get a carpenter and locksmith in and then have to chase up the police to pay for the damage. All of which was a major hassle and was to be avoided if at all possible.

At the same time, the lady upstairs was dead. Gassed! Either gassed to death by person or persons unknown, or by her own hand. Could harm have been done to Edward Higgins as well? Coal gas is heavy and falls, and if he was asleep on the floor directly below, perhaps he too could have been gassed? Kennedy couldn't be sure but he thought he could hear stirrings somewhere inside the flat. A few seconds later the door opened and who should be standing there but the resourceful PC Allaway, claiming he'd found an open window at the back of the house. Kennedy, Irvine and Allaway trouped back into the flat and in a small dingy bedroom they found Higgins alive, but only just. They'd arrived barely in the nick of time. He was taken immediately to hospital, suffering from gas poisoning. With a bit of luck he'd end up with nothing more than a chronic hangover-type headache. A hangover without the buzz of the night before.

That little mystery solved, Kennedy found it easier to return upstairs and concentrate on the SoC or perhaps 'SoS' ('Scene of Suicide'). Easier still because Coles was entertaining the two children up in the bedroom.

Irvine had discovered a small study-type room, stolen from the space that should have separated the bathroom and kitchen. While forensics scoured the kitchen with a fine toothcomb, Kennedy had Irvine fetch the nanny, Judy Dillon, to the study. The windowless room was no more than eight feet square. He positioned himself in one of the room's two seats. It was a captain's swivel chair, guarding the desk, which in turn was positioned against the opposite wall from the door. Above the desk a brown, cork noticeboard stretched to the ceiling. It was packed to overflowing with cards, torn articles from newspapers and magazines, photographs and a few picture postcards. Kennedy was immediately drawn to a family photo of the two children he'd met, a young woman (the woman now lying lifeless on the kitchen floor) and a man. All four were ignoring the camera, three of them engrossed in the antics of the small girl, who appeared to have them all in stitches of laughter. Very much a happy family. The remaining walls were shelved floor to ceiling, broken only by the doorway.

The shelves were absolutely crammed with books, magazines, files, records, compact discs, cassettes, diaries, journals, notebooks, and two cylindrical boxes containing a generous supply of pens and pencils. The shelf to the right of the desk was deeper than the rest and contained a Sony midi stereo system with cassette player, CD and radio. No record deck was visible, despite the presence of the vinyl collection. The corner away from the desk and to the right of the door housed a guitar, resting on a stand: a beautiful old Gibson L100. Beside the guitar stood the second chair, a green and purple basketwork affair with no arms. The shelf directly beside it was empty, apart from a Sony Professional Walkman cassette-recorder with a stereo microphone, and an open yellow foolscap note-pad with a felt-tip pen resting on a clean page.

Kennedy felt a strange sensation. It was as if he was trespassing in someone's very private space, a hallowed room where an artist worked. A space where magic happens and wonderful things are created and pulled from out of the sky. There was a power in the small room. The young woman, Esther Bluewood, may at that moment have been lying lifeless on the dull red oilcloth no more than three yards away, but her presence, her spirit, was still evident in her room. Kennedy was reminded of times of death when growing up in Portrush, Northern Ireland. When relatives passed away the grown-ups would tell him that the banshees would come and free the spirits of the faithful departed, and that if he didn't go to sleep early he'd be sure to hear their wailings as the banshees went about their spooky business of stealing the souls of the dead. Was Esther Bluewood's spirit waiting to be freed? Or might it still be hanging around this very study, maybe trying to tell Kennedy something? How close were the banshees?

Balderdash, Kennedy thought. Get real. Esther Bluewood was positively dead. Dr Taylor had confirmed that. She was on her way to somewhere. If she'd taken her own life, the belief was that her soul would never reach heaven. No matter where she was bound, she wouldn't be telling Kennedy anything about her untimely demise. He'd have to figure it all out for himself – and he'd better be getting on with it.

Kennedy realised that the study was a computer-free zone just as DS Irvine led the nanny into the room. The senior detective stood and offered the distraught nanny the choice of chairs. She, wisely, elected to rest her limbs in the armless model.

Judy Dillon was in her early twenties, Kennedy assessed, with a physique chunky enough to feel blessed when shapeless training gear came into fashion. Flopping-out clothes were great for flopping-out in; they saved the figure-conscious from having to be conscious of their figures. Maybe the modern attire even encouraged that additional late-night tub of Ben & Jerry's ice cream. Kennedy knew exactly how irresistible that Chunky Monkey could be, but he had a belt around his waist, and its tightness acted as a reminder.

Surprisingly, her face seemed more suited to a smaller body. It was a beautiful face, in a Jessica Lange kind of way. She used no make-up and wouldn't have benefited from it anyway. Her hair (dyed a two-tone of blonde and red) was pulled up on to her crown and held precariously in place with an electric blue plastic clasp.

'Oh, the poor kiddies, whatever will become of them?' Judy Dillon asked through her sobs. Kennedy considered volunteering something about the father, or social services when sobbing Judy continued: 'She was great to them, you know. No matter what her own troubles were, the kiddies always came first. It all must have become too much for her in the end, I suppose.'

'What were her troubles?' Kennedy asked softly.

'Now then, there's a question.' The nanny twitched nervously on the basketwork seat. Every move she made caused an aftershock of ripples, which followed through the rest of her body. Kennedy could tell she was trying to decide how candid she would be with him.

'We know that her husband was seeing another woman,' Kennedy prompted. By disclosing the single bit of information he had so far learned on the case, he hoped to convince Judy that she could not be accused of gossiping. The tone of his voice was so comforting, so soothing, so reassuring that Judy's sobbing nearly disappeared altogether as she plucked up the courage to speak.

'Yes, there's no smoke without tears. I know, it's awful isn't it?'

The nanny breathed a sigh of relief having offered her truth, even though she'd mixed her metaphors. But that was apparently as far as she wanted to go. Kennedy tried another tack.

'How long have you worked with Jens and Holmer?'

This seemed to brighten her up. 'It'll be three years this November,' she replied proudly. 'I started with them when they had a dingy basement flat up on Chalcot Square. Jen was only about four months old I think, and it was getting too much for Esther. It wasn't as if Paul was much of a help. That's Paul Yeats, of course, her husband and the kiddies' father.' Judy paused. She seemed to be assessing how the detective was responding to her negative comments about her employer. Kennedy remained impassive and, visibly encouraged, the nanny continued: 'I mean, really, it wasn't as if he was much good at anything.'

Again she paused for the effect it created.

Kennedy decided he could probably pick up this information more easily on the way back, so he continued, 'Tell me Judy, was Esther a good—?'

'She was great at everything,' Judy cut across the detective enthusiastically. 'She was a great mother. I'd love her to have been my mother. She was always doing such mumsy things. No matter what gallivanting Paul was doing, she always kept a brave face for the children. She loved them so much. She gave her life to them. It never ceases to amaze me how women do that. No matter how career-conscious or successful they are before the children, the minute they have their first child they sacrifice their entire lives for their children. And the amazing thing is, they never make it look like a sacrifice.'

That's better, Kennedy thought, we've moved on from single-sentence answers. Just then Irvine returned to the small study.

'Ah. Excuse me sir, but could I possibly have a word?' Irvine began.

Kennedy stared at his DS with a 'Really?' look.

Irvine returned the 'Really?' look and added a 'Please?'

'Excuse us,' Kennedy said, addressing the nanny, swivelling the chair in the direction of Irvine and following him back towards the kitchen.

'Sorry about that, sir, it's just that Dr Taylor wants us to release the body to him as soon as possible. The word is out about...'

'I've just realised she's *the* Esther Bluewood. I didn't even look at her face properly. You know what I'm like around corpses. I should have twigged in the study with the guitar and songwriting stuff.' Kennedy gasped in genuine shock.

'Yes, I wasn't far ahead of you. It's just the SoC people kept staring, you know, stealing more looks at her than they usually do. And it's going to get like a zoo here pretty soon. Do you mind looking at the body now?'

On this occasion Kennedy had a good reason for delaying the examination of the body – he'd been talking to a witness. He took little comfort in the fact and knew that if he delayed it any more, his questioning would be patchy at best. Viewing bodies wasn't something Kennedy found came any easier the older he got, but nor was it getting any harder. It would have been impossible for it to get any harder. This frequent acknowledgement, face to face, of the finality and surprise of death, was by far the worst recurring experience of Kennedy's life. It hurt him to have to continuously admit to himself that whenever the Grim Reaper comes calling, there is nothing anyone can do to persuade him to return alone.

Kennedy entered the kitchen.

Although some of the SoC people – photographer and fingerprints – were already packing away their equipment, the functional kitchen was still packed. Kennedy noticed that behind the door, a dark blue towel had been rolled up and placed along the bottom edge of the door. Judy Dillon, on opening the stripped pine door had, inadvertently, pushed it back. Had the towel been placed there to stop the gas from escaping to the rest of the maisonette and harming her children? Or was it there simply to give this impression?

The smell of gas had all but disappeared, thanks mainly to the open windows and the cutting fresh winds of Primrose Hill. But the smell of death was lingering longer. Kennedy thought it was like the smell of apples starting to rot: bittersweet, yet enticing to the nostrils. The kitchen was long and narrow and in two parts, with the door punctuating the longest wall. To the left of it was the functional part, dominated by a sink underneath a window, offering a beautiful view of the gable end of the house next door. Next to the sink a fridge, a washing machine, several cupboards and a cookery preparation area, rested side by side. A set of spotlessly clean utensils hung from various hooks on the bare brick wall behind the preparation top. A packed clotheshorse suspended from the high ceiling swung slightly as people brushed against it. To the right was the family living area of this very rustic-style room. At the far end was a well-worn circular oak table, surrounded by four chairs. A small island on the table housed a milk jug, salt and pepper cellars, spicy sauces, a small radio, six Clarice Cliff Solitude-design dinner place mats, stacked one on top of the other with matching cup floaters on top again. A baby's highchair, now redundant, sat deject-edly in the corner. Above the table on the end wall was another cork noticeboard, again packed to bursting with photographs, mostly of the family but some of Judy Dillon playing with the children in this very kitchen. In the opposite corner to the highchair was a small colour TV, suspended precariously on a wall brace positioned above the room's one easy chair. A pair of men's leather bedroom slippers lay on the floor, neatly lined up by the front legs of the chair, whose wine-coloured cushions were carelessly scattered with vari-ous sections of the *Sunday Times*.

To one side of the chair was a large wooden trunk, opened wide and threatening to spew out its treasure: a heap of multicoloured children's toys. The walls were adorned with children's drawings, all marked with a name and an age, as well as several Paul Yeats' album sleeves. Just to the right of the door, a telephone was fixed to the wall with a calendar, a scribble pad and pen on a string close by. The two sections of the kitchen were bordered with the gas oven – very white and very clean. It was directly below the open door of this oven that Esther Bluewood had found her final resting place.

In death, Esther Bluewood looked more like a haggard, run-ragged, mother than the glamorous popular music sensation she was. Her once proud jet-black mane appeared unwashed and unkempt. Her sharp, well-cut face enjoyed not one piece of make-up, but still the power of her beauty shone through. Her pale skin had taken on the grey translucent hue of death and, Kennedy had to admit, she looked at peace with the world. Inside the oven door was another towel, and Kennedy noted that it was the same colour (lemon) as the ones on the clothes rack. It was neatly folded and looked to be intended as a cushion. With her face turned sharply to the left, Esther looked as if she was climbing an imaginary cliff face. She was about eighteen inches away from the open oven door. She wore the standard busy mum's indoor uniform: navy blue loose-fitting trainer bottoms and a black sweatshirt. Kennedy and Irvine searched the body and found only a tuning fork in the right-hand trouser pocket. Her hands were open with palms down on the floor, nothing hidden.

'Any notes or letters about the flat?' Kennedy asked no one in particular as he continued his examination.

'Nothing so far,' Irvine confirmed. He seemed to know instinc-tively that at this stage Kennedy required only the barest of infor-mation; his mind and thoughts elsewhere.

The Detective Inspector was hunkered down near the corpse's head with his back to the oven. His black chinos were stretched tautly over his knees and his well-shined black leather shoes cracked along the toe-line and creaked as he steadied himself on his haunches. Normally he hated to be this close to death, but by now he was unaware of anything that wasn't the body of Esther Bluewood and the grievous loss to the children upstairs. He rocked back and forth on his hunkers, his black crombie overcoat bunched up on the red and orange patterned oilcloth, changing shape with every swing. Kennedy's hands were clasped in front of him, his elbows resting on his knees, his green and white tie hanging down five inches below his hands.

What were Kennedy's thoughts at this stage? How come the towel in the oven still looked so neat? Surely the fold would have been creased or disturbed to some degree with the weight of her head? The head's a heavy piece of equipment; surely it would have left at least some indentation? If she passed out with her head in the oven surely any additional movement would have caused her head to roll out of the oven and drop to the floor directly below. It wasn't the weather for the white linen shirt he was wearing today; he wished he'd worn something warmer and more functional. Why was there no suicide note as was the case with the majority of suicides? Would Esther Bluewood not have dressed up, put on a bit of make-up, tided her hair for her final exit? Was he being a bit of a sexist having such a thought? If she'd had enough of the toils and troubles of her earthly chains what did it matter what she looked like as she escaped them? Would a loving mother either endanger her children or be uncaring enough to let the little ones find her? She must have known the scars that would have left? He thought about how totally devastated his friend ann rea was going to be when she found out about this death. She was continuously inspired by Bluewood's work and took great solace in it. ann rea could get down sometimes; quite down in fact. She'd always handled it well though, by running to the refuge of her own space at such times but were there ever any moments when she considered doing this? Considered taking her own life? Was this purely and simply a suicide. How could someone do that, take their own life?

Kennedy shook his head violently a few times to try and snap himself away from such thoughts. Why was he so? Why did he have trouble accepting suicide? Was it just because he spent his life chasing those who took life and maybe he just didn't want to admit that there were some of us out there who would gladly end something as precious as their own being?

'You find anything?' Kennedy now addressed the rotund Dr Taylor, pathologist and friend.

'Well, there's no marks or bruising. Looks like gas poisoning but I'll get back to you when I've done the autopsy.' Taylor began and added unprompted, 'I'd say time of death was around midnight last evening.'

'Thanks,' Kennedy replied. 'I'm done with the body, you can take it out before it gets too crazy out there.'

'I'm going to send an empty body bag out first to draw off the hounds and then hopefully steal her away in the unmarked van we also have outside. An undignified exit I know old chap, particularly on a cold November Monday morning but…' Taylor failed to finish his sentence, uttering a few tut-tuts as he packed his bag.

Chapter 3

BACK IN the study Kennedy found the nanny, Judy Dillon, engrossed by the noticeboard. Obviously this was not a room she'd been invited into frequently, if ever.

'Sorry about that,' Kennedy began, taking up his seat again. 'They're going to bring us a cup of tea.'

'Oh, that'll be nice.' Dillon replied as she gracelessly reclaimed her seat, which seemed to groan under the strain.

'Now, where were we?'

'I'd been telling you how great Esther was with everything.'

'Yes, indeed you were. Sorry. Mmmm, before we start again, my colleagues seem to be having trouble tracking down the children's father. Have you any idea where he might be?'

'Probably living off the hat of the land.' Dillon replied rather obliquely. She seemed rather pleased with herself, clasping her hands together and using them as a crane to hike up her right knee. Kennedy was sure he could hear her chair protest with several creaks. She obviously thought better of the idea and folded her chubby arms across her chest. She then used her left hand to cradle her right elbow, raising her right hand to support her chin, forefinger protruding on to her cheek. She always seemed to be using one part of her body to support another. Kennedy figured her favourite position was on her back. For one split second he found himself trying to work out how she would get up again. He ran through a sequence of arm, leg, and head movements and had started to consider the possibilities of rolling when she continued.

'I'm sorry, I don't really know. I know Esther was expecting him in London yesterday. He'd promised to drop in on the kids. He spends most of his time up at Axis.'

'Sorry, where?'

'Axis, it's their cottage. A beautiful little place they own in the Cotswolds. I believe she bought it with one of her royalty cheques, but he, Yeats, seems to have commandeered it for himself and his floozie.'

Kennedy had heard all about the battle of the sexes but he hadn't expected such precise military action.

'Yes, we found the number for the cottage on the kitchen noticeboard,' he said, 'but all we got was an answering machine.'

'I don't really know where he is then, but I can tell you one thing, wherever he is, you can bet your bottom pound that he's not working.' Judy replied, not even trying to hide her feelings for the man.

'Are there any other family members?'

'Just Yeats' sister, Victoria Lucas.'

'Is Lucas her married name?' Kennedy asked automatically.

'Good heavens, no! Tor will never find anyone to marry her. She's destined to stay a spinster. She been grooming herself for her lonely old age all her life. No, no. Yeats is not Paul's real name. It's his stage name. God knows the last time he appeared on stage, though. No, his real name is Paul Lucas. Anyway, Tor usually sticks her nose into everything. She just can't help it. She's always instructing me on how to deal with the children. As if she'd know! I always think it's unbelievable that the people without children of their own are always the ones who claim to know the most about bringing them up. Esther's an American so her relatives are over there. I've never met any of them but I know her father died when she was young and her mother is still alive. They have a troubled relationship but they are in touch regularly.

'What about friends? Did Esther have any friends in London?' Kennedy asked just as the tea arrived. They both helped themselves to milk and sugar – the nanny three, Kennedy two.

'My very own James Bond as a manservant, complete with tweeds,' Judy gushed, flirting blatantly with Irvine. Irvine offered but a mere polite smile and returned to the kitchen. Judy batted her eyelids coyly before continuing. 'I can't believe him. Close your eyes and you'd swear it was Sean Connery talking to you. Is that his real accent or is it put on?'

'That's his very own,' Kennedy smiled.

'Oh, it makes me go weak at the knees just thinking about that beautiful voice. And doesn't he dress well?' Judy broke into a warm smile, then added, after a pause that was just a wee bit too long, 'Mind you, look at yourself as well, smart as a sin. I didn't realise the police force were so cool. Is that just because it's Camden?'

'It's certainly not because of a clothes allowance, I can tell you,' Kennedy replied, realising his remark fell flat. He didn't mind that, he was just trying to find a way to get their conversation back on track. 'Could we just go back a bit? Ahm, yes I was asking you about Esther's friends, did she have any close friends in London that you know of?'

'Well, there were the Becks, the Islington couple, Jill and Jim Beck. They seemed to have adopted Esther, Jens and Holmer as their own family. I don't know how they met and the Becks rarely came over here. I've only talked to them a couple of times, but Esther was forever going over there. They were as good as silver with Esther and the kiddies. Esther was always telling me that they tried to make her life as normal as possible by having the kids in Islington for sleep-overs and forcing Esther to have a social life. They're good people. I think you'll find their number by the phone.'

'Okay. Good. Thank you. Could you tell me what your normal day would be like?'

'Nannies don't have normal days; they look after children,' Judy said proudly.

Kennedy rarely came into contact with children. He wasn't married and he was an only child so there were no siblings' offspring to be uncle to. He tended to think that children were good as gold and didn't need a lot of looking after or attention.

'Okay,' Judy continued, sighing ever so slightly, 'I would usually arrive here just before eight o'clock, help dress Jens and Holmer and give them breakfast. Mind you, Esther always helped. She wasn't one of those, "Oh thank God the nanny is here!" types, dumping the children in your arms on the doorstep and heading off in the opposite direction. No, she liked to spend the morning with us. She liked to send Holmer out to school. He's just turned six and has been at Primrose Hill School for just over a year now. She likes him to go off to school glowing from a fun family morning. None of this rushing around balling at each other, nibbling at a bit of toast, which never gets finished. She's a very loving mother… Oh sorry… I'm mean she was…'

'I know what you meant,' Kennedy comforted.

'But she was, sir. She was such a great mother. They were very close, she and the children. He really, literally, left her to get on with bringing them up. Esther always said Paul was terrible with babies, because they couldn't communicate back to him. Shows how much he knows. But she felt that the older they became the better the father he would become. She kept saying she could see that Holmer was starting to engage his father. Paul could see this little person taking shape. Esther always thought, and never complained about it, that it was her role to bring up the children and then Paul would educate them to the finer things in life. She said she was happy with that, as he was such a well-travelled and well-read man. I knew her theory would get her into trouble; well-travelled and well-read men always seem to be frequently-bedded men,' Judy asserted, moving around in the chair. Kennedy really was worried now, as the chair seemed to shake, rattle and groan with her every move.

'So, how would Holmer get to school?' Kennedy continued.

'Oh we'd... that's Jens and myself, would take him in my clap-trap. It's a genuine Mini Minor, one of the old ones. It just about manages to get me about but the children absolutely adore it. They call it Tigger, you know from Winnie the Pooh because of the way it chugs along when it's cold in the morning and I always leave the choke out which means it's chugging forever and they just love that,' Judy said brightening up again.

Kennedy wondered about the logistics of Judy Dillon fitting herself into a Mini Minor, he wondered whether these manoeuvres were the source of the children's amusement. He kept his counsel on the matter.

'We drop Holmer off at the school and then Jens and I come back here, by which time Esther is usually in her study, working. She'll either be answering her mail (she gets a lot of fan mail) or she'll be on the phone to her record company or her publisher or solicitor finalising some deal or other. She doesn't have a manager, does it all herself. Other times you can hear her gently strumming her guitar and singing along as she works on something. We never disturb her when she's doing that. Sometimes, if Jens is having her nap when it's happening I sit out there by the kitchen door and listen to her. It's so beautiful. Her music is very sad, but at the same time, very moving. When I listen to it at home I always find I have to be in the right mood. Do you know her work?'

'I do, as a matter of a fact. I listen to *Axis* quite a bit. I too find it very moving,' Kennedy confirmed. He'd been introduced to this wonderful music by ann rea and he'd found it very comforting.

'Sorry, I was meant to be telling you about our day...' Judy continued, breaking a silence apparently created by both of them considering Esther Bluewood's music. 'I'll make us all a bit of lunch around one. After I've cleared up the dishes from that, Jens and I will be off again to pick up Holmer. I bring Holmer and Jens back home, play with them until I leave at about four, by which time Esther has finished her work in the study. And that's it until the next day.'

'But you always get here about eight o'clock?'

'I'm never late!' Judy chipped back.

'No, sorry, I didn't mean that you were. I just meant that you would have been expected to arrive here just before eight o'clock,' Kennedy found himself apologising.

'Definitely.'

'Good. Look, I think that's all for now. We'll obviously have more questions for you later. Could you leave your details with DS Irvine?' Kennedy asked, happy to have avoided the bit of awkwardness about whether or not she was late.

'Oh, you mean the Sean Connery sound-alike.' Judy momentarily perked up but then seemed to crash in flames just as suddenly. 'He's been the only good thing about this sad state of affairs.'

For once, Kennedy wondered, had the nanny unconsciously put her words in order?

Chapter 4

KENNEDY LEFT what remained of the SoC chaps tidying up their work and headed back to North Bridge House, the home of Camden Town CID. He figured he'd better ring ann rea and tell her the news. Mind you, being a journalist at the local *Camden News Journal*, she was probably already way ahead of him on this one. Either way, she was going to be very low.

It's funny how someone you've never even met can leave such a hole in your life when they die. Kennedy had felt it when Otis Redding had been killed in a plane crash in 1967. He remembered being devastated on that occasion. Perhaps it was because the classic album, *Otis Blue*, had brought him such comfort, and part of the comfort disappears when you know that the person singing those soulful songs is no longer there.

ann rea had used *Axis* by Esther Bluewood to get through many of her own personal crises.

'Aye, he is now,' Desk Sergeant Timothy Flynn said into the phone as Kennedy entered North Bridge House.

The two-storey building, on the border of Camden Town and Regents Park, is the oldest in the area, built as a monastery at a time when the monks used to tend flocks of goats on nearby Primrose Hill. The building had been through many conversions in its 250-year history, and had been a school immediately before becoming home to the Camden police.

'Ah, it's DS Irvine, sir,' Flynn told Kennedy. 'He's says it's urgent.'

Kennedy took the phone and no sooner had he placed the handset against his ear than he could hear a rather anxious Irvine, barely restraining himself from shouting.

'You'd better get back here as quickly as possible, sir.'

'What's happened?'

'Paul Yeats arrived a few minutes ago and all hell has broken loose. We've been trying to restrain him from removing stuff from the study. Look, sir, I'd better go, he's ranting and raving again. He's on about his civil liberties and stuff,' Irvine reported, clearly concerned.

'Okay, I'll be straight back up there. Where exactly is Yeats now?'

'He's in the study. Locked himself in,' Irvine replied, apparently distracted.

'Right. See you in a minute.'

The ever-efficient Flynn had been busy on one of his other phones, and by the time Kennedy returned the telephone to its cradle, there was an unmarked car at the door of North Bridge House. Just under two minutes and four blatant traffic violations later, Kennedy was running in through the front door of 123 Fitzroy Road.

Irvine came to greet him.

'He just forced his way in and ran straight into the study. When I went in he'd started to pack notebooks, journals and cassettes into a holdall he had with him. Obviously I told him he couldn't remove anything from the scene of a crime. He replied, "What crime? She's gone and topped herself, hasn't she? No crime there." He further claimed that he was her husband and legally it was his property and that he could do whatever he wanted with it. I was trying to reason with him, telling him there was still an ongoing police investigation and nothing could be removed from the premises without permission when he suddenly shoved me out of the study, slammed the door and locked it from the inside,' Irvine said.

Kennedy knocked politely on the door.

'Hello, it's Detective Inspector Kennedy here from Camden CID. I realise how distressed you are sir, but I have to advise you that you are interfering with our investigation and unless…'

'How can I possibly be interfering? My wife and I own this apartment and these are our possessions,' a self-important baritone voice replied from inside the study.

'Nonetheless, sir, we're still carrying out an investigation here and nothing, but nothing, can be removed. You're not even meant to touch anything; your fingerprints are going to be all over the place.' Kennedy was keeping as patient as possible. He knew sometimes police rules seemed to get up people's noses but they were there for a reason. Just then he noticed a whiff of smoke drift from under the door of the study.

'I'm going to count to ten, sir,' Kennedy said, raising his voice to be positively sure that Yeats was hearing him. 'Then we're going to break the door down.'

'Go to hell!' the voice replied.

'Ten!' Kennedy shouted, missing nine digits as he took aim near the keyhole on the pine door and kicked with all his might. The lock gave way more easily than Kennedy had imagined and he was surprised at how little damage had been done.

Irvine, Kennedy and Allaway charged into the study where Yeats was tearing up a black leather-bound journal and tossing the loose pages into a wastepaper basket that had flames licking the rim. Kennedy didn't want any more evidence destroyed.

'Could you please give me that book, sir?'

'Frightfully sorry, old chap. It's mine and if I can't have it, you certainly can't,' Yeats replied, his fiendish eyes glaring at Kennedy and a smirk covering his entire face.

Kennedy raised his foot and came down with all his might on Yeats' fawn shoe. The Hush Puppy didn't live up to its name, nor did its owner. Yeats screamed with all his might. Something about where Kennedy's father was when his mother conceived him. Yeats dropped the book and grabbed his foot with both hands, falling back into the swivel chair. Kennedy grabbed the journal and the wastepaper basket and ran to the kitchen. He was in time to quench the flames before too much damage was done.

On inspection, around a dozen pages were either charred or destroyed in the bottom of the wastepaper basket. Kennedy was sure forensics would be able to retrieve something from them. Irvine, who was standing at his shoulder, lifted the offending journal and flicked the pages. He let out the briefest of chuckles.

'It would seem in his haste, sir, he started at the back of the book. It looks like the book was only a quarter used. All the writing is in the front twenty or so pages. It doesn't look like there was anything at the back. You got him in time,' the DS stated proudly.

'I'll bet there'll be something in these journals. Box absolutely everything up and take it all back to North Bridge House.'

When Kennedy returned to the study a few minutes later, Yeats was seething. 'I'll sue you for every penny you've got, you bastard.'

'But I was merely reacting to the smoke, sir. I thought you were in danger,' Kennedy offered innocently.

'You might get away with that for the door but not for breaking my toes. You wait and see.'

'Oh, I think you'll find I wasn't overstepping the mark. I thought I saw some burning paper fall on to the carpet. I was simply extinguishing it before the carpet caught light. In the meantime, sir, I'm going to take you down to North Bridge House to answer some questions.'

'Are you arresting me?'

'No, sir, I'm not. You could say that you'll be helping us with our inquiries,' Kennedy replied, and on noting Yeats' apparent lack of co-operation added, 'I'm sure you're aware there are numerous media people outside. I want to avoid them noticing the deceased's husband leaving here in anything other than a proper fashion.'

The mention of the word 'media' seemed to have an immediate transformational effect on Yeats. He ran his hand through his dishevelled jet-black curly hair and forgot immediately about his injured foot, although he did limp a little for five or six steps. He was wearing a dark brown corduroy suit and a black woollen polo neck jumper. He placed the forefinger of his right hand under the collar and ran it back and forth to smooth it out.

'You realise, of course, I was protecting Esther and her estate. I'm sure you've heard all the stories about people running amuck in the Dakota Building when Lennon died, helping themselves to his possessions, which, by the way, mostly ended up sold at sky-high prices in the main auction houses. We don't want that happening with Esther's stuff.'

'But you were destroying it yourself. We saw you trying to burn one of her journals,' Irvine said incredulously.

'Well, two of her books have been nicked already, so, as I said, I was trying to protect her,' Yeats replied. He had now calmed down considerably and his voice was very authoritative. He had the air of an educated man. It was just those manic eyes that unnerved Kennedy. They looked... well, Kennedy thought they looked like you might expect Rasputin's eyes to look.

Kennedy broke away from his stare and concentrated on what Yeats had just said.

'What do you mean, "two of her books are missing already"?'

'Exactly that, her journal for this year is missing, as is another journal with notes and bits and pieces, and ideas for new works,' Yeats claimed.

'Couldn't they just be somewhere else?' Kennedy inquired.

'No. They never leave this room. Esther insisted on it. She usually kept the room locked. I've checked all the shelves and drawers and they're nowhere. That's probably why I flipped. I thought it had happened already, the rummaging had started and the body's not even cold.' Kennedy froze. He was about to say something when Yeats continued: 'In view of this I would like to remain here to log all the material. You're welcome to witness me or vice versa. Then, at least, it will all be protected.'

Kennedy couldn't, and didn't want to, refuse. He would have liked to see Yeats express some regrets about his wife or, at the very least, to check into the wellbeing of his children. He left Irvine and Yeats to complete the logging and appropriated WDC Anne Coles. Very soon they were heading in the direction of Judy Dillon's flat and, Kennedy hoped, the missing Esther Bluewood journals.

Chapter 5

'DO YOU know any of Esther Bluewood's songs?' Kennedy asked his WDC as they 'set the dials' for the centre of Park Village West.

'No, can't say I do. I know her name obviously but not the songs. What were the song titles?'

'Oh, let's see… "New Way, New Day" and "Resurrection" and "Axis" and "Autumn Poppies" but I really love the entire *Axis* album.'

'God, I'm impressed,' Coles began as she negotiated the difficult traffic lights at the junction of Parkway and King Henry's Road. 'I didn't realise you were such a fan.'

'Well, it's ann rea really,' Kennedy began, breathing a major sigh of relief once they'd crossed the junction and were turning into Albany Street. 'She's totally into that album. She's got a few other Bluewood albums as well but we mostly listened to *Axis*.'

'Have you told ann rea yet, about the death?'

'Ah no, I'm… actually, I haven't spoken to ann rea for a while.'

'Oh!' Coles said, just a tad too quickly.

Kennedy thought perhaps he should ring ann rea. He should be the one to make the call. He also thought that he should close the topic of ann rea before Coles asked an awkward question.

She didn't in fact. She asked a very sensible question, and a professional one at that.

'Do you think Esther Bluewood committed suicide?'

'I find it hard to believe that such a committed mother would take her own life. I find it harder still to believe that she would take her own life when her children were in the flat with her,' Kennedy replied quietly, the picture of the two children silhouetted hand in hand at the top of the stairs still burning clearly in his mind.

'But surely if we believe she took her own life we must also believe she couldn't have been of sound mind. She was not thinking clearly, or normally, so there has to be the possibility she wouldn't have given the children the same consideration she would have, had she not been ill,' Coles offered as she took a left and parked the car directly outside the second block of houses in Park Village West.

'Fair point,' Kennedy agreed. 'Fair point. Let's see if we can surprise the nanny and retrieve these journals.'

'Talk of the devil…' Coles replied, nodding in the direction of the rear-view mirror.

And there, larger than life and with a spring to her step, was the same Judy Dillon, mincing along with a Marks and Sparks carrier in one hand and a Regents Bookshop trademark blue bag in the other.

'Oh!' Judy gasped. Kennedy figured that she'd been miles away – this was good, no time to think or hide. 'I suppose you've come for the journals?'

Clever, Kennedy thought, attack is always the best form of defence.

'Yes,' the nanny continued. 'They were lying around in the kitchen and I thought they'd be safer with me, you know, with all those people running around. There's no point bolting the stable door when it's raining. To be perfectly honest, I was more worried about Yeats or Tor helping themselves and rewriting history. Come on in, why don't you? The journals are as safe as blouses. I'll get them for you.' The nanny opened the front door of her flat.

'Why do you think Yeats would have been after them?' Coles asked, as they followed her in to the bright hallway.

'He's obsessive, jealous, a moron, a crap songwriter and he's been struggling for years to emerge from behind her creative shadows. Perhaps he'd even nick a few of her unused ideas. It's the ideal opportunity for him to effect a change. He's always been trying to get Esther to work with Tor. He claimed she'd look after all the stuff a manager would, allowing Esther more time for the children and writing. And because Tor was family, blood as it were, Esther would never be taken advantage off and her work would be looked after properly. That's complete tosh. All he wanted to do was indirectly get control of his wife's work; work he knew was far superior to his own,' she concluded as she led them through into a little sitting room on the right of the hall.

Bags still in hand, she nodded them in the direction of a sofa and headed back out into the hall.

'Would you like a cup of tea or coffee?' she called through from an echoey room Kennedy assumed to be the kitchen. Then they could hear her rattle about in the bags and the opening and closing of cupboard and fridge doors.

'Let's risk it,' Kennedy said in a stage whisper to Coles. In a louder voice he called out to the nanny: 'That would be nice, ah we'll have…' and he raised his eyebrows at the WDC, encouraging her to make a choice.

'I'll have coffee please,' Coles replied.

'And I'll have a tea, please,' Kennedy said, finding his voice rising to nearly a shout because he couldn't physically see the person he was addressing. They heard water being poured down a sink. They heard a tap being turned on, kettle being filled, lid being replaced and a switch being flicked. They sank back into the sofa.

Suddenly Kennedy had a horrible feeling. He sprang up, half running towards the noises and then, hands deep in pockets, slowed to a casual pace as he ambled into the kitchen area. He found Judy Dillon innocently packing Marks and Sparks' life-savers into the freezer section of the fridge.

'I'm afraid it's too small in here for two,' Dillon began. 'I'll bring the tea and coffee through when it's ready.' Then she had a little chuckle to herself as she continued: 'Oh, and if you're worried about Esther's books, they're over there in that blue bag by the bread bin.'

So much for safe-keeping, Kennedy thought, as he reached over and took hold of the Regents Bookshop carrier bag that was folded around its contents. Kennedy muttered something about looking forward to the tea and returned to the sitting room, journals safely in hand.

The thing about Nash houses, or at least this particular Nash house, is that, although they look very pleasing from the outside, the inside is divided up into too many small units. The effect created is more of a Southbank Cardboard City than the special elegance Nash had intended for his Regents Park meisterwork. Judy Dillon had succeeded spectacularly in making the small room appear and feel even tinier by packing every inch of space with books. They were mostly paperbacks and they were crammed rather than packed into various makeshift shelves. There was just one print on all the walls and that was over the fireplace. It was from a painting of Virginia Woolf in a very dignified Bloomsbury-type pose and it seemed somewhat appropriate in a room filled with books.

'I just love reading,' the nanny enthused, killing the silence as she burst, subtle as a baby elephant, back into the room.

'Really?' Kennedy said, gazing once more around the shelves.

The sarcasm was lost on Judy, who replied: 'Oh yes. I just love the other worlds they take you to. I've spent many a day in here travelling around the world on one adventure or another. I much prefer books to television or movies.'

Except for a small radio-cassette recorder, Kennedy noted the lack of electrical appliances in the living room. The furnishings consisted of a small wicker coffee table; a floral patterned, coffee-stained sofa; a battered leather armchair with a free-standing reading light nearby; a black bar-stool; a fawn carpet; the Woolf print, the fireplace, and books, books and then some more books.

'Have you always enjoyed reading?' Coles inquired, as she added milk, first to Kennedy's tea and then to her own coffee.

'Yes. My mother used to tell me that was all I ever did. From when I was about three years old, she'd read me to sleep every night and I'd follow what she was saying with the pictures. I always wanted her to read just one more story. I don't know where she got the patience from but she always did. Then, as soon as I learned to read at school I was in heaven. I just adore books. My father left us when I was young and I suppose in a way I was escaping into a fantasy world. My mum and I were very close, she loved books as well, you know, but never as much as me,' Dillon proclaimed proudly as she looked about her room.

'What sort of books do you like?' Coles continued.

'Oh, absolutely everything,' Dillon gushed. 'Let's see, I like romance, horror, biography, thrillers, even some crime novels. I suppose my favourite authors would have to be Woolf, the Brontë sisters and Edna O'Brien.'

'Did Esther Bluewood share your passion for books?' Kennedy inquired. His tea was positively vile, marginally better than dishwater. He returned the blue mug to the table after one swig. It was terrible to be gagging for a good cup of tea and to be so desperate for your first drink you take a large swig, so by the time you realise how terrible the liquid is, it's too late and it leaves a foul taste in the mouth for the rest of the day.

'Well, she did in a way. But you know, with the children and her songwriting and all the time spent writing in her journals, she didn't really have a lot of time for it. She was a big poetry fan though. I've never really gotten into that, poetry. But I've always supposed it's a bit like classical music; you'd have to have an ear for it.'

'Yes, I suppose you're right,' Kennedy replied. 'Tell me,' he continued, appearing somewhat absent-minded, 'did you ever get a chance to read any of her journals?'

'Oh no. She always kept them under lock and key. As I said earlier, that's why I was surprised they were lying around the kitchen.' The nanny took a swig of her coffee and helped herself to another Marks and Sparks spicy fruit bun.

'So you've no idea what's in these?' the detective said, taking the journals from beside him and raising them to eye level.

'Well, you have to believe that they're going to be at least as confessional as her songs. I mean if she's prepared to be that honest in public, goodness knows what she'll admit and commit to paper in private,' Judy replied, as the remainder of the bun disappeared in a single munch.

'Interesting,' Kennedy said. 'Tell me, did she ever discuss her journals with you?'

'No. Never. We didn't really enjoy that kind of relationship. I mean I've nannied before for families where the mother really becomes your best mate and you kinda hang out together. But with Esther it wasn't that it was a master and servant thing, but it was getting that way.'

'Mistress and servant,' Coles offered.

'Whatever,' Dillon replied.

Kennedy could tell she was itching for another bun. He further surmised that within a few minutes of the police's departure, the remaining three buns would disappear as quickly as you could say 'Billy Bunter'. He had this flash of her sitting there in her leather armchair; book in one hand, with the other continuously offering various delights to her eager mouth.

There was a lot more information to be gained from the nanny, Kennedy felt, but perhaps not in her current mood. They'd got what they'd come for; they'd retrieved the precious journals. Questioning could continue at a more appropriate time.

Chapter 6

AS KENNEDY and Coles entered North Bridge House, Desk Sergeant Timothy Flynn greeted them with a heart-warming smile. The fifty-eight year old Belfast man was weather-beaten to the extent that he had an all-year-round tan, probably a result of his early years on the beat. His brown skin was brilliantly complemented with a full head of snow-white hair. He was, without exception, popular with his colleagues and whereas Superintendent Thomas Castle might be the captain of the ship, Flynn was most definitely the one who kept order below decks. He accomplished this with a combination of his strictness, fairness and a dry sense of Ulster humour. He was the kind of man who offered respect to all, no matter their rank or sex, as long as they earned and deserved it.

'DS Irvine told me to tell you he's waiting up in your office, sir. He's got that Paul Yeats with him. Yeats kicked up a fair bit of dust as he entered the station.' Flynn advised Kennedy, who'd stopped by the desk.

'Anything physical?' Kennedy asked as he unbuttoned his coat. He felt embarrassed: here he was feeling the cold and Flynn was dressed in his uniform – black trousers, white shirt, black tie and black boots. The detective suspected Flynn had a two-bar electric fire placed strategically at his feet, hidden from view behind the desk. He'd either that or thermal underwear, for every time the door to North Bridge House was opened the wind blowing up Parkway took a detour through the station rather than continuing the scenic route up to Regents Park. Kennedy thought that Flynn surely must have been wearing thermals. But he never dressed any different, winter or summer. On the rare occasion he visited a incident, or the scene of a crime, he would complete his uniform with a jacket.

'Nah, just a bit of prancing for the benefit of a member of the local press who was visiting Castle,' Flynn replied half distracted, apparently writing something in his book; his normal pose. He looked over his gold-framed glasses at Kennedy and continued, 'Yes, your… ah… your friend, ann rea in fact.'

'Really?' Kennedy replied, more than a little intrigued. 'What was that all about? Anything to do with this case?'

Coles had stood around for a little of this exchange but, without saying a word, vanished through the swinging doors.

'I don't know, I doubt it though. She came in, said she an appointment with Castle, he came down for her and showed her out about half an hour later, when Irvine was accompanying Yeats on to the premises. Are you and her, still... ah, you know?'

Kennedy felt Flynn's awkwardness. They'd known each other a good eighteen years but could barely be classed as friends. At the same time, however, Kennedy realised Flynn was the kind of man who would genuinely care about people but not feel a need to go blabbing about it all the time. The discreet desk sergeant's question had just naturally evolved out of the conversation as opposed to sending a line out into the wilds in the hope of hooking some gossip.

'You know what, Timothy, and this is the truth, I just haven't a clue, I haven't a clue any more.'

And at that, Kennedy too melted through the swinging doors, leaving Flynn with a look of bemusement and bewilderment upon his face.

Chapter 7

'IF ONLY Ferguson could make his team hungry again, United could win everything.'

Kennedy found Irvine and Yeats involved in an apparently civil conversation as he entered his office.

'No, no, that's not the problem,' Yeats said enthusiastically. Glancing over his shoulder at Kennedy, he continued unabated: 'The problem with English football is all these foreign players and managers. It shouldn't be allowed. If you are to play, or manage, Manchester United then you should have to be born in the Greater Manchester area. No, for the sake of English football we need to get back to basics. No wonder the English football team is so poor; there are hardly any English players on the park on Saturdays anymore. I blame the FA, bunch of tos...'

By this point Kennedy was behind his desk and seated. Yeats stopped mid-flow. Kennedy couldn't discern anything from the crazy eyes but he thought Yeats might just have felt guilty talking soccer when his wife had just been found dead. Either way he visibly changed gear with a shrug of his shoulders and announced unprompted:

'We all deal with our grief in our own way, you know.'

'Indeed we do, indeed we do,' Kennedy replied, sighing slightly.

'I never thought she'd actually do it, though, take her life.' Yeats said, as he dragged his fingers through his hair. The last three words of the sentence were spoken in a near whisper. Kennedy couldn't figure out if it was said in reverence or staged for effect.

'We're not entirely sure yet that's what happened,' Irvine said.

'Yes, it'll be a time before we can state quite categorically what occurred,' Kennedy said, rising from his desk.

'You can take my word for it, Inspector, she committed suicide, just like she said she would ages ago.'

'Really?' Kennedy said, surprised.

'Really!' Yeats replied as though annoyed anyone would question his authority on the matter. 'She tried to kill herself before, you know. It was years ago. Before we met. She was still in America and she took an overdose of pills.'

'A cry for help perhaps?' Irvine offered generously.

'An amateur psychologist as well as a detective,' Yeats sniggered.

'Tea? Anyone for tea?' Kennedy offered, hoping to defuse the conversation.

'That would be splendid,' Yeats replied immediately with a smile. 'Thanks.'

Irvine nodded positively and Kennedy began his tea-making ritual by turning on the electric kettle.

'How long ago did you meet?' He said, as he removed three white bone china cups and saucers from the eye-level cupboard.

'Mmmm, now there's a question...' Yeats began expansively. 'Let's see now...'

Irvine discreetly removed a notebook from the inside pocket of his jacket and opened it at a clean page, fountain pen at the ready, waiting for Yeats' words.

'Esther and I met...' Yeats began with a quick glance at Irvine's book. 'It would have been early 1992. It was a bit of a whirlwind romance, as they say. We met in February and were married in June. We were both with partners at the time we met. But we just clicked, it just happened. You know when it's right. You don't know why, but you just know it's right. We both felt we'd known each other in a previous life, we felt we were destined for each other. She would have been twenty-four, I was thirty-two.'

Kennedy's kettle had now boiled and the sounds of it being turned off and the detective pouring boiling water into the awaiting teapot did nothing to distract Yeats from his reminisces. He was staring at the ceiling of Kennedy's office, a hint of a smile on his face as he continued: 'I'd already had three albums out at that stage and was a bit of a veteran of the music business. Esther's first record, *Axis*, was just about to come out, I believe it was released in March of that year. She'd just moved to England from Boston. She'd suffered a troubled childhood. Her father hadn't really shown her any love and had died when she was young. On top of which her mother was completely dysfunctional. Esther just wanted to leave it all behind and start a new life. She might have been here for about eighteen months to two years when we met. She'd been writing for a couple of magazines in America – I think she said she'd edited one of them as well – anyway, she was still doing some freelance work for one of them and they asked her to interview me.'

Kennedy showed Yeats the sugar bowl and milk. Without breaking his narrative, he nodded 'yes' and displayed two fingers (polite way around) to the sugar and zero to the milk.

'Something happened during the interview, we connected spiritually. We both knew it. It happened. Some people go through their entire life without making that special connection. Some people make the connection but just aren't aware of it, nor know what to do about it, but as creative people I always thought that Esther and I were already receptive to each other on one level. It's like John and Yoko, I think; that was a spiritual meeting, they were bound for each other.'

Kennedy saw that particular situation differently: to him she was an opportunist with her claws freshly sharpened, ready, willing and able to grab the gullible Beatle. Lennon was said to have been her second attempt at the songwriting section of the band. But Kennedy felt that this may not be the best time to offer such thoughts, so he kept shtoom and delivered the tea to Irvine who smiled, and Yeats who continued unabated.

'After the interview we went out to dinner, had a few drinks and spent most of the night walking around Primrose Hill. That's where I got the idea and inspiration for my song, "Together, Forever on a Hill". We committed ourselves to each other that night on the hill. We didn't talk about marriage or anything silly like that, we just committed our souls to each other. We ended up at my place at daybreak.' Yeats noticed Irvine take a break in his writing and missed a beat before stating: 'There was nothing smutty or anything like that going on. In fact we didn't sleep together for about a week.'

Kennedy knew his DS was probably thinking something like, You showed incredible self restraint. Neither policemen spoke as the baritone narrator took them on the next part of the journey.

'After a time, on that first morning, Esther found the confidence to pick up one of my guitars and, with a lot of encouragement, she sang me a song. Now I have to admit here and now that I'm a cynic. You know everyone claims to be a singer-songwriter. I've been propositioned everywhere with songs. The famous Nashville handshake is worldwide, believe you me: taxi drivers, waitresses, waiters, window-cleaners, record company employees, people who work for my management. Hell, even my bleeding dentist tried to lay a song on me. I swear to you he was just about to start the drilling and he goes on about this girl he's found who's got a great voice and okay songs and great tits – his words not mine – and he goes to his surgery music-centre and takes off the soothing Mozart and puts on this girl's cassette. Incredible racket it was. I couldn't tell you what was the most unpleasant, his drilling, her music or his bad breath. There should be a law that dentists, at least, should be forced to have good breath. Anyway, I was prepared to deal with Esther having terrible songs, hell, maybe even okay songs. This is the baggage that goes with being a successful songwriter and you never hear Elton John bitch about it, do you? He bitches about everything else but not that,' Yeats offered with a chuckle.

Kennedy thought it was quite funny. But Irvine remained stone-faced. Kennedy could tell Irvine had taken an instant dislike to Yeats, and he felt this might be a little unfair. They were meeting and dealing with someone in a pretty unreal situation. But when Irvine's hatches came down, no amount of logic or reasoning could pull them back up.

'So she sings me a song. The first song was called "New Way, New Day", and it absolutely floored me. But I'm still acting the tight-ass cynic and I'm thinking, Okay, she is in the presence of a successful singer-songwriter so she's going to give it her best shot to start with, all the rest are bound to be crap. But no, twenty-two songs later, my jaw is still on the floor as she performs "Resurrection" and that song, I can tell you, just did me in totally. Still does every single time I listen to it. I couldn't believe what I was hearing. It was like I personally had discovered the missing link between Joni Mitchell and Suzanne Vega. Obviously I wasn't the first on the block because, as I said, all the songs on the first albums had been written and recorded and she was just waiting for it to come out.' As he spoke, Yeats'enthusiasm was building.

Kennedy had a feeling that Yeats was a fan of his wife in spite of himself. In his self-centred world (perhaps a little harsh, Kennedy thought) he'd have liked to ignore her, but her work was so outstanding his prejudices were useless. Yeats continued talking, Irvine continued writing:

'You see, Esther's work succeeds on three levels. Firstly,' Yeats lectured holding up his index finger, 'you have the music. To me it's as brilliantly crafted as any of Paul Simon's melodies. I get the feeling Paul Simon slaves over his music until it's perfect. The result, in his case, may be lacking a little soul but they are perfect modern pop songs. Esther has the same gift, but she manages to retain the soul. Next you have the lyrics. As a writer, Esther has a beautiful flow. She has such a command of the English language. It appears effortless, but it's not. She sweats over her craft. She's as economical in her lyrics as any of the great poets – Seamus Heaney, for instance. He's probably the most successful person with words that there is. Then he's a visionary as well as a wordsmith; something Esther shares, but with an obvious different insight. And finally, you have the combination of the words and music together. It just makes her better work totally irresistible; lethal in fact.'

'I'd have to agree with you,' Kennedy said in genuine enthusiasm. He accepted the fact that he could still have been blind to the magic of Esther Bluewood if it hadn't been for ann rea persistently pushing him on the journey through the American's music.

'You know her work?' Yeats said, in obvious disbelief.

'Oh yes, I'm a big fan.'

Paul Yeats seemed pleased, proud even.

'I was, too. And her work succeeds on so many different levels. Take a song like "Resurrection", for instance. That's a great song. It works well in the pop idiom. It works well on a concert stage. It works well on the radio. It works well when other people do it. I perform it some nights and it's an absolutely gorgeous song to sing. But beneath all of that, for Esther it was a very therapeutic song. When she was twenty-one, a couple of years before we met in fact, she tried to commit suicide. She talked to me about this a lot, she said she felt so hopeless. She felt helpless in dealing with her inner pain. It was unbearable and her medication made her feel like a monster, a monster under control. She just felt that she had to end it all and so she took a pile of pills and went down into the basement of her house and tried to hide there so that no one would find her until she was dead. Her brother eventually discovered her before the pills had a chance to work and she was taken to hospital where they saved her life, but she was placed in the psychiatric wing of the hospital.'

Yeats appeared as though the talking was draining him. He drank his cup of tea straight down. Kennedy had never seen anyone do that before. When Yeats' cup was refilled he did the same thing again but refused a third. He swam his fingers through his wavy hair once more and let his fine baritone voice take over again:

'But she used it to her advantage. She said she felt she *had* died in that basement. She felt that she was reborn in the hospital. She felt that she had cast off all her old pains and chains and freed herself from them and from her mother. Shortly afterwards she moved to England. To complete the resurrection, she said. Her song "Resurrection" is all about her rebirth. That's why most people find it such a rewarding, rejuvenating song to listen to. I still can't believe what it does for me when I listen to it. I suppose it must be a bit of a voyeuristic kind of thing. I mean, for example, being compelled to view someone else's pain so nakedly on display and at the same time thinking that no matter how bad I feel, no matter how great my pain is, I'm never going to feel as bad as her. But then Esther used to tell me how some suicidal people wear their psyche-ache like a trophy. Looking at other people as if to say, "Please, *this* is the real pain!"'

Yeats paused; still staring at the ceiling, the smile no longer on his face. Kennedy could tell he was gagging for a cigarette, but the detective didn't want to interrupt the flow to advise the widower that this would be fine.

'I've this thing,' Yeats started, seemingly unsure of what he wanted to say. 'Guilt would probably be too strong a word for it but I feel awkward, it's perverse in a way, I know. But I can't help feeling guilty at the disbelieving thoughts I had about her. I felt in a way that she'd never commit suicide. I'm afraid I'm one of those who feel suicide attempts are a cry for help. And when you're in the middle of it, it's so draining and sometimes you'd just get so mad that you want to burst and say, "Look we both know you're never going to do it, so why don't you just give us all a rest for a while?" Frightfully un-PC I know, but that's what I was feeling. And now, now that she's gone, now that she's gone and killed herself, it's like each and every thought I had on such occasions are coming back one by one to stab me. None will cause permanent damage, but perhaps the sum total of all those wounds will somehow harden me, and rob me of the sensitivity artists exist on.'

'Was this a permanent state for her?' Irvine asked, looking up from his notebook.

'When I first met her, it was on the agenda all the time. But she didn't tell me about her pain until she was sure we were in love. She'd just have very dark periods where she'd run off and say she had to be by herself. She felt that being loved by someone was her cure. She felt her father hadn't loved her, although she later felt he might have, but just didn't know how to tell her. She felt her mother didn't care about her at all. Her mother blamed her for Esther's father dying. Oh God, it's all so weird and I suppose it's all going to come out now. I didn't fully understand it all to be honest, but I'm sure her therapist can give you the background. Anyway, she felt in love and loved for the first time in her life, and she told me it was healing her. The dark periods were simply, in her book, relapses. My love was her cure, she said, but it was going to take time, time for her to be completely healed.'

'How was she acting in the last few days?' Irvine again.

'I thought she seemed fine,' Yeats sighed. 'But what do I know? A year after we married, Holmer was born and the bad times were behind her and she said she was completely healed. Her first record had been a complete success; slow at first but very much a word-of-mouth thing. She didn't do a lot to promote it and she didn't need to. Once the Woman's Movement and the Pink Posse tuned in to what she was doing, the word spread like wildfire. We'd money, were in love and had started a family. The following year she had a miscarriage and the dark moods returned for a time. But things got better when Jens was born. We became the perfect family. But as artists, she and I were continuously pushing our experiences; not exactly living our lives as fodder for our songs but just being aware of what was out there. Then I had a relationship with another woman.'

'When was this?' Kennedy asked, without a trace of either shock or disapproval.

'Well… Look, this is awkward. You're going to find out anyway so I'd better tell you before the "nanny from hell" does. I'm still seeing her!' Yeats said, with a double run of fingers through his hair, throwing it first to the left then pushing it straight back where the curls mingled with their less luxuriant friends on Yeats' crown

'Oh,' Irvine said, unable to hide the subtext of, 'Well, this changes everything'.

'I still loved Esther. You have to know that. Ross, sorry, Rosslyn St Clair, knew that as well. It was no secret. I was convinced that Esther and I were going to grow old together. In a way I felt that she was throwing me into Ross' arms. I don't know why, either for me to sow the end of my wild oats or for me to realise how special the love was between Esther and myself. It backfired. What can I tell you? I fell in love. Fell in love in a different way, but in a way that made it impossible for me to give up Rosslyn. So, if I'm being honest, I'd have to say that there was a chance that Esther was feeling unloved again. But then again, she was always claiming that she felt totally fulfilled caring for Holmer and Jens. Tell me, was there a note or a letter?' Yeats found a question of his own to ask, perhaps hoping to turn the spotlight away from his confession.

'Not as yet, but we did find the two journals you reported missing—' Kennedy began.

'What?' Yeats shouted, jumping from his chair, his coolness disappearing as quickly as a kick. 'You didn't tell me that. Where were they? Who had them? They are my property. You are not permitted to look at them. I will have to injunct you. Look, am I under arrest or anything?'

'No, sir, you are helping us with our inquiries into the death of your wife,' Kennedy replied immediately.

'So you're not holding me here?'

'No.'

'I'm free to walk out of the police station?'

'Well, we do still have some more questions for you.'

'And I'll gladly answer them, but not just now. I also feel I should advise you that those journals are private property and now that my wife is dead they are my property and I have to categorically advise you that under no circumstances are you allowed to look at them. You will be hearing from my solicitor immediately,' Yeats advised Kennedy and Irvine before storming out of the office.

'Well. Who was that masked man?' Irvine asked as he and his boss stared in the general direction of the vanishing aftershave.

'I don't know. It certainly wasn't the Lone Ranger,' Kennedy replied, still somewhat shell-shocked. 'But it looks like those journals could contain some powerful material.'

'Methinks you speak without forked tongue, kimosabe.'

*

Kennedy stole away to the conference room. Paul Yeats and his lawyer would not be able to gain access to the journals while the detective insisted they were vital pieces of evidence, but Kennedy didn't want the journals sealed and unavailable until such time as a judge ruled on the matter. That could take days, possibly even weeks, and there could be vital evidence in those leather-bound journals.

The conference room was unused. Kennedy sat underneath the glaring painting of PR Fenn, a former superintendent of the station who'd gone on to become a commander at New Scotland Yard. Kennedy felt Fenn's presence almost as a representative of the Establishment, saying to him, 'You may think you're catching the quick on us but we know what you're up to.' Had it been a picture of the present superintendent, Castle, up on the wall, he felt sure that it would have winked at him and added, 'Hurry up then, laddie, and make sure no one catches you.'

One of the journals was made out like a diary. No year was given, just the day of the week and the month. Kennedy checked a few of the days against the dates in his own diary and came to the conclusion that the journal's first entry would have been for the middle of last year and the most recent entry was made a matter of ten days ago.

The handwriting was very neat and easy to read. Kennedy had mixed feelings about reading someone else's private thoughts in a diary. He felt, in a way, that it was cheating her, he felt it was wrong, but at the same time he was fascinated. Everybody enjoys reading other people's private thoughts, particularly those that have not been edited with a reader in mind. It's like having a direct line into someone's head. Now, as Kennedy turned the pages the hairs on the back of his neck were at full attention: all neat and in lines like Camden Town's uniformed police turned out for Superintendent Castle's inspection. He could hear Esther Bluewood's voice in his ear. But it was her singing voice, for that was the only Esther Bluewood Kennedy knew. This voice, as with the more confessional songs on *Axis*, was plaintive and haunting, and Kennedy found some of her written words even more moving than the songs. And there were some, such as the entry for October 21 last year, that Kennedy would have preferred not to have read.

Chapter 8

Sunday Girl

Sunday 21st October

I WOKE up this morning feeling bad again. I don't know why. There were no hints of the dark clouds when I went to bed. Yeatsie and I used to have a code in the early days; if I felt the dark clouds gathering I'd tell him it was a good day for talking. I needed to talk, I needed a mood elevator. Not as a distraction but as a catalyst. Yeatsie, for all his faults, knew how to talk to me when I felt that illness. He knew I didn't want him to say things like, 'Don't worry, it'll be okay tomorrow,' or, 'You're only thinking like that because you're depressed.' He knew that he had to question my thoughts. He had to come between me and my thoughts by offering me an alternative view. And in considering that view, whether right or wrong, I, not he, sowed the seeds of doubt. I would hesitate and in my hesitation he won. Why did it take so long to find someone I would take notice of? Someone to listen to because they weren't a doctor?

It's weird. In a way, it's like writing a song at high speed, the streams-of-consciousness thing Van Morrison used brilliantly in Astral Weeks. *Yeatsie worships the ground Morrison walks on, but for me, apart from* Astral Weeks, *which I will openly admit to using as my template for* Axis, *he's much too undisciplined in his writing and his recording. He so badly needs to work with a producer, and a strong producer at that. God, I hate myself for writing that. It's like I've become a critic. I suppose it's just because I see how much Yeatsie sets Morrison up as an artist and I want more from him, want more from Yeatsie. I want him to be aware of these things but so often Yeatsie will go along with the crowd. But with* Astral Weeks *the Irishman hit the ground running as fast as his little legs would carry him. And maybe it's because of the brilliance of that work that I get so frustrated with the rest of his stuff. Yeatsie, on the other hand, feels* Astral Weeks *is enough, more than enough.*

When you work in this way, when you are writing at high speed and you're not allowing your inhibitions or reserve to get in the way of things, it's like listening to a voice as you take dictation. You're working more as a medium and letting the spirit take over. You're listening to the voice within. It's not yourself you want to attack. That's not what you fall in love with.

This process is at the expense of all else. When you're 'in the normal world' you see how selfish you must look. How selfishly you treat the children, your husband, your family, but you don't see any of that when the clouds are around you. You feel that you exist in a space and you can only be comfortable working in the space if you are part of the force and not fighting it. You don't see it as an end, it's really just a way to take away the hurt, which – if I'm being totally honest – comes from feeling unloved.

But then Yeatsie says, 'Yes, I hear you, but you have to earn love. You can't buy it in a shop. Not everyone is entitled to it by virtue of their being. People don't consciously make a decision not to love you. The potential is there and you have to fight for it, swear for it, cry for it, long for it, sweat for it and then grab it. And when it comes, don't be fooled into thinking it's going to last.' I ask him if it is so wrong to want to be loved. He replies, 'Of course not. Why do you think we write songs and release records to an unwaiting public? It's because we all feel we've been deprived of love at some stage in our lives and we want to compensate for it now. And the NOW is so real for us.' He pleads with me to accept the fact, though, that we don't get it as a birthright, we have to work for it. He tells me that we all have these thoughts; it's not just my monster.

That's the door opened and then he hits me with a list. He says okay, he accepts that the ultimate search for peace and harmony is one legitimate answer. He also wants me to consider others. Like living my life for my children. Like working for a charity and helping those more needy than myself. Like dedicating myself to writing about all of this so that it will serve as a map for others in similar turmoil that may not have the intelligence to see what is happening to them. He asks me to think for a while and then to write the above down in my order of priority. Of course, dedicating my life to my children is number one. And 'ending it all' is way down the list.

Yes, it's way down the list, but it's never last.

He never tries to change that, and the following day he sets both of us a list of tasks that reflects the priority of the list, and as we work on the list, letters, phone calls or whatever I come to the realisation that the talking day has gone. My feelings of 'Hopelessness and Inferiority' fade, to simmer underneath the surface until the next time. My fear now is that when they return, Yeatsie may not be with me to help me fight them. Is that why I feel so bad about him and Ross? Not because I hate her because I don't, I don't even know her. I pity her for I know exactly what she's getting and it's not like she can't take him back to the shop and exchange him for a newer model.

No, I feel bad because we battle well together, Yeatsie and I, especially when we are on the same side.

*

Two hours later, Kennedy put the journal down on to the large conference table and walked around the room, hands deep in his pockets, his head bent towards the floor. He returned to the journal and reread the entry for 21st October. From a quick scan of the diary, he saw that it was the only entry that dealt directly with suicide. And even then she never actually used the word. Maybe, thought Kennedy, Esther's demons had returned and this time she'd been unable to fight them off.

The other journal was more of a book of ideas. Some were for songs, others for future writings. Several times in her journal Esther Bluewood had alluded to her intention of exploring prose as a way of expressing her thoughts. In the ideas book, she sometimes wrote a single word on a page, other times a development of words. Maybe a saying, or a character, or a word and a description of the word. Kennedy found it intriguing to venture, albeit uninvited, behind the scenes, as it were, and see how an artist put their work together.

Kennedy speed-read his way through the diary journal, jotting down notes as he did so. He returned to his office and hid the journals in a secret compartment he'd found in the wall. One of Kennedy's recent predecessors had painted over the magnificent oak-panelled wall, so Kennedy had taken a lot of time restoring the office to its former glory.

Truth be told, he savoured the work and was in no hurry. It reminded him of the hours he used to spend with his father in his workshop up in Portrush. His dad was a carpenter, forever making something, if not for their house then for one of the neighbour's houses. Kennedy could easily recall the scene: fresh wood shavings spilling on to the ever-growing pile on the floor, the smell (pleasant) of his dad's sweat mixed with the aroma of the wood glue that simmered gently in the corner, it's container stained from repeated reheatings and spills. He could hear the sound of his father's plane slicing through the wood as it reduced it to invisible, but always accurate, lines, bevelled it or merely smoothed it to a surface as silky as a baby's bottom. Well, that's what his mother had always said on the rare occasion she joined them in their kingdom. The young Christy Kennedy had been prepared to take her word for it.

Kennedy wondered was it those special times with his father that separated him from Esther Bluewood. Was it the unspoken love between father and son during their bonding sessions that set him up for the path that he today strolled? He'd asked his father a million questions during these sessions; all million answered with the patience and wisdom of a saint.

A lot of the lessons he'd learned then were standing him in good stead today, even though, at the time, they didn't seem like lessons at all. Kennedy recalled one memorable occasion: it was just after the Christmas holidays and he had received a 'junior carpentry' set as his major Christmas present and he was forever going on to his mother and father about how he was going to make them some chairs for the house.

A few weeks later, his father asked Christy how he was getting on with the chairs. Christy reluctantly showed his father his effort. Well, it was all a tangled mess really, the young Kennedy couldn't effect a design that included seat, legs, back, support rims and still stood up. The elder Kennedy took three pieces of wood from his son's disaster of a chair. He nailed them together in the shape of a rectangle with the bottom side missing, like a letter 'n'. He told his son that was a chair until such a time as he could make a more sophisticated model. But in the meantime the new sample would do fine. It was a variation on the 'You got to learn to walk before you can run' theme. Christy Kennedy never forgot it and found it helpful in his police work. 'Work with what you've got' was something he was always telling his team. 'When you work out exactly what it is you've got, then you can learn more, and move on to the more sophisticated model.'

In refurbishing his office, Kennedy had found this little compartment, probably once the home of a small safe, and he had matched up the oak with some wood he'd found in a timber yard. Then he'd fitted a matching secret door, which opened with a click when you pushed the panel against its spring, clicked shut on to a magnet, and was invisible when closed. Kennedy now shut it securely and went off in search of Coles and Irvine. As a result of his recent readings he had a list of eight people he wished to talk to. Nine if you counted Jim and Jill... as individuals and not a couple.

'So,' Kennedy said, twenty minutes later, following a brief synopsis of the journal. 'We need to question, Paul Yeats (again), Doctor Hugh Watson, Jill and Jim Beck, Victoria Lucas, Judy Dillon (again), Esther's mother, the mysterious Josef Jones and Rosslyn St Clair, Yeats' mistress.'

'But…' Coles began, 'do you think Esther Bluewood committed suicide?'

'That's a question we should save until we have four legs on our chair,' Kennedy replied.

Both Coles and Irvine looked bewildered. Kennedy gave nothing away; he merely, proudly, surveyed his handiwork in the office and added, 'But perhaps Doctor Hugh Watson can throw more light in that direction for us.'

Chapter 9

Friday I'm in Love

Friday 13th November

I WENT to see Doc Watson today. I told him that's what I called him because of his funny cowboy boots. It's his one and only fashion statement. He told me he saw me on TV last night for the first time. He said I looked uncomfortable, scared, drawn, a bit like a rabbit caught in the headlights of a car. I told him just because I was breeding like a rabbit there was no need to be calling me names. I laughed, but it was too stiff. He knew I forced the laugh because I didn't want to discuss it any further. Of course I'm awkward and scared. I'm a songwriter. I'm not a TV star. I don't want to be a TV star. It's like you're not allowed to feel anything or express anything except feeling acceptable for the camera.

I know people would kill to have my opportunity to be on television, I told him. I suppose in a way I nearly did (kill) to be on it; another of my jokes that fell flat in front of the doctor. Flippancy is the spring in my stride. As usual after a few minutes, while the Doc quietly sits out all my attempts at bravado, I slow down and talk to him. I tell him I live to write my songs. I go to a place no one, or no thing, can take me to. It's better than any of the medicine my body has been subjected to for the last twenty years. I tell him this. I also tell him about a dream I had where all the medicine and pills and drugs I had ever taken in my life were all in a room and my father was there with me, but he'd only one leg for some reason, and I asked him should I take the medicine and drugs and pills and he said, 'Don't be stupid, Esh.' My father never ever called me Esh, I don't remember him calling me anything. I seem to remember the tone of his voice for some reason. But in my dreams and thoughts he calls me Esh because I always thought a dad would have an affectionate nickname for his darling daughter and I couldn't think of one which fitted with my name but after a time Esh seemed to be called out in my dreams. But my father, with his wooden leg and his one hand stiffly supporting my back as though I was a ventriloquist's dummy, said, 'Don't be stupid, Esh, if you do that you'll kill yourself.'

Doc Watson asks me why I love writing songs so much. I tell him because songwriting is the only thing into which I can totally escape, leaving all the other stuff behind. I tell him writing can help with the battle, it... When my writing is sad I'm not necessarily sad because when I'm articulate in my writing those are the times I'm dealing with it the best. He then wanted to know why I could not feel comfortable performing these songs on television. I tell him that television is not interested in capturing the performance of the song, it only wants someone looking pretty, white teeth, heavily made-up, groomed hair, eyes open – I can never ever sing a song that matters with my eyes open. I just can't, it seems to be obscene or naked. So the television wants the picture postcard look even if it's at the expense of the song. You see, it's because the screen can only portray the two dimensions. They don't have the facility yet to convey all of what you give in the performance. They can't transmit sweat, fear, smells, imagination: it all has to be done with pictures – pleasant, pleasing pictures. They can't show you being a woman.

He then wants to know if I should not feel more comfortable talking about my songs.

I tell him this feels like an interview and I further advise him all anyone may ever want to know about me is there in my songs, waiting for them to discover it. If the press would just find the time to listen to my music, then they'd also find out everything about me they ever wanted to know. What's the point in continuing to talk about it further when it's already there? It's done. I've said it in the song. People should just listen to songs. People just look at paintings, but with paintings that's enough. People never asked Van Gough to continuously re-paint his self-portrait. It was already all there, conveying all the pain you could ever wish to convey.

'Why do I do it then?' he asks.

Because I'm a vain bitch and I want to sell my records, I answer.

He laughs at this, maybe more out of relief than from the humour. Humour?

Hey, that's it. That's the truth. You work so hard at your life, at doing what you do, at being allowed to continue to do what you do. And that means selling records. You have to sell records before you can make more records, which you then have to sell before you can.... But that's the recurring story an artist has to put up with.

The truth is, I make music. I want people to love my music and by loving my music they'll love me. I need to be loved. It's so simple, really, isn't it? It doesn't cost money to be loved. You just pick anyone, like Dylan wrote, and pretend that you've never met. I *wonder, does Dylan feel a need to be loved? I thought Yeatsie loved me. I tell the Doc this and he asks, How come I'm so sure he didn't, or doesn't, love me? I tell him he couldn't love me because of Rosslyn. He says, 'What about Josef?' I tell him to shut up!*

I actually said, 'Shut your effing mouth.'

Isn't that a weird thing? I can't actually write that word. I can say it. I can swear it at a perfectly friendly doctor trying to be helpful. I can do the act with another human being; I can do it to Josef, too. He can't do it to me though (only Yeatsie can do that). But I still can't write it. That's Ma's fault, she's as retentive as the Gadobie Dam.

The Doc thought he'd hit on something, didn't he? Maybe he did. But I didn't want to go there, so we didn't. I wish it were as easy as that with Yeatsie. Yeatsie did help me, though. He loved me at a time I needed to be loved. His love healed me. It's as simple as that. But love that had to be strong enough to heal me was never going to last. It was always going to burn out. It had to be bright to save me, but, equally, it was therefore too bright for its own good, so it was inevitable it would burn out.

I tell this to the Doc. He says, 'Quite possibly, but now you think this love is gone, what's keeping you well? Or are you now so strong because of his love that it doesn't matter?'

I tell him it is the love of my children that now keeps me together. They love me. They love me unconditionally. They love me because they need to love me. They love me because they depend on me. I'm the big person who will hold their hand and look over the tall hedges and make sure there is nothing bad on the other side. I will look in the cupboards in their bedroom and under their bed before they go to sleep to assure them there is nothing bad lurking in the shadows. I am the person who will recline with them on the bed until they are safely off to dreamland.

Why do children become aware of evil spirits so early in their lives? Who introduces them to this world? I have tried to keep my children away from demons but they both discovered the world when I wasn't looking. The Doc says this is because evil rises, it never falls! He looked guilty when he made this perfectly profound statement and I asked him if he wished he hadn't said it.

He put his hands in his back pockets, Bette Davis style, and asked me if I wished he hadn't said it.

I said it was time to go, the other Dillon will need her McDonald's medication shortly.

Is there a Gadobie Dam?

*

Hugh Watson turned out to be similar to a friendly parish priest: able to listen in a kindly manner, but when push comes to shove, a man with his own agenda. Kennedy guessed he'd be in his early fifties. He was dressed in a Fred Perry three-button blue shirt, a brown v-neck pullover and a fawn button-up cardigan over a fairly wrinkled pair of grey flannels and, surprise, surprise, a pair of cowboy boots. The skin around his eyes was as wrinkle-free as smooth silk, making him look like he'd benefited from plastic surgery, though Kennedy was sure this couldn't be the case. His short, black curly hair displayed hints of Brylcream.

He took Kennedy and Coles straight through to his 'surgery', a comfortable book-lined room at the rear of his house. He lived and worked in one of the grand houses at the end of Regents Park Road, on the corner, just before the railway bridge. Watson's stride appeared to be limited by the weight of the boots, Kennedy assessed. The silver studs and blue flaked glass stones seemed like they also would weigh several pounds. He flopped down in his favourite, well-worn and even more-used leather chair. It came with some Native American patterned cushions, but the extreme angle at which Watson inclined, hands clasped in front of him, made it look as though his spine was in danger of permanent damage. Although the room appeared to be centrally heated, Watson also enjoyed a two-bar electric fire, which was working at fifty per cent capacity, affording his boots a permanent carmine glow.

Coles and Kennedy both avoided the couch and sat side by side on the leather sofa, as far apart as possible. Either they were seeking the support of the sofa's arms or the comfort of the space. Somewhat dry-throated, Kennedy began: 'We are hoping you can give us some background on Esther Bluewood...'

'I've been expecting you ever since your sergeant rang me this morning,' Watson began. He had a slow drawl, more English midlands than American Midwest.

'Yes, it's so sad, such a talented woman,' Kennedy replied.

'Ah, you knew her then?' Watson said eyes opening a little wider.

'I know her work. I'm an admirer,' Kennedy smiled. 'We know she was seeing you and we are trying to assess her state of mind. Whether or not you think it possible she might have...'

'Committed suicide,' Watson said, immediately finishing the detective's sentence as though impatient. 'On this earth humans die from a natural cause, or an accident, or a suicide, or a homicide.

These are the only four classified causes of death. That which is fact is not to be avoided. You, in your work, are used to the word homicide, but take a person whose relative has been murdered, do you think they are scared to hear the word "murder" mentioned? That is wrong, purely and simply incorrect. Equally, you are nervous of mentioning the word "suicide" merely because Esther Bluewood was my patient. But that's not all she was. I am not the patient, I did not suffer from the whatyemecallit...' and here Watson paused, rolling his eyes up as if the word was written on the ceiling, '...Ailment,' he announced with relief before continuing, 'I was not the one suffering from the ailment. I was helping her treat it.'

Watson then broke into a warm smile; Kennedy assumed the smile was meant to be a sign that he was not being reproached. Kennedy didn't know what to say next.

To fill the lull in the conversation, Coles asked: 'How long had you being seeing Esther?'

Watson looked at Coles and broke his hands apart, just slightly so that he could tap his fingers together. The tapping fingers were just below his face and occasionally brushed the beginnings of stubble on his chin. 'Esther Bluewood had been a patient of mine since she moved to London six years ago. Her doctor in Boston – Ernest Siddons – had referred her to me. He's an old chum, we meet occasionally at conferences.'

'How often did she see you?' Coles continued.

'Oh,' Watson paused and blew air through his lips, 'sometimes, as often as three times a week and at other times, maybe once every four months.'

'Why were her visits so irregular?' Coles asked.

'Okay, some people are ill,' Watson began, clicking his fingers in time to the rhythm of his vocal delivery. 'When they are ill they go and see someone about it. Now if you suffer from arthritic pains or heart problems, for instance, you will go and see a specialist doctor, someone who can look after your ailment. If your aliment is psychological, that is of the mind, then you consult someone like myself. If we do what we are meant to do – that is, help make our patients better – then there is no need for our patients to visit us often. Occasionally you get patients, and this applies as much to those with physical pain as it does to those with psychological needs, who will become dependent on their doctors; I always say that which is a crutch-cure is not healthy.' Here, Watson smiled gently but only with his eyes. The rest of his face hardly moved.

'Such patients will find an excuse to visit us as often as possible. Esther worked hard at helping herself cure her pain.'

'So would you say Esther was keen to fight her... her illness?' Kennedy asked.

'All of us play a vital role in keeping ourselves alive. In Esther's case she continuously fought to turn those self-destructive forces into life-saving enlightenment. The major part of what we all do for ourselves is to acknowledge that there are certain crises, which we cannot handle alone. We need to seek out professional help. This seeking out professional help is a major step in the treatment. There are those out there,' Watson looked briefly over his right shoulder, 'who feel that we are quacks and that mental pain simply doesn't exist, full stop. They'd like to take away our status so that they could remove our funding. But thankfully, temporarily at least, we've come out of the dark ages.'

Where did that soapbox come from? Kennedy thought. He was warming to the man, though. He loved the language Watson used to discuss that great taboo: the taking of one's own life. Few who haven't suffered mental stress can fully comprehend it, but at the same time there were few in the world who, at some time or other, haven't contemplated suicide, if only for a fleeting second.

'Ahm, I wonder... could you tell us where Esther's anguish came from?' Kennedy inquired, as he settled comfortably back into his corner of the sofa.

'What was the problem, in other words?' Watson said, eyes smiling again. It was a unique gesture, or at least Kennedy had never before noticed anyone whose face didn't break into a smile at the same time as their eyes. 'The two vital words with suicide are "childhood" and "unhappiness". A suicidal feeling never grows from happiness. We know that suicide can occur with adults who cannot stand the pain of grief or loss after the tragic death of a loved one, irrespective of a good or bad childhood or loving or unloving parents. But even then it would be my view that the fact that such people cannot withstand these adult whatyemecallit... ahm... storms, yes storms, lies in the lowest recesses of personality which are formed in a very early childhood.'

'So you're saying what happened to Esther Bluewood in her childhood has a direct bearing on how she was feeling at the time of her death?' Kennedy found himself asking.

Watson shot the detective one of his impatient teacher-to-pupil stares.

'Yes, yes. Of course.' Watson replied, picking up his pace a little.

'And this was?' Kennedy asked, offering a little of his own impatience.

'The love of her father, or in Esther's case, the lack of love from her father,' Watson replied, the smile now missing from his eyes. 'This is thirsty work, isn't it? Shall we treat ourselves to some tea?'

Without waiting for a reply, the doctor rose from his chair and crossed the burgundy-coloured carpet which separated him from the fireplace and pushed a bell on the wall. Somewhere in the recesses of the house Kennedy was sure he could hear a bell ringing. The tea must already have been prepared, because by the time Watson had returned to his chair, the door opened and an old woman, tray in hand, wobbled in. Kennedy jumped up to help her with her load but Watson said, 'No it's okay, you'll get her flustered. Won't he, Ma?'

The old woman nodded and smiled, set her tray on the coffee table between them and hobbled out of the room again.

'Your mother?' Coles asked incredulously. Kennedy felt that Coles was shocked a man as seemingly educated as Hugh Watson would have his mother, or any woman pushing eighty, wait on him.

'No no, dear me, no. My mother's long gone, God bless her. No, Ma's been here for years, longer than me in fact. She comes with the house. Lives in the basement, and knows everything about everybody. She's obviously too old to work but she feels guilty if she's not doing something to earn her keep. She always has a pot of tea brewing – it's usually strong enough to put hairs on your chest – oh, sorry.' Watson looked at Anne Coles and his eyes inadvertently wandered to her chest and he found himself apologising again, 'No offence intended.'

'None taken,' Coles chirpily replied.

Kennedy hoped that his WDC hadn't notice that his own eyes had strayed in the direction of the doctor's stare.

'Sorry, anyway, I was saying, she always has a pot of tea on the brew and with certain patients, when I ring the bell in her parlour, she troops in. I bet she'll tell me all about you when you leave,' Watson said as he helped himself to tea, leaving his guests to fend for themselves.

The tea certainly was strong but not unpleasantly so. Very refreshing, Kennedy thought. Nonetheless, he hoped it wouldn't have the hair-growing qualities Watson had mentioned. He would not want it to spoil Coles' magnificent… but best not think about things like that now. He shook his head a few times, as if to dispel the thought, and said, 'Now, where were we?'

'Her father, we were discussing Esther's father. For some reason he couldn't and wouldn't deal with her. He never let her in, so to speak. Even though she was just a young child, something somewhere deep inside of her was picking up on her father's thingamabobs... vibrations, yes that's it, vibrations.' Watson once again apparently had found the missing word floating around the ceiling.

'But aren't all of us meant to be closer to one parent than the other?' Coles inquired.

'Yes, and with girls it's usually their fathers. In Esther's case her father was rejecting her and she, in return, was rejecting her mother. I don't know why she should start this process at such an early age, we can surmise of course, but I doubt if we'll never know. The first part is simple, well relatively so, she felt unloved because her father showed her no love, or warmth, or comfort. That could have been for many reasons: sexual, reasons of ego, being too busy, or perhaps he hadn't wanted a child in the first place and the mother had somehow tricked him into it. But that doesn't explain why Esther would then reject her mother.'

'Maybe Esther picked up on the father's negative feelings towards her mother and blamed her for her father's lack of love?' Coles offered.

'Quite possibly, and a very good assessment,' Watson said, his eyes breaking back into a smile. 'So we can assume it all starts there for Esther. She thinks: I can't depend on my father, I won't depend on my mother. I certainly can't depend on them together. Therefore, I must find someone I can depend on. Answer: I will depend on myself. I must drop them before they drop me entirely. It is better for me to be the victor rather than the victim. My body is my friend, it is also a hater of my parents. My body is my only instrument with which I can get what I want in this world. I can control my world by ruling my body to do as I will, gain a stone, lose a stone. I can cut my body and let the marks show I'm in charge of it. I can do as I wish with it and the marks I give it will hurt others. And the ace is? If life gets too difficult I can turn my life off for ever.'

'So she was cutting herself?' Kennedy asked.

'Yes, a lot when she was younger, but not recently. She hadn't done that for ages; she'd found more sophisticated ways of marking her body, leaving scars on her mind.'

Coles looked bemused at that.

'Yes, they…' Watson began, looking over his right shoulder again, 'they tell us that we can see the mind. The mind, Donald O Hebb tells us, is "what the brain does", and suicidal tendencies depend largely on mental pain as created by the… the cootermegig… the… the mind. Yes, the mind. The majority of our behaviour is based on our fundamental biological needs. You know, all the basic things like oxygen, water, warmth and food. We include our sense of achievement, of domination, of self-protection, of self-control, our need to be loved and comforted. As we live our lives, we are continually chasing these essential, inherent psychological needs. That's what keeps us going. When an individual tries to commit suicide, what they are trying to do is to end the unbearable psychological pain that rises from the frustrated psychological longings vital in that person's life.'

'But surely, even in a low mental state, no one could think of death as a solution to their problem?' Kennedy asked. As he asked the question he wondered had he felt that way because he'd been brought up to believe that all life is precious. This was the very foundation of his work, the basis of his chosen career. All life is precious, therefore all who would take it must be policed by society. It's very basic, incredibly simple, but true, at least to Kennedy. He was willing to concede that he might have felt this way only because he had been brought up in a loving environment by two of the most wonderful people he had ever met: his parents.

'Now, I've found there's no such thing on this earth as a little question, but that's certainly one of the bigger ones. You need to realise that suicide is the need to abate the painful pressure by ceasing the unbearable rush of consciousness. In simple terms, it's like being able to black out the gaudiest room you'd ever seen with the simple flick of a light switch. Think of the peace and satisfaction you experience when you turn off a troubled engine after willing it those last several miles home, and you just make it, maybe even with the help of a steep hill which rolls you down to your front door. You turn off the ignition, the rumbling stops, the rattling ends and the noise is no more. You're left with beautiful silence and the people on the street stop staring at you, so you can sink back into your seat and enjoy the blissful, wonderful feeling of peace. In a perverse way it's almost worth the unpleasantness of the final few miles just to be allowed to savour that pleasurable state.' When Watson concluded, his voice was gentle and almost a whisper.

'Mind you, all that… unreliable cars, I mean, only came into being in this country when they...' Watson again nodded over his right shoulder, 'started to encourage the sale of foreign cars.'

This time his entire face broke into a big smile, which lit up all of the front room. He hiked his shoulder quickly as if to say, 'Oh excuse me, it's just another of my pet hates.'

Kennedy mulled over the information they had just gathered. Had they learned anything? Definitely. Did it help with the current investigation? Possibly – he wasn't sure. He turned to the doctor:

'Would you say, from your dealings with and treatment of Esther Bluewood, that it's possible she committed suicide?'

'I'd have to say that we are all capable of suicide,' Watson replied, clasping his hands and placing them under his chin. He was reclining so far into the seat Kennedy was slightly worried that should the doctor's anchor – his spectacular pair of cowboy boots – slip, he would fall out of the chair and on to the floor. Watson looked deep in thought as he surveyed Kennedy's eyes, perhaps looking for some clue of his own. 'Tell me,' Watson began, breaking his clasp and stealing a quick glance at his watch, 'did you find a diary or anything like that?'

'We have some journals, yes,' Kennedy replied.

'Well, if I could read through those, particularly any covering the last several days, I would be in a better position to give you my opinion on whether or not she committed suicide. That which is on paper comes straight from the soul.'

Kennedy and Coles smiled.

'I've got a patient arriving in a few minutes,' Watson announced, rising to his feet. 'Why don't I spend some time with the journals and then we could meet and talk some more?'

'Obviously the contents....' Kennedy began.

Watson shook his index finger several times from left to right. 'No question about it. I assure you 100 per cent confidentiality,' he offered as he led them to the front door.

'I'll send the journals around in a little while,' Kennedy said. 'When could we meet?'

'First thing tomorrow morning, if you like.' Kennedy hesitated, so Watson spoke in his place: 'You understand, I can't just flick through them. I have to try and assess what may lie between the lines.'

Kennedy smiled. 'Sorry. Yes of course, we'll see you first thing in the morning.'

Chapter 10

I Don't Like Mondays

Monday 8th February

I'VE JUST seen Josef. I've just been with Josef. Again. I wonder about my wisdom sometimes. Sleeping with a fan! There must be a rule somewhere in Yeatsie's as yet unwritten manual about the dos and don'ts of sleeping with fans. I can just hear him say, 'Esther, how could you sleep with a fan?' He wouldn't say, 'How could you be unfaithful to me?' He wouldn't be annoyed that I'd slept with someone, but he's be disgusted I'd slept with a fan.

In my mind it's not that I've been unfaithful to Yeatsie, it's more that I've used a person to masturbate on. That's callous I know, but that's exactly how I see it. I cared not for his pleasure, not even a little. I was only interested in my own and I know my body well enough to have manoeuvred him to my gratifying advantage. It's delightful I can tell you, everyone should have a human dildo and JJ's mine.

When I first saw him, I was convinced he was gay. He had that air young girls and gay boys have when they've just discovered the power sex can give them. They flaunt it in a brazen yet slightly inhibited way. Like at any time you could, with the right word, cut the sea legs from under them in one swipe.

Maybe that's JJ's power. By parading his apparent gayness, women feel safe. We let him closer than you would a macho like Yeatsie, for instance. Mind you, I don't seem to attract those kinds of fans. It's mostly gays and young girls. And then before you know it they are taking liberties. Mmmm, I was the one who took the liberty with JJ. I've always had the itch, and anyway, why scratch it yourself when you can get someone else to scratch it for you?

But that was all. Just someone to scratch my itch. Nothing more. It made me feel quite decadent to be as detached as that. We never once attended to his pleasure. But I know I should stop. I know what I'm doing, meaning I know I shouldn't be doing what I'm doing. Mind you, Yeatsie always left me to attend to my own pleasure. It's just that I think of him with her and I know he's not really with her because pleasuring his partner is not high on his list of *priorities. At the same time, though, I can't help imagining it's different with her and they're at it all the time, and so that's probably why I want some of my own.*

I wonder had JJ told anyone? Does he have anyone to tell? And would they believe him?

I remember when I was in high school I slept with a poet, an Irish poet who visited Boston each year. He was so rugged, not quite handsome but with a gorgeous voice and all the girls used to swoon over him, and I slept with him. But my best mate didn't believe me. Well, he had to sleep with someone, I reasoned, why not me? Physically it was very forgettable, he was only after his own plea… Now there's a thing, that's a similar report to the one Josef would give me, I'm sure.

I can imagine the scene: a café or at a stage door, waiting for someone. 'Esther Bluewood,' he'd say, 'I've done the wild thing with her. She's not much cop in bed. She only thinks about herself.' I would hope my fans would stick up for me and say, 'On your bike, you spotty little herbert. She's the most beautiful woman in the western world, maybe even the whole world. She's not going to go with a nobody like you, and if she did it would be the most pleasurable night of your entire life!' Or words to that effect.

To be fair, JJ's not spotty, neither is he a herbert, little or otherwise. He's quite intelligent, always looking dapper in his four-button black suit and white shirt, top button done up, no tie, always the same. And he can be very funny. God, I'm starting to boast about his qualities, it must be time to get rid of him.

It's like a drug. I suppose I can give him up at any time. That's not, of course, accounting for his feelings. I need to go and get some sleep. I've got to go over to Jim & Jill's early in the morning and collect Jens & Holmer.

*

By the time Kennedy and Coles returned to North Bridge House, Irvine was busy tracing the smartly dressed mystery man who'd been seen lingering around the Bluewood household during the morning of the death. The early edition of the *Evening Standard* had a piece on Esther Bluewood's death. It was a below-the-fold front-page story with a fair-sized photograph of the scene outside the house in Fitzroy Road earlier that morning. A few uniformed police were hanging around, and the beginning of a crowd had gathered.

Irvine was busy on the phone when Kennedy entered the large

office his DS shared with several others. Kennedy sat on the corner of his DS's desk, picked up a copy of the *Standard* and glanced over the story and the picture. Irvine had completed his phone conversation and was setting the phone down when Kennedy exclaimed: 'That's him, I'll bet. That's Josef Jones, aka JJ.'

'Who?' Irvine asked.

'Esther's lover, the fan… there he is. "Always looking dapper in his four-button black suit and white shirt, top button done up, no tie, always the same".' Kennedy pushed the newspaper towards Irvine.

They both studied the picture of the fan. He was looking side on at the camera. Kennedy thought he must have been half-frozen. It had been cold out there this morning and he was dressed only in a suit and shirt. Kennedy had felt the nip of the cold and he'd worn an overcoat as well. The well-dressed lad in the photograph, he was hardly a man, was fresh-faced. Kennedy seriously doubted if he had even been shaved by a blade. He'd a sharp-featured face with a tight crop of black curls falling about his crown. Kennedy couldn't be sure but he thought he could make out a hint of eyeliner, serving to emphasise the very boyish eyes.

'I would bet you our friend Judy Dillon will have the whole nine yards on this guy, James. Give her a ring and see if she can give you an address.'

'Grand,' Irvine replied and set to his task.

Kennedy returned to his office, newspaper in hand, reading the story. It was one of those news articles that revealed nothing but filled plenty of space. Basically, the only disclosure was the announcement of the death of Esther Bluewood. As Kennedy reread the story he wondered what ann rea's take on it would be. He should ring her. He knew he should. But it seemed bizarre to ring her now just because someone they both knew and admired had died. ann rea had met the singer-songwriter a few times. They weren't exactly bosom friends but from ann rea's side they'd gotten on very well and occasionally spent evenings together.

To ring or not to ring, that was Kennedy's dilemma.

He was saved from making a decision on it one way or the other when his phone began to ring, exactly as he opened his office door. Kennedy was glad of the diversion.

On the other end of the telephone, once he rescued the handset from its cradle, was the very same ann rea.

'Christy, I hope you don't mind, I just had to talk to you. Poor Esther, I can't believe it.'

'I know, ann rea. It's totally fine to call. I was about to call you anyway.'

'Listen, I don't want to talk about this on the phone. Can we meet?' ann rea requested in a quiet, feeble, almost childlike voice.

'Sure, yes, of course. Ahm, shall we meet at the Queens at eight?' Kennedy replied.

'Look, that's going to be very crowded, would you mind if we met at The Albert. If there's any chance of earlier than eight I'd be ever so grateful. Could you make it at seven o'clock?'

'Yes, of course, I'll see you then. Will you be okay?' Kennedy asked, just as he was about to set the phone down.

'Yes, Christy, I'll be fine. Now that I know that I'm seeing you, I'll be fine.'

This time Kennedy did set the phone down, because ann rea had already disconnected.

He didn't have much time to dwell on the state she was in, because Irvine came charging into his office, saying, 'We're in luck. Miss Dillon didn't know where he lived but she told me he worked part time as a barman at the Jazz Café. They gave me an address: he lives in a bedsit up in Kentish town.'

'Great,' Kennedy said. 'Well, there's no time like the present, as they say.'

And he grabbed his coat and headed out the door before Irvine had chance to say another word.

Eight minutes later, just as the BBC London Live's five o'clock news was concluding on the car radio, they pulled up outside a dilapidated, converted house on Greenwood Place, just off Highgate Road. They rang the doorbell marked 'J Jones' several times before they heard stirrings from within. Eventually, following a lot of muttering and grunting and groaning, the fresh-faced Mr Jones answered the door, looking somewhat dishevelled.

Following the presentation of warrant cards and introductions, Josef invited the two policemen into his flat. Well, more like bedsit really. Although the enterprising Mr Jones had commandeered what appeared to have originally been a washhouse or an outhouse of some kind to double the floor space offered by his back room, it looked as if he, or perhaps a former tenant, had used a window to make a doorway so that his living quarters consisted of the small back room of the house (used as a bedroom), an open entrance to a very narrow covered porch, two steps lower than the back room, and then through another doorway, a windowless room. It was in this darkened room that Josef Jones entertained the two members of Camden Town CID.

Kennedy stood, staring opened-mouth at the room's far wall. It was covered, ceiling to floor, with photos, posters, flyers, leaflets, magazine articles and adverts of Esther Bluewood. The floor was carpeted in royal blue, the wall to their right had a makeshift book-case-cum-shelving unit, made up from boxes, bricks and planks of wood. The do-it-yourself unit contained three or four hundred albums, roughly the same number of compact discs, a record deck, a double cassette recorder, a CD-player, a radio and an amplifier. The equipment was a mismatch of Sony, Hitachi and other names ending in 'Y' or 'I'. The rest of the unit contained what looked like thousands of magazines, packed to overflowing on the shelves. At either end of the shelving-unit-cum-fire-risk stood a large Grundig speaker cabinet which was gently purring and begging to be filled with sounds again.

Centre spot in the third wall, and pride of the room, was a large framed, autographed poster of Esther Bluewood. The singer was uncharactically heavily made-up, collar pulled high and hiding some of her famous mane, and she was looking at where you imagined the photographer's knees would be. In the background was water. Kennedy couldn't exactly place the shot, but he thought it might have been taken near the lake in Regents Park. He thought he could make out, although blurred and somewhat obscured by Esther's coat, the air duct that's become something of a landmark. The exact same air duct which is visible for about a minute as Trevor Howard and Celia Johnson row past in the famous boating scene in David Lean's classic *Brief Encounter*.

The poster had Esther's name at the top in blue lettering, high-lighted by a black drop shadow, and along the bottom the legend: 'Songs from the Heart. The music of Esther Bluewood exclusively on Camden Town Records. Available in all good record stores now!'

The poster had been signed 'To Josep', using a gold magic marker. The 'P' had been converted to a fallen 'F', whether by the author or by someone else wasn't obvious. The inscription continued, 'A prince of a boy! Well done! Esther Bluewood.' The hand-writing was extremely neat, tidy and very readable. Josef Jones was almost in a trance, staring at the face in the poster as if he too was looking at it for the first time. Below the poster was a shelf, holding a couple of envelopes, three or four bills, a Royal Mail 'while you were out' card, along with a paperback copy of *Lake Wobegon Days* by Garrison Keilor.

'Sorry I took so long to answer the door,' Jones began, offering the policemen a seat on the green and blue sofa below the shelf. He sat opposite on a dining chair, no arms. He seemed to want to position himself there so that he could steal a glance occasionally at the autographed poster. The sofa position afforded Kennedy and Irvine a good view of the Bluewood wall.

'I suppose it's a difficult day for all her fans,' Kennedy began. 'But one tends to feel more sorry for the family.'

'We were her family, you know, but some more than others,' Jones said in his inimitable voice.

He was dressed only in a white T-shirt and pair of black suit trousers. His feet were bare and to Kennedy's eye, his hair looked much as it had in the current edition of the *Standard*. And like the *Standard* photo, he looked like he was wearing eyeliner. Kennedy remembered now who Jones reminded him of: Posh Spice, but Posh Spice with curly hair. His small nose, thin neck and large adam's apple all conspired to give him a high-pitched whine while speaking. In an American accent, as with the Disney characters, this would have sounded funny, but with an English voice Kennedy thought it sounded positively evil.

If Kennedy hadn't already read the journals he would have pursued this line but he let it drop for now. If Jones was so obviously prepared to drop such blatant hints about his closeness to Bluewood, Kennedy wondered how long it was going to be for the story to be splashed across the middle pages of one of the tabloids.

'I don't have long to talk,' Jones began, his voice chilling Kennedy's spine and causing the hairs on the back of his neck to stand to attention. 'I've got to be at the Jazz Café by six-thirty. That's why I was trying to get some kip. I'm on until it closes tonight and by the time we tidy up and close up, it will be nearly three o'clock before I get back to my bed.'

'You're going to go to work today?' Irvine asked.

'Why yes, of course. Why wouldn't I? I've got to eat. I've got to earn money in order to live. I'm not like Lord Corduroy – Paul Yeats. I'm not going to be able to live off Esther's estate and lie around on my back for the rest of my life, watching the money flow in. Now that she's dead, I have to work more than ever. Mind you,' Jones said, seemingly realising something for the first time, 'the price of all my memorabilia will have shot through the roof now that she's dead.'

'Esther Bluewood was accessible to her fans, wasn't she?' Irvine asked.

Jones kind of smirked at that question. 'Yes,' he smiled knowingly, 'to the real fans. Not to the autograph slags.'

'Sorry?' Irvine leaned forward in his chair.

'You get a lot of slags hanging around stage doors waiting for stars. They're more interested in getting star-fucked but asking for an autograph is a good way of getting an introduction. Some of them are so brazen. They'll stick their hand down the front of the star or celebrity's trousers as they're signing and say something as subtle as, "Is there anything happening later?". There's a lot of that goes on. And mostly the pop stars are up for it, and even if they aren't there's always a roadie who'll do the business. But in the stories to the fan's mates the next day the roadies will have miraculously become leading members of the band.'

'Really?' Irvine continued.

'Oh, you're such an innocent, or you're having me on,' the high-pitched whine continued.

'No, it's just you hear the stories, but I've never heard first-hand.'

'First-hand, that's a good one. It's what the second one's doing you've got to worry about. Just hang around a few stage doors for a while, that's a real fly-opener.' Jones barely got his line finished before he burst into laughter. It was like you'd imagine a gay wolf howling would sound.

Kennedy was a little upset. He couldn't really work out why. He figured it might be because Josef Jones didn't seem in the least upset at the death of a woman he'd been so obsessive over. Who's been using whom? the detective wondered. Kennedy decided to play it dumb.

'Did you by any chance ever meet Esther Bluewood?'

'I'd say,' Jones sniggered.

'At stage doors?' Kennedy pushed.

'I knew her, detective. I knew her very well.' Jones boasted.

'Is that why you were at the house this morning?'

'I wasn't at the house this morning. I was here. I was here all the time,' Jones said.

'But,' Irvine claimed incredulously, 'there's a photo on the front page of today's *Evening Standard*, taken this morning outside Esther Bluewood's house, and you're in it.'

'No! No?' Jones shrieked. 'GOD! Are you sure?'

'Yes,' Kennedy replied simply.

'That's wonderful, that's great. All the slags will be soooo jealous,' Jones ripped. Kennedy was convinced he was about to tear his vocal chords.

'But you said you were here all morning,' Kennedy persisted.

'I was here in the early morning and then I heard on the news about Esther, so I went over, but that would have been just before lunchtime. Is it a good picture? Can you see me clearly? Are there any of the Pink Posse mourning in it, too? God, they absolutely worshipped her. I suppose they would wouldn't they, strong woman and all of that?'

'I'm sure you'll still be able to get a copy. I forget all the details. But you say you were here all morning until you went out to visit Esther's house. What time would that have been?'

'Probably about noon, maybe about ten-to-twelve, why, what's the mystery?' Jones asked.

'Nothing, really. Just checking our facts,' Kennedy said and looked at Irvine, prompting his next question.

'Did you meet Miss Bluewood personally much, sir?' Irvine dutifully inquired.

'You know, now and again. But what's this all about?' Jones asked, a little panic appearing to creep into the proceedings.

'Well, it's just that we're investigating the circumstances surrounding the death of Esther Bluewood and...'

'But why? There's no mystery. She topped herself, didn't she? Just like we all knew she would one day. Listen to her music for heaven's sake. It's all there!' Jones suggested, slightly irritated at having to explain it to the detectives.

Chapter 11

KENNEDY AND Irvine returned to North Bridge House shortly thereafter, Josef Jones blagging a lift to Camden High Street from them. Just as Kennedy was climbing the steps into North Bridge House, he met Dr Taylor travelling in the opposite direction. The friendly doctor had dropped off the autopsy report and didn't take much persuading to accompany Kennedy to his office for a cup of tea.

'So what did you find? Anything suspicious?' Kennedy asked, as he set about brewing the tea.

'I'm afraid not, old chap,' Taylor began, stretching out in the one easy chair in Kennedy's office. The chair Superintendent Thomas Castle always considered his own. Kennedy had positioned it at the far side of the office from his desk. Sometimes he will sit in the chair to see if another angle of view at the 'Guinness is Good For You' green felt noticeboard – which is usually generously peppered with information on the case in hand – might inspire another angle on the case. Now the leather armchair groaned under the strain of Taylor's ample girth.

'Spoon, spoon, who's taken my spoon?' Kennedy moaned as he searched around his tea-preparing area.

'Allow me, old chap,' Taylor said as he sat bolt upright and searched around through the numerous pockets of his brown-check patterned three-piece suit. The ability to produce, at the drop of a hat – usually his own, a green felt trilby – vital odds-and-sods was one of Taylor's specialties. He rarely disappointed.

'Thanks a million,' Kennedy said as he gratefully took the spoon. Not only had the doctor produced a spoon, and a silver one at that, but it was clean, polished and sealed in a polythene bag.

'Oh, don't mention it. It's the least I can do. What was I saying? Oh yes… No, we found nothing really out of the ordinary. I'd say she died as a result of gas poisoning around eleven-thirty yesterday evening. Apart from old scars, and there were absolutely loads of those around her arms, legs and lower abdomen, there was no bruising and no suspicious marks on the body. We did find traces of barbiturates in her blood. Not a particularly high dose: a regular amount for someone who would have popped a couple to help get a good night's sleep. I've checked and she had them on prescription.'

'So you'd say it was a simple case of suicide?' Kennedy asked, bringing Taylor's cup and saucer across to him.

'Was there a suicide note?'

'No. At least none we could find. But that doesn't mean a lot. Only about one in twelve suicides leave a note. From the little I know about her domestic politics, I am sure she would have left something, if only to instruct the authorities as to who she wanted to look after her children and how she wanted her work treated. Apparently she had a sister-in-law, Tor, who was always trying to meddle in her career,' Kennedy said, realising that he was speculating wildly.

'Could a person or persons unknown with an ulterior motive have discovered a note and removed it?' Taylor asked, settling cosy into his chair, obviously enjoying his tea.

'The nanny, Judy Dillon, found Esther this morning. We caught her helping herself to a couple of the dead woman's journals but she claims she was thinking of their safety with all the strangers who were running around the apartment.'

'Do you think she could have removed a note?' Taylor asked.

'Oh, she could have, I'm sure. But why would she?' Kennedy said, apparently distracted. 'Let's consider the kids. I have a hard time accepting that Esther Bluewood would have killed herself, particularly when her children were upstairs and, potentially, could have been in danger from the gas, not to mention that there was a good chance they might have discovered her body.'

'The little I know about it, old chap, and it is a little, is that when you're suicidal you're not thinking logically. They say...' Taylor paused for a little chuckle, 'you should never kill yourself when your mind is disturbed by suicidal thoughts.'

Kennedy enjoyed the lighter moment. 'Well, her analyst, Hugh Watson, is studying her last couple of journals this evening, to see if he can pick up any clue as to her stability, so I guess there's not much we can do until then.'

Chapter 12

KENNEDY DIDN'T have time to go home before meeting ann rea in the rarely crowded but always customer-friendly Albert. He had walked to the pub, situated on the corner of Kingstown Street and Princess Road, from North Bridge House, his crombie collar pulled up high to shelter him from the cutting winds. But the cold of the night was nothing compared to the chill he felt about Esther Bluewood's death. Particularly vivid in his mind was the scene of the two motherless children standing hand in hand at the kitchen door looking in on their dead mother. Kennedy's preoccupation about Jens and Holmer was broken when he spotted ann rea sitting on a sofa facing the pub door.

ann rea was staring towards the door, but her stare was so concentrated that she didn't notice her sometime-lover arrive. She continued looking at him as he walked towards her but she still didn't register it was him. He was right up beside her and leaning over to kiss her before she snapped out of her trance.

'Kennedy, it's you,' ann rea said, ringing out the 'you' into at least three syllables.

'It's me,' Kennedy said quietly, concluding their greeting of old. Somehow tonight it lacked its usual fun and came across as very hollow.

'Can I get you a drink?' Kennedy asked, glancing at her empty wine glass.

'Yes, a glass of white would be great. The house stuff is fine.'

'How about some food?' Kennedy asked, stopping and looking back over his shoulder as he headed for the bar.

'Maybe later, right now I just need some alcohol in my blood.'

Kennedy resumed his journey. It felt like being in a film that had been frozen on a frame and then, as the projector restarts, it comes back to life.

'God, Kennedy, whatever will the children do?' ann rea continued a few seconds after Kennedy's return.

'Won't Yeats look after them?'

Glasses touched and, first of the crisp wine downed, they sat back into the sofa, half facing each other, their knees almost touching.

'Esther wouldn't have wanted that because she knew he'd just palm them off on Tor.'

'Who would she have wanted to raise them?' Kennedy asked.

'Oh, there'd be a few: her brother, her Islington friends, Jillian and James, her mother, perhaps – but she's quite old and they weren't very close. As things are I expect the authorities will have to hand them over to Yeats, won't they?'

''Fraid so,' Kennedy said at the end of a long swig. He could tell ann rea was relaxing, so he moved back into the corner of the deep red sofa a few minutes after she'd made a similar retreat. They were now facing, one leg each up on the sofa.

ann rea was dressed all in black. Tight-fitting pants and thick woollen polo neck jumper, with a black nylon scarf still tangled about her neck. Her trusted black duffel coat was draped over the back of the sofa between them, serving as a border of sorts. She wasn't wearing a touch of make-up. Nor did she need to. Her sharp features – Beatle bob hairstyle, brown hair recently washed and full and shining (just like in the adverts, maybe even a little better); generous lips, (Kennedy knew exactly just how giving they could be); heavy eyelids, perfectly capped with strong, defined, eyebrows, slightly darker in colour than the hair on her head – all combined to create a picture so breathtakingly sensational no one could ever have done better with make-up.

They both finished their wine at the same moment and a split second later Kennedy felt a warm flush come over him. It could have been the wine successfully eking its way into his bloodstream, but he preferred to think it was the connection, that particular deep bond which he felt was starting to draw them back to each other.

ann rea reached her hand, which had been resting across her coat on the back of the sofa, towards Kennedy. As she did so she leaned over and ran her fingers through his hair. The detective's hair was black. It had a natural middle parting and fell about around his ears (barely). He rarely combed it, preferring mostly to do as ann rea had just done and run his fingers through it when he wanted a tidy. He had started the day, as with most days, clean-shaven, but the five o'clock shadow had arrived early and now there was a light growth about the bottom of his face. Kennedy wasn't really handsome, not at all in fact, but neither was he bad looking. It was just… well he had the kind of face that was going to look great in another ten or so years, when his age would begin to show.

Most women were attracted to his hands. They, and his green eyes, were his best features – according to ann rea anyway. She'd described his hands as kind. She couldn't explain why. When pushed she'd say that they just looked kind and then she'd giggle and add that she also liked what they did to her; what he did to her with his hands. He claimed his hands had a mind of their own. That was his story and as a policeman, one of the things he had learned was that when you have a story, you should stick to it.

Neither ann rea nor Kennedy were thin people; neither were they plump. Kennedy had a sweet tooth and claimed to have to watch his belt. But dressed as he was tonight, in black trousers, grey shirt, black waistcoat under his crombie – which he still hadn't removed – black leather shoes and grey socks, he looked fine. No embarrassing bulges where bulges shouldn't be. ann rea, in Kennedy's eyes (not to mention a few others around North Bridge House) had the perfect figure. Perfect in a Rosanna Arquette kind of way.

Even now, drained by a highly emotional day, ann rea looked more late-twenties than her actual thirty-three-and-one-third years on this planet. Her fingers were still combing his hair as she leaned her face in closer to him. He thought she was leaning in to kiss him, and perhaps she had started off this movement with that in mind, but at the last possible second she aborted the mission and sent her lips to within half an inch of his ear. She whispered into it, sprang up from the sofa and headed towards the bar.

Kennedy hadn't heard what she had said and when, upon her return laden with two fresh glasses of wine, he inquired as to the contents of her remark, she hiked her shoulders as if to try to find the words to explain, but instead settled for: 'Oh, just that it was my round.' But the manner in which she delivered the line lead Kennedy to believe that what she had whispered had been anything but those innocent words.

The detective let it go, for now.

'When did you see Esther Bluewood last?'

'I can tell you exactly when it was,' ann rea replied, her mood picking up a notch, apparently happy at the new tangent.

'Yes?' Kennedy prodded, stretching the words into an incredible four syllables.

'It was the 16th of February this year.'

'Oh,' Kennedy contented himself with a single syllable this time.

'Yes, it was the night of the British Music Industry Awards. I remember it well; it was so gross. She invited me over to watch it with her, saying she knew I shared her healthy dislike of all the back-slapping the industry gets up to. She said it always depressed her but that she still found it compulsive viewing, and she invited me over. She claimed, being American herself, that America was particularly to blame as they had started the whole awards ceremonies thing in the first place. We all know that you can't possible say *Titanic* is a better movie than *Saving Private Ryan* or *Waking Ned*. It's the same as saying a 747 Jet is better than Morse's XJ6 Jaguar – that's really what they're trying to do.'

'I agree, so what made it such compulsive viewing?' Kennedy asked.

'Perversity, that's probably the best word to describe it. Even though you know the awards are pointless, you still want the person or film you like to win; and maybe, and this might be an even bigger motivation, you like to see certain people lose. I have to admit this year's awards were pretty perverse by any standard. Right, you have our good friends in the music industry paying £600 each to sit and eat something like 8,000 pounds of smoked salmon, 1,000 eggs, 4,000 chicken breasts and 600 fillets of beef. They wash this down with roughly 12,000 bottles of various booze and then Bono, never a man short of a cause, parades out Stevie Wonder and poor Muhammad Ali and announces, as part of the 2000 Campaign, that we can't expect all the starving people in the world to repay their debts.'

'Well, I suppose someone has to draw attention to it,' said Kennedy, trying to provide some balance.

'Yes, perhaps, but did he really need to bring out Mohammed Ali? The man's ill, for heaven's sake. That was so undignified.'

'Oh, I'm sure he wouldn't have been there it he hadn't wanted to be on public view,' Kennedy offered with a shrug. He stole a sip of wine before continuing. 'Was Esther grossed out by it as well?'

'Totally. We were quite squiffy towards the end of the television coverage of the awards. We'd drunk lots of wine and had no food. Lethal. Bad mistake. I remember being quite mad about the spectacle but in a light-hearted way. But Esther, well she was becoming visibly upset. "Don't let it upset you," I said. "What's going on there has nothing to do with you." "The problem is," she replied, "most people think this is what the music business is all about. People sitting at home won't be encouraged to do what I do." She then went into a real spiral as yet another bland act took their turn to perform.'

'Who was it, then?' Kennedy felt obliged to ask.

'Oh, it doesn't really matter, probably someone like Michael Bolton. But then Esther said, "There's no place for people like me in the music business. They only want groups like bla bla bla who are manufactured and consequently controlled artistically and personally. People tell them what clothes to wear, what to say, what songs to sing, which producer to use. What dance steps. Everything. I'd like to think that someone sitting in Belfast or Glasgow or even Boston, who feels the way I do, would have access to a platform to express those feelings and, consequently, be able to deal with their own stuff. Instead, what do we get? We get this crap." And she pointed to the TV screen.'

ann rea broke into a laugh. Kennedy knew she was remembering something else.

'And then, guess what she did?' she said through her laughter.

'What?' asked Kennedy, desperate to know. 'What?'

'She threw the remains of a tin of cold baked beans she'd been eating at the TV screen, so hard she smashed it. It was beautiful. Here was something that was annoying us so much, making us madder and madder, and by just chucking a tin of bleeding baked beans at it, we had removed it, removed our problem as though for ever. After the screen was smashed, the television spluttered and splattered and gave up the ghost with a feeble puff of smoke. And then it was all over. The Brits were over and the silence was golden. The contrast was incredible you know, from all that crap, grossness, visual and audio pollution and obscenity to beautiful peace and quiet. And then we both rolled about the floor in stitches laughing about how decadent we were smashing up TVs. Oasis or what?'

'It was The Who, actually, who smashed up TV screens, threw them out of hotels rooms.'

'Who?' ann rea asked, a hint of devilment creeping across her face.

Kennedy was about to explain when he realised he'd been caught, or very nearly caught.

Two further glasses of wine each and forty minutes later they were back at Kennedy's house.

'I always feel safe here,' ann rea said, as Kennedy locked the door behind them. 'I don't know what it is exactly. It always feels warm and homely in here. Maybe it's the times we spent here, the memories, how close we were…'

'Fancy a cup of tea?'

'Very romantic, Christy. Here I am about to spill my heart out on to your hall floor and you want to know whether or not I want a cup of tea…'

'Well, romantic or not, the point is, after all that wine and no food we could both do with some liquid of a different kind,' Kennedy said. It wasn't what he'd meant to say, but he didn't feel it appropriate, if fact it was somewhat insensitive, to say at this point that he didn't want to get into discussing their relationship again. As far as he was concerned it had been discussed to death. There were only so many times and so many ways you could reach some invisible point in a relationship, and then, for some unexplainable reason, turn and run in the opposite direction, like someone chased by demons. Although, for ann rea, any direction at all would seem to do, so long as it was away.

For his part, it wasn't a subject that was totally resolved, either. He liked being with her. He loved being with her, in fact. At one point in the relationship he thought he might have even loved her. Actually, that was rubbish. At one point in their relationship he'd felt he loved her like he'd never loved anyone before, and he couldn't imagine loving anyone as much in the future. If there had been a battle-axe mother in the background, it would have been easier for Kennedy, giving him someone else to blame. But there was no one else, just the two of them. They'd started out on this wonderful journey together, but for some reason they'd stumbled and fallen. Maybe it was something to do with her baggage: ann rea's previous relationship with a man she'd loved (like *she'd* loved no other), a man she'd lost to another woman. Perhaps it would have been easier (for Kennedy, at least) if ann rea's previous relationship had run its natural course and withered, rather than dying a horrible death. But she had still been in love with the other man when he'd walked out, and – to add insult to injury – he'd married his new woman only two months later. And ann rea was still trying to come to terms with her loss. To add further insult to injury, the couple was still married, four years later, and the proud parents of two happy, healthy children.

Kennedy was sure that ann rea didn't begrudge her ex and his wife their happiness. No, certainly not. It was just that she'd felt herself absolutely in love with this guy and she was forever tormenting herself about it, to the point that now she and Kennedy had a… well, Kennedy wasn't exactly sure what kind of a relationship they were enduring.

They had great sex. No, scrap that! They had *phenomenal* sex, infrequent but phenomenal. The relationship would frequently start back up again following a night of great lovemaking. When they were making love and all the other crap had been thrown aside, just like their clothes scattered around the bedroom floor, Kennedy was convinced that they were in love. It was spiritual. Their souls were close, as close as two souls could possibly be. But, and it was a big 'but', every single time they got to this stage and were warming to each other again, ann rea would become more and more nervy until eventually she would take flight, like a frightened doe. And, like the frightened doe, the more vulnerable she looked, the more attractive she became, and (consequently) the more hurt and pain Kennedy felt at her leaving.

They had broken up several times now, and Kennedy was not quite weary from it, but certainly well on the way to getting there. At least that was what he felt in the cold light of day. But now, in his house at evening, both of them a few glasses over the limit even for walking, he watched as this beautiful vision relaxed in front of his eyes, her inhibitions, like her reservations, melting gently away as the alcohol took control of their minds.

'Okay. You've sold me on the idea of some more liquid refreshment. Let's see? Ahm, is there any wine in the house?' ann rea asked enthusiastically.

'There certainly is. There's a bottle of white in the fridge. Why don't you open it, while I prepare some food to soak it up?' Kennedy laughed. He realised they would drink no more than about a half a glass each, for neither of them were what you'd call drinkers, certainly not when compared to the likes of James Irvine.

ann rea struggled with the corkscrew as Kennedy struggled to make his famous psychedelic omelette, so-called not because of any mind-altering qualities but because of its colourfulness. He chucked in every brightly coloured food he could find: sweet corn; red peppers; green peppers; peas; scallions. All tossed into the omelette as it was browning in the pan, just before it was turned over. His secret ingredient, which he never allowed anyone to see him add, was half a spoonful of sugar scattered into the colours. This added the twist that caused people to comment about what an unusual and delicious combination it was. No one (but no one) had ever figured out the secret of this wonder of Kennedy's world.

Wine in hand, and half an omelette each, they moved to the first-floor living room, each spreading out on a sofa. That was ann rea's choice. She waited to see where Kennedy was going to sit before opting for the other sofa. That was another thing about ann rea Kennedy liked. It wasn't guaranteed that they would spend the night together, it was never guaranteed. They'd known each other for five years, and during that time they'd never just fallen into bed together. Kennedy liked that; he liked the uncertainty. He cherished the specialness of their lovemaking; loved the fact that it wasn't a habit. This meant that, at least from his point of view, there was always an edge of uncertainty, always a longing, always a lusting. He still found her breathtakingly beautiful in that she literally did take his breath away whenever he looked at her. She never flaunted herself, and there was always some mystery about her. They'd been naked with each other so many times over the previous five years, but she still took care to do simple things like never disrobing fully before climbing into bed with him. Perhaps that was because she remembered he liked her that way. He liked to discover the final secrets in the dark, and mostly by touch. If they had married or lived together, Kennedy would have given anything for this to remain the same. He'd heard the 'we have a shower, flop into bed, jump each others bones then roll over and go to sleep' line too many times to want to be party to it.

So, from that point of view, he had exactly what he wanted. She was now about four feet away from him on the neighbouring sofa, and he was incredibly turned on by the vision of her. She wore her clothes dark and tight, tight as in figure-hugging. That vision always excited him like no other.

A few minutes later, ann rea set her clean plate down on to the coffee table, and after taking a swig of wine announced: 'Great, Kennedy. That was really great: I was absolutely famished.' She rose and walked shakily across the room to his CD collection and carefully selected and loaded a CD. She made for her original sofa, but at the last minute changed her mind and cuddled up next to Kennedy.

From the opening chord, Kennedy knew her choice: *Axis* by Esther Bluewood.

The introduction caught Kennedy by the throat every time he listened to it. A crisp, plaintive, electric guitar with a touch of echo set on the left-hand side of the stereo, perfectly complemented by a gently soaring ambient guitar on the right-hand side. The guitar sound occasionally floated in and out as time was kept by a plodding bass and a solitary drum beat, the drummer keeping time with drumstick resting on the snare-drum and gentle beating it down with the flat of his hand. Such a simple sweet beautiful sound, but as beautiful as the "Hills of Donegal".

Then the voice comes in. A sad, soulful, haunting voice, no studio enhancements, just a full voice singing:

We have one life, and one life won't do

It was if though ann rea and Kennedy were hearing her sing it for the first time. And it totally destroyed both of them. ann rea could not hold back her tears; she didn't even try. Kennedy held himself together, but only just, as Esther went around the houses a few times with variations on 'you move much better when you're happy', singing her heart out. Voice and music as one, working so closely together, so tight you couldn't tell the join. This was all intuitive. This was not thought out for her by a producer: his job was to turn on the tapes and listen and watch in bliss to all that was happening in front of him.

When Esther sang:

There is one love but one love won't do

Kennedy lost it as well. Anyone with a heart would have lost it. The person singing the song, one of several songs she'd used to exorcise her demons, had twenty-four hours earlier either lost her battle with the demons that haunted her, or else someone had taken her life away.

Kennedy felt like he could have stayed in the space, the space created by this amazing soundscape, forever.

You move much better when you're happy

Esther Bluewood's voice was now double-tracked and sang against itself, building up to a crescendo, ad-libbing around the 'you move much better when you're happy' theme. Then one voice drops out and she gently winds down the song, singing quieter and quieter, until, almost in a whisper, it stops.

No music Kennedy had ever listened to, had moved him as deeply as that song had that night. She was an artist at one with her art and with her musicians; a brave artist who exposed her pain, while, at the same time, offering comfort to others.

It was beyond words.

ann rea was gently sobbing into Kennedy's chest. They held each other tightly and listened, maybe even lived, the rest of the album. They dozed off for a time, not having spoken since ann rea had put on the CD.

She woke him at about two o'clock in the morning and took him upstairs, where they made love like they'd never made love before. It was if their lives, their beings, depended on it. It was perfect love-making, no rushing, no slowing, no worrying, no hurting, no imagining, no wishing, no chasing the butterfly, no nervousness; just love.

They made love.

Then, contented, they fell asleep in each other's arms.

At some stage, in the early hours of the morning, as they both drifted back into consciousness simultaneously, ann rea put an arm around Kennedy and pulled him closer to her. Just before they drifted off to sleep again, she whispered, 'Oh, and by the way, thanks for the omelette, Kennedy. It was a great omelette, just a hint too much sugar in it, though.'

Chapter 13

EARLY ON the second morning of the investigation into the death of Esther Bluewood – and incidentally, the second morning of the week – Detective Inspector Christy Kennedy walked the four hundred or so yards from his house at the foot of Primrose Hill to Hugh Watson's house-cum-workplace. The genial Watson greeted Kennedy with a smile and a firm, warm handshake. A handshake so firm Kennedy was tempted to check his fingers afterwards to make sure they were still intact. If Kennedy was not mistaken, Dr Watson was dressed exactly as he had been on the previous day's visit, right down to his rhinestone cowboy boots.

Kennedy was led through to the same room he'd been in on the previous day. The two-bar fire was alive and there were hints of what smelt like burning dust in the air. This time, before flopping down in his chair, Watson went immediately to the fireplace and rang the bell. Three minutes later, right on cue, the old woman arrived, somewhat more steady than on the previous day, bearing a tray with not only tea, but piping hot buttered toast.

'So,' Kennedy began, once the formalities were out of the way. 'Did you have a chance to study the journals?'

'I did,' Watson replied, as he munched on his toast. He looked slightly uncomfortable having to sit upright in his chair in order to drink his tea.

'And?'

Watson sighed a sigh that signified it wasn't as easy as that. 'What we first have to accept is that the motivation for suicide consists of both an inner... inner whatyemecallit? Turmoil yes, that's it turmoil. The motivation for suicide involves turmoil, inner disturbances, if you will, and the belief that death is a solution. A solution in as much that it is an escape from the inner bedlam. To a sufferer, this is as violent as any physical violence could ever be.' The doctor finished his cup of tea and happily sank back into his chair.

Kennedy, feeling he was about to receive the 'long version', settled back comfortably into the sofa. It wasn't the same corner he'd occupied the day before, but the spot Coles had nabbed, which was closer to the electric fire.

'Each year in this United Kingdom of ours, there are approximately 3,000 suicides. Around 450 of them take place in London and a third of the London total are women. Every single suicide is the act of a mind-tyrant. A little Napoleon lurks in there, ruling the roost and making decisions that are often against the person's own interests. Though I'd have to say I wouldn't be altogether sure in Esther's case that a tyrant was actually in there.' Watson clasped his hands in front of his chin and, breaking his index fingers away from the clasp, used them as a single pointer to caress his lips. His eyes, though none of the rest of his weather-beaten face, were smiling just as they had the previous day.

How does he do that? Kennedy wondered.

'Let's discuss suicide for a moment,' Watson continued. 'It's a multi-faceted event which encompasses cultural, interpersonal, logical, biological, biochemical, philosophical, conscious and unconscious elements. But its fundamental nature is psychological. In simple terms, imagine you are a tree. These elements I've just mentioned would be the roots, the leaves, the branches, even the subtleties of the camouflage is an aspect to be considered. Now, unlike ourselves, a tree can't think. There are no mental problems a tree can solve. It can die because it catches a... a whatyemecallit... a blight; or, someone cuts it when it's young; or its roots can't get a grip in the earth, problems like that. But if the tree could reason, say it suffered from psychological problems, then perhaps it would think, My roots aren't strong enough to hold me up so I'm going to fall. So, if it thinks it's going to fall, it does fall.'

Kennedy wasn't entirely sure he was with the doctor on that one, amusing though the concept was.

The doctor seemed to sense the scepticism, and he elaborated: 'No, let me explain it another way. Dying is the only thing on this earth that men and women don't have to do, they don't have to arrange, we just stick around long enough and nature does it for us. But...' Watson continued energetically, his eyes smiling again, 'conversely, it is the only thing you must do. All of us have serious responsibilities in life – but there is only one responsibility from which we can't hide, death! There are positively no "ifs" to death. The only questions are where, when and how? Suicide decides the time, the place and the method. It is the only type of death where the victim supplies you, the investigator, with the details required for the death certificate.' Watson paused, as if to consider the weight of his own words. He turned to face Kennedy, looked him straight in the eyes and continued:

'I'm telling you all of this because I want you to have a little understanding of what might have been going on in Esther Bluewood's mind. If you can grasp that, then hopefully you'll also understand my logic when I tell you what I learned from Esther's journals.'

'I'm with you so far, doctor. Or at least I think I am,' Kennedy offered in encouragement.

'Thinking you are is always a good start,' Watson said, his entire face breaking into a complete smile. He looked over his right shoulder, repeating another of yesterday's habits. 'We are not encouraged to think much for ourselves. *They* tell us it's better if they do our thinking for us... anyway, back to suicide. With suicide the goals merge into one aim: escaping the turmoil, the pain. This escape is considered relief. That which is peace, is desired above all else. By taking your own life, you believe that the unbearable pain will become tranquility. All your suffering will disappear. At least that's what the suicidal person hopes.' Again Watson paused, he looked unsure about what to say next. 'I think it's worth pointing out, though it's obviously not entirely relevant to this case, that there are other occasions where we take our lives or...' Watson nodded back over his right shoulder again, 'when we may be encouraged to take our own lives by means of ideological methods: *hara-kiri, suttee, seppuku* and, more recently, by suicidal terrorism. But back to Esther Bluewood: let's look at what people are trying to achieve when they commit suicide. They are looking for a solution. Suicide is never an accident; it is never committed without some hope in mind. It becomes an answer, invariably the only solution to the problems of the suicide's world. To understand Esther's earlier suicide attempt we simply need to look at her relationship, or lack of relationship, with her father. Now she fought hard to overcome this lack of love. All of the album that made her name was about starting over again. One of the songs was actually called "Resurrection". And in terms of her life that's what it's all about. When her brother found her in the basement and she was taken away for treatment, she felt as though she'd started a new life. Now the great thing about Esther is ...' Watson stopped dead in his tracks, smiled a sad smile and dropped his eyes.

'Forgive me.' He paused for twenty-three ticks of the large clock on the mantelpiece, then sighed. 'I meant to say, Esther was... the great thing about Esther was that she wasn't naive enough to think that her illness was cured and that she could then live happily ever after. She knew there was still a disease somewhere deep inside her, and if she wasn't aware of it, if she ignored it, it would eat away at her until, eventually, it would destroy her altogether. "New Way, New Day", again a song from that album, examines exactly that.'

'So her songwriting would have helped her come to terms with her unhappiness?' Kennedy asked, trying to get a proper grasp.

'Perhaps. They say there's always a great song at the end of a teardrop. In Esther's case her songwriting certainly gave her a voice through which she could articulate and exorcise her demons. It wasn't exactly that writing songs cured her, it was more that the songs are the diary of her need for help, her cry for help, her acceptance of help, her own help as well as the help of others. She became an important person in her own life again. At the time of her death she was in charge of her life. She was successful, she was in a non-competitive situation. That's one of Paul Yeats' qualities. Although he's a fellow artist, he saw the greatness in her work. He wasn't threatened by it, the opposite in fact, he was extremely supportive and generous with his time and praise. In her eyes, Paul loved her and as a fellow artist, he loved her work. He wasn't in the least bit jealous.'

'But they were about to split...' Kennedy paused to correct himself. 'Hadn't they already split up?'

Again Watson offered another generous eye smile. Kennedy couldn't figure out if the doctor's smiles were of encouragement or reproachment. 'You see, the thing about Esther was that she was ill. She was aware of her illness, she wanted to deal with it, and she *was* dealing with it. She also recognized illness in others.'

'What? Yeats was ill as well... you mean, like Esther?' Kennedy asked.

'No, no, no, nothing like that. Well, in point of fact he was a compulsive womaniser. When she met him he was with another woman. She went around to their... their thingamabob... their flat, yes, their flat, in response to an advert. She went around to his flat with the aim of renting a room. They fell in love and the then girl-friend was cast aside for Esther. Perhaps, as an older-looking man, he was replacing her father. Although I personally doubt that. I think she'd already dealt with her father's rejection by that point. But the honest answer is, we'll never know and it certainly didn't do any harm for him to take up that role, if that's what he did. Unfortunately though, he in turn met someone else and the process repeated itself, this time with Esther being the one cast aside in favour of a newer model. I'm not sure she felt it was entirely over, though. It was certainly unresolved and that which is unresolved is never over. Esther reports him as saying something about their growing old together. And he probably meant that. Now, we don't know the politics of the relationship between Paul and his new girl-friend and how that might make him think about and deal with Esther. Some women never come to terms with their partner's ex, they are forever seeking signs of preference, but for this conversa-tion, that needn't concern us. Let's talk about the emotions involved in suicide…'

Kennedy, like a dutiful student, mentally opened a new page.

Watson continued: 'The dominant emotion in suicide is help-lessness, the feeling of being useless, hopeless. The feeling that the only way out is suicide. Looking through Esther's notes, I don't think she felt any such emotion. She wasn't overjoyed with life but she was in charge of it. She was successful. She had a very comfort-able income drawn from her art, and that generated a very satisfy-ing feeling of fulfilment.'

'I can see that,' Kennedy said, recalling ann rea's satisfaction with money earned from her freelance writing.

'Okay. Now we come to ambivalence. People who commit suicide claim they don't care whether they live or die. "What's the difference whether I live or die?" they'll say. "I'd be better off dead." Now there have been some very literal suicide victims over the years and they have left a very elegant trail of words, and so, in some instances, suicide might even appear to be attractive. But my point would have to be that people who want to commit suicide, do so, so that they can enjoy a better "life". That which is without turmoil is preferable,' Watson continued, the lecture now in full flow.

'Sorry, can we stop there for just a minute? I was with you, pretty much up to that point,' Kennedy said, intrigued by Watson's latest remark. 'People want to commit suicide because they want to enjoy a better "life". Surely that's a contradiction?'

'Yes, if you look at it literally. But let's look at it from another perspective. Someone is suffering considerable turmoil. Their life is a complete misery due to intense psychological pain. They experi-ence an overwhelming desire to escape the pain and the pressure. They want release. They want to feel better. They want to enjoy their lives just like the people around them do. In their minds, their mental pain is much greater than any physical pain their friends or colleagues might suffer. So, why do they want to commit suicide?

Simple. They want to commit suicide because they want to feel better. In other words they want a better "life", don't you see?' Watson proclaimed. He continued in a sadder tone. 'Suicide is a very lonely act and always an unnecessary act. There are ways to heal yourself and enjoy a better life.'

'How?' Kennedy asked simply.

'By asking for help, that's how. In many ways a suicide attempt is exactly that, a cry for help. Yes, there is medication, and don't get me wrong, medication is vitally important, but equally important is therapy. Getting to the root of the problem by asking the right questions. "Where are you hurting?"; "Can you describe your turmoil?"; "What is it you need to escape from?"; and so on. The objective being to work out exactly what the problems are and to show that, perhaps, suicide is not the only answer. It all sounds very simple, but you've got to show people that suicide is not the only route available; that it's not the only way out. By focusing on the problem, you can broaden the range of options available to them. Again, from reading her journals, I have to tell you Esther was most definitely not in that corner when she died. She was dealing with her problems in an adult fashion. She wasn't running from them. Far from it, in point of fact, she was prepared to endure the pain of a divorce in order to deal with her situation with Paul Yeats.'

'Do you really think she'd have gone ahead with a divorce?' Kennedy asked.

'Who knows? She might just have been shooting a warning shot over his bows. He was always saying that they were going to grow old together and maybe she wanted to call his bluff, to let him know she wasn't going to hang around while he continued having his affairs. She writes in her journal that she didn't consider herself to have been unfaithful to Paul when she went with Josef—'

'But surely—' Kennedy cut Watson off, only to be cut off mid-sentence himself.

'She never cheated on their love. She never stopped loving him and she believed that he had never stopped loving her. In her mind's eye, they were both seeking physical release elsewhere. But that's exactly how she considered it, you've read her words. "Josef didn't require batteries", or words to that effect. But back to the point I was making. At this juncture in her life, Esther Bluewood was in charge. A second common trait of suicide is the prior communication of intention. People communicate their intentions, dropping subtle, and sometimes not so subtle, hints to friends and colleagues.

They attempt to seek professional help. Again, nothing like this from Esther and don't forget, she had attempted suicide once before, and she'd marked herself, cut herself very badly. In fact, her mother, brother and friends were concerned about her. On that occasion when she attempted suicide, she could just have easily have gone into the forest and cut her wrists and no one would ever have found her, at least not until after she was long dead. But she didn't: she chose the basement of her family home. I personally think if Esther had intentions on her own life, those around her would have been aware of it. People who are intent on committing suicide behave abnormally; they don't know how to live otherwise. Stands to reason, they've never done it before – successfully. Medical doctors, colleagues of mine, have told me that people who are in the final stages of a fatal disease, cancer for instance, behave normally over the final few weeks or months, even an exaggerated normality, if you know what I mean. But with suicide cases, well, there's an inherent need to survive. So, by their actions they will betray themselves, or betray their intentions. There were no such signs from Esther. She knew the pain could be reduced by psychotherapy yet she never sought it. She knew that as well as reducing the pain, psychotherapy would help her see clearly again, would dissolve her cloud of mental anguish and lighten the pressure on her. At such times, a little help can bring salvation.'

Watson paused again and Kennedy found the doctor staring deep into his eyes, as if challenging him. It was quite unnerving.

'You don't believe she committed suicide, either, do you?' the doctor asked.

'No. I don't,' Kennedy replied truthfully. 'What made you ask that?'

'Well,' Watson began, and his entire face broke into a generous smile. 'I see you sitting here, watching me, listening intently, never moving a muscle, except that is for continuously flexing the fingers of your right hand, wanting me... no, willing me to prove to you that Esther Bluewood did not commit suicide. You want so badly for her not to have committed suicide. Why is that?'

Kennedy described the sad scene back at the Bluewood maisonette with Jens and Holmer, hand in hand, looking down at their dead mother.

'I can't believe she would have killed herself if she thought there was the slightest chance she could have done harm to her children, or if there was a chance they might have seen her body.'

'Fair point, but I should point out to you that when people are intent on committing suicide, they sometimes feel that they will be doing their children a favour by getting out of their lives. You see, they are so preoccupied with their own pain that simple logic is forgotten. Professor Edwin Shneidman has the view that suicide stems such a deep psychological pain. He believes that when pain comes from frustrated psychological needs, those needs are of mental, rather than organic, origins. He tells us that suicide is prevented by changing our perception of the situation and by redefining that which is unbearable. Esther, in my mind, had long since mastered this.' Kennedy felt the doctor's tone implied that he was starting to wind up.

'There is a need to belong. She belonged,' Watson continued, raising his thumb. 'There is a need to be loved. She was loved. She mentions it in her journal. She felt her children loved her unconditionally. She was aware of the loyalty and commitment of her fans, a different kind of love, I know, but a love nonetheless, and a love which will bear one gladly upon its shoulders. Paul Yeats, she thought, had many faults, one main fault, in fact, but deep down she believed he loved her in his own way. In her journal she concedes he was the bridge over which she walked from troubled waters back to dry land.' Watson held out his third finger to emphasie his third point. 'Esther made no cry for help. Neither did she feel helpless. She certainly cared about whether she lived or died. As we've already discussed, there was no apparent heightening psychological pain and certainly none is evident in her journal. She sought to solve her mental problems.' By this time Watson had stopped counting. 'I would have to tell you, Inspector Kennedy, that there is not a shred of evidence available to me to suggest that Esther Bluewood committed suicide.'

Chapter 14

A FEW minutes later, Kennedy was walking across his beloved
Primrose Hill, going over doctor Hugh Watson's words in his mind.
As he reached Magpie Corner, he spotted two magpies.

One for sorrow, two for joy. He took this as a positive sign. A
sign perhaps that the spirits of Primrose Hill were happy that Esther
Bluewood's death was going to receive a full investigation. She
deserved nothing less.

He could see the beginning of a small crowd milling around the
corner of Regents Park Road and Fitzroy Road. Possibly fans on a
pilgrimage to pay their last respects, to voice their disbelief and to
take comfort in the fact that others were feeling the pain as much as
they were. ann rea certainly was taking Esther's death very badly.
ann rea, being ann rea, and honest to a fault, would never have
claimed to have been a friend of Esther Bluewood, but Esther had
felt comfortable enough to have invited ann rea around to her
maisonette a few times.

During the night, as Kennedy and ann rea lay in each others
arms, she, just like Doc Watson, had claimed – no, claimed was too
weak a word for it – ann rea had positively asserted that Esther
Bluewood had not committed suicide. She didn't have Watson's
expertise to prove her case. She'd only met the songwriter about
seven times but she knew her work and she'd seen her with her children and that was enough to convince her that this woman would
not have taken her own life.

The last time ann rea had seen Esther Bluewood had been when
they had watched the Brit Awards together on television, when
Esther had smashed the screen with the tin of baked beans. That
was only just over a week ago and ann rea said she'd seemed
mentally and physically strong. She'd discussed plans for her next
album and had claimed she had a dozen new songs. Esther had
played ann rea some of them, trusting the journalist's instinct as a
sounding-board. ann rea said Esther had been very enthusiastic
about the new direction of the songs. She had been writing for some
time but all the new songs had sounded like material she'd done
before, saying things she'd already said. The record company had
loved them because they were in the same vein as the hugely success-

ful *Axis*. But Esther had shelved the new songs, not content to furrow the same ground again.

She told ann rea she'd had a troubled six months following this decision, when no songs would come. During this time she'd written more and more in her journals and had happened upon an idea for a novel. She was going to make a new record, because there was something inside her bursting to get out. Then after the album, she was going to write the novel and try and find a publisher for it. She was very enthusiastic about this and drew a promise from ann rea that she would read it for her before it went to an agent or publisher. ann rea felt confident Esther would get her book out.

Just before Christmas, Esther was playing songs for the children on her guitar. Singing silly songs with simple singalong melodies for Jens and Holmer to join in with. Maybe it was because it was so close to Christmas but the first song she sang to them – which she later played on cassette to ann rea – had a joyous and infectious sound. Esther claimed it had just come from nowhere and had literally taken as long to write as it had taken her to sing. She tidied up the words afterwards, but basically, how it came out of her mouth was how it ended up. She was so pleased with it that she fetched her Sony Walkman and recorded in on the spot, with the kids in the background, singing along, and their mother getting more and more confident as the song progressed.

Then, according to ann rea, a very strange thing happened. In the space of the next thirty minutes or so, encouraged by her two young children, Esther Bluewood had written another five songs. And there she stopped. She didn't try and push it to write a seventh. Two days later, the same thing happened and a further six songs flowed out of Esther. The ones ann rea had heard were short, snappy, uplifting songs, with something of the feel of the poppier Paul Simon, with hints of The Beatles and Cat Stevens' *Tea For The Tilerman*. They were the kind of songs you were convinced you'd heard before, known all your life, in fact.

The singer was so enthusiastic about these new songs and this new direction that she couldn't wait to get into the studio to record them. ann rea loved the songs and had had Esther play them over and over again. She was convinced Esther Bluewood was going to make a great album. ann rea's point was that even forgetting this new bunch of songs, if you just took Esther at face value, it appeared she was dealing with whatever demons she had. Then, taking the tone of the new songs into the equation, there was absolutely no way the songwriter was of a mind to have considered taking her own life.

Kennedy loved the passion ann rea had displayed when she told him of this. At the time, he also felt that Esther's enthusiasm could have been a proud front for ann rea. However, Doc Watson's corroborating conviction added weight to the argument, and Kennedy found himself wondering just how Esther might have been murdered. How would it be possible to make it appear as though someone had gassed themselves? And who'd want to go to such lengths? Was the method of murder a clue in itself?

Kennedy remonstrated with himself as he passed the Feng Shang Restaurant. He was breaking his own golden rule by getting ahead of himself. He was trying to solve the puzzle before he had the pieces in place. A few minutes later he reached North Bridge House. He immediately buzzed Irvine, instructing him to get the troops together and meet in the basement conference room in thirty minutes.

*

Thirty minutes later, just as the eleven o'clock news bulletin was beginning on radio BBC London Live, Kennedy's team were milling around the conference room. Kennedy was uncharacteristically late, as he'd wanted to hear London Live's news update on the Esther Bluewood story. The Bluewood section of the news bulletin was short and sweet: the Music Business was coming to terms over losing one if its greatest writers, shocked fans gathering around the songwriter's house, police were still investigating the death but understood from the gas company that they were called out to turn off the gas, implying a suicide. In other words, a 'no news' news story.

'Okay,' Kennedy began, noticing that Superintendent Castle had crept into the room and had found a high profile spot in the centre. 'I'm not convinced that Esther Bluewood's death was a suicide...' His statement drew sharp intakes of breath and whispers from the team.

Those present were WDC Anne Coles, DS James Irvine, recently promoted DS Derek Allaway, WDC Jane West, DC Donald Gaul, and DC Julien Lundy. Not forgetting Superintendent Thomas Castle and Detective Inspector Christy Kennedy himself. Kennedy noticed Coles nod positively in apparent agreement with his assessment. At the other extreme Castle was giving it one of his 'wait until I get you into my office!' looks. Everyone else's reaction was somewhere in-between.

'So, are we treating this as a murder inquiry?' Irvine asked, clearing the air.

Kennedy looked to Castle for a sign. Surprisingly, Kennedy's look was returned with a shrug. The Super was giving nothing away. Actually, Kennedy didn't have the usual relationship with his Super. Castle wasn't a horn-rimmed-Harry. No, generally he was very supportive of his team. Perhaps that was why Camden CID was one of the most successful teams in London: Castle allowed his detectives to detect.

'No,' Kennedy began awkwardly returning the smile. 'At this stage we are still carrying out a general investigation into the death of Esther Bluewood. Let's gather as much information as we can before we start looking at possible charges. People out there assume she committed suicide. Perhaps under the cloak of that particular darkness we might be able to pick up some valuable information. If her death was anything other than suicide, then we are obviously meant to think otherwise So let's use this red herring, if red herring it might be, to quietly compile as much information as possible. What I'd like to do is put together a picture of Esther's last days alive, focusing particularly on Sunday, from her waking up to evening.'

'There's going to be plenty of leg work. We might need more people,' Irvine suggested. 'The longer we take, the colder the trail will grow.'

Practically everyone in the room attempted to steal a look at Castle, all very casual, but the nonchalance evaporated when everyone did it simultaneously. Castle merely nodded to Kennedy.

'We've got the help we need, DS Irvine. I've made a list of the people who can give us background and hopefully more.' And Kennedy revealed his mental list:

'The nanny, Judy Dillon,

'The neighbour, Edward Higgins,

'The husband, Paul Yeats,

'The fan, Josef Jones,

'Friends from Islington, Jill and Jim,

'The Doctor, Hugh Watson – though I've already spoken with him twice.

'We'll also need to chat with Tor, Victoria Lucas, Yeats' sister, and Rosslyn St Clair, his new lover. Then you'll need to interview the usual neighbours and local shopkeepers, as well as people at her record company, Camden Town Records. DS Irvine here will give you details and allocate duties. Let's get through as much of this as we can today. As Irvine said, the longer we sit here, the colder the trail becomes. We'll regroup here at the end of the day and pool our information. Let's go to it.'

Kennedy left his team mingling around Irvine, awaiting instructions. He was halfway to his office when Castle, hands deep in pockets, caught up with him.

'Very sad, this matter, isn't it?' Castle began. Without waiting for a reply, he continued: 'So you don't think she took her own life?'

'No, I don't actually,' Kennedy replied, not elaborating, and crossing his fingers behind his back in the hope that Castle wouldn't push.

'Well, see where you go with it and keep me posted,' Castle replied, head bowed, staring at the red-tiled corridor as they walked along. 'I wanted to talk to you about another matter, Christy.'

Oh no, it had been too good to be true, Kennedy thought, sighing inwardly.

'Do you have a minute?' Castle persisted.

'Yes, I was about to start on the Bluewood interviews but of course I've got time, sir.' Kennedy was worried about Castle's tone. Whatever was troubling his superior, he didn't appear anxious to spit out the details.

'It's my boy,' Castle began cautiously. 'He's...'

At that point he stopped talking having spotted someone approaching from the opposite direction.

'Why don't we just nip into my office, sir? We'll have some privacy there,' Kennedy offered hopefully.

'Yes, yes. Good idea, Christy,' Castle replied, enthusiastically.

Kennedy was intrigued and fearful of the worst. Had his superior's son found himself in trouble? If so, how serious was it? Drugs? Armed robbery? Why was Castle coming to him about it? If it was a professional issue, his superior was putting him in a compromising position. Kennedy had a reputation for doing everything by the book and had no sympathy for the 'soft-shoe brigade' who policed his or her own.

He adamantly believed that members of any police service should not feel above or beyond the law. The general public certainly would be happier if internal investigations were independent and carried on from outside the force. There were enough private firms around these days for the government to hire one to carry out any necessary investigation that may arise. But Kennedy worried who would take responsibility for financing it. The government? And then who'd police the government? The Met? And on and on it would go until, if we weren't careful, we'd be back at square one.

Much as he hated the 'soft-shoe' boys and all they stood for, he hoped that Castle wasn't about to put him in an embarrassing position by either asking him to get his son off something or other, or expect Kennedy to sit in judgement on Castle himself, because of something his son had done.

Once back in his office, Kennedy automatically headed straight to the sanctuary of the tea-making area. Castle opted for the comfort of Kennedy's leather chair. Contrary to his normal disciplined posture, Castle just flopped into the chair like a lifeless puppet.

Kennedy had always thought that, for a sixty-year-old man, his superior was in incredible shape. His thick and full head of hair might have turned grey and yes, he did have a whiskey flush around his nose and cheek, but he was still as sharp as a needle. Castle, uncharacteristically, unbuttoned his jacket and Kennedy noticed, for the first time, the beginning of a paunch attacking his belt.

Kennedy slipped his Super an extra half spoonful of sugar; he looked like he could use a bit of a lift. Castle held off as Kennedy prepared a couple of demon cups of tea, served up in white bone china cups and saucers.

'Very civilised,' Castle offered in appreciation. 'I have to say you're very civilised, Christy. Always have been.'

Oh Jesus, Mary and Saint Joseph, Kennedy thought, civilised! He now thinks I'm civilised. That probably means he's found out that his son is gay and he is going to ask me what he should do about it.

'Oh, I like what I like, sir,' Kennedy replied, choosing his words carefully.'

'Ah, but it's more than that. I've noticed you. I've observed things. You have impeccable manners. You like your rituals. You like your systems. You see, just now, you were enjoying the whole procedure, the ritual, of making your tea, maybe even as much as you enjoy drinking it. I feel...'

'Oh, I don't know about that, sir,' Kennedy cut in. He always disliked talking about himself. It made him feel extremely uncomfortable to be the centre of attention, even when there was just one other person in the room. This dislike of attention even extended to the way he dressed. He was always smartly turned out, as his mother would have said, and, yes, his 'clothes awareness' was a lot keener since he'd met ann rea, but even then he always liked to be dressed in as low-key a fashion as possible. Kennedy didn't like to draw attention to himself when he walked into a room. He'd also (conveniently) found that being this way generally ensured people ignored you, which helped greatly when you wished to observe others. Whether or not that was the reason for his reserve or, a result of it, he'd never really worked out. He didn't choose to figure it out. His logic was that if he'd come this far in his life without that particular knowledge, then he could pretty much continue to survive without it.

Kenedy took a generous gulp of his tea and continued: 'There's nothing as good as a refreshing cup of tea.' He was screaming with all the body language available: *Can we get on with this please?*

Castle must have picked up on it, because he said: 'You might be correct there, Christy. You might very well be correct. Look, I wanted to talk to you about Tommy. You met him a couple of times, didn't you?'

Kennedy nodded positively.

'Well, it is my fault, I suppose, but really, Mrs Castle and me… well we'd been hoping he'd follow me into the police force. He just won't hear of it, though. He wants to quit university immediately.'

'Oh,' was the only word Kennedy felt it appropriate, but he spoke it as much out of relief as anything else.

'Yes, he wants to throw away all his educational opportunities. And you know, Christy, you and I are the last of the old breed. We're the last to have been able to work our way up through the ranks. These days you need a degree in the *A to Z* before they'll let you be a bobby on the beat and even more if you're going to be ambitious and seek promotion.' Castle was slumped in his chair and in great danger of spilling his cuppa over his crisp white shirt. 'He's a good boy, is Tommy,' he continued, the pride glowing through again. 'He's given Mrs Castle and myself little or no trouble so far. But on this one, he's firm. He wants to quit university. Drop out.' Castle pronounced the final two words with such utter contempt and distaste that Kennedy was sure this was his superior's worst nightmare.

'Tommy seems a sensible enough lad to me. Has he mentioned anything he'd like to do instead? Has he made any plans?' Kennedy asked. He felt sorry for being so relieved the conversation had taken this turn. Up to a few minutes before, he'd ideas of drugs, police corruption, homosexuality, and a life of crime.

'Oh yes, he has. That's one thing about our Tommy, he's still very ambitious. He wants to get into some sort of show-business management.'

'Oh,' Kennedy said.

'Yes. He's always had a passion, particularly for music and loves some of these new groups. Ahm, let me see now he was telling me about some them over the weekend. Oasis, he reckons there're the new Beatles, better than The Beatles, he claims. Could anyone be better than The Beatles, Christy?' Castle asked in all innocence.

'If there is anyone, sir, I certainly haven't heard of them.'

'Quite. Exactly. Let me see if I can remember some of the others, Blurred, Pup, Verve and Stereophones, do they sound familiar? Anyway, Tommy's point is that they've all been great bands and it's been a good time for music but that they've all burnt themselves out. He reckons it will soon be time for a new wave of bands and he wants to be in on the new wave.'

'Right. Well, that seems like very sound logic to me, sir.' Kennedy offered encouragingly.

'But he doesn't know how to start. He wants to try and get some experience first, working for a record company or something similar. He's written off to a few companies but none of them have even bothered to reply.'

'I see,' Kennedy said, but he couldn't see where the conversation was going.

'So, Christy, I was wondering, this young lady of yours, you know, the one without any capitals, the journalist ....' Castle was on a route through his mind trying to locate her name.

'You mean, my friend, ann rea?' Kennedy offered, casting Castle a lifeline.

'Yes, that's her. She knows all these people?' Castle asked a slight hint of distaste creeping into his voice again on the 'these people'.

'Some of them sir, yes.'

'Well, I was wondering, could you possibly ask her if she could check out whether there were any positions going in any of these companies and, you know... maybe put in a word for Tommy? He doesn't mind starting at the bottom. He'll work hard, Christy. I can guarantee that,' Castle concluded, the proud father once more.

'Yes. I mean, of course, I'm sure she'd be happy to ask around. You know, ah... yes,' Kennedy said. It was all he could think of to say.

'Good!' Castle declared. It had been another of his famous 'one cup' meetings. The minute the Super got to the end of his cup of tea, the meeting would be over, whether the other party liked it or not. He jumped to his feet and buttoned up his uniform jacket. His few moments of vulnerability had vanished along with the dregs of his tea. Kennedy was left standing in the middle of his office, holding both his own cup and saucer and that of his boss, wondering exactly what had just happened.

Castle stopped at the door and turned. 'You know,' he began, as if remembering an order of his own, 'you and miss ann rea must come over and have tea with Mrs Castle and myself. Sometime soon.'

At that, Castle turned on his well-polished heels and was gone in a heartbeat.

Chapter 15

I'VE JUST *been downstairs for another of my ever-growing number of late-night treats with Higgy. I leave my door open and he leaves his door open, so I can hear if anything is wrong with Jens or Holmer, and we have a right royal charge at his bottle of sherry. I have to admit to feeling quite squiffy right now, so this will probably read like a bunch of sparrows have dipped their feet in ink and run riot over my page. And to think, I used to think he was a right old miserable bastard!*

He was very cold and snotty with me at the beginning, and if he did talk, I couldn't understand a single word he was saying, thanks to his thick Scottish accent. Actually he doesn't talk, he shouts. He shouts because he's going deaf and his hearing aid doesn't work properly. He claims it never did work properly, not since the day he got it. I tell him to take it back and get it fixed or else get a new one, and he tells me it's on the National Health and they might not take it back. He then proceeds to tell me how Thatcher ruined Bevan's dream. I didn't quite realise what he meant at first. Here was I thinking he'd a pervy friend called Bevan who was forever having an erotic dream about Thatcher but that she'd always ruin it – or something along those lines.

Anyway, it turns out he was pissed off with me when I first moved in because he thought he was on a promise for my apartment. He claims the landlord told him he could have it when the old tenant moved out. He wanted the extra space for when his grandchild came to stay during their holidays. Apparently it's not really his grandchild: it's the child of this woman he's been having an affair with for about twenty years. She's a teacher and only comes with her child in the school holidays. She's a lot younger than him. God, she must have been a child when they first got together. Anyway, when the landlord had showed me the flat he asked me if I'd like to see downstairs because that was the one he preferred I took. I told him it was too small and the discussion ended there. So, it took some time for Higgy to forgive me. I don't think he'll ever forgive the landlord.

Higgy is quite strange in his own way. A few times I've opened my front door and he's just been standing there, doing nothing. Said I'd taken him by surprise and that he was just about to knock on my door. Every time I think about it, it gives me the creeps. But then when he invites me into his flat for a sherry and I forget all about that because it's company, and at the end of the day I need someone to talk to. You do, don't you?

Higgy's great, he just lets me rabbit on and on. Maybe he turns off his hearing aid completely and joins Bevan and Thatcher in the dream. I hope he's not imagining me in it. That would be too weird, wouldn't it? But he's got that look in his eye. I thought old men couldn't do it any more. But he certainly can, I can tell. When his young teacher comes over, they go at it hammer and tongs (hammer and tongs!!! ??– I've been in England too long). How can you go at it hammer and tongs? I've seen an English hammer and tongs and I can't for the life of me see how they could go at it like that. They just don't fit. Obviously Higgy does – fit that is – because I keep thinking he's going to wake up the entire neighbourhood with all his grunts and groans. Mind you, that's only ever on her first night. They're as quiet as church mice after that. There I go again: church mice! Why would they be quieter than ordinary mice?

Do you think a racket could be red? I love the idea of a red racket. I love red. I love the deep red of poppies, all that blood in those poor dainty little flowers. I dream a lot about poppies. Why? I told Higgy tonight about my poppy dreams. He seemed to pick up at that. You know the way people break temporarily out of their zombie-like state while watching television once the news comes on. They'll pick up for a bit and then when the headlines are over, they'll nod off again.

Anyway, he asked me what I thought my poppy dreams meant? Blood. Must have something to do with blood, he said. But I hate blood, I told him. I love poppies!

He then mumbled in his heavy accent again about Americans, and football and cricket. He lost me to be honest, probably because I was quite squiffy. Now there's a good English word. It describes the state perfectly. Anyway, so I thought I'd come up here, write and dream a bit more. Hopefully my dreams will be of poppies, fields of poppies, not Thatcher, not Bevan and not Higgy. Certainly not Higgy.

*

Irvine was as keen as Kennedy to get the investigation into gear. Like Kennedy he was convinced that Esther Bluewood hadn't committed suicide. Which meant, of course, that someone must have killed her. The more they stood around debating, 'did she or didn't she take her own life?', the more time the killer had to cover up his – or her – tracks.

Esther Bluewood's downstairs neighbour, Edward Higgins, was a fifty-six-year-old Scot who'd been living in London for just over thirty years. His hearing had been seriously impaired after a childhood accident. Apparently, in his early teens, his brother had leaned a shotgun on his shoulder 'to get a steadier shot', and the repeat of the gun had done irreparable damage. He just about managed to decipher Irvine and Allaway's questions, thanks to his archaic hearing aid. He'd checked himself out of the Royal Free Hospital that morning, against the doctor's wishes. Higgins claimed he'd recoup better in his own home. There was a lot to be said for that. Generally people do recover better in their own homes, but Higgins had no family to tend to him.

He was still feeling queasy when the police came calling. He brought them into his small living room, where he returned immediately to the comfort and safety of a bed he'd made up for himself on the sofa, pulling it closer to a cosy fire.

The room was bright and the walls uncluttered. It was sparsely furnished with a sofa, one armchair and a small coffee table. A television set and an old valve radio sat precariously on a wickerwork basket, which had been adapted for use as a shelving unit. This haphazard arrangement was propped up in the centre by a four-by-two plank and every available inch of space covered with copies of the *Standard*, *Telegraph*, and the Culture Section of the *Sunday Times*. No books or records, no CDs or cassettes, no paintings or pictures, not even a photograph. A room to watch the telly in and, by the stains evident on the coffee table, Edward Higgins had had his fair share of telly dinners in front of its flickering screen.

Allaway, glowing from his recent promotion, was being caring and considerate. Did Higgins need anything? He didn't. He couldn't keep anything down, he claimed. 'Just water,' Higgins added as he patted the bottle of Ballygowan beside the sofa.

Irvine thought Higgins looked impatient for them to begin, recalling that while under the weather, he too preferred only his own company.

Higgins continued: 'It's a terrible shame about Miss Bluewood, isn't it?'

'Yes. Yes, indeed it is,' Irvine replied.

'When was the last time you saw her?' Allaway asked.

'Sorry lad? You're going to have to speak up a bit,' Higgins replied.

'I said, When was the last time you saw her?'

'Yes, there's no need to shout. I can hear you clearly now. I saw her at the window on Sunday afternoon. She had that faraway look in her eyes. Do you know what I mean?' Higgins said to a red-faced Allaway.

'Yes,' Irvine replied. 'I think I do. You didn't actually speak to her on Sunday, then?'

'No. I'm not sure she even noticed me, to be honest. We had a wee sherry together on Friday evening. We'd do that now and again. I have to admit, at the beginning, when she moved in, I was a bit standoffish. Well, I mean, she'd nicked my flat, really, hadn't she? Aye, she had. Our trusted landlord had promised me that when the previous tenants moved out, I could have their flat. It's bigger you see, bigger than this one. That's why I've never done much in here. I'd always been planning to move to a bigger place. The problem is, I've been planning for going on nine years now, and I'm still here. Anyway, I heard the old couple were moving out. Nice people, in their sixties, very quiet. Kept themselves to themselves. The O'Sullivans, yes, that's it, the O'Sullivans. They were moving back to Wexford. His father had died. Ninety-three he was. That's great, isn't it. Ninety-three and apparently sharp as a needle the day he died. Aye, anyway, they told me they were expecting to get the house and it had always been their dream to move back. So I went to see the landlord and he said fine, no problem, as I'd always paid my rent on time, I could have it. But then in the middle of it all, Esther had her own opinion. I think he wanted her to take my place but she felt it was too small. Esther was quite persuasive, you know, in a very quiet way, and before I had any say in the matter she had moved in upstairs.'

'So you weren't exactly friends at the beginning?' Irvine smiled, sympathetically.

'Well, no, not really, to be honest. Then I realised it wasn't exactly her fault. She was looking after her own. Holmer was only a baby then.'

'Was Paul Yeats not around?' Irvine asked.

'No,' Higgins stated firmly. 'She moved in by herself. Yeats was on a tour of America, I didn't even see him until about three months later. Then he'd be back for a time and then he'd be off again. In the middle of all of this she became pregnant with Jens, and I think she was worried about being by herself. So, I mean she'd always been polite and friendly to me, but she seemed to start to make an effort to get through to me. As I said, I realised it hadn't been her fault. I'd been stiffed by the landlord. So what's new, eh? Anyway I suppose eventually we warmed to each other.'

'That would make Friday the last time you spoke to her?' Allaway asked, somewhat more at ease now that his blushing had vanished.

'Yes, Friday evening. Quite late it was, maybe about eleven o'clock. Yes, I think it was about eleven o'clock because it was during the last part of *The Late Late Show*, you know, with that guy who think's he's as good as Gaye Byrne, but he's not. It's on RTE but Tara broadcast it here for the cable. And I remember, sometime later, hearing the end music as we were still chatting.'

'How did she seem to you?' Irvine asked.

'Well, you have to realise that Esther was never as jolly as Mrs Merton, if you know what I mean?' Higgins replied, seemingly proud of his comparison.

'Yes, she's a bit of a hoot isn't she, old Mrs Merton,' Irvine responded, wondering were all of Higgin's reference points going to come from television-land.

'But she said she was happy. She was a songwriter, you know, so she could be a bit up and down. She'd apparently just finished work on some new song, which she was very happy about. Aye, she was very proud of her new songs,' said Higgins, staring off into space, as if trying to recall the scene.

'I could never quite work that one out', he continued. 'I'd see her after she'd just written a new song and she'd be buzzing, walking on air. Then, other times she'd be very down; when the songwriting wasn't working out and I'd remind her about other songs she'd mentioned to me she was so proud of, hoping she'd allow herself to take some solace from them. But she was a bit like a fisherman in that respect: once the fish are in the nets it's the next catch that's the important thing.'

'I see what you're saying,' Irvine replied, wondering whether songwriters were also like fishermen in that the ones that got away were always the biggest ever. 'But would you say her mood was dark?'

'Nah, not at all,' Higgins grunted. 'She was like the rest of us. Well, not really like all the rest of us. To all intents and purposes she was a single parent. Yeats was off being intellectual somewhere or other. That was his bag. He liked to project the image of a college professor. Have you met him, yet?' Irvine and Allaway shook their heads. 'You'll see what I mean when you do. He even dresses like a professor. He's got this permanent pose. Even when the kids are weeing, he'd be standing close by, very pensively, arms folded, one hand supporting his chin, studying the action intensely as if the meaning of life was going to emerge instead of some smelly urine.'

Irvine was starting to view his fellow countryman somewhat differently. The older man was dressed well in grey flannel trousers, a check shirt, blue (possibly old school) tie, and a royal blue V-neck sleeveless pullover. He had the classic pregnant male look – small frame with a protruding beer belly. Irvine was always amused at how men like Higgins never seemed to add weight anywhere else apart from on their stomachs. Perhaps it came from too much drink and not enough food. Mind you, Irvine thought, if it was a beer belly, Higgin's skin was remarkably clear for a drinker. He had a good head of brown hair, cut army style: short back and sides with a sharp parting. His eyes were blue and uninteresting, but it was his eye for character which Irvine found intriguing. His impression and description of Paul Yeats had been spot on.

'Was it usual for you and Esther to go a weekend without seeing each other?' Allaway inquired.

Higgins battered his museum hearing aid and cocked his ear in Allaway's direction.

'I said…' Allaway repeated uninvited.

Higgins banged again, then jumped with apparent shock. 'Aye that's it. It's back again. Sorry, what were you saying?'

Allaway smiled, unflustered. Promotion will do that for you, Irvine guessed, put you above things that would normally niggle.

'I was wondering, were there many weekends when you wouldn't see each other?' Allaway asked through his smile.

'Oh, yeah. Quite a lot. Most weekends she would take Jens and Holmer over to Islington and base herself there. Occasionally she might come back by herself to do some entertaining,' Higgins replied. He appeared to be discreet to a fault and didn't embellish or pepper his information.

'Do you know who it was she entertained?' Irvine asked, quickly picking up the point.

'Oh, a few friends,' Higgins replied simply.

'Male friends?' Irvine pushed.

'Well, yes, why wouldn't she? Yeats was shacked up in their cottage with his piece. Esther... ah, Miss Bluewood I mean, she was young. She was beautiful. She was very beautiful. She could be good fun and let her hair down when she wanted to.'

'Would you recognise any of these "friends"?' Irvine asked.

'Oh, come on. Really.' Higgins roared with laugher. 'Do you see me as being one of those old biddies who sit staring out from behind the curtain? Watching all who come and go. It was none of my business.'

Irvine decided to change track. 'What about Esther's health?'

'She was fine the last time I saw her. She seemed to catch an awful lot of colds and doses of the flu, but then again lots of our American visitors do. This wet weather, you know?'

'Aye, you're not wrong there,' Irvine replied. He paused now, seeing how uncomfortable Higgins was becoming. 'Are you okay?'

'To tell you the truth I'm feeling a bit queasy again,' Higgins replied with great effort.

'Just a few more questions and then we'll leave you in peace. We'll make them quick,' Irvine promised.

'Thanks,' was Higgins' simple reply.

'On Sunday night last, did you notice anything suspicious?' Irvine asked.

'No, with my hearing I tend to have to turn the telly up a bit. I had an early tea myself and settled down here about seven o'clock for a night with the telly. Sunday night's not as good as it used to be, but I've got cable and there's always something to watch.'

'So you didn't hear anything upstairs?'

'Sorry, son?' Higgins replied, dismissing Allaway's rank and recent promotion with one word.

'What about front doors opening and closing?' Allaway continued, wings now slightly clipped.

'Sorry, nothing but the television. I'd love to help, I really would. If someone else has hurt Esther, I'd like to help you find them.'

'Someone else?' Irvine asked, immediately picking up on what the man had just said. 'You just said, If someone else hurt Esther. What did you mean? Someone other than whom?'

'Than herself. I meant anyone other than herself,' Higgins replied, annoyed at having his word questioned or maybe he knew something he wasn't passing on. Irvine couldn't work out which it was.

'So you think she killed herself?' Irvine asked.

'Well, that's what they're all saying,' Higgins replied, looking out of the window in the direction of the crowd of diligent fans who were keeping vigil outside.

'Do you believe that's what really happened?' Allaway asked.

'I'd find it very hard to believe that she'd take her own life, with the kids and all. But you never really know about folks do you? You think you know them. You see them every day and you discuss the price of fish one day and the state of the universe the next, but you never really know what's going on in their heads. My uncle's wife committed suicide when I was growing up and I remember all the family being in total shock because no one had expected it. In those days it was a big disgrace to have someone in your family do that, you know, take their own life. It was as if there was something wrong with the family. But with Esther, are you now saying that she didn't commit suicide? It's just that, Judy, you know, the nanny, she said Esther put her head in the oven and gassed herself. Is that not what happened?' Higgins asked, looking intrigued.

'Well, that's why we're continuing our investigations, Mr Higgins, to try and ascertain exactly what did happen,' Irvine said, rising to his feet. Allaway followed suit. 'If you think of anything, anything at all, just give us a call at North Bridge House,' Irvine said, scribbling the number on a piece of paper. 'You might not think it's relevant, but no matter how trivial you think it is, please give us a shout, won't you?'

'Yes. Oh yes, of course,' Higgins replied, seeming evangelised, testifying to his maker, or just happy that they were finishing their questions.

'We'll leave you in peace,' Irvine nodded, and he and Allaway let themselves out of the house and made their way through the growing, but orderly crowd outside.

Irvine stared into the faces of the fans, looking for something, anything. Then he spotted a fresh-faced, sharply dressed, curly-haired young man. He recognised the face from the photograph in yesterday's *Evening Standard*.

Chapter 16

JOSEF JONES was there, mixing with the fans for the second day in a row. He didn't notice Irvine slip up to him and whisper in his ear, 'We'd like to ask you a few more questions.'

Neither Irvine nor Allaway were prepared for what happened next. Without warning, Jones turned on his heels and ran. He ran down Fitzroy Road, narrowly missing a green VW Beetle as he crossed Chalcot Road and turned right into Gloucester Road, where for some reason known only to himself, he slowed to a walk. By the time he reached the gate of 121 Gloucester Avenue, Irvine and a panting Allaway had caught up with him.

'What was that all about?' Irvine asked, barely breaking sweat.

'God, it's only you. You scared the living daylights out of me up there. I thought you were someone else. What on earth were you thinking about?' Jones said, looking somewhat relieved.

'We're doing our work. Do you owe money to someone or something?' Irvine continued. It would take a few moments more for Allaway to compose himself sufficiently to speak.

'What?' Jones asked in an obviously guilty manner.

'Who's after you?'

'Two members of the Camden Town CID, as far as I can see.' Jones replied, his attempt at humour falling short.

Irvine decided to give up on that line of chat. 'Anyway we'd like to ask you a few questions. Let's go to the Engineer and we can have a coffee as well.'

'Or something stronger,' Jones added, as they headed off down Gloucester Avenue.

The Engineer pub was empty except for an Australian couple; easy to spot, you didn't have to strain to hear their accents. Irvine and Jones sat in the front corner of the pub and Allaway went off to order two cappuccinos and a double espresso for himself. He needed something to kick-start his engine.

'So, Josef,' Irvine began, studying his man carefully. 'You and Mrs Bluewood were quite close, then?'

'Well, she was quite friendly with me,' Jones admitted.

'I'd say taking you to bed with her was a lot more than "quite friendly"!'

Jones' eyeballs nearly burst from their sockets. 'God, keep your voice down in case one of this bunch hears you,' he urged, nodding in the direction of the staff, 'or it'll be around Primrose Hill faster than Eddie Irvine's Jaguar.'

DS Irvine knew now that Jones was rattled. He wondered why the fan had bolted outside Bluewood's house. It was obvious that he was scared of someone, but who? He wouldn't have known about the journals, and worrying about Yeats would come later. If indeed he'd ever worry about Yeats. Yeats was playing away from home as well, so the husband would have little justification in seeking revenge on the one his wife was sleeping with, unless, of course, it was a matter of public relations?

'When did you see her last?' Irvine asked, as the drinks arrived.

Jones waited until the waitress with the 'I'm also an actress' air moved out of earshot before answering.

'Do you mean "When did I last see her?", or "When was the last time I *saw* her?"'

'Look we know all about the relationship so we don't need your boasting, just some facts please,' Irvine said, his voice quiet but firm.

Jones seemed a little disappointed. 'I was meant to see her on Sunday evening. But she never showed.'

'Showed where?' Allaway inquired, having found his breath again.

'At my place.'

'Sorry?' Irvine asked in disbelief.

'That was the thing,' Jones continued in conspiratorial tones. 'When she wanted sex, and I know that's all it was, she'd suggest meeting at my place. If she just wanted a coffee and a chat we'd meet at her place. We never had sex at her place. Never! She was very strict about that.'

'Did she always show up when she said she would?' Allaway asked.

'Always!' Jones replied quietly.

'Were you worried when she didn't show?' Allaway asked. Irvine thought the recently-promoted constable had discarded more than his uniform with his elevation. His new skin – a dark blue four-button suit and a black button-neck pullover – was giving him an unmistakable air of confidence.

'Well, no, not really, *really* worried. You see I knew she wanted me for the one thing only. I knew she thought I was harmless. Esther was a beautiful, passionate woman with needs, and, quite frankly she wasn't scared to go chasing those needs. I also realised if Yeatsie came back to her, I'd be dropped like a hot potato. Hey,' Jones said, 'I certainly wasn't complaining.'

'Did you try and contact her?' Irvine asked.

'No, it was also part of our agreement that she'd always contact me. I wasn't going to break our agreement, was I? I'd too much to lose.'

Allaway again: 'So what do you think happened?'

'I kinda though, she possibly might have been writing. I'd been with her a few times when she'd started to write and when she did she blotted everyone and everything else out. She just went some-where else.'

'Where, her study?' Allaway interrupted, in search of his facts.

'No!' Jones replied, annoyed and just about avoiding the word 'fool' from his short reply. 'No. I meant she went somewhere mentally when she was writing. It was like she was in a trance. She'd keep her tape recorder running and the songs, the music would just flow out of her. She told me afterwards, after I'd seen this happen once, that she felt she was just the channel through which these songs flowed. She told me it happened two or three times a year. She didn't know when it might happen but she felt all her attempts at playing bits and pieces and messing around in the meantime, all of this helped for when the songs came flowing through. When the time was close she became aware that it was close and when the songs started to come they would flow through her for sometimes up to a month, and then nothing...'

'So you thought she'd got lost in her writing and that was why she didn't make your rendezvous?' Irvine asked.

'Something like that,' Jones replied, taking a sip his cappuccino. Irvine joined in, the very hot drink frothy, with just the correct amount of chocolate on top... a perfect cappuccino.

'When was the last time you actually did see her, then?' Allaway asked.

'That would have been one day last week. Let's see... It would have been Wednesday. Yes, she told me to come round about seven-thirty, saying the kids would have been in bed by then, and she usually fancied a chat at that time of day. She loved her children but she said she also loved the peace that fell when they went to sleep. She spent a lot of the time on the phone in the evening, talking to her friends. She complained that on some days, such as Wednesday, she couldn't get them on the phone until after eight o'clock because every one of them watched *Coronation Street* on TV. That was one of the reasons she liked me, she claimed. I had no interest in *Coronation Street*. Can't stand the programme. Never watched it in my life.'

'Did she seem okay on Wednesday?' Irvine asked, wondering how Jones couldn't stand the programme if he'd never watched it in his life.

'Oh, God, you're not going to, how shall I put this, you're not going to ask me to assess her mental state?' Jones asked quietly.

'No, no nothing like that, but generally did she seem, happy, sad, up, down? Just her general mood. Did anything seem to be bugging her?' Irvine searched for the key that would start Jones rolling again.

'What exactly is all this about? Surely she committed suicide?' Jones asked.

'Well, we don't know for certain,' Irvine began.

'But Judy said she was found with her head in the oven,' Jones said in a matter-of-fact tone. Irvine felt that if he'd been seeing someone, even it it was just a physical relationship, he'd surely be more cut up about it than Jones was. But Mr Jones seemed to have all his emotions in check. He was either a very well-balanced individual, Irvine thought, with a chip on both shoulders, or else a man too busy dealing with his own demons to bother much about others.

'You know Judy Dillon, then?' Irvine asked.

'All the fans know each other. It's a little network. We all keep in touch,' Jones said. He finished his drink and glared over his empty cup towards the bar, hinting he'd like another one. Irvine noted this but chose to ignore the hint, and pushed on.

'But Judy's the nanny, not a fan.'

'No. No. She was a fan who became the nanny. Lucky cow,' Jones replied, his cup still in his hand.

'And when did you last speak to her?' Irvine asked, sensing a wee breakthrough.

'Yesterday evening, a pile of us got together down in the Landsdowne. Nice place, but the cappuccino's not as good as it is here.'

Allaway offered another cup, but as Jones was about to accept, Irvine said, 'No. No need, Derek, we're nearly through here and we don't want to detain Mr Jones any longer than we have to.' And before Mr Jones had a chance to speak up on his own behalf, Irvine had continued. 'Tell me, Josef, exactly what did Judy tell you about the scene of Esther's death?'

'Well,' Jones began, 'she said when she went into the house it smelled of gas. She closed the door and ran downstairs to the ground-floor flat. As she couldn't get a response from Higgins, she rang for the police. The police rang the gasmen. They all arrived at once. She let them into the flat with her keys and when they went into the kitchen they found Esther lying with her head in the oven, her chin resting on a lemon towel. Judy said she collapsed in a heap with shock when she saw Esther.'

'That's exactly how she described it, Josef?' Irvine pushed.

'Yes, words to that effect. Yes. But what does it matter? Surely the point is that Esther committed suicide. Why all the fuss?' Jones persisted with his earlier line.

'No matter how it might appear, Josef, we still have to investigate her death to ascertain exactly what actually happened. Appearances can be deceptive, you know. Tell me, what did you do with yourself on Sunday evening?' Irvine asked in his politest tones.

Jones smiled an enigmatic smile.

'Look,' he began slowly, 'how should I put this? By the way, has anyone ever told you that you sound just like Sean Connery?'

'It has been mentioned, Josef, yes. Just once or twice. Now back to my question. What were you doing on Sunday evening?'

'But I've just told you,' Jones moaned. 'I was at my place, waiting for Esther to show up.'

'And you waited in all night for her?' Allaway asked.

'Well, by the time I realised it was a no-show, it was too late to organise anything else. I watched a bit of telly and hit the sack early.'

'No other callers?' Allaway continued.

'No. Luckily for me...' Jones began confidently, but then looked as if he'd thought better of what he was going to say. 'Luckily for me, because I was in need of some serious sleep.'

Irvine considered Jones carefully and let it be known he was considering him. He didn't say a word. Allaway must have sensed something was going on because he too kept shtoom. The only noise was the clink, clink as staff washed glasses.

Josef Jones was not even fazed a little. He sat at the table, hands clasped in front of him, returning Irvine's stare.

After about two minutes, Irvine announced: 'Oh well, that's all for now. We may need to talk to you again. But if we—'

Before Irvine had time to finish his sentence Jones was up and out of the bar, leaving the door swinging behind him.

'Ah, no, Josef, it's okay, we'll pay for the drinks,' Irvine announced, deadpan, to the door. 'You're welcome.'

Chapter 17

Saturday Night's All Right For Fighting

Saturday 14th January

I'VE JUST *put down my guitar. Sometimes it works and sometimes it doesn't. Today I've been trying to make it work. I've put on some-one else's music, my favorite song in fact: Emile Ford singing 'What Do You Want to Make Those Eyes at Me For'. Should there be a question mark there? It is a question. What do you want to make those eyes at me for? Are you trying to hurt me? Are you trying to turn me on? Or, are you just being downright silly. Emile sang it so sweetly. My Mum used to play this record all the time. That's where I first heard it. It's such a simple song, but it gets me close to sobbing every time. I don't know why, but it does. So there.*

I've just checked the label and there is no question mark, just 'What Do You Want to Make Those Eyes at Me For' by Emile Ford and the Checkmates, Pye Records. I recognise the label because it's the same one all the classic Kinks hits were on. I just love Emile's song, though; it is so moving. I've just put it on again. Why does it connect so with me? I liked it before I met Yeatsie. Although when I met him first, I have to admit these words where the first words which sprang into my mind. His eyes! No wonder his Raybans are never far away. He has such power with his eyes. It was like he could summon up, and concentrate, all his energy through his stare.

Even in the early days he was always kidding around about hypnotizing me and I'd let him try. I'd kind of go a bit woozy and pretend to be dropping under. But then when I was having Holmer he did something to me with those eyes. I was in such pain. You try having this nine-month growth removed from your body through that orifice! God, I get the shivers now even thinking about it. I know mothers-very-soon-to-be are meant to be the salt of the earth, Earth Mothers or whatever, and pop out the old man's heirs at the drop of a hat, but I was dreading it. The pain was excruciating, getting worse and worse, when Yeatsie grabbed my hand very tightly. At first I thought it was to distract me from the pain, but he moved his face until it was about eight inches away from mine, we were literally eye-to-eye, and I was yelping with the pain, and he caught my stare and held it. He started whispering to me. I found that I'd stoppped crying just so that I could hear what he was saying. His voice was as smooth as the Fifth Dimension's harmonies. He was telling me we were together and we were lying on the beach at Martha's Vineyard. The sky was a sweet, pure blue, apart, that is, from the occasional fluffy cloud that gently floated by. The breeze was gentle, but enough to take the sting out of the sun's rays. The water was lapping gently at our feet. We were lying in each other's arms looking up at the bluest of skies, just the two of us, perhaps the last two people in the world. He said we were together and we'd be together for always, and very soon a miracle would take place and this miracle would change our lives. The miracle, he said, would complete the healing process and everything would be perfect.

Yeatsie kept on painting his picture, our picture. I wanted to hear his voice forever. I wanted to lie in his arms on that beach forever. He'd taken away my pain. I remember waking from my dream and being disappointed, when I heard the nurse slap Holmer's bottom and the little cry from him. At the time I didn't think I'd been hypnotized, but the doctor said that Yeatsie had put me under. The doctor said he was relieved that he'd done so, as I was making such a racket.

So that's when I started to believe that maybe he could hypnotize me. Perhaps he was a very clever hypnotist who said to me as I was about to go under, 'When you come to, you will think I have only pretended to hypnotize you.' Okay, okay, I know what you're thinking, but just because I'm paranoid doesn't mean that there aren't people out there trying to get me!

It was so beautiful at the beginning with Yeatsie, I suppose I realised it wouldn't last forever. I think a man and a woman together are like a river's bed and banks. The marriage is the water that flows through them. No matter how sound the banks of the river are, if the river flows too quickly it will surely burst them. Some little twist or turn will appear from nowhere and the river will fight to hold its course, but in the end the water will go with the path of least resistance. Sadly, once a river bursts its banks you can never get it back in there again. No matter how much you want it, or how hard you try, it just won't work. That's when the powerful river transforms into feeble water. I've often tried to work that into a song, but I've never quite got it.

Songs like that that never quite get written are the great songs, the ones that got away. Yeatsie's more mercenary about it. He claims all songs are fodder to fill what is the true work of art: the CD pack. I don't think he was always like that. I wonder, does he think like that about a marriage, about our marriage? That it's only to fill up a few years of his life. He keeps saying that we were meant to be together. That's fine for him. I'm stuck here in a tiny apartment raising the kids, while he's away, doing Ross in my cottage. So listen, Paul Yeats, your words are not a comfort to me any more. I don't believe you. This sham may be a career move to you, but it's become purgatory for me. I need to end it. I have all the papers from my lawyer, Leslie Russell. He says all I need to do is sign and serve them and the marriage is as good as over.

That seems much too simple a way to end the meeting of two minds, doesn't it? The new Romeo and Juliet, the Melody Maker *called us. Eff them, what would they know, don't they realise that Romeo was a little shit who wore tights and poisoned his lover before taking the strange brew himself? Do you believe that? I don't. She probably told him to get real, forget getting in touch with his feminine side and be a man for a change. He couldn't take the criticism, or the rejection, so he did both of them in. Yeatsie as Romeo, I can't see it. He has the voice for sure, but he was more interested in us talking about him than he ever was in love. Mind you, two out of four is not a bad batting average. Hey now, there's a juicy piece of gossip for the fans to exchange. I wonder what that one would be worth? But he'd never forgive me for it. Even Josef thinks Yeatsie is a super-stud.*

Yeatsie has other things going for him, I'm sure – and when I find out what they are, I'll tell you. Ha! So, I suppose I should just end this sham. I feel strong enough now to sign those papers and end it. I should do it. I couldn't bear him coming to me when I'm on medication, looking to end it because he wants to wed Rosslyn. He wouldn't do that to the children, would he? He seems aware of his responsibilities on the one hand, but on the other, he is quite prepared to leave them here with me, despite the fact I'm struggling on all fronts. They're his kids (for definite), so come on, Yeatsie, it would be brilliant if you rolled up here some Friday evening and told me you wanted Jens & Holmer for the weekend.

Wouldn't that be a dream? But on second thoughts, I don't want Jens growing fond of Rosslyn. That would be just too confusing for everyone... including me.

As I hear Emile Ford and the Checkmates sing 'I'd Love To Get You On A Slow Boat To China', I wonder when my true love will come. I did think at one point it was Yeatsie. He hates me calling him that, he thinks it's disrespectful to the master (his claim not mine), I'd have thought it was more disrespectful for a bleedin' failed pop star to be nicking the name. Anyway this is all old ground. I've ploughed it so many times before. Enough: I have to end it. The furrows are prepared; they've been ready for ages. It's time for the new seed. We all need a new crop, me more that most. I need to be happy. This time I'm prepared to compromise and not expect to be swept off my feet. I'll settle for a dependable man who'll be my friend, look after Esh & Jens & Holmer – a man who'll care for us. Caring for us would be enough. Well, at least it would be a start, not to mention a change to the current situation. I'll call Russell in the morning and let him know I'm going to sign and return the papers.

There... I feel such a relief having made that decision. It shows the absolute power of words on a page, I feel completely rejuvenated. It's like a resurrection, not as powerful as first time around, but hopefully it'll work just as well the second.

*

Paul Yeats had checked into a hotel and been considerate enough to leave his details with the ever-reliable and efficient desk sergeant, Timothy Flynn. He was holed up at the Britannia Hotel on nearby Primrose Hill Road. A suite, no less. As Kennedy approached the accommodation, his path crossed with that of a photographer and a hack, heading in the opposite direction.

'They found you quickly enough,' Kennedy offered as his opening greeting.

'No, no, you've got the wrong impression. They're okay, they're the good guys. I agreed to do one interview to clear up the details so that the rest of the pack will leave me alone. The record company are paying for the suite, and they wanted their pound of flesh in return,' replied Yeats, as he lounged in a sofa. The room was trying to be up-market Holiday Inn. Everything was convenient, functional, but perhaps suffering, Kennedy thought, from 'bulk-buying syndrome'.

The suite enjoyed a spectacular view of hundreds of roof-tops, but, in true Elvis fashion, Yeats had chosen to close all the drapes and turn on some table lamps. The TV was humming in the corner and Kennedy could hear a second one blaring away in the bedroom.

'Does it not upset you to be talking to the press now?' Kennedy asked, feeling that maybe it should.

'Listen, Inspector, the secret of success in the music business is sincerity. Once you can fake that, you've got it made. In other words, I perform. I tell them something they want to hear, the situation's defused, and they leave me alone,' said Yeats, without batting an eyelid. He then added, as an afterthought, 'Hopefully.'

'I just thought most artists hated the press,' Kennedy continued.

'I can't abide all of that nonsense,' Paul Yeats said. As he lifted the phone to order some room service, Kennedy noted that he was either dressed in yesterday's clothes or else he had bought an identical set to change into. Yeats put his hand over the mouthpiece: 'I'm having some coffee and sandwiches sent up, would you like some?'

'Brilliant. Tea and a couple of hot egg sandwiches would be perfect,' Kennedy replied, not knowing why he was whispering.

Yeats concluded his business with room service and replaced the receiver. 'Sorry,' he said to Kennedy, 'as I was saying, I can't abide all that star crap. Those who complain about the press were happy enough to use them on the way up. Dead grateful for the attention, if they're prepared to be perfectly honest. For Christ's sake, the press is the most important tool to get news of your music out to the fans. How else are they going to pick up on you, for heaven's sake, telepathy?'

'Radio, TV, concerts?' Kennedy, asked.

'Sorry, no move with this throw,' Yeats announced loudly, TV quizmaster fashion. 'In fact, go to jail and you'll have to throw another six before you can move back into the game. If the press isn't writing about you, the radio is most definitely not interested in what you have to say. Well, all radio except maybe some specialist show on at three o'clock in the morning in Grimsby, listened to by the odd insomniac and fishermen keen for the weather. If the press isn't writing about you and the radio isn't playing your music, then you can bet your bottom dollar there won't be too many offers for TV work. And, if you're not in the papers, not on the radio and never on the TV, you can guess how big the audience is going to be at your next concert.'

Kennedy was about to try the line, 'But what about building up a live following through word of mouth?' In his mind, this was a valid approach and ann rea had told him how effective it could be. Paul Yeats, however, seemed to think he had a fix on all aspects of the music business and given an opportunity to step up to that particular microphone, Kennedy was sure he'd be there all night without answering any questions regarding Esther Bluewood's death. Time to move on to a more personal level, Kennedy thought. And he did.

'I have to say you don't look too upset to me, you know, for someone who has just lost his wife,' the detective began, and then, deciding it was perhaps a wee bit insensitive, took the sting out of the tail with: 'I'd have to say you're coping well.'

'That's exactly it, Inspector,' Yeats said, leaning back in his seat. The basketwork support to the lush cushions creaked under the strain of the movement. 'That's exactly it, I don't look upset. I'm trying to deal with it in my own way. I'm trying to get beyond this. I didn't kill myself. I'm not going to let this hurt me. Why should I suffer because of what my wife did? Her final grandstand, attention-seeking act has only served to deprive her children of their mother. Don't get me wrong, they'll be fine. My mother absolutely adores them, as does Tor.'

'Who are they with now?' Kennedy asked.

'My mother came into town yesterday and took them to her place. She lives near our cottage in the Cotswolds; she's in Burford, we're in Fulbrook. They'll be in the country. It's a small village but there are other kids to play with and we have a few cats and a dog and some ducks, and they always get a hoot out of the ducks. Esther's mum absolutely dotes on them as well, and I'm perfectly fine for them to go visit her as often as she wants them. As long as they get their education in England, they can go to Boston during the holidays. I spoke to her, Mrs Bluewood, on the phone yesterday evening. She's not as upset as I thought she'd be. She's a very strong woman. She's had to be. Her husband died when the family was very young. Esther had a very troubled childhood. She tried to kill herself before, you know. She'd cut herself a lot when she was a teenager, but nothing life-threatening, and then, about three years before I met her, she took an overdose of pills and hid in the basement of her house waiting to die. Fortunately, her brother found her on that occasion.'

Yeats paused for a time. Kennedy felt more was to follow, so offered no interruption.

'You know,' Yeats continued, 'I keep thinking about what would have happened if she'd been found by Holmer. Or worse still, what if the silly cow had gassed the lot of them in her search for immortality. That's the problem with all these Sylvia Plath/Virgina Woolf types, they glamorise suicide. They make it seem like an elegant literary event, where their grandiose performance supplies the final answer. For heaven's sake, the only thing it supplies is food for the bleedin' worms six feet under. There is no glory in any of this. You don't even get to read your final reviews, those glowing obits. You don't get to see the TV specials or hear the radio tributes. You don't get the royalty cheques all this new attention generates. All you do is put an end to your own life and cause untold misery to those you leave behind.'

Kennedy was going to ask, 'But what about *her* pain?' but decided against it. It would probably have brought on another tirade, perhaps at a later time.

'You are talking as if your wife committed suicide, sir,' Kennedy started, about to offer another side of the coin. 'When, in point of fact, Dr Hugh Watson claims that she wouldn't have.'

'What? Is he now convinced that divine intervention caused Esther to stick her head into an oven and keep it there until she was dead? Where's that man's head?' Yeats said, sitting up rigid in the seat. Just then the door chimes announced the arrival of their snack.

Kennedy had prepared himself for the worst with regard to the tea and sandwiches. But to his pleasant surprise, the tea was superb and the egg sandwiches were not only hot, but freshly made. The brown bread was soft and the eggs were half scrambled, half fried; exactly the way Kennedy loved them. He rarely asked for hot egg sandwiches in cafés or breakfast rooms, preferring to enjoy them in the privacy of his own home. His father had first shown him how the make the perfect hot egg sandwich and it was one of the mysteries of the world he was happy to have mastered. Like he was sure that it would have been great to know all about the Hanging Gardens of Babylon, you know, really great, but it wasn't the same kind of pleasure you got with washing down the perfect egg sandwich with the perfect cup of tea. His father's method began with melting a generous amount of butter in the bottom of a saucepan. When it sizzled, he'd break in two eggs per person, and, once they'd started to fry, he'd scramble them. You could add a few scallions or herbs to taste, but basically that was it. Kennedy preferred it to a hanging garden any day of the week.

In comparison, Yeats' cheese and ham looked positively boring, but Kennedy was careful not to show too much enthusiasm about his stash, for fear of having to share it. The tea and sandwiches had arrived at the perfect time for Yeats, Kennedy thought. Assuming he needed to, he was able to use the interruption to collect his thoughts.

'Watson is definitely sure Esther didn't commit suicide?' Yeats inquired, mid-munch.

'Yes, I mean as far as he can be sure,' Kennedy replied.

'So, that means you guys are convinced it was murder?' Yeats said, finishing his first cup of coffee and refilling his cup.

'Well, we have to keep an open mind until we've concluded our investigation. I'd like to ask you about the last time you saw Esther.'

'That would have been on Saturday. On Saturday at lunchtime. I dropped in on them all, over in Islington.'

'How did you get on?' Kennedy asked.

'Well, okay, you know, we were in company, Jill and Jim's, so we were civil. I mean, in all of our dealings, particularly in front of the children, we've always tried to be civil to each other. Particularly with the children, you know, in front of the kids, we were very well behaved. We'd actually gotten to the point in the relationship where it was over, emotionally and physically, but there were other things that tied us together. In a way, we were both trying to tread the path of least possible resistance with each other.'

Was that what it always came down to in a relationship, Kennedy wondered, the path of least possible resistance? Paul Yeats and Esther Bluewood had once shared such strong feelings for each other that they'd gone through a marriage ceremony in front of their friends. On two occasions they had loved each other enough to want to create a child together. How could the relationship have possibly ended the way it did? They were both – apparently – intelligent adults. Where had it all gone wrong? More importantly, *when* had it all gone wrong? Could either of them, when pushed, have been able to pinpoint the exact time they realised that their partner was no longer the one they loved or the one they wanted to spend the rest of their life with?

It was obvious from the journals that Esther was going to instigate divorce proceedings. Had Yeats hurt her one time too many? Had she perhaps finally decided that he wasn't her perfect partner? What could she have done to avoid making such a terrible mistake? Should she have spent more time getting to know him? Or was it predestined that their time together was not forever? If Esther hadn't met Paul Yeats, would she have met her genuine soul mate and avoided her untimely death? Or maybe without Yeats' support in the relationship, would she have tried, perhaps successfully, to end her life earlier?

Kennedy knew he could not afford to forget the fact that Esther

Bluewood had once before tried to end her own life. Doc Watson may have been convinced that at the time she died she was not in a suicidal state, but neither he nor Kennedy – not even ann rea with her heartfelt conviction – could be absolutely certain that Esther had not taken her own life. Quite possibly Watson, Kennedy and ann rea, for their own reasons, didn't *want* to believe that Esther had ended her life. Why was that? Might it have made their own journeys through life more precarious?

Paul Yeats, for all his faults, had come into Esther's life and had loved her at a point where, more that anything else, she needed to be loved and feel wanted. Yeats had certainly fulfilled that role, so did that mean that because of Yeats' involvement, Esther Bluewood's life had been prolonged? Or was it simply a case of when the Grim Reaper comes calling, appeals are useless?

'Tell me, sir, 'Kennedy began, 'when you saw Esther on Saturday in Islington, did she leave at the same time as you did?'

'No, no. I was just visiting. I left about five o'clock. That was the last time I saw her alive,' Yeats replied. 'I find it weird, you know, thinking about the possibility that Esther may not have committed suicide. That creates a whole different field of possibilities. Like who, for instance, could have wanted to murder her? Do you have any suspects yet?'

'At this stage we are merely collecting information, sir, and trying to make sure we keep an open mind over the whole affair. I am sure once we are in possession of all the relevant facts we will be better equipped to consider any suspects and methods that may arise. What did you do for the rest of Saturday, sir?' Kennedy inquired, looking to amass an important piece of information.

'I caught a train to the cottage, Axis, immediately after I left them. I rang Rosslyn from the station in Charlbury and she collected me. We had a quiet night in,' said Yeats, in a matter-of-fact manner.

'And Sunday, sir?' Kennedy pushed.

'Lay in bed. Read the papers,' Yeats said, leaning forward in his seat. 'I'm aware that this could turn out to be my alibi, Inspector, so I'm trying to remember the sequence of events in detail. I went down to the pub, the Mason's Arms, had two or three pints while Rosslyn made lunch. Returned around two o'clock for lunch and a couple of glasses of wine. Then I had a snooze in front of the telly. It's all a bit hazy – *Eastenders* or something was on. I'm afraid I'd a bit too much to drink if the truth were told. Then I went out for a long walk around five to clear away the cobwebs.'

'Did your girlfriend go out with you?'

'No, ah, you see, the point of the matter is we had a bit of a row. She was annoyed I'd been to see Esther the previous day. She wouldn't believe that I'd only gone there to see the kids. She said if I wanted to see Jens and Holmer I should bring them up to the cottage for the weekend. So you know…' Yeats rolled his head from side to side and clicked his teeth in a 'You know what women are like' way, before continuing: 'I couldn't be having all of that. I'd been down to London to see the kids and Esther gives me a hard time for not spending enough time with them; then I come home and Rosslyn gives me a hard time about spending too much time with them and not enough with her. It got to me and I just had to get out of there. So I tore off in a rage, you know.' Again Yeats hammed it up.

'And you were out for the rest of the evening?'

'Pretty much,' Yeats replied.

'Did you see or speak to anybody?'

'God, this really is turning out to be my alibi. I saw a few people. No one I specifically remember… as I say, it's all a bit hazy. Probably down the pub for the major part of it I suppose. God, it's sad, isn't it? I mean, if there were more happy marriages the pubs would probably go out of business.'

Kennedy felt that nothing would be gained by taking this line any further for the time being. It was time to change the direction of the questioning.

'Was there ever a chance that you and Esther would have gotten together again?' he asked.

Yeats looked slightly relieved at this new line of enquiry.

'I have to be honest here and tell you that I had hoped so, but the more time that passed the more I doubted it. I'm sorry to have to admit that. I always thought we'd be together forever. I kept saying that. Even when our relationship was cracking at the seams I kept telling Esther, not to worry, that it would all work out, that we'd grow old together. And for the sake of the children I wanted that to be so. But the truth of the matter is that we had both changed from how we were when we met. That happens.' Yeats stopped talking and stared at the detective for a few seconds. He seemed to be considering his next words carefully.

'Look, Inspector,' he began, in a conspiratorial whisper, 'the truth about Esther Bluewood was that she was hard work, really hard work. She was selfish. She required too much attention. She gave absolutely none back. Take, for example, a star like Elton John. By reputation he is meant to be demanding, and moody, and temperamental, and everything else. Did you see that TV documentary on him? I thought he was very courageous to allow that to go out. But at least with a star like Elton what you see is what you get. You can deal with it. You always know where you stand. But the Esther Bluewoods of the world, well they're a different kettle of fish altogether. The impression they give is one of "I just love my fans. I haven't changed. I don't want to be treated any differently to anyone else." But at the same time Esther would be screaming about her limo. You know...' —and here Yeats effected a high-pitched whine— '"Oh, by the way, I know I told you I didn't want a limo to meet me, but the next time you're going to send a car to pick me up at the studio, at least you could try and make it one from this decade. And could it possibly also have air conditioning and a scratch-free bumper? And I know I said I didn't want a chauffeur with a peaked hat and all, but could you possibly get me a driver with a suit and a shirt and tie? And could you please tell him I prefer not to talk?".'

Yeats really threw his all into the car and driver sketch. Kennedy imagined it was one of his regular routines.

'And that was Esther. Yes, she was a woman of the people but she still liked to be pampered like a star and boy did she throw a wobble or three when things didn't go the way she wanted them to. She'd be nice as pie and then quietly go off into one with one of her menials and she'd read them the riot act about what was wrong. Then she'd come back into the room as if nothing had happened and as if butter wouldn't melt in her mouth. Meanwhile the poor "yes man" would be scurrying around trying desperately to right the wrong. And if his actions crept into the group consciousness she'd put him down with an "of course that's all fine, please leave things just as they are. I don't care for any of that star attention stuff". Yes, very demanding, I can tell you. And the reason I know all this is because I was the "yes man" if no one else happened to be around. Agh! She could be so dammed infuriating when she wanted to be. But in spite of myself I wanted to help her. I wanted to try and make her life easier. I wanted to try and ensure that she didn't make the same mistakes I did at the beginning of my career. And mine were expensive mistakes. And, bit-by-bit, I was helping her get it together, putting everything in order. I was trying to set it up so that eventually Tor could run the business stuff for both of us, a little cottage industry. She could have saved so much money. All the copyrights would have been under the one roof and under our control.'

'Was Esther happy for Tor to do that?' Kennedy asked.

'Well, we were still talking about it, to be truthful. And it was hard, especially for me. I'm a brother and I'm a husband; really I was just a middle man,' Yeats replied. Kennedy noted which of the two roles he mentioned first.

'And so, inevitably, all the goofier stuff began to creep into our personal life,' Yeats continued. 'I wouldn't treat a servant, let alone a spouse, the way Esther treated me. Yes, as an artist I was from an older generation. There wasn't really too much different in our ages but five years in this business is like two generations in any other. The thing is I really do like to look after myself. All this help doesn't come cheap you know and they're all on their own little power trips. You know, they don't feel they're really important enough until they have to have an assistant or two of their own. And who pays for it? Muggins. And all it does is put two or three interpretations of what you want done between yourself and the person who actually does it. It's so much easier to do it yourself, and of course it's a lot less expensive. I don't sell out Wembley but I can bet you, with my one-man operation, I come home from my gigs with a lot more money in my pocket than some of the boys who play Wembley take home. I pay an agent to get my gigs, that's it. He's on ten per cent. That's my most important relationship. He gets me my work and I'm civil to him and thankful for the work he puts my way. I pay a solicitor by the hour to do the rest. And that's it.'

Had Yeats, through this tangent, been trying to steer Kennedy off the track? If so, what track was Yeats trying to divert him from?

'Did you know that Esther was about to instigate divorce proceedings against you?' Kennedy dropped what he hoped would be a bombshell.

'Oh, that's been floating around for... You've been reading the journals. I warned you, I've been co-operating with you and here you are breaking our trust, not to mention my legal instructions. Sir, I have to tell you that this interview is terminated!' Yeats shrieked at the top of his voice.

With that the singer jumped up and pushed his chair back with such force that he knocked it hard against the table. Kennedy just about managed to save the empty sandwich plates from crashing to the floor. Yeats stormed out of the room, slamming the door violently behind him.

'Well,' Kennedy said to himself, 'you certainly blew that one, old son. I guess that means a signed CD is out of the question.'

Kennedy heard a few gentle taps on the door a couple of seconds later. Shit, he thought, it must be the hotel management come to see what the disturbance was all about. Kennedy rose from his chair, crossed the room and opened the door, whilst simultaneously searching inside his jacket for his warrant card. As he opened the door he was more than a little surprised to see Yeats standing there. He'd composed himself in a classical theatrical pose: one foot raised on toe and stretching across his other leg, one hand on hip, and the other outstretched, resting on the door post. He looked like he was one degree this side of breathing. Paul Yeats stood there frozen in his pose as though Kennedy was a photographer and he was impatient to be captured before the inner thought of the outward expression was lost forever. The outward expression was 'I'm seriously pissed off'. The inner thought, Kennedy guessed, was somewhat more humiliating.

Kennedy barely managed to keep a straight face as he said, 'You'll be looking to come into *your* room, then. I'll leave you to it, sir.'

With that, Kennedy left the star furiously spluttering. As he entered the lift, he heard another ferocious crash come from inside the hotel room. As the thunderous sound echoed around the corridor, Kennedy aloud said to the row of almost identical bedroom doors, 'Now that would have been a classic scene for the Elton John documentary.'

Chapter 18

Tuesday Morning

Tuesday 18th March

WHAT WOULD I do *without you, darling Jim and dear Jill?*
You've just been around to collect the children. You give me some
space, and enable me to sit in this tiny room and write. I'd like them
to be funny, these jottings in my journal. Should they ever be
published? How pompous is that? 'Should they be published?' I'd
hate to think they would ever be published. If anything ever
happens to me, these writing are to go directly to Leslie Russell, and
Leslie, you are to destroy them. There is too much hurt and pain
and spite in these pages. I'd love them to be witty and sharp and
colorful like Alan Bennett's Writing Home. *But they're not. So*
there. I want them to go to Leslie because I trust that Leslie will
destroy them as per my wishes. I don't trust anyone else as much.

Welcome to the nineties. I'm a married woman, thirty-two years
old, two children, one mother, one mother-in-law, one sister-in-law,
one father-in-law, one husband, one lover, and yet who is the only
person in the world I can trust? My lawyer. Well, that's not strictly
true. I do trust Jim & Jill, too. But I know they'd buckle under pres-
sure from Yeatsie and Tor. Tor is so desperate to have a successful
career and, unfortunately for me, the only way she can see of having
one is by using mine.

I suppose Jim & Jill have unofficially adopted me as the daugh-
ter they never had. That would then make Jens & Holmer their
surrogate grandchildren. They are so wonderful with them. If I was
really their daughter and anything happened to me, I'd be content
knowing they'd be looking after my children. I know Jens &
Holmer would be happy with them. I love the way Holmer is so
protective of his little sister. That's such a beautiful thing to see.
Where does he get it from?

Not from me. I've been preoccupied with myself since I first
became ill and that is for as long as I care to remember, if not longer.
Yeatsie doesn't even pretend to care about them. He's never even
changed a nappy. He'd just hold them away from him at arm's

length and say, 'It's soiled!' expecting me to clean up the offending child and present 'it' back to him, as good as new.

Jim & Jill, they prove that 'someone up there' has concerns about me. I know 'someone up there' orchestrated our meeting so there would be someone out there to care for me. We met, bizarrely, in Sainsbury's in Camden Town. Holmer was misbehaving because I wouldn't buy him more chocolate and he ran off. As ever, when he loses me he starts to cry. He wandered around crying and wiping his eyes, until we met up again. He bumped into Jim & Jill, who comforted him and stayed with him until I turned up. It was as simple as that: a thoroughly modern meeting.

That was over a year ago and we've spent so much time together since. We meet up most weekends and occasionally they baby-sit for me during the week. They have this wonderful old house over-looking Myddelton Square in Islington. It's just opposite the church. And sometimes when I'm over there at the weekend I'll go into the church and just sit. I find it very spiritual. I don't know if I'm just confusing a bit of peace and quiet for spirituality, but it's spiritual to me. Just outside the church is a children's playground with lots of multi-colored apparatus to occupy Jens & Holmer. Occasionally they'll take the children there and if I've just been in the church, I come out into the sunlight and find the kids happily enjoying themselves, not needing or missing me, and that in itself is like a religious experience.

If I'm not around, Jill & Jim mostly keep Jens & Holmer in the back garden, which is large and rambling and offers endless oppor-tunities for adventure. The children actually leave some of their books and clothes over at Jim & Jill's. I notice Jill and Jim never tidy them away. It's like they like to leave them lying around the house, maybe they get comfort from them. Whatever, it's great, they're great. There're very unselfish and I love them lots. They are the reason I can afford the time to write this.

I've just now felt in the mood to work on my music. The muse – or whatever it is – comes as fast as the next elevator and it vanishes even quicker, so I'm going to go and get started before it vanishes...

*

Immediately she met them, Coles realised exactly what it was Esther Bluewood liked so much about Jill and Jim Beck. The second she walked through the door she felt totally at home in their house. Coles imagined Esther and her two children would have wandered around the spacious house in Islington like it was their own. It was the kind of place you could fantasise about visiting for the traditional family Christmas get-together.

At the same time they were the only witnesses in the case, so far, who showed any signs of grief over the death of Esther Bluewood. Both seemed equally upset, but not so upset that they forgot their manners. Jill left Coles and Lundy in the sitting room with Jim, before returning five minutes later with a tray laiden with a pot of fresh coffee, warm milk, brown sugar, homemade biscuits and a delicious looking layered sponge cake.

The room was very light, very airy, with a high ceiling, cream-coloured walls and curtains. One end had a built-n wall unit. The bottom section had a brass grille hiding a radiator. Above that were two glass doors with red curtains on the inside, guarding what could have been rows of rare books. Or perhaps the only providers of wisdom inside came in the smooth shape of bottles of malt whisky. Each side of the cupboard contained wall-to- ceiling units neatly packed with books: paperbacks, hardbacks, old and new, Dickens to Dexter. Above the fireplace were prints of plants and vegetables, probably more suitable for the kitchen. On the far wall, lit by natural light that shone from the window during the day and from its own spotlight at night, was a beautiful Tom Carr painting. It was a winter seaside scene of a small crowd, including a nun and a dog, presumably going to church.

A number of pale-coloured vases holding dried flowers were dotted around the room and against one wall stood a three-legged oak coffee table on which sat three stacks of antique books. A flower vase and a needlework box were cleared away to make room for the refreshments tray. The whole room was spotlessly clean, from the straw-coloured woven carpet to the floral patterned three-piece suite. It was, however, noticeably without a television, or a hi-fi system. It was a room for conversation.

'This is just lovely,' Coles said, as she took the first sip of coffee. 'And your room is just beautiful. You've done amazing things with it. All so simple but very effective.'

Lundy wriggled uncomfortably in his chair.

'Aye, you're right. That's Ma for you,' Jim announced proudly. 'She does have a good eye for colour. Always did.'

And Ma Beck blushed ever so slightly beside him.

'Esther and the children just loved it over here…' Ma started, setting her coffee cup and saucer back down on to the table and helping herself to a generous portion of the cake.

'...And we've had them over here as often as they've wanted.' Pa Beck completed Ma Beck's line, and showed a little more restraint than his wife by choosing a plain digestive biscuit.

Their respective figures bore testament to their choice of food. Jill, if not exactly plump, was full-figured, with rosy cheeks, blue eyes and blonde curly hair, which Coles was convinced was a wig. She was dressed in a grey skirt which was stretched to the limits, white frilly-collared blouse and a red cardigan, completely buttoned with the exception of the bottom one. Jim was wiry and fit. His brown, fading to grey, hair was thinning on top. Coles was intrigued by how aged his hands appeared. He was dressed as a favourite grandad should dress, in light blue shirt, dark blue and green school tie and green v-neck pullover. He sat beside his wife on the sofa, and as he crossed his legs, you caught a glimpse of brown and cream as areas of his golfing socks emerged out of his brown leather shoes and disappeared under white chino trousers.

'The children were over here a lot, then, were they?' Coles asked.

'Oh yes,' Jill said.

'All the time,' Jim added.

'We loved to have them,' Jill said.

'They were always more than welcome,' Jim added.

'When were they here last?' Coles asked, nudging the conversation in a slightly more specific direction.

'Sat...' Ma opened.

'...Afternoon,' Pa closed.

'Were you baby-sitting, or was the mother here as well?'

'Oh, all three were here. In fact...' Mr Beck started.

'... at one point, the whole family was here,' Mrs Beck finished, successfully completing her first sentence since they arrived.

'Really?' Lundy felt compelled to say. Coles could see he was happier now the conversation stood at least a chance of providing them with a few facts.

'What time would that have been?' Coles inquired, nodding in the direction of Lundy's notebook in the hope he was recording the conversation.

'Around five o'clock, I'd say,' said Jim, showing the slightest hint of remorse.

'You know it was five, Pa. You'd just sat down to watch the football results ...' Jill smiled at her husband and patted him on the leg.

'You see,' Jim continued with a hike of his shoulders, 'I love to do the football pools...'

'It's his one vice,' Jill prompted.

'It's my one vice.' Jim smiled at his wife.

'I hope it's his only vice.'

Coles felt she could hear Lundy's subconscious voice scream, *Oh for heaven's sake just get on with it!*

'So, Paul Yeats was here a five o'clock,' Lundy checked, betraying a hint of irritation.

Jill and Jim raised their eyebrows at each other in a well-rehearsed routine which probably meant 'Who rang his bell?'

'Yes,' Jill replied, stretching the word to a full three syllables.

'Yes,' her husband confirmed, with a shorter, snappier version of the same word.

Coles worried that Lundy's impatience had thrown the conversation, so she tried to smooth the troubled waters.

'Was that a usual occurrence, you know, for Paul Yeats to come over when they were here?'

'Well, he most certainly would never have been made welcome on his own,' Jill replied quickly.

'Oh, Ma, it's not for us...'

'Don't, "Oh, Ma" me, Jim Beck,' Jill replied sternly. 'Paul Yeats was out of order in the way he treated the three of them. That's a fact and it needs saying, police or no police.' As she finished her sentence, she stared straight at Lundy.

'We don't know all that goes on...' Jim started. He uncrossed his legs and sat back into the full comfort of the sofa and the support of the cream-coloured cushions generously scattered about it, as on all the chairs in the room.

'How can you say that, Pa? A man and a woman, a husband and a wife, that's sacred. But the kiddies, what he has done to them is unforgivable if you ask me, totally unforgivable.'

'Oh come on, Ma,' Jim said, as he reached out to give his wife a hug. 'Not everyone has been as lucky as we have.'

'Luck doesn't come into it. You're a good man, Jim. That's the plain and simple fact. That's the difference.' Ma replied, softening a little and allowing herself to surrender to the effect of his cuddle.

Coles and Lundy looked on as the couple snuggled up close and kissed each other gently on the lips.

Jill Beck pushed him off playfully and brushed down her skirt.

'Did Paul Yeats stay for long?' Coles asked. For the time being at least, Lundy had tuned into her line of questioning and had obviously decided not to interfere.

'Same as usual.' Jill replied.

'He'd come over here ...' Jim said.

'He'd never sit down...' Jill prompted.

'Yes, that's right, Ma,' Jim replied, as if realising it for the first time. 'He would never sit down.'

'He'd always stand over there...' Jill said.

'By the fireplace...'

'Yes, by the fireplace,' Jill continued. It was as though they were both duelling to take up the thread of the conversation. 'Hands deep in pockets ...'

'Leaning against the wall...' Jim interrupted, seeming to recall the scene in his mind's eye.'

'Humph,' Jill grunted, agreeing. 'Some people have no respect whatsoever for other people's homes. He'd stand there, hands deep in pockets, leaning against the wall. I'd have to wipe the wall down after he left, every time, in case it had smudged. Anyway, he'd stand there lecturing her about something or other in front of us. Part of me would want to leave them alone...'

'But the other part of you wouldn't want her to be left alone with him, isn't that right, Ma?'

'Yes. I'm not nosy by nature. But it's our house. And if he's coming over here upsetting her, well...'

'We weren't having any of it, were we?'

'No, we weren't, Jim. Be a dear and get us a refill of coffee, Pa?' Jill said sweetly.

Coles didn't want another coffee and she was sure Lundy didn't either but she kept quiet, silently urging Jill to continue talking.

'He's very sensitive you know is Pa. He's so very upset about all of this. You know he always thinks the best about people. But that Paul Yeats got under his skin. Pa just loves Jens and Holmer. We both do. How are the poor little mites? Where are they?'

'Right now they're with Paul Yeats' mother,' Coles replied. 'The social worker stayed with them for a good few hours before reporting that they were perfectly happy with their granny. They don't fully realise what has happened yet.'

'Probably won't for quite a while. Goodness, I hope it doesn't upset them, you know, in the long term. There are so many people going around these days who are just sick in the head. That's the only way I can describe it. I know it's an illness, but it's an illness they have in their brain. Perhaps when these people were growing up, well, maybe... if they had been better looked after, more loved,

they wouldn't have turned out that way. That's all I'm saying. I'm
sure they'll be fine just as long as Victoria doesn't get them. Just as
long as she's not involved in anything related to Esther. Esther
couldn't abide her, you know. I'm talking about Tor Lucas. Why
couldn't she be like everyone else and call herself as she was chris-
tened, Victoria. Or even Vickie. But "Tor"! I ask you. Thinks she's
better than the rest of us, that's what.'

'Did Paul Yeats play with his kids when he was here on
Saturday?' Coles asked.

Jill Beck laughed.

'You've got to be kidding. He wouldn't know how to. They
weren't old enough to be of any amusement to him yet. It was funny,
though, to see Holmer and his dad together. Holmer would immediately adopt that quiet, withdrawn look Paul had perfected over
the years. But the moment his dad was gone he'd snap out of it and
be back to being a fun child. Bit worrying that, if you ask me,' Jill
said downheartedly.

'So, he wasn't alone with the children?' Coles affirmed quietly.

'No, he'd no time for his kids on Saturday or any other day. He
spent most of the time pestering Esther,' Jill replied.

'So, did you hear what they were talking about?' Coles asked.

'Not really. He was always on at her, trying to get her to do
something she didn't want to do,' Jill said briskly. It was incredible
how fluent her conversation had become without Jim around to
start or finish her sentences.

'Like... for instance?' Coles asked. Lundy sat, pen poised at the
ready, willing to record her response.

'Oh, lots of things, like letting Tor manage both of them; like giving him some of her hard-earned cash. For heaven's sake, she was living in a small flat with her children and supporting them on her own
and he was always sticking his hand out, hitting her for a sub,' Ma
Beck answered, just as Pa Beck returned to the room, tray in hand.

'You're not still talking about Paul Yeats, are you?' Jim said,
gingerly lowering the tray on to the table.

'Afraid so,' Coles admitted, with a shrug. 'I know you've told me
how they normally behaved, but when they came over last
Saturday, did they speak to each other in front of you?'

'No, they didn't. Did they, Pa?'

'No they went into the kitchen for a short time by themselves.'

'Were they there long?' Lundy ventured, his first question for
quite a time.

'Maybe ten minutes or so,' Jill said.

'Yes, no more than ten minutes,' Jim confirmed.

'How were they when they returned to the room?' Coles asked.

'Well, he didn't come back in…' Jill started.

'He let himself out the front door,' Jim completed.

'How did she seem when she returned?' Coles asked. She couldn't help hoping that they were on the brink of uncovering some vital piece of information.

'Disturbed and concerned,' Ma Beck replied.

Pa smiled. 'Obviously not something I would have picked up on.'

Ma smiled meekly as if to say, Men. They're just not with it.

'Did Esther and the children stay the night?' Coles fishing again, hoping for something – anything would do at this stage.

'The kids stayed…' Jim continued.

'Esther left about an hour after Paul,' Jill continued further.

'She returned before midday on Sunday to pick up the kids,' Jim offered.

'Wasn't here but a few minutes. She didn't stop, just whisked them off.'

'So, you didn't see her again?'

'No. Sadly not,' Jill said, ever so quietly.

'What about Paul Yeats?' Lundy inquired, attempting to keep Ma Beck away from her darker thoughts.

'Well, funny enough he called back here late on Saturday, looking for Esther's car keys,' Ma said.

'She's got this clapped-out Morris Minor Traveller,' Pa said.

'The one with the wooden frame,' Ma said.

'And it works about one time in ten,' Pa said

'It's still outside. He came around here about eightish,' Ma said.

'To see if Esther had left the keys here,' Pa said.

'We told him, no,' Ma said.

'Even if they were here we wouldn't have given them to him,' Pa said.

'Pa kept him standing on the doorstep,' Ma said.

'If I had my way, I'd never have allowed him inside the door, no way,' Pa said.

'He walked away, no warmth from that man. He walked away, hands deep in pockets, staring at his shoes,' Ma said.

'Well,' said Coles, 'thank you. Very illuminating. We'll be off now.'

Lundy was in such a hurry to get out, he nearly tripped over himself. He hastily shoved his notebook into his pocket, crumpling the pages and he nearly stabbed himself as he tried to put his pen into his top pocket.

Coles wondered whether the Ma and Pa, carpet-slippers-and-pipe life was so distant from Lundy's current life that he was offended by it. Or was he merely dreading the inevitability of old age?

Chapter 19

Thursday's Child

Thursday 21st December

I'M WRITING *in my study and I can hear Dillon outside the door. I keep thinking she could be the sort of person who lingers outside doors with a tape recorder, hoping to capture me singing my songs. If that's so, she could play the songs back to her friends. I'm not entirely sure I like her. Jens & Holmer do, though. I think it's funny they like her. Mind you they say they like her; they never say they love her. How do they know the difference? Do they know the difference?*

I have to assume that because they like her, she has never mistreated them. I suppose we can't help but be worried about our children, after the recent spate of nannies murdering children in their care. Do children grow up thinking that adults – yes, even their parents – are going to treat them badly? Sometimes I think so. When children look at you and you are not doing what they want you to do or if they are not doing what you want them to do, the look in their little eyes is so unforgiving. As if to say, 'I expected no more from you.'

And the other thing is that with all her extra weight, Dillon will appear cuddly to them. Like Pooh Bear's mother, but with not quite as good a dress sense as Pooh Bear. Whereas Pooh loves his honey, Dillon loves her sugar, in the shape of candy bars. Any candy bar, all candy bars. Is that her love? Is sugar her healer? You see we all need something and before we can afford to lose that something we have to substitute it with something else. In my case, by the time Yeatsie went off, I was addicted to Jens & Holmer. So, if she had to, what would Dillon willingly substitute for her sugar? Her books? My looks? God how vain of me, I meant to write 'my books?'.

And what would she do in-between? I mean in that gap, say between giving up sugar for the love of a man or a woman. Let's assume she'd first have to lose weight to attract a partner. She'd have to give up sugar for – shall we say, three months? – before she went out to find a man (or woman). With Dillon I really don't know which – what would she use as a crutch during this time? Or would it happen another way? Could she find someone to love her as she is? I often think that her fondness for food is also her excuse. 'I don't have a man because I'm so overweight,' therefore, 'I have an excuse for not having a man'.

Friends can be so unintentionally cruel to their partnerless friends. For some reason people in relationships feel compelled to match up the solo members of the community. It's like, if we haven't escaped, why should you? Or something. I know, I've been that warrior. I've been that interesting solo female strategically placed beside the solo interesting man at a dinner party. If you were a car without petrol the joint mental energy of all the other people at the table willing you together would push the car with the couple in it up Primrose Hill. But either one, or both, of them have been to the movie before, and whereas when we were younger we would gladly have taken a chance, now all our prejudices instinctively cut off any potential relationship at the pass. Give yourself one excuse not to go ahead, that's all you need, one simple little excuse. And, if you can't find that excuse, you can bet your bottom dollar he will. I still think of income in dollars: advances, royalty cheques, gifts from mother (ha!), whatever. If they're in pounds, I will translate them into dollars. Expenses, on the other hand, I see in pounds. Perhaps that's why I'm not as well off as I should be.

But back to Dillon: do her friends leave her alone at this stage? Does she have any friends? She behaves weirdly sometimes. Last week I caught her standing outside her Mini Minor, talking to it. She was there for ages. When I saw her at first from my living room window, I thought she was talking to someone across the street or on my blind side. But I couldn't see or hear anyone. Then I went to the door. I opened it a little, so that she wouldn't see me and I swear I saw her talking to her car. Probably trying to coax it into letting her climb on board. The kids call her car 'Tigger', and I never know whether they are laughing at the chug-chugging of the car, the fact that it's continuously lopsided, or the ritual she has to go through to climb on board. But all of that paled into insignificance when I saw her talking to her car. Who would talk to a car? And why?

Eventually I had to go outside and ask her if everything was okay. She said it was, and got in (eventually) and drove off, huffing and puffing, like she does when she's under pressure. I can hear her breathing now outside my door. It's more like a wheeze than breathing and she must know I can hear her. Perhaps she's lived with her wheeze for so long she can't hear it anymore. But I can hear clearly. I am writing this to her 'beat'. Breathe, one, two, three, four. Breathe, one, two, three, four. What is she doing out there? Maybe she's doing nothing, just listening to me. If I wasn't writing this I'd probably be scared, because you have to admit, it's quite spooky behaviour.

She's quite spooky a lot of the time. I'll catch her standing at my bedroom door. Just standing there looking in the room, taking in everything. Is she imagining what I do in my bed – and I don't mean sleeping and dreaming? My bed doesn't have many stories to tell, but I do love it. Dillon's like a fan, you know. That's it! She behaves like you'd imagine a fan that's broken into your flat would behave. They'd sneak around, drinking in everything for the hit of just being there; then they'd go and swap the experience with another fan. The swap might involve what looks to you and me (whomever you are, dear reader) like a plain white piece of paper, but in reality I'm assured, is a signed Japanese limited edition CD jacket with luminous ink you can only read when you've got a UV light. Pretty abstract, a bit like a Canadian art-house movie.

No fan that I know (except Josef) has experienced my home, so how would the other fan know if Dillon is telling the truth? Not unless she takes things, things like pillowcases, sheets, some of my rubbish? Aggghh, even the thought grosses me out. But I understand from Yeatsie weirder things have been swapped.

As gross as you want to think – now hold that thought – because, according to Yeatsie, it's been swapped.

Mind you, at least fans claim to like the music (my music), but I get the feeling the same people are waiting outside the stage door every night saying the same things to different artists. You know, just like it's their job. Their job is to get an autograph, and the harder the autograph is to get, the more they want it. They have their little tricks, too. If you don't feel like signing all this weird memorabilia they seem to find, one of them will shout at you, but mainly for the benefit of the waiting journalists and photographers: 'Oh, too big to sign for the poor fans who supported you all these years and got you to where you are now.' It's bad, I know, but then I usually smile, take his photograph or whatever, and write 'I wasn't here' on it and leave it unsigned. By the time he works out what I've written, I'm gone. Yeatsie says that the best way to defuse these situations is to scribble anything, give them their quick photograph opportunity. Then you're done, you're outta there, no negative energy. He also says that some day you'll be happy to have someone ask you for an autograph.

I remind him that Mark Chapman asked for John Lennon's autograph just before he shot him!

Dillon, even Yeatsie calls her the 'nanny from hell', lurks around giving off a kind of Chapman vibe. Or am I just being stupid now? She really does spook me, though.

*

Kennedy and Coles completed their respective interviews around the same time – shortly after three pm – and went together to visit the nanny. This hadn't happened by chance: the ever-efficient James Irvine having fitted it into the interview timetable. For her part, Anne Coles would happily have slipped Irvine a fiver, as she treasured the time she and Kennedy spent together professionally.

'We're ahead of schedule,' Kennedy said as they exited North Bridge House. 'I don't know about you, but I'm famished. Fancy a quick bite of lunch?'

'Don't mind if I do,' Coles replied. She was conscious, probably because she was nervous, that she might have sounded flippant. Why, she thought, do I always behave like a schoolgirl around this man? She was convinced that were anything ever to develop between them, she'd be able to handle it. But as soon as she'd have such a thought, she'd give herself a hard time. 'He's your boss,' she'd say to herself, 'for heaven's sake, forget it. It's never going to happen.'

Even that was a cop-out, she knew. She was making the assumption that if he weren't her boss he'd be interested in her. Wrong. Kennedy's type, if Kennedy did in fact have a type, would always be of the ann rea variety: a dark and troubled soul. But why should ann rea be dark and troubled? She was certainly beautiful, definitely intelligent, and she must have something major going for her to have Kennedy still interested in her years down the line. Recently there seemed to be a bit of a problem between them, Coles noted. Just little things that were said and done and little hints that were dropped. In fact, at one point, Coles was convinced that her superior and his journalist girlfriend had split up. Worse than that, Coles was equally convinced that on one occasion, when Irvine had said something about Kennedy and ann rea going out together again, she had let down her guard and shown her disappointment. If Irvine had picked up on it, as Coles figured he must have, he'd been too much of a gentleman to comment.

Coles also liked Irvine, but not in the same way she liked Kennedy. With Irvine it was more as a mate. She liked him, she trusted him, and he'd never tried anything on with her. He certainly had an eye for the women and appeared to be incredibly successful with them, but from the little they'd talked about it together, it seemed he always lost interest the minute they said yes. Anne Coles had been too much of a lady to inquire as to what exactly the host of girls had been saying 'yes!' to.

But this daydream was about her and Kennedy, and as they walked down Parkway together, she let her mind race through all the possibilities. Her next train of thought was: Even if this man is attracted to me, why would he want to consider being unprofessional? Of course, part of his attraction was his professionalism, the fact that he'd never ever come on to a member of the team. Therein lay the inconsistency. Coles thought he was absolutely gorgeous. He wasn't an ounce overweight, he had such kind hands, such soulful eyes, such a gentle voice, sharp features, lovely hair... 'Oh for heaven's sake, stop this rubbish!' the sensible part of her brain interrupted. 'It's never going to happen. Not in a million years!' 'But if it were to happen,' the romantic part of her brain cut in, 'would I be disappointed in him if he did ask me out?'

'So,' Kennedy said, interrupting her thought process, 'what are you so deep in thought about?' They had just passed the off-licence, and a few spits of rain had started to fall.

'Sorry?' Coles replied, thinking, (a) I hope I'm not blushing, and (b) my hair is going to look a mess if this rain continues. She was forever giving herself a hard time. Her blonde hair was either too long or too short, it never seemed just the right length. Legs a bit too fat, she presumed, for the rest of her body, and she swam for forty minutes every day as a corrective measure. Well, that wasn't entirely true. She swam every day because she enjoyed it, enjoyed the exercise. The fact it might be keeping her in trim was a bonus. The main thing she absolutely adored was the feeling of tranquility, the tuning out of the rest of the world during her thirty-four lengths.

'You seem deep in thought. Esther Bluewood?'

'No, Judy Dillon,' Coles lied. Well, it wasn't a real lie. She'd found that the overweight image of Judy Dillon had helped spur her on to swim an extra few lengths that morning, up at the O2 Centre, Finchley Road. It was handy for her. She lived in Dynham Road in West Hampstead and travelled in to work by moped, all her gear in her backpack. The O2 Centre was on her route. Parking was a pain, but parking was a pain for everybody, everywhere in NW1, now they had a new, stupid system. Yes, it was even stupid for the police, but they were not allowed to comment on it or its fairness. But then when was fairness ever allowed to get in the way of the council relieving you of your hard-earned money?

'Oh,' Kennedy said, appearing a little surprised. 'And what exactly were you thinking about our favourite nanny?'

Coles was convinced now that she was blushing. Was Kennedy such a good detective that he could detect what people thought? Don't be such a dimwit, she cautioned herself.

'Well, I always try and get a fix on someone before I go to talk to them. I try and think of their lives and how their days are,' Coles replied, this time telling the truth. 'If I can get a clue about their life styles and their daily routines, then I feel it helps me read between their lines.'

'Like if they're lying, for instance?' Kennedy offered, nodding in agreement.

They arrived at George & Nikki's Golden Grill, known in North Bridge House as the 'Golden Gorilla'. Kennedy held the door open for Coles. As she passed him she could smell him, smell his cleanness. Not a hint of aftershave or cologne, or smoke, or anything other than pure soap and the intoxicating smell of clean-shaven skin.

'Like they're lying for instance,' Coles agreed and chastised herself for the sin she'd just committed – if indeed it were a sin to imagine yourself kissing your superior.

'So how are you and DS Sandy Johnson getting on?' Kennedy asked, as they hungrily started on their snacks. Coles (ever weight-conscious) had ordered a baked potato with cheese and coleslaw and Kennedy a sweet corn omelette with hash browns and baked beans.

Coles swallowed the wrong way and coughed and spluttered. Kennedy rose from his seat, came behind her, and patted her on the back six times.

'God, that was hot,' she lied, taking refuge in a long drink of mineral water. 'I'm okay now. Thanks.'

She couldn't believe it. She had dated Sandy Johnson three or four times a few years back. He was from another section completely, the Fraud Squad at New Scotland Yard. She'd been checking illegal comings and goings in the music industry when Camden CID, led by DI Kennedy, was investigating the disappearance and death of Peter O'Browne, Managing Director of Camden

Town Records, located in the blue building directly across the road from North Bridge House. Nothing had come of the relationship. It had been good fun but that was all. And all they had in common was fun. Short term had been great enough, long term it would never have got off the ground. But the man she had just been daydreaming about, the man she spent a considerable amount of her day dreaming about, not only remembered the name of her ex, he'd also picked up on one small point in her personal life. She didn't know whether to be impressed or disappointed.

Coles had calmed down again. As she forked another helping of potato she said, 'Goodness me; Sandy. That was such a long time ago. I'd nearly forgotten about him.'

'It wasn't serious then?' Kennedy continued.

'Oh, I could never be serious about someone who wears slip-ons,' Coles said flippantly.

She hadn't realised the potato was hot and she found herself taking another large gulp of water. The friendly, cosy café was nearly empty. It was that lull between late lunch and the beginning of early dinner. The great thing about the Golden Grill, apart from its consistently excellent food and the friendly banter from Vange, the head waiter and all-round entrepreneur, was the fact that it was open midday to midnight. Perfect opening hours for the local police force and for employees of the numerous music business companies in the area. People who were always on the way to or from a gig or a recording studio would just about always have somewhere to stop for a chat, a bite and a drink. The walls were adorned with write-ups about the café, photographs of the celebs who had visited it and autographed photographs of cast members of soaps like *Eastenders* and *Coronation Street*. Coles searched these photographs now, desperately looking for a distraction for their conversation.

'Really?' Kennedy pushed.

Why is he pushing this, Coles thought, or is it just my imagination?

'Yes, and grey slip-ons at that,' she continued, trying to up the humour level and thereby (hopefully) turning the spotlight away from herself.

'No! Never,' Kennedy said, now laughing. 'I bet he wore white socks with them too?'

'Yes. In fact he did wear white socks.'

'Oh, that's it then. I'll have the fashion police pick him up immediately,' Kennedy said, much to Coles' relief.

*

Seventeen minutes later they were buzzing Judy Dillon's doorbell. Judy opened the door, showing no sign of surprise at their visit.

'Goodness, it never rains but it snows. Oh, come in, why don't you?' The nanny said, walking away and leaving them standing on the doorstep.

Coles looked at Kennedy as if to say, 'What's up with her?'

Kennedy hiked his shoulders as if to reply, 'I don't know.'

'I'm in here,' they heard her voice announce from the book room, as Kennedy closed the door.

'Will this take long do you think? You see, I'm just about to listen to something important about childcare on the radio, and if you're going to be here for a while I'll tape it. A stitch in time saves the crime,' Judy said, hovering around her radio-cassette recorder.

'I'd tape it if I were you,' Kennedy said.

Coles thought that she wouldn't have chosen that option. She would have said that they weren't going to be long. That way Judy would have been impatient to get the questions over with, so she just might have allowed something to slip out.

It became apparent that Kennedy had picked up on something she hadn't. Dillon appeared to be upset. Perhaps that had been it. Perhaps her boss had picked up on this and had decided not to risk upsetting her further.

They started with questions about Esther Bluewood and were getting nowhere fast. Judy Dillon's answers were short and snappy, nothing of substance was being given away. Coles noticed Kennedy give a slight twitch of his head at the way Dillon answered a question about Paul Yeats.

'Have you seen Paul Yeats since yesterday?' had been Kennedy's starter for ten.

'Oh yes, I have. Large as life and twice as shitty,' came the dead-pan reply.

'Where did you see him?' Kennedy asked. Coles noted the casual way he kept the conversation going, his voice always gentle, soothing, encouraging. He'd obviously sensed something in the air and was homing in on it. Not that he was being transparent about it. Judy, in her state, would have thought it was merely the flow of conversation.

'He came around here, didn't he? Pretends to be the nice guy all the time. But I can tell you he's a sheep in wolf's clothing if ever there was one,' said Dillon.

Coles was losing count of the number of times the nanny mixed her metaphors. The last one was also quite amusing, the thought of a good guy posing as an asshole. Could there be some clue there to the real Paul Yeats? He didn't seem to have many supporters in the Bluewood camp, but could he really be all that bad?

'What was he after?' Kennedy continued.

'He only came around to give me the sack, didn't he? Said my services were no longer required. "Who's going to look after Jens and Holmer?" I asked. "None of your business," he replied. "Don't come around the house any more," he said. "What about my stuff?" I said. "I'll send it around," he said. "Just make sure you don't come around Fitzroy anymore," he said, as he turned around and walked out. "What about my wages?" I shouted after him. "Take it out of all the things you've helped yourself to over the years," he shouted, slamming the door. I swear to you on my mother's grave, I never took anything which wasn't mine or that I wasn't given as a present. The jumped-up, sixth-form-poet.'

'Did they owe you any money?' Coles asked.

'Well, she paid me every Friday, but they must have to give me some kind of notice, wouldn't you think?'

'Was it all through the books?' Kennedy asked, Coles thinking that it probably wasn't.

'No, of course not, I could never afford to pay taxes on what she could afford to pay me. But if he'd not been using her money to keep him and his fancy woman on, well, it would have been a different thing wouldn't it? Oh yes, there was enough money for all of that. But money for clothes for the kids and food and all of that, well now, he didn't give a shit about any of that. Let me tell you, what comes around goes back again.'

'But surely he must have been okay for money?' Kennedy asked. Coles noticed the way he was upping the pace of the questions, not so much fishing for specific answers, but more to see what else came out.'

'Please,' Dillon replied, raising both her hands and making claws with them in front of her. 'He's never sold a record in anger. It was an insult to even Michael Bolton to call Paul Yeats a singer. He'd have been better off as a bin man; and that's not a slight on bin men. It's just that Yeats was no stranger to rubbish. Perhaps it was time he collected it rather than try to sell it. Yes, that would have been a pleasant change.'

Coles felt like asking the nanny how she knew Yeats made so

little money, but Kennedy seemed to be going somewhere, so she sat back, observing Dillon. Strange thing was that the nanny rarely, if ever, looked at Coles. All her answers and body language were directed towards Kennedy. Coles was aware how ever so slightly at first, then more and more blatantly, the nanny was flirting with Kennedy. A wee smile here, a pose there, a come-on stare. How could someone so obviously overweight, Coles thought, fancy her chances with the detective? Not just any detective either, but – in Coles' eyes, at least – the most eligible bachelor in London. The brass-neck of her, Coles snarled to herself.

'I thought Paul Yeats was moderately successful?' Kennedy asked, oblivious to the vibes being given out. Was that how he did it, by ignoring what wasn't relevant to the questioning? How was it Kennedy was so good at questioning witnesses? By breaking the police stereotype and being a genuinely nice bloke? He always seemed to care about the people he met, to be concerned about them, to listen to what they had to say. Yes, Coles confirmed to her inner self, Detective Inspector Christy Kennedy actually listened to people. He was warm, he was friendly and he didn't come across as the enemy. How had he been in the force for so long and not become as jaded as everyone else? Coles had been a member of Camden Town CID for a relatively short time and even she found herself regularly losing her patience with obvious offenders. She found herself thinking, You're lying. You know you're lying, I know you're lying, and you know I know you're lying, yet you still persist with this whole charade.

But Kennedy never seemed to adopt a similiar attitude. It's not that he believed everything he was told. He didn't, Coles knew, but he's prepared to take it all in. He was forever telling his team to amass information, as much information as possible. 'Don't try and guess the identity of the criminal, or the method of the crime until you have as many facts on the table as possible,' he'd say. 'That way you won't be trying to fit your facts on to the suspect or the crime.' And here he was, collecting facts, right in front of her eyes, with the generously built Judy Dillon flirting with him, and he was too much of a gentleman to acknowledge it.

'Oh please, he was as successful as a cabby in a candy store,' Dillon replied to Kennedy question about Yeats' supposed success.

That one nearly cracked Coles up and she was sure Kennedy would burst out laughing. Incredibly, he continued undeterred.

'So, you don't think he was selling many records any more?'

'Well, firstly forget the "anymore". He never sold many records. And who do you think his record label, Goodwords Music, was?'

Kennedy shook his head with a 'I haven't a clue' look.

'Paul Yeats was the chief, and only, executive. That was apart from Esther who had to write all the cheques. I saw the bills, you know. I know a lot about that man, a lot he may not want me to know. Him and his vanity records, he was playing the part of a pop star even down to the dolly bird on his arm. Well, he's not advertising the fact that his dolly bird, Miss Droopy Drawers, Miss Rosslyn St Clair, is up the shute,' Dillon blurted out, her fury now in full flow.

'Up the shute?' Kennedy said, a question mark raising his eyebrows.

'Preggers, with seed, a bun in the oven, impregnated, about to drop one, with child,' Dillon taunted proudly.

That certainly got Coles' attention. Kennedy, however, never batted an eyelid. He continued, his voice as soft and friendly as ever.

'Are you sure about that?'

'Absolutely,' Dillon replied.

'Did Esther know?' Kennedy continued.

'No, not as far as I was aware.'

'Do you mind me asking how you found out?' Kennedy continued. Coles was proud of him. His continued fishing into the unknown had turned up an important clue, possibly the most important clue in the case.

'The fan network. There's not much that goes on we don't know about,' Dillon boasted.

'Was Paul Yeats aware you had this information?' Kennedy asked.

'I think he might have been,' Dillon replied, looking a little worried for the first time.

'Really?' Kennedy said, acting surprised. Coles was convinced it was stage surprise.

'Yes, I think he might have a connection with one of the fans,' Dillon replied, still concerned.

'Oh, and why's that?'

'Just that some of the information we get, it seems just a little bit too "insider", if you know what I mean, and there's rarely any bad stuff about Yeats floating around.'

'This fan club, are there many members?' Kennedy asked.

'You realise here I'm not talking about the official fan club where you send in your eleven quid and you get your 10 by 8 and a news sheet twice a year?'

Kennedy nodded: this wasn't the club he was thinking about, either.

'There are about fourteen regulars in the inner circle,' the nanny boasted. Coles thought that as nanny to the star's children, she must have been their most prized member. She was yet to share Kennedy's information about Esther sleeping with Josef Jones.

'And you're pretty sure Esther didn't know?' Kennedy persisted.

'When I last saw her, which was Friday, she definitely was not aware of this information,' Dillon replied.

'Where would you have been on Sunday evening?' Kennedy asked, as Coles stared around at the hundreds of books.

'I was here by myself, reading.'

'All evening?' Kennedy said, a hint of firmness in his voice.

'All evening,' Judy replied, making a feeble attempt at fluttering her eyelids. 'Quite a sad state of affairs for a single girl I know, but there you are.'

Coles couldn't believe the nanny was actually fluttering her eyelashes at Kennedy.

Kennedy either didn't notice or chose to ignore it, and pretty soon he and Coles were out on the street, walking back up towards Parkway.

'Bit of a conquest there, sir,' Coles said, plucking up a certain amount of courage to cross the line between personal and police business.

'You think so?'

'Oh yes, she was like putty in your hands. Surely you noticed?' Coles said, taking another step over, and away, from the line.

'I wouldn't be so sure that our nanny was giving away anything more than what she wanted us to know. Her motive for telling us that Rosslyn St Clair was pregnant, now that's what interests me.'

Two minutes later, they were bounding up the lamp-lit steps at North Bridge House. They were slightly late for the information-sharing meeting with the rest of the team.

Chapter 20

'OKAY, LET'S look at what we've we managed to ascertain so far,' Kennedy pronounced. As he started to speak, those gathered in his office quickly brought their conversations to a halt. The following forty minutes were spent going through the information gathered thus far.

'So,' Irvine said, 'our suspects are plentiful.'

'Apparently so,' Kennedy agreed, moving across to his 'Guinness is Good For You' noticeboard. 'Okay, let's list them...'

And under the main heading of Esther Bluewood, written in a green felt-tip pen on a white cue card, he placed a second card, headed up with Paul Yeats' name.

'Okay, Paul Yeats... Let's hear about Paul Yeats. What do we know about him?'

'Failed pop star,' Coles offered, adding, 'deserted Esther and their two children.'

'Took up with a young girl, Rosslyn St Clair,' Kennedy continued, picking up the thread. 'And Miss St Clair is supposedly carrying Yeats' child. Esther had begun divorce proceedings against Paul Yeats. He was keen for his sister, Victoria (Tor) Lucas, to become his and Esther's manager, but Esther resisted this. Yeats appeared quite desperate to deny us access to Esther's journals. Motives are plentiful but mainly he was about to have his primary source of income cut off and I believe there was also a good chance – considering there were two kids involved – that he would be thrown out of the cottage.'

'When he called at the Beck's place in Islington on Saturday evening he was acting very suspiciously and looking for the car keys. This would have been at the same time he told us he was in his local pub in the Cotswolds,' Coles offered. 'Could he have been trying to get a lift home? Was there something of Esther's in the car he badly wanted? Was the car meant to be part of his alibi? But how could he have committed the murder and made it appear she had gassed herself?'

'A good question,' Kennedy enthused, as he rose from his desk to add another name card. Before pinning it to the board, he added: 'A very good question but we don't have enough information just yet to go tackling big questions like that. Let's move on to the next suspect on the list.'

Under Yeats' he pinned a new card, this one bore the legend, 'Josef Jones'.

'What do we know about Josef?' Kennedy asked his team.

'Evil-sounding voice, I can tell you,' Irvine began. 'A fan, a groupie in fact, and for some reason Esther Bluewood took him to bed.'

'She took him to bed for the same reason Paul Yeats took Rosslyn St Clair to bed,' Coles surmised. Kennedy noticed that her voice was slightly shaky. 'Esther had her needs too. He was available, he looked good – well, at least he looked youthful – and I think Esther would have thought, being so much of a fan, she could have controlled him.'

'Perhaps,' was Irvine's only concession. 'Either way, maybe he was looking for more out of the relationship than she was? Male rock stars have married their groupies, there are some extremely famous cases, so perhaps Josef Jones was thinking that it was time for a role reversal! Perhaps he saw Esther as his gravy train?'

'Interesting concept,' Kennedy said, quite deadpan. 'What was he up to on Saturday evening?'

'He claimed he was out with some mates,' Allaway offered, rifling through the notes from the meeting he and Irvine'd had with Jones. 'He behaved very suspiciously when we approached him outside Esther's flat.'

'Yes. He hightailed it, big time,' Irvine agreed.

'Did it take you long to catch up with him?' Kennedy inquired.

'A matter of minutes,' Allaway said proudly.

'At any time during the chase was he out of your view?' Kennedy asked.

'Just a few seconds as he turned into Gloucester Crescent from Fitzroy Road,' Allaway confirmed.

'Did he seem to slow down when he turned the corner?'

'A bit, yes…' Allaway began.

'I see what you're getting at sir,' Irvine said, interrupting. 'We were idiots.' He looked at Allaway to find the penny still hadn't dropped. 'Sorry, I was an idiot. He was obviously taking the opportunity to dump his stash of drugs the second he was out of our sight.'

'Exactly. But it's not important. This time we're not interested in his drugs and in the cold light of day these things are always easier to assess. When he started to run, no doubt your adrenalin was pumping and you were thinking you'd found the killer of Esther Bluewood,' Kennedy replied.

'He was also outside Esther's flat on the day she died. He's unmistakable in the *Evening Standard* photograph in his regular outfit of a four-button black suit and white shirt, top button done up,' Coles added.

'But there were a lot of other fans in the same photograph,' Lundy suggested. Perhaps we should check everyone who appears in it?'

'Can't do any harm,' Kennedy said, encouraging Lundy to do that very thing. 'Next name: Edward Higgins.'

And the detective wrote out another card.

'We spoke to him too,' Irvine started. 'Didn't give much away really. He'd originally had a bit of a gripe when Esther took the flat he was waiting for, but I'm not sure that would be sufficient reason to drive him to kill her. He seemed to quite like her, as a matter of fact.'

'And she him,' Kennedy revealed, recalling Esther's journal. 'However, she did note him standing outside her door one night behaving a bit suspiciously,' Kennedy said, recalling another bit of information from the precious journal. 'A long shot, but what was he doing on Saturday night?' Kennedy said, writing another name on a card.

'Watching telly,' Allaway confirmed.

'Must have been a great night for the television,' Irvine announced.

'Judy Dillon,' Kennedy announced as he stuck the newly written name on the board.

'Yes, she was also watching televison on Saturday,' Coles confirmed, looking directly at James Irvine.

'She's a bit weird, if you ask me,' Irvine said in response. 'I know it's much too early in the case, but if I was a betting man, which I am, I'd put a few bob on our Judy as an each-way bet.'

'You don't get paid for backing second or third in a possible murder enquiry,' Kennedy reminded him. Then, addressing everyone: 'What do we know about Judy Dillon?'

'She was the children's nanny, also a member of the inner fan club. Perhaps she pinched the journal. She claims she was protecting it, but in the fan club circle it could have counted as a major coup to have Esther Bluewood's final journal,' Coles started.

'Esther was concerned about her as well, I think,' Kennedy said, taking up the thread. 'Judy used to hang around outside her study door while Esther was working. There were also several times when Esther caught her standing at the bedroom door, staring in.'

'She's obviously not very fit, so if it was her, it couldn't have been any kind of physical murder.'

'Unless she had an accomplice,' Irvine said, apparently thinking out loud. 'Maybe a few of the fans got together.'

This gathered a few mutterings from around Kennedy's packed office.

'Okay, okay. I know. Far-fetched,' Irvine continued, raising his voice a little to dispel the mutterings. 'But stranger things have happened at sea. I mean, let's be serious here. Anyone who focuses their entire lives around a celebrity can't be all there in the first place. Scouring dustbins for trinkets, hanging around stage doors for an autograph. Now come on, what's that all about? Does it get them closer? If I'd a few grand to spare, I could buy an autograph of JFK. Wouldn't mean I'd ever met him. Wouldn't mean I was ever close to him. It would just mean, as my mother would say, "A fool and his money are easily parted". These artists release their music on records—'

'CDs these days, Detective Sergeant Irvine,' Coles jibed, raising a laugh from all in the office.

'—Fine, whatever, I'm sticking to my record player and my vinyl, so if they want to get me to buy their music they're going to have to release it in record form. But my point is that artists release their music on records, CDs, cassettes, bleedin' 8-track – if that keeps you happy – and the fans should be content to go into a store and buy the music and take it home and play it. Why do they want more? How much better does it make the music if there's a squiggle, which is meant to be an autograph, on the front cover? Does it raise the enjoyment factor? I'll tell you something about music and then I'll stop, sir...' Irvine continued, looking in the direction of Kennedy, who waited in good humour for his DS to continue.

'...For years I've collected the works of Frank Sinatra, Nat King Cole, Tony Bennett, Dean Martin, Paul Anka, Brendan Quinn, Matt Monro and I have to say, they've given me so much pleasure, but, I've absolutely no interest whatsoever in doing anything but listen to their music. I'm not connected to these people, I'm moved by their music. The point is, when Frank Sinatra died I wasn't upset, I wasn't particularly hurt. I didn't even know the man. I couldn't abide all this public grieving by people who'd never even been on the same continent as the man. I found it all a wee bit sick to be truthful. People who are prepared to act that way in public must have something drastically missing in their personal lives. Me, I've still got all the classic Frank Sinatra albums and I know they will continue to give me pleasure as they, quite simply, just get better with age...' Irvine paused. No one spoke so he continued.

'My point would have to be that obsessive fans like Judy Dillon and Josef Jones have so much shit going around their heads, stuff we can't even imagine. You know, in the normal course of your day someone does something to upset you, steal a parking space, take your seat in a busy bar, nearly run you down when you're trying to cross the road and you swear under your breath. Of course we don't mean it. But, then we're a well balanced group of people, aren't we?'

Irvine swung his outstretched arm, with its finger pointed, around the room.

'But what if we were the kind of people who spent their lives hanging around stage doors, waiting for a glimpse of our idols? The glimpse is not important. The documenting of the glimpse with a quick snapshot, a quick autograph, that's the thing isn't it? That's the big thing. Now believe me, I've seen some of these fans with their idols at the Odeon, when I was working the Hammersmith patch. They are not pleasant; actually some of them are downright rude. Ordering the stars about, shouting at them. Letting the air out of their car tyres just so they can't effect a speedy getaway. These people do not lead normal lives, they live their lives for someone else, but it's not really *for* someone else. It's for themselves and for the other people in their circle, so that *their* talking points will be bigger and better than those of their mates. That's got nothing whatsoever to do with the music. These people never actually go into the concert venues. They just hang around the stage doors, for heavens' sake. Yes, there are genuine fans that will buy the records and the concert tickets and they will also, sometimes, try to come backstage to pay their respects. Nine times out of ten, if the real fans ever manage to get through the security, they'll be scared off by these weirdos, and believe you me, they are one weird bunch of misfits. They are obsessed with their own ideals of their idols and if they, the stars, don't live up to these high standards or do anything, directly or indirectly, to upset these fanatics then my point simply is, who knows what they'd do to get their revenge?'

'Yes, quite,' Kennedy said in agreement.

'Thank you, Robbie Coltrane,' Coles added, lightening the atmosphere by the one or two notches it needed.

'Nah, he'd be too big for my shoes. When they film my life story they'll have to get Sean Connery to play me. He wouldn't have to change his accent in the slightest,' Irvine laughed.

That was the first time Kennedy could ever remember James Irvine himself drawing attention to the fact that his voice sounded identical to the best actor ever to fill the 007 shoes.

'I suppose,' Kennedy began, as the laugher died down, 'we should also add both Tor Lucas and Rosslyn St Clair to our list.' And Kennedy did just that. He added each name to a card and pinned them up on to the noticeboard.

'We need to speak to them both urgently,' he continued. 'They are both connected with Paul Yeats. I think it's going to be easy enough to find Tor, but Yeats is keeping Rosslyn out of the way. He says she's upset and he doesn't know where she's disappeared to. I'm not so sure I believe him, however, and we do need to talk to her and to Tor as soon as possible. Okay? How have we been getting on with the scene of the crime? Any new witnesses or any new information come to light?'

'Nothing sir,' Irvine started. 'Absolutely nothing, apart from...'

'Yes?' Kennedy said, outstretching one of his hands, trying to encourage his DS to spit out his little titbit. Every little helped, at this stage they couldn't afford to discard any information, no matter how trivial it may appear.

'Well, I have to say that absolutely every single person we speak to is of the same opinion...'

'Which is?' Kennedy asked. In a court of law, they say, you should never ask a question unless you know the answer. But this wasn't exactly a court of law and Kennedy was prepared to risk not having a clue what Irvine was about to say.

'Well, sir, everyone is of the opinion that Esther Bluewood committed suicide,' Irvine said, in rather more subdued tones than he'd employed on his previous monologue.

'Yep, I got that feeling too. And that, I believe, is the cloak our murderer is hiding behind. So, ladies and gentlemen, let's get out there and lift this cloak and find out who exactly is lurking behind it. We've a long way to go, and although the killer has won the first couple of rounds, we've got the stamina to see it through to the bitter end.'

Chapter 21

Happy Birthday To You!

Wednesday 18th November

IT'S MY *father's birthday today, Wednesday18th November. The year was 1928. He died when I was only five and there is still not a day goes by that I don't think about him. I remember sitting on his knee, the knee of his good leg. He was always tense and awkward with me, a wee bit like I see Yeatsie behaving with Jens & Holmer now. It's kind of like, 'This is my child so I should be close to her; I don't feel anything, but I'm going to act as though we're close in the hope that we might become close.' Is that why I wanted his affections so much, because I didn't have them?*

Here I am, all these years later, twenty-seven to be exact, and I'm still anxious for his affections. Is that why I feel, still feel, mad at my mother? Do I blame her? And if I accept the fact that I blame her, does that mean that I must therefore accept responsibility for the fact that Yeatsie behaves exactly the same way with Jens? He's a bit more parental with Holmer, especially the older Holmer becomes. There's a bit of bonding going on there now. Is that because Yeatsie can see this small child forming into his own person with his own mind and independence and that, intellectually, stimulates him? His creation is developing a mind that won't accept everything said and is not scared of questioning. Yes, that's it, I'm sure. I've noticed the look in Yeatsie's eyes and it's pride, I'm sure of it!

Yeatsie keeps telling me that he doesn't like putting Holmer to bed, because not only does he (Holmer) want stories read to him but even when they've been read, Holmer doesn't want to surrender to the night, to sleep, fall into darkness, slip into unconsciousness. Yeatsie says that the more tired Holmer becomes, the more positively he fights against sleep, and the more inevitable it becomes the more dangerous it is. His eyes get heavy and he knows he is falling asleep but for some reason he doesn't want to. Why is he so scared of sleep? Yeatsie asks. Holmer's not scared of the dark, he's not scared of what's under the bed, he fears neither what's in the wardrobe nor what's out in the hallway. So why then is he so scared of going to sleep? Then, when Holmer is about to drop off, he insists on having his father lie in the bed beside him so that he can inter-twine his little legs with his father's. He won't hug his father as he falls asleep. He usually lies with his back to him, Yeatsie tell me, but he always makes sure their legs are intertwined. Is that a safety net for when he falls deep into slumberland? Does he believe his father will soften the blow of sleep?

Yeatsie wants to know what Holmer sees when he goes to sleep. He says it's such a drain to take him to bed. He'd like to be able to just tuck him in, kiss him on the forehead and say, 'Goodnight son, sleep tight and don't let the bedbugs bite.' This hurts me because I remember it being exactly the same with my father. Even through all my counseling and therapy, I didn't remember it. Not until Yeatsie told me about Holmer. Then it all came back to me. I remembered when I was a little girl, needing my father to be close to me when I was going to sleep. I have vague memories of him saying goodnight. But I also seem to remember that it was my mother's chore to put the kids to bed.

Isn't that sad? It's considered a chore to send your children off to dream. These little people want so much from us as parents, but we are so intent – and I'm equally as guilty here as Yeatsie – on wanting them to have their independence. I try to learn from my own father. I try to celebrate my children's childhood. I'm never going to say to them, 'Be a big girl or be a big boy. It won't bite you' or 'You can do it yourself now'. We have just one childhood and it's much too short for the small time we have on this earth.

I try to remember how much my father disappointed me by not showing me a father's love. Oh, how that would have helped me. I would have been the best daughter for him. I would have made him proud. I spent my life trying to make him proud, even though he wasn't there. Then I spent the darkest years, trying to hurt him by hurting myself. I didn't feel like a person then. I felt like someone or something else. I would watch myself as a black-and-white charac-ter in a movie, but it was bizarre because everything else in the movie was in color. Then for some reason, I wanted to make him feel proud again.

I remember wanting to be a clever girl for my father but equally I remember him not even noticing it when I was. I remember how bad that made me feel. How empty it made me feel. It was as if there was no reason for my life because my father didn't see me as special. And even with all my success in writing songs and selling records,

Yeatsie says it is all, still, to prove to my father that he was wrong. 'Look at me,' Yeatsie claims I am shouting with my songs, 'I'm special and I'm proving it!'

He probably got that bit of wisdom from the back of a beer-mat!

But my father went so quickly. He just died one day, out of the blue. In my dreams it has to do with his leg. In my dreams he only has one leg but my mother keeps telling me both his legs were perfectly okay. He died, she says, because he wouldn't look after himself. He was meant to go into hospital for an operation, something to do with his insides. It was a simple operation but he kept putting it off, he just wouldn't go. He couldn't! It was a simple case of adults behaving like children. In some instances we are no better than our children, at least they have the excuse of not knowing. But my father, he just wouldn't listen to his doctor. Apparently the operation would have been simple and non-life-threatening. But he kept saying to my mother, 'Don't worry I'll be okay, it'll get okay by itself.' He was a great believer in the healing powers of the body. That's one of the things my mother goes on about in her long rambling letters: 'Remember you father,' she warns, 'He wouldn't look after himself, or go to hospital and look what happened to him. Make sure you keep up your treatment, Esther. You may think you feel better but I'm afraid you may still be ill. So take good care of yourself and get attention.'

My father didn't. Seek attention that was. And something simple developed into something complicated, and by the time he was taken to hospital, unconscious, it was too late. He died the following day on the operating table. My father had always wanted to be an actor so he would have been happy to die in the theatre. Cruel, Esh, cruel.

My father's other claim to fame? He was born on the same day as Mickey Mouse! Top that!

That says a lot about my father, he was born on the same day as Mickey Mouse, the creation that has possibly given more joy to children throughout the world than anything, or anyone, else, and my father couldn't even communicate with his own daughter. And he died and left me alone, but not so alone that he doesn't terrorize my thoughts each and every day.

So today, I'll toast you my father, and I'll also raise my glass to Mickey Mouse!

*

Kennedy was back in his home later that evening, rereading Esther

Bluewood's journal. Although it pained him, he listened to her music as he read. He listened to her voice and could almost feel her breathing through his Sony speakers. The voice singing the songs became the voice that now spoke the words of the journal into his mind's ear. He imagined she was right there beside him, talking to him, pushing herself to catch her breath so she could deliver her words. It was that breathlessness which gave her voice such charm and soul; a voice so much deeper and richer than most other female voices, Kennedy observed.

It was intriguing for the detective to listen to her singing, whilst simultaneously he imagined her speaking voice. The singing voice vehemently throwing out the words she desperately wanted the world to hear. The speaking voice reciting only the most intimate thoughts of the writer. It was interesting to try and parallel the words of her songs with the words of her journal.

Kennedy felt that all Esther Bluewood's pain originated with her father, or at least her father's inability to communicate with her and convince her that he loved her. Could any of this have been Esther's fault? True, she was a child when all this was going down, but maybe her father could see something in her eyes that scared him off. Could he have sensed that, even as a child, Esther was one who could only deal with honest feelings? Maybe he saw that it wasn't ever going to be enough for her to be kissed and cuddled and told, 'There now, dear. Everything is going to be okay.' Did Esther Bluewood know, even as a child, that everything wasn't going to be okay? Did she know that a kiss and a cuddle weren't going to make everything okay? That the bogeyman wasn't going to disappear just because her father blew him away?

Or maybe his never even taking the trouble to try and blow the bogeyman away was what started her feelings of inadequacy and vulnerability. Esther was trying to equate her own children with her own childhood. Perhaps that's why the relationship between her mother and herself had thawed in recent years. Perhaps now, looking at Paul Yeats, she saw his inability to be a good father to their children and, more importantly, her complete lack of power over that situation made her understand her own mother's powerlessness during her childhood years. The saddest thing for Kennedy was that we, none of us, learn from the mistakes of our parents. We all have to make our own mistakes. But then no one taught Holmer to be scared of the dark, or to be even more scared of sleep. Why should he develop this phobia? Was it in his genes? Was it passed down to him through his granny, then his mother? Who might Holmer pass it on to? Is it possible ever to break away from the cycle?

Why, Kennedy wondered, was he one of the well-balanced ones? Or did he just think he was well-balanced? Maybe this was his foil. That he considered himself sane, in no need of the mind doctors? He wasn't exactly cynical about them, but his opinions weren't far short. Was it the fact that he could see the wood from the trees – the simple vision Esther Bluewood was always struggling with – did that set him apart and make him a stronger person? He didn't think so and knew that without the music he was then listening to – Esther Bluewood's stunning *Axis* – his life would not be as full or as beautiful.

Kennedy was desperate for a sign, confirmation from the journal, from the music, that he and Hugh Watson were correct in their certainty that Esther Bluewood had not taken her own life. The confirmation for him was that Esther had lived her life for her children. Every decision she made seemed to be based on how it might affect her children. She knew, better than most, exactly what it would mean for Jens and Holmer not to have their mother around as they grew up. She must have known that, in her absence, Tor would have a major influence in their upbringing. She must have known that Paul Yeats would only ever be a figurehead kind of father.

On the other hand, Watson had told Kennedy that sometimes people who consider committing suicide feel that they will be doing their family, parents and/or children, a favour by getting out of their lives. This would definitely not be the case with Esther Bluewood. She knew too well the alternative. She had already made plans to get Paul Yeats out of her life, and by direct association, out of their children's lives, at least to some degree. She had already made it known to all who would listen that she did not want Tor Lucas involved in her career and she certainly didn't want her involved in any way in the lives of her children.

But who would have wanted to murder this woman? Kennedy wondered about this as he put the journal down, allowing the music to take over. Was there anything Esther was saying to him through her music? How could its creator become mixed up in anything that might have cost her her life?

Was Josef Jones a spurned lover? Perhaps he'd been cut off in his prime just once too often. But then, surely, such an obvious act of frustration would've resulted in a brutal on-the-spot murder? Strangulation? Stabbing? But was this crime of passion? No, it certainly was not. This was most definitely a calculated, cold-blooded murder. Time had been taken over the planning and execution of Esther Bluewood's murder. Kennedy wasn't even sure exactly how it had been carried out. He had a theory or two but none of them fitted the facts – so far.

Could Paul Yeats have planned and executed such a murder? Could he have found out that Esther was planning to divorce him? He'd tried, unsuccessfully, to tie their business dealings together. That coup, if he'd managed to pull it off, would have set him up for life. As her sole legal heir, he'd have been able to achieve the status he'd been unable to achieve whilst she was alive. But surely, if he were so calculating, he wouldn't have taken a lover? Everyone, including Esther and even the kids, knew about Rosslyn St Clair. He'd not even tried to conceal it. Or was he just a baboon with his brain in his trousers?

Maybe when Rosslyn became pregnant it brought matters to a head? Could Rosslyn have planned the pregnancy for that sole reason? Did that action move Rosslyn into the frame? What if she still couldn't draw a commitment from him, even though she was about to bear Yeats' child? Perhaps she thought the only way to finally win this man was to remove what she considered to be the obstacle. Kennedy knew Rosslyn St Clair must have known she would have been a prime suspect in any murder investigation. But in an apparent, credible suicide, she could have covered up her tracks well enough.

Did the killer think up what they thought was the perfect murder? A murder they were convinced they could get away with? Did the murderer have the victim in their sights first of all, or was it the method of murder that came first?

If Esther Bluewood was always the intended victim, as Kennedy suspected, who could have wanted her dead enough to kill her? Tor Lucas? She seemed to be quite the schemer from the little Kennedy had heard. He was due to see her the next morning. Out of the blue she'd rung in to North Bridge House and fixed up an appointment to come in and see Kennedy. That should be interesting. Then there was Rosslyn. Kennedy was determined to speak to her also by the end of the following day.

That only left Esther Bluewood's mother. Kennedy felt it was vital to speak to her. He would have tried to call her then and there but he knew she was on a transatlantic flight, expected to land at Heathrow in the morning. He reopened the journal and searched out the bit where Esther wrote about her mother.

*

Mother's Day

Sunday 22nd March

Another of Ma's rambling letters arrived today. It was so long I wouldn't have been surprised if she had been still writing the end of it on her kitchen table in Boston when the beginning arrived in England. Doesn't she realise that it is too long? I'll never start, let alone finish it. I wouldn't mind, but she never actually says anything. She writes and writes away, I don't know anyone who can go on for so long without actually saying anything. I can picture her, in my mind's eye, scribbling away in her tidy kitchen in Boston. I can nearly hear the sound of the nib as she scratches across the paper.

Why am I still without feelings for her? Now, with Jens & Holmer, I realise the importance of a mother in a child's life. Is it because of my earlier illness that I ceased to be a child, and, no longer a child, she thinks I have no need of a mother? Or is it that I blame her for my father's demise? God this is such old territory and all straight out of Doc Watson's textbooks at that. But when I think of my own children I wish I could feel differently. But I don't feel differently. That's a fact I can't ignore. I'm avoiding a guilt trip on all of this. I was so relieved when Doc Watson gave me permission to hate my mother. He said it was fine, okay, to hate my mother. That was like a ton weight lifted from my shoulders. Why couldn't someone have told me that fifteen years ago? And if they had, would things have turned out any differently?

My mother ignores all this negativity. I can see her sitting there thinking, 'Daughter. Oh yes, I have one of those. Now, what should a dutiful mother do for her daughter? Yes. Of course, I'll write a letter. Just jot a few things down and send it off to her. Yes, that's what a mother would do.' Then she could go to her PTA meeting with a clear conscience and drop into the conversation about the devotion she has to her daughter.

I just had a flash while thinking about my relationship with my mother: she never hugged me, or held me, or kissed me. Isn't that so sad? I cannot remember a single occasion when she hugged me.

When we meet up again after a time apart it's like I've just been down to the shops. She behaves so awkwardly, rarely looking me in the eyes. Is she scared of me because of what I've done? Does she fear what I might do to her? I have no wish to hurt her mentally or physically. It's just that she is called my mother; it's only a name I suppose. But I have to accept that she bore me; through her pain she gave me life. She was a vessel. Maybe I should treat her like that, like a milk jug. I actually like our milk jug, it's pretty pink but I'd never go around all day feeling guilty about it. I dwell on my problems and I accept that there are more than a few of them, but I can't help feeling that if I had a mother, a real mother and not a vessel, I wouldn't feel this way. These are not my problems; these are her problems, all of this shit. I've got all this weight on my back because of her. I thought she'd be sad when I left America. My considerations, the last I had, were for her. She was the only reason I didn't leave immediately after the basement illness. I needn't have worried; she was happy for me to go. Sure, I was taking all her problems – or most of them, at any rate – away to a foreign country. How considerate of me. Is that my sign of love for my mother?

I simply adore Jens & Holmer, I love them to death. They're so cute you could eat them. What a bizarre thing to say. I love my children so much I could eat them. I'm sure they appreciate that – not the cannibalistic tendencies – the love. I so much want them to grow up to love me in a way I can never love my mother.

I tore her letter into little pieces and put it in the box with all her other torn (and unread) letters.

*

Kennedy seemed to recall the piece being a little easier on her mother than it turned out to be. Perhaps he was assuming, because of her love for her own children, she must have had a soft spot for her mother, however hard she appeared to be on her. Why tear every letter she'd received from her mother into little pieces and keep them together in a box?

Just then two things happened. The Esther Bluewood CD finished, plunging Kennedy's little study into silence. He enjoyed the silence for only a few seconds before the telephone rang.

It was ann rea and she sounded upset.

Chapter 22

IN THE thirty minutes it took ann rea to reach Kennedy's house in Primrose Hill he had prepared some food. In that short time he'd done them proud, well, thanks of course to Mr Marks and Mr Sparks. Sadly though, Kennedy's enthusiasm was dampened somewhat by ann rea's lack of appetite. She seemed to be seeking solace in one of the two bottles of Saint Veran she had brought with her.

'I still can't get over the fact that Esther is dead,' ann rea said, as she finally stopped playing with her food and pushed her plate, still piled with oval minced meat pie, potato gratin and peas, to one side.

She poured herself a second, equally generous glass of the crisp dry white wine and topped up Kennedy's glass with a thimbleful of the same. Kennedy was hungry, but he found himself picking at the pie – normally one of his favourite treats.

'We're convinced she didn't take her own life,' he began.

'Oh my God,' ann rea cried out, 'that means she was murdered.'

In some ways she was stating the obvious, but in ann rea's state it was being uttered in self-realisation.

'God, Kennedy I can't believe it. What's the world coming to? Who'd want to murder Esther Bluewood, knowing they were leaving two children without a mother?'

It wasn't really a question that needed to be answered, at least not in the short term, and Kennedy figured ann rea was asking herself as much as she was asking him.

'It just suddenly hit home this afternoon. You know, that she wasn't around any more? We weren't great friends, we probably couldn't even be termed friends in the true sense of the word, but we always got on great and recently we'd been meeting up at least once a fortnight.'

'How did you meet?' Kennedy asked gently. He too had given up on his food, only half finished. He'd eaten all of the potato gratin, though; it was just too delicious to waste. He took both their plates, emptied the contents into the rubbish bin behind the kitchen door and placed the dirty dishes in the sink. As he did this, ann rea, ignoring his movements, appeared to slip into a trance, and began to talk.

'I'd been sent to interview her. It was a complete disaster, due to a domestic crisis. Her nanny hadn't showed, apparently a regular occurrence. Rather than not come to the interview at all, she'd brought the kids along with her. She was in her battered-up Morris Minor Traveller. We'd tried to do the interview in the offices of the *Camden News Journal*, but the kids were too distracted by the noise and activity going on around them, and so Esther was distracted too. I was so in awe of her. Here was the woman who'd created *Axis*, probably the best album since *Astral Weeks* or *Blue*. For me she was the missing female link between Joni Mitchell and the New Wave. You know, Suzanne Vega, Tracy Chapman, Joan Armatrading and Tanita Tikaram. We're talking here, Kennedy, about a time when 'girl power' was judged by how short their skirts were. Here was this near genius – in my book, at least – and I've got all these vital spiritual, mystical questions to ask her, and she was more concerned with wiping her children's noses or making sure that Holmer was taking proper care of Jens. She wasn't exactly tatty, but equally she didn't exactly fit the look of a glamourous pop star.'

Kennedy smiled at the picture ann rea was painting. He felt happier now that she was occupied recalling her story. He quietly tidied up and fired up the kettle, just in case ann rea should decide she needed coffee to dilute her wine. His kitchen was comfortable, very comfortable. It had the country cottage kitchen look, centred around a large table.

ann rea continued uninterrupted: 'Instead of me asking her questions, she was asking me what it was like to make a living out of being a writer. What it was like working for a local paper? Did I choose my topics or was I assigned them? Why did my newspaper by-line have no capitals? She was amused when I told her it was a steal from kd lang and it was just a way to draw attention to myself. She told me that she'd been listening to kd lang for the first time recently because all her friends had been talking about kd's music. She said she loved her voice but that she didn't quite get the original songs. I told her about *Shadowlands*, the album produced by Patsy Cline's producer, Tom Bradley. I told her about the amazing duet kd sang with Roy Orbison on his song "Crying".'

'You turned me on to that one as well,' Kennedy said in encouragement. He sat down again at the table to enjoy his wine. He enjoyed seeing ann rea relax and uncoil from the tight wire ball she'd been when she walked into his house, almost an hour before.

ann rea continued: 'The next time we met, she'd listened to both recordings and was more convinced about kd's voice, but... well, let's just say she was merely polite about kd's self-penned lyrics.

Anyway, on that first day I'd decided we weren't going anywhere with the interview, so I suggested we take the kids out somewhere, and so we headed to the children's play area at the foot of Primrose Hill. And that was fine, it was a nice spring afternoon and we bought them a couple of lollipops, we even treated ourselves as well. I remember Holmer wanting to taste everybody's before he eventually returned to his own. We sat on a park bench in the play area and watched the children leaping and running around. She talked mostly about them and how she could never have guessed how important these two little people would become in her life. She said she still loved writing songs, but whereas writing songs was once her life, it was now secondary to her being a mother. She didn't even feel it to be a sacrifice; she didn't think she was giving anything up for them. First and foremost she wanted to be a good mother. All the time we were talking, her eyes followed her children around the playground. Holmer was fearless and was tackling everything successfully. Esther had to persuade Jens she shouldn't be trying to follow her brother until she was at least a couple of years older.'

ann rea broke into a smile at this point, she held the mother of the memory for a few seconds, took another drink and continued: 'Jens is so cute, you know. She really is like a little person. She's always busily going about her business, always laughing and smiling, a very happy child. Holmer is a bit more serious. He's a protector, always looking after his sister. Anyway, we had a great afternoon. We were in the park for practically two hours. The time just flew by. We all piled back into the Traveller, which refused to start, so I walked home with them. It wasn't very far, and then I caught a cab back to the office.'

'Did you have enough material to do a piece?' Kennedy asked, as he poured the remains of the first bottle of wine into their glasses.

'Yes. Yes, I didn't really do it as a piece about the time we spent together. I felt she'd want to keep her personal life out of the papers, so I did the article about her music and about how revolutionary I felt *Axis* was. How important a work it was, still is. I know at the time some people labelled it a depressing album, but they'd missed the point entirely. Although her music was sad, in places, she was dealing with her own demons, so, when she wrote it she was in a good frame of mind. I could never think of her music as depressing. Sure, it's sad, mournful, soulful, uplifting. But I'd never categorise it as depressing. Time you opened another bottle, Kennedy,' ann rea suggested as a gulp revealed the bottom of her third glass.

'Do me a favour first. Have some water. Eat something solid or you're going to pay for it in the morning. Yeah?' Kennedy said, more as a plea.

'Okay, Mr Wise Man, what have you got?' ann rea replied, as she eyed the unopened wine bottle near the fridge.

'Hummus and pitta bread?'

'Brilliant, Kennedy. As ever the perfect host.'

Kennedy went over to the fridge, took out a bottle of mineral water and poured ann rea a large glass. Next he took out hummus, placed some pitta bread in the oven and made to open the bottle of wine.

'Do you know if she liked your piece?' Kennedy asked, picking up the threads of their conversation.

ann rea took a seriously large gulp of icy cold mineral water and then an equally large gasp for air before continuing.

'Yes, she did actually. She rang me up the day it was published. She said she was shocked I was talking about the same dishevelled person who'd turned up in a mess, with two kids in tow. She said she was happy because she felt I understood what she was trying to do with her music. She suggested we have a drink one evening, away from the kids this time, and we went out on the first of our regular little meets. Sometimes when she couldn't get a babysitter, we'd stay in her flat and just open a bottle of wine. On several occasions we'd go to a gig together. When it came to live music though, she wasn't interested in anything like her own stuff, she just wanted good-time music when she went out. I think one of the best nights we had was going to see the Mavericks at the Shepherd's Bush Empire. They're such a good-time band. We had a brilliant night.'

'Did she ever talk about Paul Yeats?' Kennedy asked, fetching the pitta bread out of the oven and placing it and the hummus on a plate in front of ann rea, together with a knife and napkin. He poured her another large glass of water.

'Yeah, a lot,' ann rea said. She was so eager to satisfy her alcohol-induced hunger, she nearly burnt her fingers on the pitta bread.

'And?' Kennedy asked, as ann rea blew cold air on her fingers.

'Sometimes she liked him, sometimes she thought he was a shit. I think she was basically grateful to him for getting her through a particular troubled time in her life. He was the father of her two children and she forgave him most things because of that. She no longer loved him. She thought he suffered from the common weakness most men suffer from – being unable to say no to a woman, any woman. She thought that in the early days he'd like to have been able to give them up. She felt it was similar to being an alcoholic who knows that life would be improved if they could just give up the demon drink. But the next time a bottle is placed in front of them, they are helpless, they've got to have it. It's as simple as that. Well, Paul Yeats was like that with women. And, Esther claimed, it wasn't as though he was a great lover or anything. He'd like the conquest of sleeping with a woman once or twice, but once he'd shared that special intimacy he felt satisfied and ready to move on, you know? She felt it was something primal like that. He'd be close to them for a time and then another woman would come along.'

ann rea tore up some of the pitta bread and dunked it in the hummus. She savoured the irresistible taste, licked her lips to catch some that was trying to escape. What, in its right mind, would want to escape those lips? Kennedy wondered.

'You've never been like that, have you, Kennedy?' she asked, changing tack.

'Ah no. That is definitely not my style. Not that I'd be as attractive to women as Paul Yeats obviously is, mind you.'

'You see, there are two of your finest qualities in that one sentence. One, your faithfulness; and two, your modesty.'

Kennedy didn't like discussing himself. He was far more interested in the morsels of info he was getting from ann rea about Esther and Yeats.

'Aye, as my mother would say, I've a lot to be modest about,' Kennedy said, and ann rea smiled a doey kind of smile. 'Talking about Yeats and his women, did you know Rosslyn St Claire is pregnant?'

ann rea spluttered, sending pitta bread, hummus and wine in an arc over the table.

'You're not serious?'

'I'm perfectly serious,' Kennedy replied. 'At least as far as the gospel according to Judy Dillon goes.'

'Kennedy, that's just unbelievable, unforgivable.'

'Do you think Esther could have known about it?'

'You know what?' ann rea began, rising and fetching a piece of kitchen towel to clean up her chin and another for the table. 'I'm shocked and all that, but I think she might just have grown to expect anything from him. She might just have shrugged her shoulders and thought that Rosslyn was welcome to him. What about the poor kids? What was he thinking? Does he need to go sowing his wild oats everywhere just to prove to himself and to the rest of the world how virile he is? You know, "I may not be able to produce songs but boy can I produce children". Would you like children Christy?'

There, right out of the blue, she'd dropped a bombshell on him. Or was it a bombshell? Perhaps she was merely asking him a question, the general sort question that would naturally come out of a conversation about children and babies.

'I've no definite thoughts on it one way or the other,' Kennedy confessed. 'I mean, obviously I've thought about it over the years. I've often thought if I was with someone and we were in love how great it would be to have a baby, particularly if the baby were born at, say, two-years-old. Now, that would be perfect. Beyond that, I haven't given it much consideration, to be truthful.'

'Would you want to have a child with me, Christy?' ann rea asked, her voice so quiet he had to strain to hear what she was saying.

Now, that was most definitely a bombshell!

How do you answer such a question? Should you take a hypothetical line? More importantly, how do you answer that question to someone currently in a highly emotional state, due to the death of her friend, not to mention, more than a little squiffy?

'Could you guarantee it would be born at least two-years-old?' Kennedy ventured.

'Kennedy, I'm serious.'

'Look, ann rea, we've a lot of other things to get through first,' Kennedy said, feeling there was no use in trying to be easy with her just because of the circumstances. Honesty was the best policy.

'Such as?'

'Such as every time we seem to be getting remotely close, you turn and run for the hills. Then you come back like it never happened and we start all over again. The problem Paul Yeats and Esther had is that they were obviously totally unsuitable for each other. Surely, if there was just the slightest chance of that, they should never have gotten married, let alone have two children,' Kennedy said.

'But...' ann rea started.

'Yes, yes, I know Esther was a great mother. But that still does not compensate for the fact that to all intents and purposes Jens and Holmer were going to grow up without a father. Aren't we led to believe that a similar situation was one of the contributory factors to Esther's early mental illness? Children need both a mother and a father. If you are going to bring a child into the world you have to do it for them, and not for yourself.'

'God, that's very profound, Kennedy, who've you been reading?'

'But it's true, ann rea. It's so true. And so... we.... we should...'

'We should what? We should get married? Is that what you're trying to say, Kennedy?'

'That's not what I'm trying got say. It's never been about that, ann rea, you should know that.'

'What's it been about then, Kennedy? Go on, you tell me what this has all been about. What have these last four years been about?'

'Listen, I was happy going on as we were. I was enjoying being together; that in itself was enough for me. It might develop into something, it might not. We were just what we were and we didn't spend too much time contemplating our navels and talking about it. Then you came up with the idea that I loved you too much. You felt, perhaps because of this, I was crowding you too much. I was asking nothing from you. I was happy with things as they were. You said you felt bad because you didn't love me as much as I appeared to love you. We went around those circles a few more times. Then you were off, and next you were back as if nothing had happened. Then we enjoyed a few months of no commitment and lots of chasing the butterfly. Then instead of discussing it, you panicked and ran away again because you felt we were getting too close *again*.'

'Ah, Christy, you have so much anger in your voice when you're talking about all of this. Is that anger directed towards me?'

Kennedy thought for a moment. He poured himself another glass of wine. He doubted he would drink it; he just wanted something to do to fill the space.

'No. No, ann rea. It's directed towards myself. You see, when I started going out with you, I so much wanted it to work. I wanted it to be so right between us. I felt so warm towards you. I felt like I had known you all my life. I wanted to spend the rest of my life getting to know you better. I convinced myself I wasn't going to do anything wrong. I convinced myself we'd make it work. You seemed reluctant at the beginning, so I didn't push you. You seemed to want your space, so I stood back and gave it to you. It's like I was trying so hard to make it work I fecked it up. I'd always known I wasn't much of a ladies man, that I couldn't, wouldn't and didn't chase every woman simply because she was a member of the opposite sex and I could be naughty with them. Never in a million years could I have done what Paul Yeats has been doing, creating perpetual drama and tension around him. I love peace and tranquillity. I love space to think, to figure things out.' Kennedy laughed. 'All this talking is thirsty work. Cheers!'

And he succumbed to his glass of wine.

'You've started, so you'd better finish,' ann rea said, misquoting the television quiz-master.

'Yeah,' Kennedy started, as he put the wine glass back on the table. He drew liquid circles on the table-top, where he'd spilt some wine. 'You see, I really thought I had it right. I thought, I'm not like the Yeats' of the world. I'm okay. I respect women. Pure vanity, I know, but if I'm being honest, that is exactly what I did think. I thought if I did all the right things at the right times, then, by the simple laws of nature, it would work out. I so badly wanted it to work out with you. But, and here's the important bit, I didn't have the experience to carry it off. If I'd only spent more time in the company of women, and particularly the intimate company of women, I'd have been better equipped to deal with it all. Wouldn't I?'

'Kennedy, you lovely, lovely man, it's not about making it work. It either works or it doesn't. You can't control human nature. You can't control natural instincts. Let me tell you something: I've got these friends, Rodney and Cathy, two wonderful people. They have two children, a boy just about to become a teenager and a girl of eleven. Rodney's a musician and Cathy's a teacher. They are the perfect couple, they love each other dearly and they adore their kids. They've always wanted to be the perfect parents. They saw the mistakes all their friends had made with their children and they were convinced they were not going to make the same mistakes. They weren't going to be too hard on them, they weren't going to be too lenient with them. They weren't going to hide things from them. They were going to be perfectly honest with the children all of the time. Their logic was a simple one – the children would grow up into well-balanced adults. Okay, so far?' ann rea asked, and as Kennedy nodded, she continued:

'Over the last few years, as teenage years approached, along came peer pressure from school-friends, hints of rebellion and the flexing of muscles. These two ideal kids have turned into two of the most troublesome children of their set. All that love and care and attention has meant jack-shit. The children are uncontrollable. They are little adults with their own opinions, opinions most certainly not shared with their parents. Their friends are considered cooler if they are friends their parents disapprove of. Smoking and drinking are musts. Rodney and Cathy thought they'd win the battle lost by all of their peers by being liberal parents. "Of course you can smoke, I prefer to see you smoke at home than hiding behind some corner in a shopping mall." Then what did they do? Or at least what does the son do? He invites his friends home and they roll up joints in the living room. Honest! There's more… Cathy allowed them the occasional glass of wine. Same logic. "I prefer you to do this in my house than at some party or in some dirty pub." The next thing she catches both of them drunk as skunks before Sunday lunch. The father sends them both to their rooms. The son stands up and takes a pop at his father; it's a clean punch, he connects, breaks his father's glasses and gives him a black eye Barry McGuigan would have been proud of.'

'And the point?' Kennedy asks, deadpan.

'The point, Christy dear,' ann rea started, a hint of irony showing in her voice, 'is that you can't control, or calculate, anything as far as people are concerned. Our magic is that we are all individuals. You see, those two parents were trying to remove that individuality by controlling the environment, on the premise that the children would grow up to be perfectly happy and well-balanced. What the children are doing, by their actions, is screaming at their parents, "It's our life, it's our right to feck up". Perhaps in a way I was doing the same with you. It was too perfect. Here you are – a really nice guy, good-looking, with no apparent vices, a good steady job, a great house. I mean what is there not to like? And maybe I was going, "Hey, hang on a moment, don't I have a say in this?"'

'You did have your say every time you ran away.'

'Thanks, Kennedy. Thanks a bunch. Didn't you learn anything from my running away?'

'Oh, so it's my fault now? Kennedy said and immediately wished that he hadn't opted for such a childish retort.

'This is not about fault, Kennedy, this is about dealing with stuff. This is what happens, Kennedy. This is what people do.'

'What, you mean, make each other miserable?' Kennedy asked, taking another low punch and regretting it. But, just like in the boxing ring, every time you made a low punch, you exposed your chin.

'Well, we can stop making each other miserable right now!' ann rea whispered.

'That might be best. You know I think we've dissected and examined this thing so much that we'll never ever have a chance to put it back together again properly. Maybe it just wasn't meant to be and we're both tired of it and…'

'Don't say what I think you're going to say. And a few minutes ago I asked you if you wanted to have a baby with me,' ann rea said, all the fight gone out of her.

'ann rea, this is all because of what happened to Esther. Because you're aware of your own mortality, there's an emptiness that won't go away. This baby thing is for a hundred reasons I'll never fully understand, but it's not for the right reason is it? It's not because you and I are in love and we want to have a child together. That's the only right way to make a baby. Every other reason is selfish, and should be avoided at all costs.'

'So does that mean it's over?'

Kennedy sighed. He pushed his half-empty glass of wine away.

'Well, these repeat performances are too painful for both of us. Perhaps we should agree that it's over once and for all, and we can each be free to get on with our lives and concentrate on trying to become just good friends, which is what you wanted in the first place, wasn't it?'

'Aye, Kennedy, you might be right,' ann rea began, rising from the table. 'It's just that when you kissed the sky it's hard to return to the unshaven faces.'

Kennedy wasn't sure ann rea had nailed that one. She might work out a better simile in the cold light of tomorrow morning.

'Look, it's fine for you to stay tonight, there's no need to go home,' Kennedy offered, as hospitable as ever.

'No, you know what would happen. It would be too convenient, and you know we'd end up in bed together, and that's been one of our problems. It's been just a little bit too convenient to be together.'

Kennedy had lost all his fight. He barely looked after ann rea as she gathered her things together and vanished into the hall. A few seconds later he heard his door close. It wasn't slammed in anger but it was a firm closure. ann rea had pulled the door strong enough after herself to ensure it was shut. Perhaps to ensure there was no turning back.

Kennedy hoped there was no going back.

Chapter 23

THE FOLLOWING morning, Wednesday, Kennedy felt remarkably calm in the early morning stillness, as he walked over Primrose
Hill. He'd been here before, three times in fact, with ann rea and
once again he found himself feeling good about the fact that it was
finally resolved. There was not a trace of remorse in his heart, probably because he'd had a few practice runs at life without ann rea. To
be honest, part of him, a major part of him, was happy. Kennedy felt
this was no way for adults to behave. Adults are meant to have this
relationship business sussed. But here he and ann rea were, still
behaving like teenagers.

Teenagers, Kennedy felt, had their emotions better sussed –
much better than adults. For one thing, they were free of baggage.
He remembered Esther Bluewood having sung about having 'one
love, but one love won't do'. In the same song she claimed that 'we
have one life and one life won't do'. ann rea had been the love of
Kennedy's life. It had taken him until his early forties to meet her,
but even with all those years of practice he still hadn't got it right. So
why then, did he not feel worse about losing her?

He kept thinking about Esther's lines, 'one love won't do' and
'one life won't do'. Was the 'one love won't do' an encouragement
to him? Did that mean the next love *would* do? In Esther's life, one
life hadn't been enough. She'd had a second try after her attempted
suicide. But for Esther, her second life hadn't been enough either.
Someone had robbed her of it.

He heard Esther's singing voice in his head as he walked over
Primrose Hill. It looked so beautiful this morning. The early morning unused air was clean, clear and sharp, and he found it made his
mind remarkably clear and sharp as well. Focused. He found it so
easy to focus this morning. Even the early morning dog owners,
aiding and abetting their animals to soil this wonderful space,
weren't going to annoy him this morning.

He spotted two young men in their early twenties, both jacketless,
with shaven heads walking in the direction of the lodge near the Zoo
zebra crossing. They were walking hand in hand, laughing away, very
happy in each other's company, obviously oblivious to the winter elements. Now if they had been two girls of similar age, walking hand in

hand, no one, including Kennedy, would have thought twice about it. Because they were male, though, they obviously had to be gay.

He smiled to himself, as he spotted a middle-aged lady decked out in designer running gear, gear that would never be run in. She was talking to a disobedient snub-nosed dog. The dog looked like he'd once been trapped between a rock and a double decker bus. Kennedy couldn't help thinking, no *hoping*, that the double decker bus had travelled the extra fifteen-and-one-half inches before stopping. The lady with the blonde beehive hair-do, protected under a flimsy scarf, persisted in talking to her dog as if it were a young child. Chastising it, reprimanding it, for not obeying her.

Now, Kennedy was quite prepared to accept the fact that the ugly, over-fed mutt – no doubt complete with large pedigree that could be traced back to a Russian poodle crossed with an orangutan – might be able to recognise the tones of its owner's voice when she screamed 'Bobbsey' across the divides of Primrose Hill, disturbing the peace as far away as Chalk Farm. He was, however, equally convinced in his heart and soul that Bobbsey could not decipher the additional directive: 'Come here immediately. We need to go and get a cappuccino and *The Independent* and go home and do my Jane Fonda exercises'.

When Kennedy entered North Bridge House, the lady waiting for him in reception looked like a younger version of the fool on the hill. Victoria, 'My friends call me *Tor*', Lucas was over-bred and freckled. She might look brilliant when she reached the age of fifty. What she was trying to carry off now, and Kennedy imagined, had been trying to carry off since she was a teenager, would all sadly fall into place when there wasn't going to be a lot of her life left.

'I'd like to get this over with as quickly as possible,' she announced, plum firmly in mouth. 'I've got an appointment with the hairdresser at nine-thirty.'

'Well, let's see if we can help you make that, Miss Lucas. It is miss, isn't it?'

'Why, yes, of course,' Tor announced, indignantly unbuttoning her high-collar electric blue coat. She followed Kennedy through to his office.

'Tea?' Kennedy asked, as he opened the door.

'I'd love some coffee really, but I can't abide instant, so perhaps a mineral water?'

'Oh, let's see what we can rustle up for you,' Kennedy said, showing her into the office.

Victoria Lucas, Kennedy thought, gave herself such a hard time. Unnecessarily in all probability. She'd obviously been playing mum since she was young, so young she'd never had an opportunity to enjoy her childhood. Could she have been forced to behave like this because her mother had been permanently absent? Could Tor have been the predominant force in Paul Yeats' life for so long that his dysfunctionalism with women was due to her? Had his sister warned him off women because of their mother deserting them? Had she done all in her power to prevent her brother from being hurt in the same way her father had been?

She was wearing a black pair of slacks and electric blue leatherette shoes to match her coat. She wore a white shirt embroidered with little Swiss men dancing. Over this she wore a black woollen waistcoat with a single brown button positioned at waist level. Her hair was brown, and it looked frizzy and brittle from too many coats of lacquer. It was flat at the top and came out at the back and sides, returning in just below the ears. It looked a little like a rugby ball plopped on her head, broadside on. Miss Lucas had a weak and forgettable face and her eyes were laden down with much too much blue eye-shadow.

She had the breeding but not the class to carry off what she was trying so hard to achieve: the classic forties look.

Victoria Lucas fidgeted for a bit as Kennedy made her coffee. She puffed up her hair at the back and sides; she ran her finger around the back of her collar, separating it from her neck. She kept sticking her chin out, as if to relieve her throat from the tightness of the collar. Kennedy wondered whether all her little mannerisms were because she liked to be in control of situations, and here, on his turf, to answer *his* questions, she was not in charge.

Mind you, if Kennedy thought he was going to run the interview freely, he was sadly wrong.

'So, Inspector,' she began, taking her first sip of coffee. She seemed to enjoy it and she used the third finger of her right hand to dab away the liquid at each corner of her mouth, ensuring it wouldn't ruin her lipstick. She ran her tongue over her lips a few times and then pushed her lips hard together before continuing: 'I'm here to see what is happening about Paul's journal.'

'Paul's journal?' Kennedy replied, with a 'forgive me' smile. 'But surely you mean Esther's journal?'

'Sadly Esther is now dead. Paul is the administrator of her estate and as such he is the administrator of all of her property. The artistic rights are not in dispute in this case; we are not claiming those at this juncture. But legally the journals are the property of the estate and as such I demand you return them to us immediately.'

'Sorry, no can do,' Kennedy replied firmly. No trace of the surprise he felt was evident in his voice.

'Our lawyers will be in touch and believe you me...' Tor started, rising from her chair, clearly preparing the end the conversation and leave.

'Listen, miss,' Kennedy began, very slowly and calmly, 'you and your team of expensive legal eagles can huff and puff all you want, but those journals are vital evidence in this case and will remain in our ward until such time as we deem them fit to be passed back to the estate. I should also advise you that until such time as the will is read and we have established *exactly* who is the executor of the estate, they will be passed to no one.'

'In that case, we have nothing else to say to each other. This meeting is over,' Tor said, pulling her coat about her shoulders.

'Well, that's entirely up to you, madam. However, I have reason to believe you can help us with our inquiries, and whilst you are certainly free to walk out of here at this moment in time...' – Kennedy paused to check his watch – '...I should warn you that we do need to speak to you, and by the time you are sitting down to have your hair done, I'll have a warrant drawn up and ready for execution. So, if you could just leave me the name and address of your hairdresser, we'll be along presently to pick you up for questioning.'

Kennedy stood up and pushed his chair under his desk signifying that, as far as he was concerned, the interview was also over. The next one, he knew, would certainly be more formal, if not a lot more embarrassing for Victoria.

'And how do you feel I can help with your inquiries,' Victoria announced in a 'Mr DeMille, I'm ready for my close-ups' voice.

They both returned to their respective chairs.

'If you're absolutely sure, Miss Lucas?'

'Well,' Miss Lucas began, demurely puffing up her hair at the back, 'if it will save both of us time. And...' she paused again to retrieve her still steaming cup, '...this coffee is positively delicious, it would be such a shame to waste it.'

'It's very kind of you to give us your time,' Kennedy wanted to make sure there was no way that it could be claimed that Miss Lucas was being held against her will. 'Let's start with Esther Bluewood, shall we?'

Tor Lucas nodded agreement. She crossed her legs and the swish of her tights mixed with the irritating click of her tongue.

'First of all, I'd like to know how you initially met,' Kennedy said. He took his notebook out of his pocket and cocked his pen in readiness. He had a perfectly good memory without taking notes but the distraction, he felt, might work to his advantage in this interview.

'Well, Paul introduced us, naturally. I knew of her and her music long before that, of course. To be honest, I thought, Oh God, two artists together, it's going to be a nightmare. I mean one of them, my brother for instance, can be more than a handful on his own, thank you very much, but two of them in a relationship, ye gods! But Esther wasn't like most artists. Let me explain what I mean exactly: she was interested in her writing. She was so preoccupied with her writing that she didn't really have much time for the rest of the razzamatazz that goes with it. I loved her for that. In theory they should have been perfect for each other. They'd have made the perfect duo. Paul loved the press and the promotion and found it hard to apply himself to the hard graft of writing songs; Esther was in heaven when she was writing and happy to take a back seat on the promotional front.'

Tor took another sip of her coffee and repeated the gesture of dabbing the corners of her mouth with her finger before continuing:

'I knew what she was going through and I... well, I'll admit to you here and now that I tried several times to become her manager. Paul had been after me for ages to become his manager. He kept saying that the only people you can trust not to rip you off in the music business are family. I kept pointing out that he wouldn't be able to support my overhead from his income. However, if we could have made Esther's songs part of the package, well, that would have been a different matter altogether. I could have made that work.'

'Have you had any managerial experience?' Kennedy inquired.

'Come on. Please! We're talking pop music here. You don't need to be the brain of Britain to work in that industry. All I needed was a phone, a fax and an assistant. The rest would have been a doddle.' Tor sighed, as if Kennedy was stupid to have thought otherwise.

'What happened?'

'Well,' Tor began, 'basically Esther wasn't interested. I could describe the situation in detail, but that's the long and short of it: she just wasn't up for it. I tried to tell Paul that he couldn't behave the way he did and still expect Esther to get into bed with him, financially speaking, as well.'

'Did you ever discuss the situation with Esther yourself?'

'Ahm,' Tor began hesitantly, 'I didn't have what you would call a dialogue with Esther.'

'Sorry?'

'We didn't actually communicate with each other.'

'Yet you wanted to be her manager and you expected her to consent to that even thought you didn't talk with her?' Kennedy asked, his eyebrows rising automatically from having trouble believing what he was hearing.

'Well, she wouldn't have had to deal with me directly if she hadn't wanted to. She could have done it all by fax, or through Paul,' Tor offered by way of explanation.

'But she had separated from Paul. For heaven's sake, she was about to divorce him,' Kennedy declared. He couldn't believe that there were people like Tor still in existence, head buried firmly, not to mention deeply, in the sand.

'So some people say,' was Tor's only concession to reality.

'So Esther herself said,' Kennedy claimed. Tor seemed totally nonplussed at the detective's disclosure, so he continued. 'When was the last time you actually spoke to Esther?'

'Oh, that would have been at Holmer's christening.'

'Sorry?' Kennedy was rarely shocked and rarer still were the occasions when he displayed his shock. 'You hadn't spoken to her for what… six years?'

'Yes, about that,' Tor agreed, still barely batting either of her blue-painted eyelids.

'And what exactly happened at the christening?'

'Oh, really. Must I go into this? Truth. We'd a bit of a fight.'

'A bit of a fight, it must have been more than a *bit* of a fight for the fall out to have lasted six years?'

'Oh, I'm sure it was all a big misunderstanding. What happened was Esther overheard Paul and myself making plans for Holmer. We were talking about which school we'd be sending him to. And she just flipped. Started screaming and shouting about Holmer being her child and any decisions about his education would be made by her. I told her, when she'd proved that she was capable of being a fit mother we'd leave her to it. I mean she was hardly the most stable of people. She'd already proved that. And now, after Sunday night, she's proven me correct. Where is those children's mother now? Now that they need her.'

'Ah, I think you seem to be under the popular misapprehension that Esther Bluewood committed suicide. I'm here to tell you that she didn't,' Kennedy offered, feeling it was important to clear up that vital point before they continued.

'What do you mean, she didn't commit suicide? Of course she killed herself. She gassed herself. Everyone knows that Esther Bluewood committed suicide by sticking her head in a gas oven.'

Kennedy leaned over his desk and stared directly at Victoria Lucas. He rested his elbows on the desk and placed his hands together. He pulled his hands slightly apart and tapped his forefinger together, once, twice and three times before he said: 'All Chinese whispers and all untrue. Esther Bluewood did not take her own life.'

'You mean she was murdered?'

'Looks that way,' Kennedy replied, studying Tor's face closely.

'You... don't... You don't think it was Paul? Of course it wasn't Paul. You realise of course it wasn't Paul, don't you?'

'It's early days in our investigation. Tell me, Miss Lucas, where were you on Sunday evening?' Kennedy asked, still gently tapping his fingers. His notebook lay between his elbows, open on a clean page with the weight of his fountain pen resting lifelessly on top.

Tor Lucas broke into nervous laughter. 'Oh, this is quite preposterous. This is developing into a farce, Inspector Kennedy. You can't possibly suspect me. That would just be too ludicrous for words.'

Kennedy continued to stare without uttering a word, his head tilted slightly to one side, and a hint of a smile forming in his dimples.

'Please! Come on. Detective. Oh, very well, then. On Sunday afternoon and evening I was with a friend. We met up at about six and he dropped me off at my house just after midnight.'

'And his name?' Kennedy asked, lifting his pen and unscrewing the top, ready to take down the precious details.

'I'm afraid I can't tell you.'

'Well, I'm afraid I need to know. If you've an alibi, we need to rule you out of our investigation.'

'I'd rather not say, to be honest.'

Kennedy kept on staring at her, his pen hovering half an inch above the page.

'Please, Inspector. A lady has to be discreet. You see, I was out with a married man,' Tor Lucas said, a red hue gathering in her cheeks, a hue that clashed drastically with her blue eye-shadow.

'Mmmm,' Kennedy said, staring down at his page in order to avoid eye contact. You dark horse you, he thought. He had to force himself not to smile. 'I can assure you, Miss Lucas, that we will treat this information with total confidentiality. If you just give me this man's details, we'll simply check to see he concurs with your story. If he does, that will be the end of the matter. No one else will ever hear about it.'

'For heaven's sake, Inspector,' Tor replied, forcing a generous smile. 'If I was going to falsify an alibi don't you think I would pick a girlfriend or even my mother or brother or anyone other than a married man. Can you imagine the embarrassment for me if anyone should find out? You couldn't possibly imagine the embarrassment for me, especially if my brother should find out, for heaven's sake. No. There has to be another way.'

'I'm afraid not, Miss Lucas.'

Tor appeared to slump in her chair. 'This mustn't get out. Paul must never hear about this. You must promise me that Paul will never hear about this.'

'As I said, Miss Lucas, I see no reason why this information should need to go outside these four walls.'

'Yeah. You see, there it is. All I need is a gossip in the police force to talk to a friend and the friend knows somebody who knows somebody who will undoubtedly relish telling Paul.'

'Does that mean that Paul knows the gentleman in question?' Kennedy felt compelled to ask.

'I'm afraid so. You see Roger, Roger Walker that is, well he's a good friend of Paul's. It's all so long and complicated and sordid and I don't really see that it's of any relevance whatsoever. But I'm sure if I don't tell you, you'll go poking your nose around until everyone finds out about it.'

But is it relevant? Kennedy thought to himself. He said nothing.

'You see, Roger, Paul and I grew up together. We were chums. All hung out together. When we got to a certain age, well Roger and I took a different kind of interest in each other, and then he and Paul went off to college together. I went to university. When we met up again, Paul and I continued our affair…'

'You mean Roger and you, of course…'

'Yes, stupid, that's what I said.' Victoria replied.

'Ahm, no… sorry, yes, please continue,' Kennedy said, deciding mid-sentence to change course. 'So you and Roger met up again?'

'Yes, we resumed our relationship. It was very serious. At one point we decided to get married and I told Paul. He'd been unaware all those years that Roger and I had been seeing each other. Roger was as keen as I was to keep it quiet. He was even scared of telling

Paul we were getting married. He said we should just run away, do it quietly and then tell everyone when we got back. But it was going to be my big day, for heaven's sake. Anyway, I told Paul and he went absolutely ballistic. Totally ape! He started ranting and raving about how Roger had behaved at college with a non-stop stream of girls. He went off and had a bloody fight with Roger. He persuaded me that it would be unwise to marry Roger. Mmmm... and we called it off.'

'Just like that?' Kennedy asked in disbelief. He was wondering what happened to the course of true love and all that.

'Of course it was more complicated than that. Life is always more complicated than that. We can't always put ourselves first can we? Anyway, to cut a very long story short, Roger went off and got married to someone else. I didn't. I never really got over it to be honest,' Tor said sadly. She sounded so sad, Kennedy started to feel sorry for her.

Tor Lucas looked like she needed time to compose herself.

'Oh, how silly of me. Do you have a handkerchief?' she asked, as the beginning of a tear rolled down her cheek.

Kennedy never ceased to be amazed at what baggage people carried around with them. Here was this wannabe aristocratic woman with an apparent attitude. She'd been well brought up, was obviously not short of a few bob, dressed well. Yet her history was as intriguing as any movie you could see or any book you might read. Everyone has a story; we all have regrets. Every one of us carries this stuff around, Kennedy thought. If he was to swap the story of his relationship with ann rea, would that make her feel good or would it make her feel worse? Nah, he decided, she'd never believe it; she'd just think he was trying to make her feel better. Even he had trouble believing what he and ann rea had been through sometimes.

And then there were always two sides to every story, both told with equal passion and both told to sympathetic sets of ears. ann rea's friends would console her with, 'Really, how could he be so inconsiderate? Men they're all the same really, when you get down to it.' And his mates, if there were any, would say, 'Women! They just don't know what they want, do they? Treat them mean and keep them keen. That's what I say.' But there wasn't really anyone Kennedy would confide the ann rea story with. He didn't have that kind of blokey relationship with any men.

It seemed to Kennedy that everyone was wandering around in

minefields of domestic and social disharmony. Did Paul Yeats' inability to have a long relationship with a single woman have anything to do with his sister? Even James Irvine – definitely a better chap than Yeats in that he never cheated on his women – but for him the chase seemed to be the most important part of the relationship. Once he'd won his woman, once she'd committed to him, he lost interest. Irvine knew it was a flaw, but he was unable to do anything about it: he hoped it was because he'd never truly been in love. Kennedy knew that Irvine was getting fed up making a career out of saying goodbye.

And Rose Butler. Kennedy hadn't thought about Rose since the Ranjesus Affair. That issue was still unresolved but Kennedy was convinced that their paths would cross again some time. Camden Town was a village in that respect. Dr Ranjesus was another case in point. Outwardly respectable, beautiful wife and family, successful career and there was the good doctor, pursuing a non-stop series of affairs with young nurses, some of whom he'd even managed to get pregnant. One of whom he had murdered – well, Kennedy and Rose Butler were convinced he had.

Everyone Kennedy could focus on carried some baggage or other around with them. Kennedy found himself wondering, not for the first time, about Anne Coles. What was her story?

Tor Lucas interrupted his mental free-fall with a little sniffing and a blowing of her nose, courtesy of the Kleenex supplied by Kennedy.

'I'm sorry, please forgive me,' Tor continued, pulling Kennedy back from his thoughts.

'No, it's fine,' he replied, his voice as kind and soft as ever.

'It's just that I've never really discussed this with anyone before,' Tor said, composing herself, a signal that she was ready to continue. 'Roger got married. It was all very civil, Paul and I went to the wedding, and then about five years ago, I literally bumped into Roger in the street in Chelsea. We went for a coffee and then to a bar for some wine. He told me how unhappy he was. We drifted back into the relationship, which of course now had to be classed as an affair. I see him once a week. To be truthful, that is enough for me. I hadn't dated any other men. After Roger married, I lost all interest in men. So this affair is really the perfect compromise for me, to be perfectly honest. I escape all of the grief of a full-time relationship.'

She paused, reached across the desk, took Kennedy's notebook and pen and wrote down the name Roger Walker and an out-of-town telephone number.

'Please be discreet,' she said.

The interview had reached its natural conclusion. Kennedy helped her on with her coat and saw her to the door of North Bridge House. She turned to face him and kissed the air beside his cheek, before turning on her blue high-heels and running off down Parkway.

Kennedy, hands deep in pockets, watched her go. He couldn't help wondering if maybe that had been one of the best theatrical performances he'd ever witnessed.

Chapter 24

MEANWHILE, WDC Anne Coles, her trusted DC Lundy in tow, was making her way by train to Fulbrook, in the wilds of the Cotswolds. Her intention was to interview Rosslyn St Clair, who had mysteriously reappeared at Paul Yeat's mother's house. Actually the local police in Witney had advised them that there was no railway station in Fulbrook. They'd have to catch a train to Charlbury (one of England's best kept stations), where a local squad car would pick them up and ferry them on to Fulbrook.

Yeats' mother was conspicuous by her absence. Particularly as Coles and Lundy had found the back door of the picture postcard cottage open, hinge creaking ominously, when they'd knocked. Coles pushed the door open further and called out. There was no response. She called out louder, pushing the door fully open and stepping into the cottage. Coles was sure she could hear groaning from somewhere deep within. Lundy shadowed her every movement.

Gingerly, they walked through the kitchen, with its low oak beams, and opened a rickety latch door into a hallway. The groans were growing louder and seemed to be coming from behind a door to their left. Lundy tapped on the door and announced that they were from the police. Again someone groaned, this time louder. Coles pushed open the door with some force to find a young woman lying full length on the sofa. The only part of her body visible above the Black Watch tartan woollen rug, was her head.

Her long black hair was matted with perspiration.

'Is that you, Paul?' a weak and obviously delirious voice said. 'I've done what you wanted... I got rid of it.'

The room was cold, cold in colour and cold in temperature. The walls were a light blue and the wood – rafters, skirting boards, doorframes and door – were all dark varnished pine. Coles figured the room, and probably the cottage, was more Yeats than Bluewood. His rebellion against her natural taste, perhaps. Even the sofas and two floral patterned easy chairs were mostly hidden under dark, grey and brown, covers. The hearth was still wealthy from a previous day's ashes, cold and grey and smelling somewhat damp in the cold air. A blue earthenware vase filled with dead flowers, was placed on a wooden sideboard. Coles figured Yeats used the place as a stop-off rather than as a home. Or perhaps he was just incapable of creating a homely atmosphere?

'There, there,' Coles said, as she sat down on the edge of the sofa to comfort the girl. Lundy, meanwhile, was busy on his mobile telephone, calling for an ambulance. Coles feared the sickly sweet smell could be the smell of blood. She gently removed the blanket to reveal the body, and breathed a sign of relief to not find a speck of blood. The girl was drenched from head to toe in sweat, which accounted for the earthy, salty smell.

Coles did what she could to make the young woman as comfortable as possible. She wondered where Yeats' mother was. Who was meant to be looking after this young woman? If Coles' assumption was correct and the young, distressed woman was in fact Rosslyn St Clair, then Mrs Yeats Senior definitely knew she was in the house. She had informed Sergeant Tim Flynn of this while he was engaged in telephonic backup work for Kennedy's team.

About twenty minutes later, an ambulance arrived, responding to Lundy's 999 call, lights flashing, siren shrieking like a CD player stuck on some obscure Beatle harmony backing vocal. A neighbour, attracted by the racket, invited herself into the cottage to see exactly what all the commotion was about. She positively identified the young woman as being Rosslyn St Clair.

The paramedics advised Coles that the young lady had recently undergone what had all the appearances of a backstreet abortion. They complimented the members of Camden police for alerting them, stating further that if they hadn't been called out when they were, it was certain Miss St Clair could have died from internal bleeding. That said, they made her comfortable and transferred her by stretcher to the ambulance, snuggly wrapping her in a red blanket. Coles realised that the blanket would act as camouflage to patients who might otherwise panic when they saw the sight of their own blood, particularly if smeared on something as betraying as, say, a virgin white blanket. She sent Lundy off with the ambulance to monitor proceedings and to make sure she was off the critical list before he returned to London.

The train carrying Coles back to London passed a never-ending parade of back gardens. They varied in size, shape and what they revealed, but even these numerous glimpses into people's lives could not distract Coles from the image of Rosslyn St Clair lying helplessly on the sofa, her life draining away from her. Paul Yeats' new girlfriend had nearly died from the effects of having their baby aborted, and all of this only two days after the murder of his wife. Her mind went through an endless stream of possibilities.

Every time she passed a new row of rear gardens, another theory hit her. But the main thread, the one she kept returning to, was: what is it with this man? What did he have that made all the ladies in his life jump through hoops so?

Could he possibly have told Esther Bluewood that Rosslyn was with child? Surely not. Maybe Esther had found out of her own accord and confronted him about his sordid life. Either way, a quarrel had ensued which had resulted in Esther Bluewood losing her life and Rosslyn St Clair nearly having lost hers.

Had that been the plan? Had Yeats organised the low-key abortion so that he wouldn't be publicly connected? Or could the second part of his plan have been to be 'careless' with Rosslyn during her convalescing period in the hope that she too would expire? Thus solving another of his problems.

Had Esther threatened to cut him off? Maybe she'd even warned him that she was considering taking the children back to her mother's home in America. Had his usual effective powers of persuasion not worked with her on this important occasion? Kennedy had advised Coles and the rest of the team that Esther had claimed in the journal that Yeats had hypnotic powers. Had these powers stopped working? Desperation can help destroy natural powers. Coles followed that train of thought for a time, only to replace it with an equally vivid memory from her youth.

The memory involved an older man, a much older man, in fact – a widower who was a friend of her father. She had always been comfortable in his company and he was always quite fresh with her. She liked that. She was seventeen at the time and she remembered he'd made her feel like a woman. He was fifty, not quite ancient, but definitely old. Sandy was his name. She always felt in control. Once, when her parents were out and she and Sandy were alone in the house, she asked him to kiss her. Just straight out of the blue, she couldn't believe the words she was saying herself. She'd been with boys before, but she wanted to see what it would be like to kiss a man, a real man. She felt so naughty, but at the same time she yearned to get away from her immaturity. She felt that for the young, sex is such a long and complicated process. You hold hands, you hug, you kiss, you feel, and that entire process can take two months to achieve. When you get older – well now, that's a different thing altogether. Sometimes a single kiss can unlock the doors of mystery all at once, and in seconds, without those months of planning and scheming, you can end up in bed together, making love. When she and Sandy kissed, she was completely turned on. So was Sandy. It seemed he was as eager for her young, fresh, firm body as she was for his older, more experienced one. She surrendered to her desires, but was vexed to hear a few minutes later, 'Sorry old girl, there appears to be no lead in the pencil.'

She supposed the one positive thing about it happening with one so experienced was that, on his part, there was little or no embarrassment. A mere 'Oh, these things happen, old girl' would do. The barrier had been broken, and it was only a matter of time, two days in fact, before they did make love. Their lovemaking was sweet, the sweetest thing of her teens. She was lost in thoughts of such pastimes, when the image of Paul Yeats flashed into her head as quickly as the telegraph poles flashed by her train window.

The big niggle Coles had about the case was the ginormous jump between Bluewood finally losing her patience with Yeats and him killing her. Yes, he'd behaved a bit suspiciously. What was all that rigmarole about Yeats turning up in Islington on the Beck's doorstep and demanding the keys to the Morris Minor Traveller? There was obviously something going on, but what on earth was it?

On and on the train thundered. Coles tried to tune back into her Sandy daydream but found that daydreams occur naturally or not at all. Instead, other ideas on the case flashed through her mind. As they pulled into Oxford station, she wondered how Kennedy and the team were getting on back in London. She'd spoken to him on the phone and told him about her discovery. He agreed Lundy should stay behind but said he needed her back in Camden Town.

The thought that Kennedy needed her in Camden Town made Coles feel good. Before she managed to become too hung up on that thought – pleasant though it was – Kennedy had qualified it by saying he needed her to talk to Esther Bluewood's mother who'd just arrived at Heathrow. Kennedy had also advised her that he and Irvine were going to be tied up for several hours talking to Josef Jones and then to Judy Dillon, who even Paul Yeats had referred to as 'the nanny from hell!'

Chapter 25

KENNEDY WAS never an admirer of the mobile phone. He figured humans were meant to be free from technology for at least part of their time. If this were not the case, then surely God would have fixed an aerial beside those ineffective wings he'd stuck on the sides of our head to hang our spectacles on. Kennedy was lucky enough to be passing through the reception area of North Bridge House when Coles rang in. Eagle-eyed desk sergeant Tim Flynn called to Kennedy, just as he and DS Irvine were about to descend the steps.

'Right, we're off!' Kennedy announced, handing the phone back to the silver-haired sergeant. The call had taken a matter of two minutes.

'See you later, then,' Flynn called after them, as he automatically and unconsciously picked up the recently-replaced receiver, answering another in a never-ending audience of calls: 'Hello, Camden Town police station, Sergeant Flynn here, how can I help you?' Then a pause… 'Oh, just hang on a moment, please.' Then another pause, this time no more than a heartbeat, then: 'Detective Inspector Kennedy!'

Kennedy turned around for the second time in as many minutes, sighed and shouted, 'Who is it? No, whoever it is, tell them I'll ring back later.'

'Mmmm. It's miss ann rea for you, sir,' Flynn called back, hiking his shoulders in a 'What should I tell her?' manner.

Kennedy hesitated.

ann rea obviously knew he was there. So, if he didn't take the call she'd read something into it. Kennedy didn't know exactly what she would read into it, but he didn't want it to be rudeness. He was still running through the various possibilities of what to do when Irvine made his decision for him.

'Look, I'll go get the car, sir. You go back to your office and take the call, and I'll meet you outside in a few minutes.'

'Yes, good,' Kennedy stammered, still hesitating. 'Yes, why don't you do that. Tim, give me a few minutes to get back to the office and put the call through.'

It had been an awkward and embarrassing moment for Kennedy, but he imagined most of the self-consciousness was down to his personal guilt. In reality neither Irvine nor Flynn would have given the incident a second thought.

'Hi,' Kennedy said tentatively, now comfortably seated in his chair.

'Hi, Kennedy. Look, sorry to ring you and it's a little bit weird to be honest, but I should tell you up front it's nothing whatsoever to do with us. It's not about us at all, it's about business. This is an official call.'

ann rea seemed, to Kennedy, to go to great lengths to get that point across, even to the point of repeating herself. He also figured she could be sharing some of the same embarrassment he'd just gone through.

Embarrassment was too strong a word. He and ann rea had (supposedly) just spilt up for the final time and, all things considered, they both would have been much happier speaking to any other living soul at that moment.

'Really?' Kennedy replied, and then thinking that maybe he'd sounded just a mite disbelieving, continued: 'Yes. Yes, of course. And... ahm.... what, what was it you wanted to talk to me about?'

'God. This is awkward isn't it?'

'Yes,' was Kennedy's single word reply.

'Look,' she announced. Kennedy could hear the confidence in her voice growing, 'let's deal with this in a professional way, shall we?'

'Absolutely,' Kennedy replied, feeling that some of the charge had been taken out of the atmosphere. 'Good idea.'

'Okay, I'm a journalist; you're a policeman.'

'I'm with you so far.' Kennedy forced the one liner to try and ease things up a little more.

'Good. I always knew you were quick on the uptake.'

Great, Kennedy thought, they'd made it to the end of round one.

'You're investigating the death of Esther Bluewood,' ann rea continued, this time not leaving a space for a Kennedy quip. 'Earlier today we were offered her journal for £50,000. We were advised that there was lots of explosive material in it.'

'Did you take the call or was it someone else?'

'It was me. They asked for me by name,' ann rea answered simply, all nervousness gone from her voice.

'Who was it?'

'I don't know. They wouldn't say.'

'Man or woman?' Kennedy asked. In his greed for information

he had forgot all about his domestic disharmony with this particular journalist.

'Woman,' ann rea replied quickly, and then added: 'But I think her voice was heavily disguised – muffled or something.'

'No one you recognised? Kennedy asked.

'No. Not really, not at all, in fact. But it must have been someone who knew that I knew Esther,' ann rea replied, now sounding somewhat distracted.

'Why do you think that?' Kennedy asked, doodling with a pencil on a blank page of note-pad.

'Well, think about it. They rang *Camden News Journal*. As I said, they asked for me. It's all a bit amateur really, isn't it? I'm sure we'd have trouble raising fifty quid let alone fifty thousand! One of the male children of the gutter press would have been a much better bet.'

'Would any of them pay fifty big ones for the journal?' Kennedy asked.

'I should think so. If there was dirt in it the *Sun* might have gone higher. But going back to my original point, I think if someone knew I'd known Esther, they might also think I'd know what to do with the journal.'

'Taking that point further... surely they would also know that Paul Yeats would be very keen to get his hands on it?' Kennedy said, drawing a hangman as he scored off the letters to Paul Yeats' name, which he had printed in large letters at the top of the page.

'Perhaps they also know he's one of the few people in this world worse off than the *Camden News Journal*,' ann rea replied, attempting to laugh. It didn't really come off.

'So if this person knows that you were friendly with Esther and also knows that Yeats doesn't possess the proverbial pot, then it must be someone quite close to Esther.'

'Correct. I knew you'd get there without me having to spell it out for you,' ann rea said.

'Which means you can't really talk. There's someone there with you?'

'Camden CID. God bless them... right on the money every time, you've just kissed the pink...'

'Judy Dillon?'

'In the pocket, not exactly a Hurricane Higgins shot, more of an interesting Steve Davis, solid and sure, but eventually gets there.'

'Okay, then. How did you leave it?' Kennedy said, recalling how when they first met she couldn't stand snooker.

'I stalled them until I'd a chance to call you, told them I'd have to see could we raise the money. They're going to ring back in an hour.'

'Okay, here's what we do: I've got to go and interview someone,' Kennedy said, looking at his watch. 'Tell the mystery caller to ring back at, say, four o'clock. Tell them you're trying to raise the money and they should call you back at four. Okay?'

'Good, that sounds like a plan to me. Ahm...'

'Look I really do have to go,' Kennedy interrupted, knowing he was risking hurting her feelings but he felt he knew where the conversation was going.

'Yes, of course,' she said, then in a quieter voice, 'Tell me, Kennedy, how are you doing?'

Up to that point it had been fine. He'd been dealing with a voice on the phone and not the woman he'd split up with the previous night.

'Oh, you know. Trying to be professional,' he said and cursed himself for being so flippant the moment the words left his lips.

'Okay. Bye,' ann rea said, in a reply she just managed to get out before she returned the handset to its rest.

Chapter 26

FIVE MINUTES later, Kennedy and Irvine were in Josef Jones's apartment (well, part apartment, part shrine to Esther Bluewood, to be more accurate). Josef let them in immediately. This time he was obviously clear of incriminating substances, Kennedy thought; no need for his now famous greyhound impression. Kennedy knew that Josef Jones – his person, his apartment and his work place – would all be totally 'clean' until the Esther Bluewood investigation was done and dusted.

Jones invited the police into his living area.

'We're here to clear up a few facts with you, regarding Esther Bluewood,' Kennedy began, looking for something that resembled a comfortable chair. When he thought he'd found it, he sat down.

'Oh!' Jones said. The host was the last to be seated and he chose to sit cross-legged on the carpet between Irvine and Kennedy, completing a lopsided triangle.

'Yes, we want to know more about your movements on Sunday,' Kennedy continued.

'I'm happy to go through it all again,' Jones replied, betraying no sign of impatience. If he felt aggrieved, he was certainly doing a great job of hiding it.

'So, let's just recap,' Irvine began. 'You were meant to see Esther on Sunday. She didn't show, you hung around waiting for her, you didn't try and make contact, and you stayed in all night. You didn't make contact with anybody or see anybody at all?'

'In a word, no. I saw nobody.'

'So you didn't go out on Sunday?' Irvine persisted.

'No.'

'Then if someone told us you'd been in the Spread Eagle, they'd have been mistaken?' Irvine said, appearing not only to have a list of questions, but to have them racked up in order.

'I mean, I was out before I was supposed to see Esther, of course I was. But I was back here by seven-thirty to tidy up before she was supposed to arrive at eight. She was a stickler for tidiness you know. It would put her right off if the place wasn't spic and span.'

'Let's just backtrack a wee bit here,' Kennedy said, picking up Irvine's thread and showing that he wasn't particularly worried, at this stage, about Esther's fetish for tidiness. 'You got back here at seven-thirty?'

'Yep.'

'So, what time would that have made it that you left the Spread Eagle?' Kennedy asked.

'What's all this crap about the Spread Eagle? It's a pub, man, nothing more. Surely your spies told you what time I left. I wasn't exactly looking at my watch. Probably about half an hour before I got home which would have made it about seven o'clock.' Josef replied. He appeared bemused with the questions, perhaps a tad cautious as to where they were going.

'How did you get home, then?' Kennedy asked.

'I travel home from Camden Town so often, if I told you I remembered which way I travelled on Sunday I'd be lying. Could have been a 29 bus, which you catch just outside Rock On Records, or it's one stop on the overground from Camden Road, or maybe I walked. I really can't remember,' Jones sighed.

'If you'd walked, what way would you have walked?'

Jones looked like he was getting worried. 'Look, what's this all about? What does it matter which way I travelled home? I travelled home some way. If I had realised it would have been important for me to get an alibi, I would have hired an open-top double-decker bus and got Frank Bruno to join me, and waved at everybody, and then maybe you'd be happy. Hey, I got here around seven-thirty, maybe ten minutes either way, and I was ready for her to be here at eight. She didn't show.'

'How did you feel when she didn't show?' Irvine asked.

'It's the worst feeling, isn't it, being stood up?' Jones started. 'Initially you give them the benefit of the doubt. You know, kids playing up, she couldn't get them to bed. Ahm, she couldn't get a taxi. The nanny wouldn't baby-sit. It could have been any one of a million good, legit excuses. But all that vanishes after, say, ninety seconds and you start to have doubts. Lord Corduroy is back; she'd decided to dump you. But you really feel the pits. It's incredible how early in the wait it hits you that you've been stood up. As a rule of thumb, my gut instinct is always spot on, but you keep giving them the benefit of the doubt, as I say. You know, you say to yourself, "I'll give her another fifteen minutes and that's it". And the fifteen becomes thirty, becomes an hour. After an hour, you are usually forced to accept the worst. I mean, any more than an hour and you'd be silly to wait around, wouldn't you? I mean, if I thought someone was prepared to wait around for an hour for me, I'm not sure I want to go out with them anymore. Do you know what I mean?'

'Mmmm,' was the only reply Kennedy could think of, mainly due to the fact that his mind was elsewhere. 'Yeah. Look, I don't think you told us what way you would have walked home.'

Jones sighed. Now he was impatient and he wasn't scared of showing it.

'Okay. I would have come out of the Spread Eagle and immediately crossed to the other side of Parkway. The reason I would have done this is I would either have had to cross Arlington Road and then I still would have had to cross Parkway at the bottom. Now, if it was in the middle of the week with the heavy traffic, I would have walked down Parkway on the same side, because there is a zebra crossing just before Arlington Road. So, now we go down to where Camden High Street crosses Parkway. I cross to the tube station, turn left, walk up Kentish Town Road, past Rock On Records, keep on up Kentish Town Road up to Highgate Road, and right into my street.'

'Very interesting. You're right, that's probably the best way than go, and would you mind telling me how long it takes you to walk that distance?' Irvine asked.

'Probably about twenty minutes, but I've never timed it,' Jones replied.

'Okay, I'll accept that, probably closer to twenty-five minutes to thirty, but let's, for the sake of this discussion, say it's a twenty minute walk.'

'Whoa,' Jones breathed a large breath through his teeth. 'For a moment there, I thought you were going to charge me with speeding on the pavement.'

'No, not at all,' Irvine began, 'but I was wondering if you could explain to me how you managed to leave the Spread Eagle at seven forty-five.'

Irvine paused for a millisecond and waited until Jones was about to protest. 'You see, as one of our officers was going off duty on Sunday evening, he visited the Spread Eagle for a well-earned pint, and spotted you leaving. It was seven-forty-five exactly, because he says he checked his watch when he ordered his first pint. This officer has also seen you in there before on several occasions and he recognised you from your picture in the *Evening Standard*. The price of fame, you see.'

'So fecking what? What's the point? I confused my times by

twenty minutes or so. So, what does it matter? What did I do for twenty minutes? What on earth is this all about? I've told you before and I'll tell you again. Esther committed suicide. What does it matter what time I got home? What does it matter what time she was meant to show? She didn't, she stayed at home, stuck her head in the oven and topped herself, and now we're all paying for it.'

'Well, 'Kennedy began, 'my main point would have to be that if you were going to see Esther Bluewood in your house at eight and you only left the Spread Eagle at seven-forty-five, then you would have at least had to catch a taxi to make sure you were there on time. You're not going to be late to see Esther Bluewood are you?'

Kennedy looked around at the posters and photographs on the walls.

'You know, what you say might well be correct. Now that I think about it, I did catch a cab home. I must have forgotten the time or something. Yeah, you're right, I caught a taxi. There, that's that settled. Anything else?' Jones said, breaking into a grin.

If only he didn't have such an evil sounding voice, I'd find it easier to believe him, Kennedy thought, but said: 'Yes. Let's talk about Monday morning. Okay?'

'Sorry?'

'The last time we spoke to you, you told us that you were here all Monday morning,' Kennedy continued.

'Ahm, yes, if that's what I said.'

'Well, how do you explain this then?' Kennedy said, rising from his chair and walking across to the large Esther Bluewood poster. He searched around the shelf for something he'd spotted on his earlier visit. 'Ah, yes here we are…'

Kennedy picked up the Post Office card he'd spotted earlier, he read aloud: 'We called at (and here has been filled in "10.30am") to deliver a package. You weren't in. Could you please contact us so that we can arrange for delivery…' Kennedy paused and looked over at Josef. 'You see, the delivery driver filled in the time.' Kennedy turned the card around so that Jones could see the neat handwriting.

Jones was about to say something. Kennedy beat him to it:

'We've heard how loud your doorbell is, so there's no way you could have slept through that.'

'Again,' said Jones, 'I have to say, what does it matter if I was in or out? I was in; I slept through it, I couldn't be bothered to get out of bed. I was out; somewhere doing something. I was in or I was out. It doesn't really matter. I don't live a life where I jot down all these boring details. There's a life to be lead, man. I haven't time for this domestic crap. Anything else?'

'Yes, there is, in fact. Did Judy Dillon know you were seeing Esther Bluewood?' Irvine asked.

'Do you mean, did she know I was seeing Esther, or did she know I was *seeing* Esther?' Josef said.

'Oh, I'll settle for either, to be honest,' Irvine replied.

'No, of course not. What, do you think I'm stupid? That was surely the quickest way to lose the relationship, wasn't it?' Josef replied.

Kennedy stepped in: 'Tell me, has she said anything to you about it recently?'

'About what?' Jones had his hands held high in front of his chest in apparent exasperation.

'About your intimate relationship with Esther?'

'No,' Jones replied, and then stopped, appearing to consider the implications of the question.

'You're sure?' Irvine asked this time.

'I have to tell you, these are just the weirdest questions I've ever heard. It's like we're both in different movies and someone's mixed up the scripts.' Jones said, now rubbing his hand on his legs.

'Yeah,' Kennedy started, 'life's a bit like that sometimes.'

Jones rose to his feet, stretching his legs and shaking each in turn.

'Paul Yeats,' Kennedy began, ignoring Jones' leg stretching exercises, 'has he been in touch with you or have you been in touch with him since Esther's death?'

'Oh, Lord Corduroy. He was on the phone yesterday, huffing and puffing about some journal. He was in one of his usual superior moods and I haven't a clue what he was on about. I eventually set the phone down on him. I'd have loved to have been in the room with him – you know, fly on the wall – when that happened. I'll bet there was steam coming out of his ears by that point.'

'We may need to see you again, but I think that's all for now,' Kennedy said, by way of conclusion.

'You may need to see me again? Who's behind all this? Is Lord Corduroy pulling your strings? Is that what this is all about? What's he after? He's got all her money now. That's all he was ever after. What more can he want? What is going on here? Esther Bluewood committed suicide and you guys are behaving like someone's murdered the heir to the throne. What's with all this about the

Spread Eagle, the walking, the taxis, the nannies, the journals, anyway?'

'We're just carrying out our investigations, sir,' Irvine said, as he and Kennedy prepared to leave.

'Wasting public money. There's no crime to solve here,' Jones replied, as he showed them out.

There was something sinister about the way his high-pitched whine delivered the word 'crime' that grated with Kennedy. As they walked back towards the car, he said to Irvine: 'He's a cold fish that one, isn't he? He's supposedly a fan of Esther's and he's so matter-of-fact about her and her death. Supposedly a lover, and yet now he's incapable of displaying any feelings for her other than contempt.'

'We know for certain he'd told us two lies, and although it was obvious he'd been found out in both cases, he didn't seem to care,' Irvine replied, opening the car door. 'Where to, now? Judy Dillon's?'

'Mmmm,' Kennedy said, nodding. He got in, sank deep into the car seat and deeper into his thoughts.

Irvine was happy to leave Kennedy alone as he drove. He too had thinking to do.

Chapter 27

KENNEDY AND Irvine drove straight to Park Village West and parked the unmarked police car outside Judy Dillon's house. Kennedy was sure he noticed a flick of the curtains.

'Let's just sit here for awhile,' he said to Irvine. It was the first words they'd spoken since they'd left Kentish Town. After a few minutes and several more flicks of the curtains, Kennedy said: 'Let's go for a wee spin, James.'

'Okay, where to?' Irvine bemusedly asked, turning the key in the ignition.

'I fancy a bookshop, myself. Let's try the Regents Bookstore.'

'Okay, whatever you say,' Irvine replied, starting off on the short but complicated drive to Parkway. It took eight minutes.

'Good day,' Kennedy said to Peter, the ever-helpful and friendly store owner, as he walked into the shop.

'Hello,' Peter said, breaking off momentarily from his ceaseless conversation with the previous owner of the bookshop, his father. Today's conversation seemed to be concerned with the ever-growing number of people who go into bookshops but who never seem to purchase any books. As far as Kennedy could gather, they'd compiled a list over many years that included: people who look up at the ceiling as they walk into the shop; old ladies in black suits; people with backpacks and rucksacks; people with filofaxes; people with banknotes in their hands (a cunning breed this); and people who walk in saying, 'What a really nice store you have here'.

'Just a quick question,' Kennedy said, providing a much-needed diversion to their conversation. 'You do offer a photocopying service?'

'Yes we do and we could tell you a thing or two about the people who come in here to get photocopies.'

'Would you remember a young lady coming in here… it would have been some time on Monday morning, and photocopying a notebook?' Kennedy asked.

'Yes, I do, as a matter of a fact. A lady of generous proportions, as I remember,' Peter answered diplomatically.

'Did she photocopy part of the book or all of the book?' Kennedy asked.

'I'd say, all of the book, judging by the number of copies she made,' Peter replied.

'Great, that's all I need for now. See you later.'

'Okay, see you,' Peter replied. He turned and said to his father, at a level he knew Kennedy would hear: 'I think we can add "detectives on investigations" to our list of people who never buy books.'

*

Five minutes later, Irvine pulled up outside Dillon's flat in Park Village West for the second time in twenty minutes. It was eighteen minutes to four, enough time to ask a few questions before Dillon's four o'clock call to ann rea was due. Kennedy was interested to see how the nanny would react as the deadline loomed. For the second time the curtains twitched nervously, as though there was an actress hiding behind them who suffered from first-night nerves.

'Okay,' Kennedy began, as he unclipped his seat-belt and opened the car door. Rain had started to fall, a gentle but dampening mizzle. 'Let's put her out of her misery.'

No sooner had Kennedy's index finger connected with the doorbell than the door sprung open. The fingers of his left hand twitched by his side, as the lady in black greeted them from inside.

'Oh, what a surprise,' Judy Dillon said.

Not a great opening line, Kennedy thought. Perhaps just a little too over-rehearsed.

'We'd like to ask you a few more questions,' Irvine said.

'Oh, come in,' Judy began. 'Would you like a cup of tea?'

'Ah, no thanks,' Kennedy replied, perhaps a little too quickly.

Judy responded the way a dentist's patients have a habit of doing when the dentist drops a hint that they aren't going to be long in the chair. Obviously, Kennedy thought, from the nanny's perspective, refusing tea implies that the interview's going to be short and painless. The simple truth was that the refusal was based purely on the fact that the nanny made a vile cup of tea.

'Esther Bluewood,' began Irvine, as they all sat down. Once again Judy chose a seat Kennedy felt was barely able to take the strain. 'Would you know if she'd been involved with anyone?'

'What? You mean apart from Paul Yeats?' Judy asked, fidgeting in her seat.

'Wasn't it all over between her and Paul Yeats?' Irvine suggested.

'It's not over until the chickens are hatched,' Judy announced. 'Or at least that was the case as far as Yeats was concerned.'

'Yeah. I meant, did she have any other relationships?' Irvine said.

Judy leaned in towards them to the point where her chair was fighting the laws of gravity.

'Well, now you come to mention it, she had me do quite a bit of baby-sitting over the last six months or so,' the nanny offered, a few decibels above a whisper.

'So, you think she might have been seeing someone?' Irvine said. He was speaking, Kennedy was observing. They looked more like an odd couple than two policemen, with Irvine in his country tweeds and brogues, and Kennedy in a dark blue two-piece suit, crisp white shirt, green tie, black highly-polished shoes and crombie coat. Neither were smokers and so didn't have anything obvious to do with their hands during conversations – though Irvine was more demonstrative with his gestures.

'Well, if she'd been going out with a girlfriend I'd have known about it, wouldn't I? She'd have come round the flat, for instance.'

'Perhaps.' Irvine said. 'Was there anything more definite than that, you know, to make you think she was seeing a man?'

'Well,' Judy began, leaning back in her chair again. She clasped her hands together around her knee, using it as a form of crane to raise her legs off the ground, all the time leaning back further and further in the frail basketwork chair. Kennedy was convinced it was either going to tilt over, or collapse into tinderwood as she fell into a heap on the floor. 'I think… the thing I was thinking was, and it's not an original thought, I know, I don't know which book it comes from, but she didn't really seem to be missing her man – Yeats, that is. You know, for sure she was sad that the children had lost their father, but she wasn't missing out… if you know what I mean.'

'Okay,' Irvine said, continuing in the driving seat, 'do you think there is a chance that Paul Yeats knew that Esther was having an affair?'

'I didn't say she was definitely having an affair!' Judy barked.

'Sorry, of course you didn't. Let me rephrase it. Do you think there is a chance that Paul Yeats *suspected* that Esther was having an affair.'

'No.'

'Why do you say that so positively?'

'Simple. He'd didn't care a fig about anyone other than himself, so he wouldn't have been tuned into what was going on in her life or what kind of vibes she was giving off.'

'Did the kids ever say anything to you about there being another man around?' Kennedy said, breaking his silence.

'Oh, what do children know? They live in a fantasy world all the time anyway.'

'Oh, I wouldn't be so sure about that. I would have thought Holmer was old enough, not old enough to understand, but old enough to know something was amiss,' Kennedy continued.

'It's not something I ever discussed with them,' Judy replied, shutting down the subject.

'Tell me,' Kennedy continued, searching for the right question, one that would bear fruit, 'who were Esther's friends?'

'Friends. That's interesting. It's like I think she didn't really have any real friends. She used to tell me that she felt she was like a black-and-white character in a colour movie. She seemed to find it hard to make a connection beyond the initial words. I mean I could dig that. It's hard for people who think a lot to go into a pub with their mates and talk about the weather or the price of fish. I'm a bit like that myself, no time for small chat. Never been able to do it. I know it's terribly anti-social but I much prefer to come back here and read my books and maybe have a glass of wine or two.' Judy looked longingly at Irvine as she finished this.

'So, Esther wasn't really a pub kind of person?' Irvine asking, implying directly that of course she wasn't.

'I mean, you can't possibly write an album as beautiful or as confessional as *Axis* and then go out and discuss how many goals Beckham should have scored on Saturday,' Judy said.

Kennedy felt that she was shifting the emphasis from herself back to Bluewood for Irvine's benefit.

'So, she'd no friends?' Kennedy asked.

'Well, no buddy-buddy friends I'm sure. But she liked Hugh Watson; she got on well with him. She liked that journalist, the one with no capitals in her name... ahm...'

'ann rea?' Irvine offered helpfully.

'Yes, she seemed to come round to Fitzroy Road regularly. Esther seemed to like her and was always happy to have her come around. Let's see who else? That's sad, you know, no one else springs to mind. Of course, there was Jim and Jill Beck, but apart from that, she pretty much lived her life for her children and her songs.'

Kennedy didn't bat an eyelid at the mention of ann rea, and he was impressed that Irvine didn't steal a glance to see if he was batting an eyelid.

'Did you ever work for her at the weekend?' Kennedy asked.

'Rarely,' Judy started. 'I like to have some space to myself. It's important; it enables me to do my job better. I think so, anyway. But occasionally I would break my rule and help her out if she was doing something or needed someone and no one else was around.'

'Were there other people who'd baby-sit for her?' Irvine asked.

'I think she was just comfortable leaving them with me and Jill and Jim. Even Yeats wasn't high on the baby-sitter list. She kept saying that Paul got distracted too easily and she was scared of something happening to the kids. Paul wasn't really a kiddie kind of person, all the hoochie-coochie-coo embarrassed him.

'So what did you do with your Sundays?'

Judy swung around in her chair. Kennedy prepared himself to catch her. She swung her arm around in an arc. 'These. I get lost in my books.'

'Don't you ever go out?' Irvine asked. The DS hadn't meant it to be a put down, but Kennedy felt it sounded like that.

'I sometimes meet friends, yes,' Judy said, very defensively.

'A certain group, or just various people?' Kennedy asked.

'Pardon?' Judy said.

'I mean, do you hang out with a regular group of people or are there other friends you see from time to time?' Kennedy said, stepping up the pace of questioning now.

'What does that matter? I can't see the point? You're not suggesting I'm part of a gang or something are you?' Judy said, obviously on her guard.

'No, it's just that Josef Jones… you do know Josef don't you?' Kennedy said interrupting his own question.

'Yes, I know Josef.'

'Well, it's just that Josef said that there were a group of you, and you all were fans of Esther's and…'

'Excuse me,' Judy replied, interrupting Kennedy. 'I worked with Miss Bluewood. I admired her work, immensely in fact. But I was not a fan the way that group of Jones's were fans, swapping and all that. I loved her music and her work, that was enough for me.'

Kennedy immediately thought of the journals.

'No, I don't think Josef was implying anything,' he began. 'He was just suggesting that some of you, who shared a common bond in a love for Miss Bluewood's music, occasionally met up.'

'Well, I did see some of them from time to time. But most of them are anoraks; they tend to upset artists in their search for the rare and the unique. They'll literally go through rubbish bins looking for stuff – ugh! Gross!'

'I'm intrigued about all this, you know. How did Esther meet up with these people? At her concerts, at TV stations?'

'Esther hadn't done a live concert for about three years, since Jens was born, in fact,' Judy stated.

'You're kidding,' Irvine said. 'I thought it was impossible to be in the pop business and not appear on TV and on the concert stage.'

'She hated it. Made her feel physically sick. And then she decided if it was making her feel so bad, why do it? She told me she couldn't work out why someone, anyone, would ruin their lives just to sell a million records. She sold a million records on *Axis* and the high she felt from selling a million didn't balance out how bad she felt doing the never-ending stream of concerts and TVs, so she just stopped doing them. All her records sold comparatively well. Enough that the record company wanted her to continue to make records, which was all she wanted. So long as she had a genuine outlet for her work, she was happy.'

'So, why did she have such fanatical fans?' Kennedy asked.

'Because the more of a recluse someone is, the more a certain group of people will chase them. That's not everyone, mind you. Some of the fans received enough from her music and were prepared to leave her alone, others wanted more.'

'So how did she promote her work?' Irvine said.

'She'd do an exclusive with Radio 2 for one of their specials and she'd talk to one person from the press she liked, and that was it. The record company took a few ads and the word of mouth spread,' Judy said. She seemed happier with the conversation now that it had moved on to this topic.

'So would you call Josef Jones an "anorak"?' Kennedy asked.

'Well, he looked better than most of them, but that voice. Goodness, it sends a shiver up my spine. I mean, I'm not slagging him off or anything like that, and he certainly followed and supported Esther, but you got the impression that his support had little or nothing to do with her music, more to do with her celebrity. Do you know what I mean?'

'Mmmm,' Kennedy said with a certain degree of uncertainty in his voice. 'These anoraks, as you call them, they usually hang around dressing room and stage doors and places to see their idols?'

'Yes…?' Judy said.

'So, where would they hang around to see Esther?'

'Well, sometimes they'd stop by Fitzroy Road, but mostly they gathered in the Landsdowne, out of the way,' Judy replied.

'Did Josef ever hang around Esther's house, hoping to see her?' Kennedy asked.

'I mean, from time to time you'd see all of them, not just Josef. There were about nine in the crew. Do you think one of them had something to do with this? I saw her, you know. I found her. I'll never forget that scene for the rest of my life, her lying there dead. The oven was open. I just thought she'd committed suicide but you're still busy asking questions. Do you think it was one of her fanatical fans? Was she not gassed?'

'Oh, we're still checking that entire situation out. Still carrying out our investigation,' Kennedy said, looking at his watch.

'What time is it, please?' Judy asked.

Kennedy, as ninety-five per cent of the population would, looked at his watch again, even though he'd checked the time a matter of a second earlier.

'Three fifty-six,' he replied.

Judy began to twitch ever so slightly.

Kennedy pretended to be intent only on his ongoing investigation, and continued with his questioning: 'So, where do you go from here? What do you do for a living now your job's gone?'

'Oh, I'll continue to be a nanny, no doubt.'

'Is there much work going for a nanny in this area.' Irvine asked innocently.

'Oh there's always work for a good nanny,' Judy began, as she tilted her head to a forty degree angle, so that she could read Kennedy's watch.

'How would you go about getting a job?' Kennedy inquired, prolonging the agony.

Oh, there are agencies that secure that kind of work. Which reminds me, I've got a couple of calls to make, you know, chasing up work...'

'Sorry, you'll have to forgive us,' Kennedy said, all of a sudden the voice of concern. 'James, please loan Miss Dillon your mobile so that she can make the call.'

'No, no, it's okay,' Judy protested. 'There's a communal coin box out in the hall. I can do it when you've gone.'

'Oh, we've a few more questions to ask you yet,' Kennedy began, starting to feel bad for pretending so with the nanny. If only she wouldn't lie like this. 'But we don't want to spoil your chances of a job. Why don't you make your calls and we'll talk here amongst ourselves until you're done.'

'No, I prefer to wait until you're gone, to be honest. What time is it, please?' Judy asked, just about managing to keep her cool.

'It's now one minute to four,' Kennedy replied.

'Ah,' Judy replied, now literally and physically twitching in her seat. 'Actually, I do have an important call I have to make at four o'clock. It's rather private, though. I wondered, could I possibly go outside?' Judy was now beside herself.

'Certainly, shall I dial the number for you?' Kennedy asked innocently.

'Sorry?' Judy asked, every ounce (and there were plenty of them) of her being confabulated.

'No, sorry, I just thought it would be quicker for you if I dialled the number.' Kennedy, every ounce, and there were but a few to spare, the straight man.

'Pardon?' Judy said, getting more rattled by the millisecond.

'ann rea's number. Should I dial ann rea at *Camden News Journal*'s number for you? Just to save you a bit of time so that you can see if she'd been able to get your money.'

'What!' Judy was now totally distraught. 'What's going on here?'

'Listen, Judy, we know you visited Regents Bookshop and photocopied Esther's journal on your way home on Monday morning. We know you've been trying to get £50,000 from *Camden News Journal* for it. So why don't you save us all a lot of time and hand it over and then we can keep the fuss to a minimum?'

'But...'

Kennedy simply stared at the nanny, as if to say 'Please, we both know what's going on here.'

Although she said nothing, Judy Dillon seemed to agree this to be the case, and she started to panic.

'No, you don't understand, I can't give it to you. I need to be able to give it to him. He's going to be mad at me. I don't like him when he's mad.'

It didn't take much stone-walling from the detectives before Judy went to the fridge, followed closely by Irvine, and returned with a cold set of photocopies of Esther Bluewood's unique but very readable writing.

All Judy's continued protests were in vain. Kennedy thought, She dost protest too much, as he and Irvine escaped the rain for the comfort of the car and the return to the comfort and safety of North Bridge House, where a proper cup of tea would only be minutes away.

Chapter 28

CONSIDERING THAT Mrs Violet Bluewood was (a) at least sixty, (b) had recently lost her daughter in circumstances which could only be described as suspicious, and (c) had just spent seven hours breathing in recycled air at 35,000 feet, she was in remarkably good fettle. Added to which, Anne Coles was surprised at her mildness, as – thanks to the stories she'd heard about Esther and her mother – she'd half been expecting an ogress.

'You know,' Bluewood senior began, immediately adopting a familiarity usually reserved between friends of several years' standing, 'I have this emptiness inside of me, I keep feeling I should break down and cry or something. Sadly, I haven't the capacity for that. Edna, that's my good friend in the States who took me to the airport, didn't really need to do that, you know, I could have just as easily got a cab, but she wanted to, so I thought it would have been a little ungracious not to have allowed her; anyway, Edna she was saying to me, "Vi," my real name's Violet, but my friends all call me Vi, I'll never know why, but where were we? Yes, Edna said, "Vi, you're just going to be strong and then the dam will burst and the tears will come".'

Violet 'Vi' Bluewood could have won any glamorous granny competition she chose to enter. She was wearing an ice-blue two-piece suit with a waisted jacket. It looked good but the effect was spoilt by the brown shirt she was wearing. She didn't have the kind eyes one usually finds with grandmothers, more those of a neighbour you tolerate rather than become friends with. She sported an auburn, short-haired curly wig, or at least Coles thought it was a wig. Violet's make-up was thick, as though she first covered all visible facial area with a base and then painted a face on top. The overall effect was, Coles thought, a presentation of who she wanted to be, rather than who she was: something like Hillary Clinton. Yes, a lot like Hillary Clinton, Coles thought.

They were sitting in the hotel lobby of the Marriot at Swiss Cottage, formerly the Holiday Inn, sharing coffee and biscuits. The illusion of space, which the hotel tried to create by dividing the lobby into lots of small areas, hadn't really come off, and unless you actually sat in the reception area, it could be quite stifling. Coles was thankful, nonetheless, that they were occupying one of these small compartments off the main area, as it afforded her and Mrs Violet Bluewood complete privacy.

'Have you spoken with Paul Yeats, yet?' Coles asked.

'What, since the death, or since I got here? If both, the answers would be yes and no, in that order,' Violet replied.

'How was he?'

'Well, he seemed a little like myself, shell-shocked. Not really knowing how to feel, if the truth be told,' Violet said. 'I think that may be because I rarely saw Esther these days, different continents, let alone spoke to her, different time zones. So, you see, in a way, she was out of my focus, awareness, as it were, so it's hard to miss her. What I mean is if she lived around the corner and I saw her every day and was always nipping in for coffee and a chat, then it would probably be a much bigger loss and maybe I'd be feeling differently now. But she is my flesh and blood and I should be feeling differently, shouldn't I?'

'You know,' Coles started, not sure what she should say, 'we all deal with our grief in our own private ways.'

'I think Paul is numb because he feels he failed her, you know, wasn't around when she needed him. He's convinced she took her own life.'

'And you?' Coles asked.

'No way,' was the stern and firm reply.

'Even with her earlier…' Coles searched for the correct word.

'Sickness?' Violet was polite and generous with her assistance, helping Coles out of a tricky situation.

'Yes.'

'No. Sorry. That was a bit of silliness that Esther had to go through. I know, and God knows, I've paid for most of her therapy, that she talked to people until she was blue in the face and she dealt with her problems and resolved them. But that was all when she was much younger. You have to realise that Esther's a much changed woman since she'd had her songs on the radio and was married and had children. She's very resourceful and determined. She was no longer one to waste her life. I always thought that's why there was a bit of an air between her and me, you know, because I've known both of the Esther Bluewoods. Few people did. Maybe she's rather ashamed of the younger one, and when she dealt with me she'd be acknowledging the younger one existed, and I think she was rather ashamed of the way she dealt with things in those days.'

'Did you ever talk about it?'

'Oh, my dear, you obviously didn't know Esther,' Violet began, warming to the memory of her daughter, 'Everything was black and white with her. She would have totally disowned me years ago if I hadn't kept persisting, refusing to go away, refusing to give up on her, as it were.'

The waiter brought the bill. Violet took a pair of pink horn-rimmed glasses out of her bag and put them on as she checked it. 'What's the rate of the dollar to the pound these days? I need to know what this costs in real money, honey.'

The waiter didn't know. Coles suggested it might be around $1.40 to a pound sterling.

'Would you like anything else?' Violet asked Coles.

'No, I'm fine, ta.'

'You don't fancy a cigarette, do you?' Violet asked, a hint of desperation creeping in.

'No, thanks, I gave it up a few years ago.'

'Do you mind if I do? I'm actually gagging for a ciggy, as Paul Yeats would say.'

'Totally fine,' Coles said, and a pack of something American and a new pot of coffee were ordered.

'I hate to smoke by myself and I hate others doing it in the same room. Sorry, where were we?' Esther Bluewood's unlikely mother asked.

'You were saying you didn't agree with Paul Yeats on whether or not Esther committed suicide.'

'Yes, that's right. I mean, it's not right. She didn't commit suicide, positively not,' Violet said, as her cigarettes arrived. They'd already been opened and presented more like a box of delicious chocolates than the leaves of tar and nicotine destined to eat and eventually destroy the cells of the human body. The waiter offered her a cigarette, she accepted, and he extended his other hand with a lighter already in flame. She held his hand to steady the flame close to the tip of the cigarette. She took that first important drag and closed her eyes as she did so, continuing to keep a hold on the waiter's hand. She blew the smoke out, turning her head to the right, away from the waiter and Coles, and guarded it behind her hand. 'Thank you, honey, that was just great for me,' she said to the waiter. 'Sorry, that was crass, wasn't it?' she said to Coles, as the waiter walked away.

'Ah...'

'Not to worry,' Violet continued, unperturbed, 'let's get back to

Esther. Look, to tell you the truth, Esther didn't really try very hard the first time. She could have killed herself, if she had wanted to. I know that must sound terribly cruel to you. But she could have gone to the forest behind our house and no one would ever have found her. I do mean ever. Instead, she cut her wrists, a very slow way to kill yourself, you know, and went and hid in a place she and her brother had always gone to: the basement. No, that was just Esther crying for attention. She was forever seeking attention since way before her father died. He was a cold fish; I don't even know what it was I ever saw in him. Maybe it was his brain, it certainly wasn't...'

The 'glam gran' had obviously thought better of finishing her sentence.

I'll bet she's a wild one after a few G & Ts, Coles thought, but asked, 'When was the last time you and Esther spoke?'

'She rang me on Thursday of last week.'

'How did she sound?'

'She sounded fine, same as usual. She was even threatening to come over soon with the kids. She said it was going to get a bit hot in London and she'd be better out of it until things quietened down.'

'Did you have any idea what she was referring to?' Coles asked.

'Not really, not at all, in fact. She never really went into personal things with me. She kept most things to herself. She'd be quite obscure, saying things like "Paul's not around much", which I took to mean he was cheating on her. But there was nothing new in that. He was doing that in America early on in their relationship.'

'What do you think she was talking about, when she said "Things might get a bit hot in London"?' Coles asked.

'Again, I assumed it must have something to do with Paul, maybe she was planning to leave him. But I learned never to ask her personal or potentially embarrassing questions. If I got into stuff she didn't want to talk about, she wouldn't ring me again for ages, and all the letters I'd write would go unanswered. So I used to write letters without questions, which pretty well made them ramblings. But what else could it have been, other than Paul? She'd no business problems to speak of, or at least that I was aware of. She always talked about stuff like that. I think it was because she thought it was above my head. When Esther and I spoke on the phone it was like making a duty call. We both felt we should be making some kind of effort to stay in touch, but we had little time for each other really. I know it's horrible to admit, but it's the truth.'

Coles felt that was very sad. Violet may have been honest, but her honesty didn't hide the sadness of the situation. As Coles left the hotel, she resolved to ring her mum that very evening and have a good old-fashioned natter with her.

Chapter 29

'OH NO, not again.' This was Paul Yeats' greeting to Kennedy and Irvine as he opened the door to 123 Fitzroy Road. It was five o'clock on the Wednesday evening, and Kennedy was keenly aware that the third day of the case was drawing to a close.

'Oh yes,' Kennedy announced. 'I'm afraid so.'

'How did you know I was here?'

'We didn't. We tried on the off chance,' Kennedy admitted.

'I shouldn't have answered the door. Ah well, you're here now, you might as well come in,' Yeats announced, finding some manners hidden in the dark recesses of his mind.

The kitchen, the very same one where Esther Bluewood had met her end, was still sealed with police 'do not cross' tape, and Yeats had camped in the small living room. Kennedy couldn't work out how Yeats had managed to stay there, so soon after the death of his wife. Was there anything to be read into that, he wondered? The living room reminded Kennedy of a hippie squat in the sixties. Yeats was sleeping on the sofa, but had not tidied away the bed linen. Nor had he cleared away a few days' worth of pizza boxes, polystyrene coffee cups, ashtrays filled with pipe scrapings and burnt matches, soiled shirts, dirty socks, newspapers. A guitar case was lying open on the table, a guitar resting half in and half out of it, with a sheaf of pages scattered all around.

'I've been trying to do a bit of writing, to be honest. I felt it was important I did it here. The songs are about here and I felt I needed to do them in her space. I realise that's quite morbid. But in literary circles it's not unusual for one writer to tune into the muse of another,' Yeats said. He was dressed in his usual uniform of brown corduroy suit with crew neck jumper. The suit was a constant but the jumper colour varied to suit his mood. Today it was bottle green.

All three stood in a relatively small space. There were no seats available to sit on. Yeats had them all burdened down with bric-a-brac. The sofa, with the worn bed linen, looked about as inviting as a pot of stale Irish stew. So, with Yeats' hands deep in pockets, occasionally taking out his right for a few seconds, to enable him to run it through his curly hair, they looked like two students (Irvine and

Kennedy) summoned to the master's untidy study for a dressing down.

'How's it coming, then?' Kennedy felt obliged to ask.

'Ha, talk about struggling for your art,' Yeats began. 'The song-writing lark is not as easy as it used to be. Perhaps I'm too old to rock and too young to die.'

He paused to think about what he'd just said. It seemed he'd impressed himself, because he wrote down the line 'Too old to rock and too young to die' on his legal pad. He viewed it, tried to hum some melody to fit, gave up and returned the pad to the top of the guitar case.

'Tell me, did you and Esther ever write songs together?' Kennedy asked, fighting for Yeats' attention.

'Sadly not, I mean in the early days when we met we used to write loads in each other's company, and sometimes she'd tighten up some of my stuff and I'd do the same for her. But they were never really co-writes. I don't think either of us was capable of that. It seemed somewhat too calculated. Even the great Lennon & McCartney wrote their own parts of their songs. Sometimes, even though their songs were always credited to the both of them, one of them would have been responsible for the lion's share of, if not all, the writing.'

Kennedy felt something wasn't right about the situation. He still couldn't understand how the husband of a young woman, the mother of his two children, who had died very recently (not to mention in such tragic circumstances) could carry on as normal, business as usual. Well, not even business as usual: he was writing songs, 'in her muse' he claimed. But, apart from all of that, Paul Yeats hadn't even mentioned the situation with Rosslyn. Nor had Kennedy. At the beginning of the conversation, Kennedy had avoided the issue in the hope Yeats would introduce it. Now it was getting to the point of embarrassment. If Yeats genuinely didn't know about the recent developments, then Kennedy felt it was cruel not to enlighten him.

'Tell me, have you spoken to Rosslyn St Clair today?' Kennedy asked, as if the idea had just dawned on him.

'No. To be honest, all things considered, I thought it important we put a bit of space between each other,' Yeats answered, hand out of pocked and scratching his chin in a 'how about this for a theory?' pose.

'So you didn't know she was in hospital?' Irvine asked.

'Hospital? Where? Why? What happened?' Yeats said, apparently panic-stricken.

'Well, sir, from what we can gather, she'd an abortion and, well... it was not done professionally, and she was found by two of our colleagues just in the nick of time. They got her to hospital,' Irvine added, sympathy creeping into his voice.

'Abortion? Surely there's some mistake? Abortion? Impossible. She wasn't even preg... It must be a case of mistaken identity,' Yeats spluttered.

'No, sir, it's definitely Miss St Clair. One of the neighbours confirmed it, before she was taken to hospital.'

'God, I've got to get to her. I've got to get to her immediately. Poor Ross.'

'We'll take you to the railway station,' Kennedy offered.

'No. No, I'll be fine, thanks. If you're done with me?' Yeats said, as he started packing some of his dirty clothes, the sheets of paper from the top of the guitar and his mobile phone which was still lying beside his makeshift bed, into a Marks and Sparks bag.

'Sure. Sure, that's fine. We can finish this later. I'm sorry, sir, we thought you knew...' Kennedy started.

'Knew? Sure, if I knew I'd be there. I wouldn't be moping around here,' Yeats replied, not looking at either policeman. He grabbed the bag and left the house without bidding them goodbye.

'Well, 'Kennedy started, 'what did you make of that?'

'He's either sincere, or else he's missed his vocation,' Irvine replied.

'Yeah, anyone that good should be on the stage, and I'm not sure I mean singing.'

'You think he knew, then?'

'I'm convinced he knew. I have the feeling that people like Paul Yeats live on the telephone, the same way Warren Beatty and Van Morrison are supposed to. Connecting with their inner circle regularly. I bet he knows everything there is to know,' Kennedy speculated.

'But what's to be gained by appearing not to know?' Irvine said.

'Well, for starters, so he'd not be connected with the abortion. Also, it would allow him to pretend he doesn't know about the pregnancy. If, as Coles suspected, there is a chance Rosslyn St Clair was left to die, he would remove himself from any suspicion in that area,' Kennedy said. Then he stopped and thought about what he had just said.

'Does that put him in the frame for the death of his wife, then, sir?' Irvine asked.

'Now, there is a question, James,' Kennedy said, turning to lead his DS out of the untidy room. 'I suppose it does in a way. He's lots of motives; maybe even too many. His wife was about to divorce him. Cut him off. He was living way beyond his means. His girlfriend was pregnant. If his soon-to-be ex-wife found out, perhaps it would have speeded things up. Perhaps it would have given her the grounds for kicking him out of the country cottage as well. Maybe he'd lived too long in her shadow, maybe he basked in her reflected glory and knew that was all the glory he was going to enjoy for the rest of his career. And by murdering his wife, he puts himself in a much better financial position, i.e. as the surviving spouse he more than likely inherits everything. When we're back at the station, remind me to check with Tim Flynn if he managed to track down a will. But also, and maybe more importantly, he gets to control her work. He can remaster and remix her recordings, taking some of the credit for himself.'

'But would he need to do that? Would it be so important for him to have his name on her recordings?' Irvine asked.

'I think so, yes,' Kennedy said, stopping outside the kitchen door and looking inside the room. He turned his back on the room of death, leaned against the doorpost facing Irvine and continued: '"Too old to rock, too young to die". I think Yeats is desperate for credit. I think he craves the sort of critical acclaim his wife received. It probably aggrieved him that she got so much acclaim and yet seemed disinterested in it. I think he's the kind of artist who makes his every move in the hope of the attention he's going to receive. Whereas Esther just had something she desperately needed to say and she said it in the verses of her songs. She wrote and sang songs not because she wanted to propel herself up the charts, but because she needed to.' Kennedy stopped and laughed. 'I don't believe it, I'm on one of ann rea's soap boxes.'

Irvine laughed. 'Well, I suppose it makes a lot of sense.'

'Yes, he'll change things around so he'll appear to have some artistic input. He'll maybe put together a compilation of his own choosing and write the sleeve notes for it. With his new-found power he could eventually control what's out there of Esther's. This way he'll have the final say on how she would eventually be judged. There might even be some unfinished work, demos or whatever, that he'll finish, giving himself a co-songwriting credit.'

'Nah. He'd never be allowed to do that, surely?'

'Well, look at The Beatles: they did it to John Lennon's demo of "Free as a Bird". Yoko was obviously in the thick of it, but we've come to expect that from her. But the other Beatles, how could they do that to their mate?' Kennedy asked. It wasn't really a question. 'The other thing Yeats may choose to do, is to release inferior material never planned for public airing, just to water down the strength of the legend. You know, "The genius who created *Axis* was also responsible for this". He'd obviously argue that the fans had a right to it. A right to it when Yeats deemed appropriate.'

'Or when his bank balance needed it?' Irvine chipped in.

'Exactly,' Kennedy replied.

'But how could he have managed to murder her and make it look just like the classic suicide case everyone is claiming it is?'

'And that is another question altogether, James,' Kennedy said, turning to look into the kitchen again. He stood in silence for a few minutes without saying a word.

'Look James, I'm going to stay here for a while, you go ahead. I'll walk back to North Bridge House later when I'm finished.'

'If you're sure,' Irvine said.

'Positively. Look, check with Tim Flynn on the will situation when you get back. I'll see you and the rest of the team in about three-quarters of an hour, and we'll go through the new info we've picked up since last we met.'

*

Kennedy was picking up a weird vibe in the kitchen. He took a pair of plastic gloves from the inside pocket of his crombie. He pulled them over his hands. He always had a slightly uncomfortable feeling when doing this. Not quite as bad as when someone scraped a pane of glass with their fingernails but perhaps number two on that particular Richter scale. He turned on the gas tap; the one he assumed would release the gas to the top right rim of the hob. There was nothing, no reaction. No evil hissing to interfere with the silence of the lonely room.

The taps had been dusted for fingerprints, brush-coated with metallic powder. He wondered if any had been found. What if Esther Bluewood's fingerprints were the last set of prints on the taps? That would almost certainly mean that she had committed suicide. Kennedy went through the procedure in his head. He realised that the prints of the person who turned the gas off, Judy Dillon, would be on the tap. But in her statement she hadn't said that she'd turned the taps off. She'd discovered the body ahead of the police and gasman and collapsed into a heap. Had the man from the gas company turned the tap off? If so, it would be his prints, or (if he was wearing gloves) his smudges, that would be on the tap. Kennedy made a mental note to check the report and confirm with the man from the gas company. Either way he couldn't remember anybody saying they'd turned the gas taps off. So, if the gas had been escaping all night, how come there hadn't been an explosion or the children harmed by it?

Yes, the downstairs neighbour had been affected, but only in a minor way. The heavy gas had obviously fallen and found its evil way to the storey below. The children, contentedly sleeping above, had been totally unaffected.

Kennedy returned that tap to the off position and tried the three others that controlled the remaining rings. Again nothing, nothing foul and sickly to contaminate the fresh, cool air. Kennedy could imagine that in the right mood, the sickly smell might be quite intoxicating, in much the same way a cheap bottle of wine would be, or even, he supposed, the way meths appealed to a meths-drinker.

If one was gassing oneself, at what point in the procedure would you feel in danger? Would you be so enraptured with the power of the poison filling your eager lungs, you'd willing give yourself up to the feeling? Could there become a point in the procedure where you wouldn't resist 'surrendering to the rhythm'?

Kennedy guessed that if you gassed yourself it wouldn't be a cry for help, it would be because you felt a compulsion to kill yourself. Hugh Watson had told him about the difference. The likeable therapist had said Esther's earlier American suicide attempt had been exactly that, a cry for help. Other people, Watson had assured the detective, were sadly destined to take their own lives and were beyond help. Some even went as far as to seek out help and flirt with redemption for several months, sometimes even years, before eventually ending their lives. When they'd finally succumb to the lasting peace they felt death brought.

Why was there no gas escaping now? Kennedy knew the gas company had felt it safe enough to turn the supply to the house back on, and had done so. He looked behind the cooker, as close as he could get to the wall. He saw a thick pipe come out of the back of the cooker and he followed it behind the cupboard and out the other side, where it connected to a coin meter.

There was no gas because the money had run out. Why hadn't it expired in time to spare Esther Bluewood her life? Kennedy sat on the floor in front of the meter and stared at it. Why hadn't Esther enjoyed the luck of the gas running out? Had someone ensured there was enough gas available to pollute her body? How would they have done it? Same way as with a parking meter, his inner voice answered him: someone had fed it.

Kennedy studied the gas meter. It ate 50p pieces. Surely if the meter was fed, there must be a chance that the 50p pieces would have fingerprints on them? But then for someone to carry out a murder as clever as this, they'd obviously have worn gloves, wouldn't they? Maybe not. Kennedy resolved to have the meter emptied the following morning and have the coins dusted for prints.

That also could have been the mechanism the murderer had used to turn off the gas when the deed was done. The meter would have done the murderer's work for him. How would he have known how many 50p pieces it would take to kill someone? Why was Kennedy continually referring to the killer as 'him'. Could it be that the 'him' in question might have had a conscience and wanted to ensure his children's safety, by minimising the risk of the building blowing up or his children being gassed?

Clever though, Kennedy thought. But how had he turned it on, activated the flow of gas in the first place? Some mechanism that dropped the coins into the meter, maybe using a timer? Kennedy's mind raced through various devices, including candle wax, chewing gum, lollipop sticks, rubber bands, pieces of paper folded into funnels which might have been dismissed as scraps of paper when the police where doing their investigation.

Whoever had killed Esther Bluewood knew that Judy Dillon would have been the one to find the body. Probably even concocted the plan with her in mind. Wouldn't it be convenient if Judy Dillon herself was the murderer, then she would have been in the best position to destroy any and all evidence? But Kennedy chastised himself for making the mistake he so often reprimanded his team for. He was racing ahead of himself, making the crime fit the facts. He'd a lot more work to do yet; he'd a lot more information to collect, before he was going to be in a position to start making choices.

But having thought all of the above, he had to admit that Judy Dillon's position as nanny afforded her the best opportunity to remove evidence from the scene of the crime. He then started considering her possible motives. His mind was racing ahead of itself again. As ann rea kept telling him: 'Your head's got a mind of its own.'

Kennedy decided it was time to get back and compare notes with the rest of the team. Perhaps he was closer to solving this case than he'd dreamed possible just twenty-five minutes earlier when Irvine had left.

Chapter 30

KENNEDY RETURNED to North Bridge House, only to find no mention in the file about either the gasman or Judy Dillon claiming to have turned the gas taps off. That was something that would have to wait until tomorrow – as would the news on the will, as Tim Flynn had gone off duty.

Kennedy and his team then spent an hour swapping the information they had learned during the day. For the next day, Thursday, they were assigned to follow up leads on the gas tap, check the will and hopefully interview Rosslyn St Clair and see what her side of the story was.

The Detective Inspector was surprised to find that ann rea had telephoned twice in the late afternoon. He checked his watch as the last of the team, Coles and Irvine as usual, departed his office. Eight-twenty. Too late to ring her at the newspaper. Should he continue to try and stay professional and leave it until the morning, or should he ring her at home?

After all was said and done, he claimed to be her friend and she might well need him as a friend. She, like him, didn't have a generous scatter of friends to call from. With a solitary image of her burning in his mind, he dialled her home number.

'Kennedy?' she said immediately, before he'd even had a chance to offer a word of greeting. Was she so lonely that no one other than Kennedy rang her at home? Or was it just a wishful reflex?

'Hi,' Kennedy said, trying to sound as friendly and as casual as he could possibly.

'God, Christy, I miss you so much,' ann rea gushed. 'There, I've fecked up already haven't I? It's okay to think that stuff, it's not okay to say it, is it?'

'It's best to be honest when expressing your feelings, ann rea. It hasn't exactly been a bed of roses for me either, you know,' Kennedy said. He'd just been saying, as in the last few seconds, that it was best to be honest when expressing your feelings and here he was saying, implying, that he was missing her. The truth, as ever, was that he was consumed on his case.

Kennedy felt it was very important not to lose sight of the edge of the pit in case you fell in. He felt you could do better work if you were able to 'turn off'. It was easier to be rational if the demons of the working day weren't constantly inside your head. Even so, he had an inkling that at some point in his life all the corpses he'd ever looked at were going to return to haunt him. Was that why he was so scared of all these corpses? Scared was the only word that really expressed how he felt.

When he'd started on the crime squad, he'd been rendered so distraught by the sight of his first corpse, he thought he'd either have to quit the police or else move to traffic or some other equally boring branch of the service. In the 1970s he'd been stationed in Hammersmith, and a nineteen-year-old girl's body had been found behind the Odeon, which – according to *The Guinness Book of Records*, at least – is the biggest cinema in Europe. Kennedy had just joined the crime squad as a DC, and he was proudly accompanying his detective inspector, a compassionate Yorkshireman, to the scene. Everything went well until it came time to examine the body. The vision still burned a hole in Kennedy's mind. She lay lifeless on top of a pile of rubbish bags, micro skirt (not much more than a belt) tucked up around her waist, thigh-length platform boots and arms sprawled in a lazy X-shape. Eyes wide open and a look on her face Kennedy interpreted as 'Why me?'.

It wasn't so much that it made him want to be sick, he was repulsed, and his stomach heaved a few times. But the overwhelming emotion he felt was anger: he wanted to go and find the person who had done this terrible thing. Seek out the animal who had ended this young life, shattered her dreams and the dreams of her parents, her friends. He wanted to find this person and kill them. Actually he wanted to find a way to not just kill them, but to make them suffer more than she had suffered, more than her parents and friends had suffered.

"Don't get mad, get even!' the Yorkshire DI had come up and whispered into his ear, only too aware of what was going through Kennedy's head.

"You're no good to her and you're no good to me if you're going to want to satisfy the fire I can see burning in your eyes. We can never ever make up for the loss of this life. Listen to me, and listen to me good. All we can do, all we must do, is be logical and method-ical about this and go out and forget revenge and use the brains God gave us along with our eye, and find out who did this. We must use our guile and our cunning to track them down and hand them over to the courts. That's it, that's where our job ends. If we do this and do it good, perhaps in some small way we send out a message that says, "Do this on our patch and you're not going to get away with it". That's all we can do. To do it any differently, no matter how popular they make it appear in movies, makes us no better than the scum we are up against.'

The Yorkshireman's words didn't make dealing with corpses any easier for Kennedy but it did give him the resolve as to what he wanted to do in the police. Perhaps that initial drive and enthusiasm had carried him along to the extent that he didn't need or want to get mixed up in the world of police career politics. He was happy to get on with his work as long as he was allowed the freedom to do what he was best at: solving crime, leaving the politics to the likes of Superintendent Thomas Castle.

'Kennedy?' the voice at the other end of the phone called out, 'You still there? You still with me?'

'Sorry, yes, of course.' Kennedy hoped his reply didn't sound like a sigh.

'Kennedy, I don't want to be by myself. Can I come over?'

He wasn't sure of the wisdom of such a visit, but he could hear how much ann rea wanted it.

'Of course,' he replied.

Eleven minutes later, after she rang his door bell at ten-twenty-five, the first thing she said was, 'Thanks, Christy.'

'No. No, no, goodness, no thanks,' he said awkwardly.

'No, I meant thanks for saying, Of course, and not saying, Yes, but I'm tired so can we not talk about us and all this stuff between us?'

'Oh.'

'Let's just have a pleasant evening like we used to and forget about all this stuff. Can we do that, Kennedy?' she said, inter-linking their arms and snuggling up close to his shoulder, making it diffi-cult, but not impossible, for him to shut the door.

'I'll drink to that,' Kennedy announced.

'Great idea,' ann rea replied and they went through to Kennedy's family-room-cum-kitchen. ann rea always said this was her fav-ourite room in Kennedy's house, his room of food, chat and music. She was always suggesting to him that if he discreetly managed to fit a mattress somewhere in his kitchen, it would surely be the perfect room!

Kennedy uncorked the chilled wine, poured a couple of glasses and set about cooking one of his specialties: fresh bread rolls stuffed with crispy bacon and baked beans.

ann rea wandered through to the adjoining front room and fired up the stereo system. Soon Esther Bluewood's deep voice filled the speakers. The opening electric guitar chords, so hypnotic, so compelling, with the repeat echo effect teasing before the big drum sound introduced the lead guitar, which, in turn, played across the echo guitar, heralding the arrival of the most comforting of voices. Although the voice was comforting, the lyrics were always stimulating and sometimes disturbing. Now she was singing about how the body was in trouble. This song got to Kennedy every single time he listened to it. It never ceased to move him. That was before Esther Bluewood had been found lifeless on her kitchen floor. Now the song totally destroyed Kennedy. Now some of the feelings he'd felt behind the Hammersmith Odeon returned and he found himself wanting to grab hold of Paul Yeats' neck and twist.

Kennedy sipped on the wine, trying to concentrate on HP Sauce-flavoured bread roll, leaving ann rea to dance gently around the front room, totally engulfed by the music, her panic attack now apparently over. Kennedy had to admit, no matter what bad stuff went down between them, at that moment he still felt a lot better knowing that she was there with him.

Was that to do with his insecurities? He'd accepted that ann rea was the woman he'd wanted to spent the rest of his life with. He'd equally accepted that this was not the case for her. He even gone further than that and accepted the fact that it was time to deal with it all and get on with his life. Coincidentally, Esther Bluewood started singing 'New Way, New Day', which dovetailed perfectly with Kennedy's thoughts. It was time for the new way on the new day, but the new day could wait until tomorrow. Today he was happy to be sharing this time, and space, and music, with ann rea, the woman he'd been closest to in his life.

In the front room, ann rea drifted on in her dance: she needed this time as much as he did. Kennedy went through and refilled the wine glass in her hand, and he was sure she didn't even notice. Her movements were so gentle she barely caused a ripple in her drink. Her dance might have been gentle, but it was also sensual. Now Esther was singing about one love not being enough, but how there is only one love. The song was about moving much better when you're happy.

It was just when she sang:

When you know why you're happy

It sounded like a plea, like a cry. The power of her voice at that point was so effective she pulled you into the heart and soul of her song. Right into *her* heart and soul. Esther was so brave she held absolutely nothing back from her listener. All of this was set to a gently semi-reggae beat. That was the thing about Esther Bluewood's music: it was so beautifully melodic with concise, perfectly visual lyrics, but, at the same time, intensely rhythmic. It drew you to your own natural dance and a little movement was enough to make you feel that your body was being washed by and immersed in her glorious sound.

All too soon the music was over and ann rea looked as drained as Kennedy felt. They recharged with food and more wine.

'It just gets better and better,' ann rea said.

'Thanks, it's just practice and the magic ingredient,' Kennedy replied.

'Not the sandwich, you fool, her music,' ann rea laughed.

'Yeah, I know, I know. I mean it's such a great record it must have been hard, in a way, to live with it.'

'No, I think she was okay about it. She didn't make the mistake that a lot of people make of trying to re-make it. In her book she'd made it, she was very proud of it and she had no wish to make it again. She was happy to move on to pastures new. It's the sign of a truly great artist; one who can co-exist with their great work. Van Morrison made the classic *Astral Weeks*, and to my humble ears, he's been rewriting it ever since.'

'Oh that's a bit unfair isn't it? He's done lots of great stuff. What about *Moondance*?'

'Don't get me wrong, Kennedy. He did make *Astral Weeks* and yes, there have been several other high points along the way, but in my humble opinion, he's always re-writing his songs. It's like he's lazy or something and you just wish that he'd put some of that creative energy he was enjoying at the time of *Astral Weeks* into some of his other work. Mind you, with a voice like his, a voice to die for, what should he worry what I think?'

'But even Esther's songs…'

'Oh, come on now, Kennedy, she'd been covering other territory. This new set of songs of her were absolutely gorgeous. Probably the most commercial thing she'd ever done. I'm not sure how she would have dealt with all of that pressure.'

'What'll happen to all those songs now?' Kennedy asked.

'They're the property of the Esther Bluewood Estate. They'll make all the decisions. Maybe they'll give them out to other people to do cover versions – and they're certainly strong enough to stand up to a variety of interpretations,' ann rea said, pushing her Beatle fringe back from her forehead, and (as ever) it fell back into an identical position.

'You mean Paul Yeats?' Kennedy asked.

'I hope I don't,' ann rea replied.

Next Kennedy put on The Beatles' *Rubber Soul* album and they listened contentedly to that. By now it was half-past midnight and getting close to that awkward time of deciding who sleeps where. As they were on a promise not to discuss their relationship (or otherwise), this too was an issue to be avoided.

Twenty-eight minutes later, they were in bed, semi-clothed and remaining so. Neither felt like pushing the issue a step further, but both seemed content to take comfort in each other's arms. Kennedy was dropping off. He could hear ann rea purring. Last night they'd spilt up. Supposedly for good. As ann rea purred gently, seemingly feeling very safe and comfortable in his arms, Kennedy resolved they would have to do something about it and do something soon: 'New Way, New Day' and all of that. But the new day would be another day. In his semiconsciousness he thought he heard someone, probably ann rea or it might even had been the ghostly singing voice of Esther Bluewood, saying something about love. He fought to try and recall what was being said and by whom. But it was useless: he was falling under the spell of sleep. All issues of love would have to be resolved in a new way on a new day.

He'd finally fallen under – he thought it was a matter of minutes but in fact it was about two-and-a-half hours – when he was woken up by someone kissing him. Someone? It must have been ann rea. Or was it a dream? He felt unable to wake up completely from his sleep. He was being undressed. All the time, a shower of gentle kisses was raining over him. Head to toe. It was a blissful feeling and he still didn't want to shake the sleep from his head. Perhaps he was scared it was a dream and he'd ruin it. He wanted to prolong and enjoy. For the second time that evening he felt he was experiencing the best there was to experience: once from the lips of Esther Bluewood and her beautiful music, and now this, from the lips of ann rea.

He felt her climb on top of him and the sensation was like never before. Perhaps the 'butterfly technique' had finally paid off, but now he was neither chasing nor resisting, not concerned about being too early or too late. He was simply lying there and he and ann rea were floating together, pleasuring each other. He knew what he was feeling, still not one hundred per cent convinced it was a dream; and he could hear her groans of pleasure as well. On and on they chased the butterfly, drinking in the rich, vivid scenes of the pleasures they were passing along the way. They got closer and closer to the butterfly. It had slowed down to the point it was merely hovering. They were in the meadow and all was as they thought it should be, and, when there was nothing more left to look at and enjoy, they exploded together.

In the afterglow, Kennedy drifted off back to sleep – if indeed he'd ever been awake. If indeed it had ever happened.

A few minutes later, he heard sounds in the room again. This time he was sure it wasn't a dream. This time he wanted to enjoy it more, if that was possible. He considered it for a moment, whether it's possible to enjoy love more in an unconscious state than in a conscious state.

The disturbance in the room wasn't ann rea; this time it was the ringing of the telephone.

Kennedy checked the clock beside the phone: 3.10am.

'Hello?' Kennedy said. He knew he sounded very groggy, he knew he was waving the butterfly goodbye for the night.

'DI Kennedy, it's Desk Sergeant Bell here at North Bridge House,' Flynn's night-shift opposite number announced. 'Sorry to wake you, but they've just found a body. DS Irvine said I should contact you immediately. He felt you'd want to get over there right away.'

'Who is it? Whose body have they found?' Kennedy asked, his voice still sounding groggy, but his brain perfectly clear.

'It's Judy Dillon, the nanny in the singer-suicide case, sir. Irvine said you'd want to know.'

Chapter 31

KENNEDY LEFT ann rea to the remainder of her dreams. He hoped she was enjoying the peaceful sleep of the innocent.

On his walk to Park Village West, the sharp, cold night air helped Kennedy shake the sleep from his head. There was a hive of activity outside Judy Dillon's flat. Strong shafts of light from the house and the various police vehicles, spilled out into the night air, turning from white to cream. Kennedy had never been able to work out how that happened, or if in fact it was an illusion.

The fingers of Kennedy's left hand were twitching furiously by his side as he honed in on the light. He had a habit of doing this at crime scenes and whenever he knew the sight of a corpse was imminent. He used it to delay that final moment, walking in to examine the corpse.

But Kennedy could never have properly prepared himself for the sight he was about to see.

Judy Dillon, the nanny of Esther Bluewood's two children, was lying, eyes still open, staring up at the Virginia Woolf painting above the fireplace. She was on her side on the sofa. Old coffee stains and fresher dark brown patches now contaminated the pretty floral pattern.

Judy Dillon's eyes had frozen in their final view. Whatever she had witnessed last had obviously been unpleasant. The panic she had experienced was recorded and frozen in her stare, testifying to the fact that this particular nanny had not passed willingly or without a struggle into the next world. Kennedy saw that a mixture of chocolate and spittle caused the new stains on the sofa. The stains were still damp. The offending objects were three bars of Chunky Kit Kat, which were protruding from Judy Dillon's mouth. Two still fresh and unwrapped, the third uncovered and rammed further down her throat.

In her final moments, Judy had been dressed in her usual black: elasticated black pants, half-covered with a pleated black skirt – part of the new style, Kennedy was assured by Irvine, but much more flattering on someone carrying half of Judy's fifteen stone. Her black sweatshirt had been hiked up in the struggle, revealing her midriff and the bottom of a black bra. Her stomach seemed to carry folds of loose skin. Perhaps she'd been losing weight faster that her skin could tighten. Kennedy wondered whether Judy had always been overweight, and if she'd ever considered herself to be overweight in the first place.

There was slight bruising on either side of her nose, and her hands were frozen in front of her, giving her the look of an amply proportioned opera singer, going for the final high note of the evening.

She looked as though she was balancing precariously on the edge of the sofa. Kennedy wondered if maybe her murderer had moved her from her death position. There was a strong logic to this as the rest of the small living room was an absolute mess. Her prized books had all been pulled from their shelves and were now strewn carelessly around the room, some open mid-book, pages up, others similarly opened but jacket up.

The journal!

Kennedy recalled Judy words of protest several hours earlier as he and Irvine had confiscated the photocopied version of the journal: 'No, you don't understand, I can't give it to you. I need to be able to give it to him. He's going to be mad at me. I don't like him when he's mad.' Kennedy hadn't paid much attention to her pleading at the time. Who had she been talking about?

Had the detective signed Judy Dillon's death warrant by confiscating her copy of the journal?

Kennedy wandered around the small room, taking everything in. The Scene of Crimes officers quietly and respectfully went about their work, seemingly ignoring the corpse. Perhaps that's how they dealt with the continued presence of death in their work place, thought Kennedy. The wickerwork coffee table, which for some reason, had managed to remain upright during the struggle, held an open blue cardboard shoebox, stuffed to the brim with Judy's private stash of goodies. It was like she and the girls had been down to raid the tuck shop for a midnight feast in the dorm. She seemed to have a preference for Bounty Bars, Mars Bars and Kit Kat – original and Chunky. There were also packets of M&Ms and Rolos. The problem, Kennedy imagined, with both of these was that for someone of Judy's girth, a packet of M&Ms wouldn't seem all that filling, so she'd have to satisfy her hunger with Bounty Bars, Mars Bars or Chunky Kit-Kats.

Kennedy himself had a sweet tooth, possibly even two, but he used them to taste not to consume.

The murderer was either planting a misleading clue by stuffing bars of chocolate down her throat, or he was making a statement. Did this mean that Kennedy was looking for someone who, like himself, found Judy's eating habits gross? Or was it merely someone who felt cocky enough to introduce a little confusion?

Dr Leonard Taylor was kneeling on a cushion. A little blue number he always carried around with him for such occasions. Like a magician, he had a habit of being able to produce from either his person, or from his bag, an endless supply of useful items. Once he and Kennedy had been on a case and tea had been available in the police site wagon, but there were no cups. Taylor, quick as a flash, produced two polystyrene cups from inside his bag, not only saving the day in that regard but also providing two plastic spoons to transport and stir the sugar.

Taylor was examining the corpse, humming away to himself as per normal. Was this his way of distracting himself from the reality of death, Kennedy thought? Kennedy recognised Taylor's tunes to be classical or operatic, but that was as much information as he could have offered.

'James tells me our victim was Esther Bluewood's nanny, old chap.' Taylor delivered his lines with theatrical precision so economical you'd have thought he'd an inbuilt editor.

'Yes, indeed, Leonard, I'm afraid her light fingers may have been her downfall,' Kennedy replied.

'How so?'

'Well, we visited her yesterday afternoon and confiscated a photocopied version of one of Esther's journals. She hinted that someone was going to come looking for it and that they would be enraged when he couldn't find it,' Kennedy said.

'So, you're feeling responsible, eh?' Taylor replied, stopping his work momentarily.

'Oh, you know...' Kennedy began.

'Don't!' Taylor lectured. 'We must all take responsibility for our actions, old chap.'

'I suppose so,' Kennedy said quietly, but already his mind was elsewhere. Either Taylor knew this or else he'd completed his lecture. Either way, he returned to his humming and to the examination of the body.

Kennedy considered the picture of Virginia Woolf staring down from over the fireplace, looking very grand, authoritative and educated: every inch the mistress of feminine literature. There wasn't even the slightest hint of the insecurity that would lead to her downfall. Kennedy couldn't help thinking about Esther Bluewood, another of her flock, one with her own set of insecurities, who had fallen prey to the evils of the world.

Kennedy wondered whether Esther Bluewood had also admired Virginia Woolf. He found himself thinking about what he'd just said to Dr Taylor. 'He'd be mad' when he couldn't find the journal. This meant, of course, that if Kennedy believed such a person called at the nanny's flat and couldn't find the journal and consequently murdered Judy Dillon then that person was a man. If the detective pushed this envelope even further and accepted the fact that the self-same person who had killed Dillon had also killed Bluewood, then Esther Bluewood's murderer would most definitely have been a male.

But this was pushing the bounds of credibility far beyond levels acceptable to Kennedy at this stage. He reminded himself he was an information collector and that he should only accept such a conclusion when the evidence in its favour was overwhelming. Which meant that he couldn't just yet remove the names of Rosslyn St Clair and Tor Lucas from the original murder's suspect list. Mind you, he could definitely rule out Rosslyn St Clair as Judy's murderer, as she'd have been tucked up in her hospital bed.

But Tor Lucas, that was a different matter entirely. And equally if the 'he' Judy Dillon referred to had been Paul Yeats, then he could very well have sent his sister, Tor, to do his dirty work. Could he also have sent her to do his dirty work with Esther Bluewood? Yeats had already demonstrated, on more than one occasion, how desperate he was to get his hands on her journal. What was the big deal? Kennedy had read it through and had found several unflattering references to Yeats within the pages, but probably not enough to justify killing two people over, even considering Paul Yeats' exceedingly large ego.

'I'd say,' Taylor announced, breaking Kennedy's thought process, 'that the victim was killed no more than five hours ago. I'll be able to pinpoint a more accurate time after autopsy but for now, a guesstimate would be between 10pm and midnight. She was very crudely suffocated, probably leading to a heart attack. Someone blocked her wind pipe with all this chocolate and pinched her nostrils together, probably with thumb and forefinger. I imagine our murderer sat on top of her and the poor victim's weight would have worked against her. I would also guess that death wasn't immediate.

She would still have been able to gasp in some breaths of air via her mouth. The chocolate bars wouldn't have provided an airtight seal, which would have meant she probably struggled for some time. I doubt if she put up much of a fight, though.'

'Mmmm,' was all Kennedy could find to say.

'The fact that someone was trying to kill her, old chap, would also have been a contributing factor in her death, especially if it was a heart seizure.'

'But wouldn't that have made her fight more violently to save herself,' Kennedy asked.

'Normally yes, but you have to remember that she was very unfit, very unhealthy. She probably would have felt totally helpless and eventually her heart would have given out.'

Kennedy had an idea.

'Is there a chance someone could have been torturing her?' Kennedy asked. 'You know, while trying to get information out of her, she died by accident; I mean, before the murderer meant her to die? That is, if they did mean for her to die at all.'

'Quite possibly, old chap, that would also give a better explanation for the presence of chocolate bars. I mean, you're hardly going to try and kill someone by shoving bars of chocolate down their throat, are you?' Taylor replied.

'Precisely,' Kennedy said, a hint of excitement creeping into his voice. 'Whoever it was just pushed it too far. In searching for the whereabouts of the journals, they just went that one step beyond. The poor girl probably kept protesting that she didn't have it any-more, he didn't believe her and she quite possibly died accidentally.'

'Now, you're back to thinking that if only you'd left the journal there, she'd still be alive,' Taylor said.

Kennedy made to protest.

'Don't,' Taylor reprimanded his friend for the second time that night. 'Who's to say that if you had left the journal and she had surrendered it to our suspect that they wouldn't have murdered her anyway to hide the evidence of the journal's whereabouts. They've already shown how desperate they were, or still are for that matter.'

Kennedy knew full well that Taylor was correct. Wasn't he constantly lecturing his team about not breaking police rules to accommodate individual theories? That can lead to the police breaking the law and where is that going to end?

'What's in this journal that is so explosive?' Taylor asked, packing his instruments into his magic bag.

'Well, I obviously missed something. I've read it through, but apart from Miss Bluewood being brutally truthful about certain people, there's really nothing I'd consider explosive in it,' Kennedy admitted.

'Maybe you should have another read through, old chap?' Taylor suggested, as he struggled to his feet. First he rose so that one knee and one foot was on the ground and then he pushed down with all of his might on his raised knee to hoist himself into a vertical position. He was still stooped over at waist height, so he put both his hand behind himself and massaged the small of his back. (Quite a difficult task owing to his girth and the chubbiness of his arms.) Eventually he worked his body into the fully upright position.

Taylor okayed Judy Dillon's remains to be placed in a body-bag, and as he squeezed past Irvine to leave the small room, he called across to Kennedy: 'I'll give you a shout with the results later.'

'Fine,' Kennedy replied absently, waving his friend goodbye. He then turned to DS Irvine: 'Who found the body?'

'The upstairs neighbour,' Irvine replied, checking his notes. 'A Mr Bill Cunningham. He says he was woken from his sleep by noise from downstairs. He said he couldn't be sure if what he was hearing were groans of pain or pleasure. That's why he thought it all might be a dream. Some time later the groans sounded more like someone in trouble. Again he thought he was dreaming, then he was woken for sure by someone causing havoc below. It went on for several minutes. He thought it might be a lover's tiff. Usual thing, he didn't want to interfere. Then several more minutes of wrecking noises, quiet for a few moments, then someone walking down the hallway, then the front door opening and closing. He waited a few minutes but couldn't hear any further activity. He thought everything was okay again so he tried to get back to sleep but he couldn't. He was troubled, he said. He didn't want to be accused of being an interfering busy-body. He said neighbours never thanked you for it. They tell you to mind your own business and, he claimed, never politely. But tonight he said he had a bad feeling and that he'd never have forgiven himself if he'd not called us. So he rang about 3am, sir.'

'And here we all are, James,' Kennedy said, surveying the SoC people on their hands and knees, tweezers in hand, searching for something, anything, just as long as they could stick it into their little plastic bags and label them up.

Kennedy hoped they were going to put some vital evidence into these little bags. If, as Dr Taylor suspected, this was not a planned murder, then there must surely be something within the reach of a pair of tweezers that could lead Kennedy and his team to the murderer.

Chapter 32

ON THAT Thursday morning, Kennedy walked the short distance from Dillon's flat to North Bridge House along tree-lined streets, wet with rain. As he avoided a water-logged mess on the pavement, he wondered whether, as the original inhabitants of what was now the headquarters of Camden Town CID were monks who had kept goats, goat do-do was as big as hazard then, as dog do-do is now.

He pulled up the collar of his crombie to shelter him from the cold, dark and lonely November morning. For the first time since he'd left ann rea in his bed, four hours earlier, he thought about her. He thought about *them*, him and her. What a weird relationship it had turned out to be.

Would he have bothered chasing her in the first place if he'd known how it was going to turn out? But where exactly were they now? Yesterday he would have described the relationship as in the dumper. But was it now back on again? And if so, what level were they now on? Physical seemed to be the operative word. At this time in their lives Kennedy and ann rea were enjoying a very physical relationship. Kennedy wasn't complaining. Oh no! He was counting his blessings.

During the 'off' sections of their on/off relationship, Kennedy was convinced that he had slept with a woman for the last time. He was convinced there would be no one after ann rea; that he wouldn't want anyone other than her. But he felt deeply disappointed by her inability to conduct or finish a relationship, and he suspected that this might have had some bearing on his thinking.

But the more regular became their periods of inactivity, the more he found himself regretting the times they could have made love and hadn't. If you'd have told him, when he was first chasing her, that there were occasions in the future when he and ann rea would be in bed together and would not be making love, he would have said, with 100 per cent conviction, 'No way!' exclamation mark and all.

It had happened, though. They had been together several times when, for one reason or another, they hadn't made love. He found himself recalling each and every one of those occasions. Had he known what was going to happen, had his crystal ball been working then he would surely have taken better advantage of the situation each and every time. If Kennedy were now to enjoy a loveless life then he would need a reserve of memories to see him through the lonely times.

Perhaps last night had been an opportunity to add another to the memory bank. What an addition it was, too. If that had been the final one, then that was fine, because there were few, if any, love-making sessions which had been better. The fact that there was no border between dream and reality made his reality open to inter-pretation. Then he had a thought. ann rea had asked him only a couple of days before if he'd wanted to have a child with her. Was that was this was all about?

Kennedy had just tuned into this thought when he arrived at the steps of North Bridge House. He was surprised when entering the reception area to find Josef Jones waiting for him.

'I've got to talk to you, urgently,' Jones announced immediately. He was dressed in his usual four-button, two-piece black suit and white shirt, top shirt button done-up, but no tie.

'Sure,' Kennedy said pleasantly. 'Come on through.'

'Ahm, I'd like to make this official. You know, with a witness and a tape recorder type of scene,' Josef announced. The few people in the reception turned to stare at the smartly dressed young man with the sinister voice.

'Oh?' Kennedy replied, slightly taken aback. He opened the buttons of his crombie and continued. 'That's fine. Should we also send for your solicitor, Josef?'

'Crikey, no, Inspector.' Josef smiled clumsily. 'It's not a confes-sion or anything like that. It's just a piece of information really. I just think we should keep it all official.'

'By all means, Josef,' Kennedy began. 'Tell you what, you wait here, Sergeant Flynn and I'll go and set everything up. Round up a witness or two.'

*

'For the record,' Kennedy announced to the microphone, which was suspended like a giant dead daddy-longlegs from the ceiling, 'we are here to interview Josef Jones. He has some information he wishes to volunteer. Josef, would you confirm, for the record, your name and address and the fact that we've read you your rights and offered you a solicitor.'

'I'm Josef Evan Jones of Kentish Town and I'm here of my own free will to give the police some information I think may be relevant to them in a case they are currently investigating. I—'

'Don't get carried away just yet, Josef.' Kennedy felt he should interrupt the young man in case he gave away the entire plot of the movie before they'd a chance to roll the opening credits. 'Those present are myself, Detective Inspector Christy Kennedy and...

'Detective Sergeant James Irvine,' the DS announced in the space Kennedy had left.

'I wanted to tell you—' Jones made a second attempt to tell his story.

'Sorry, Josef, could you also please confirm that you have been offered, and declined, a solicitor.'

'Hmmm,' Jones cleared his throat, he was clearly bursting to start. 'I can also confirm that I was offered the services of a solicitor. I was further advised that if I couldn't afford one the court would appoint one for me. Now can I start?'

'Yes, Josef,' Kennedy said in his usual soft, quiet, calm voice. 'Please tell us what you need to tell us.'

'Phew,' Jones blew air through his lips. 'I thought we'd never get started. I wanted to tell you that I saw Judy Dillon yesterday evening.'

Now that was worth waiting for, Kennedy thought, and worth getting down correctly.

'Tell us more,' Kennedy said, no more formalities to lay out before the young man.

'Ah, I saw her yesterday evening. We were in her flat.' Josef whined.

'Okay. I assume you realise the relevance of this?' Kennedy asked.

'Of course I do. I know she's dead.'

'How do you know that, Josef?'

'I went back to her flat this morning and saw all the police there. A neighbour told me that you'd taken away Judy's body in the middle of the night,' Josef replied innocently.

'Okay,' Kennedy continued. Irvine and the tape recorder listened on. 'Let's go back to yesterday. What time did you see Judy?'

'Let's see now, I went around to her flat about... must have been after ten o'clock last night,' Jones replied.

'Why did you go around to see her?' Kennedy asked.

'Oh, you know. I was missing Esther. We're all missing Esther. It's a hard time for all of us.'

'Did she invite you around or did you just drop in?' Kennedy continued.

'Well, a bit of both really.'

'Come again?' Kennedy said.

'Well, I'd been speaking to her earlier in the day and she'd said if I wanted to, I could come around and see her any time. We had a nice chat about Esther, you see. It was very friendly, very non-competitive. We fans are always trying to get one up on each other and now really there's no point. I think Judy was completely misunderstood. Because of her weight and that, people tended to assume there's not much going on. But she was a very bright girl, very well read. You can see why Esther would hire someone like Judy to look after her children. You know, she'd be happy that they'd grow up in an atmosphere of books and things. Anyway, for the first time I saw another side of her. She's usually quite coarse and hard but I think that's because she's always had to be on the defensive because of her weight. You are either a "Look at me I'm such a jolly fat person" or else you're hard and have a chip on your shoulder. I always thought she was hard and one-dimensional. Quite frankly I used to think she was completely useless. About as useful as a stylist with Abba.'

Jones stopped to laugh at his own joke. When it became obvious the police weren't getting it, he said: 'You know, Abba, the Swedish group, renowned for their poppy songs but not for their dress sense.'

'I got it, Josef,' Kennedy replied deadpan. 'But, anyway, what did you and Judy do around at her flat yesterday evening?'

'We listened to Esther's records. We talked about the old days, we watched a few videos of Esther's rare television appearances. We discussed her lyrics. Judy had a few signed sets of lyrics she showed me. I never knew they existed. She didn't want to sell them. I told her she'd probably get a fortune for them from someone in America now.'

Jones stopped talking for a minute, appearing remorseful. 'You know what she said?' he started in his high-pitched whine. It was hard to tell, because of the texture of his voice, if he was being emotional or not. 'She said that the lyrics were worth nothing to her because she'd never ever sell them. She'd keep them forever, no matter what she was offered.'

Near-quiet reigned in the interview room. The only noises beneath the white-washed high ceiling were the ticking of the clock on the wall, the gentle hum of the tape recorder, and the faint buzz of the neon strip lights.

'And that was it? That was all you did? Just talked, listened to music and looked through her collection of Esther's signed lyric sheets?' Kennedy asked.

'No, we had some wine and... ah... then we made love.'
Kennedy and Irvine looked at each other in disbelief.

'Then you made love?' Irvine stammered, his first question of the interview.

'Well, yes. I mean, it wasn't planned or anything. It just kind of happened,' Josef admitted shyly.

Kennedy held this thought for a few seconds. 'It just kind of happened.' By any stretch of his imagination he couldn't imagine how it could 'just kind of happened' with Judy Dillon. She was probably a nice girl and all that, but Josef Jones wouldn't have been sitting beside the nanny, talking one minute and getting naked the next.

Who would have done what? And how? That was one of the world's major mysteries to Kennedy – how people managed to get it together. The whole scenario was pretty preposterous, when you thought about it. What we all do to each other physically and then on top of that, if that weren't enough, what we use to do it. Come on, really! Sometimes, Kennedy wondered how mankind had managed to last so long. Other times – usually when he was with ann rea as in *with* ann rea – he wondered how the population managed to stay so low.

'Really?' was the only word Kennedy could find to say, and in saying it, he returned to the broadest Ulster accent he'd ever used.

'Yes. Really!' Jones replied in a high-pitched, indignant whine.

'No, it's just...' Kennedy was flustered now, aware that the recorder was catching his every word and inflection. '...It's just that the last time we spoke, well... you betrayed none of this affection, where did it all suddenly come from, Josef?'

'Grief,' Jones replied. 'It came from our united grief. We'd both lost a very important part of our lives. I shared something special with Esther. She hadn't been with too many men in her life, you know. She wasn't like some of the slags in the music business. She wanted me. She picked me to spend time with. I was special to her. I cared for her more than that ass Yeats ever cared and now he'll get control of everything. Bit by bit he'll start to rewrite history. In ten years time people like Judy and myself... Oh feck!'

Jones checked himself at what he was about to say. 'You know what I was about to say. I was about to say that in ten years time even people like Judy and myself will doubt our memories of Esther. Then it hit me Judy's gone, she's not going to be with us in ten years time.'

'So you and Judy got together because of your mutual grief?' Irvine asked. Kennedy sensed a spot of lip-biting.

'Yes. I'd have to say simply and honestly, yes. I didn't go around with the intention of making love to her. As I say, it just happened and neither of us regretted it,' Jones said.

'How much time did you spend at Judy's flat, yesterday evening?' Irvine asked.

'A few hours, I'd say.'

'What? Say, two hours? Three hours? Just how many hours, Josef?' Irvine continued.

'Maximum of two-and-a-half, I'd say.'

'Ahm, I know this is a delicate question and I hope you won't take offence but can I ask you how many times you made love during that two-and-a-half hours?' Kennedy elected himself to ask the question both he and his DS were leaving up to.

'Pl—ea—se!' Jones screeched. There wasn't much variation from his normal tone; he was just an octave higher.

'I know, call me insensitive if you must, but it is important, Josef,' Kennedy said by way of explanation.

'Why just once of course,' Jones admitted.

'Okay. Okay. We've got that part out of the way now. You came around about seven-thirty and left about ten then?' Kennedy asked, hoping to move right along.

'Yeah, pretty much.'

'And when you left, did you see anyone else loitering around?' Kennedy asked.

'No.'

'Anything suspicious?' Kennedy said.

'Nothing at all.'

'Tell me, Josef. This love making between you and Judy, did it happen at the beginning of the two-and-one-half hours or did it happen at the end?' Kennedy asked, swinging back to pick up a few stragglers.

'Towards the end, I suppose.'

'And, ahm, did you have a drink of anything?' Kennedy said.

'We'd some wine.'

'A little wine, a lot of wine?' Kennedy pushed.

'Sorry? What does it matter?'

'Well, you'll have to forgive me, Josef, but the way I see it, you're a well-dressed, handsome young man. You are, I believe, what your contemporaries would define as "cool". So you're not exactly short of women friends now, are you? You admitted to us you've been to bed with Esther Bluewood. Now with the greatest of respect, Judy Dillon was no Esther Bluewood.'

'Some of us hide our beauty within, detective,' Josef said, cutting across Kennedy's flow.

'Exactly, Josef; that's my point exactly. I would agree with you that Judy probably did conceal her beauty. Now a little drop of wine might possibly have loosened both of you up. Can you see what I'm getting at here?' Kennedy asked, grateful for the lifeline.

'I had a few glasses of wine. I was merry. Yes. I wasn't drunk.'

'I have another question I need to ask you, Josef. Again, it's not meant to upset you,' Kennedy said, hiking his shoulders into a 'Can I ask the question?' pose.

'Yes?'

'Ahm, did you wear any kind of protection?'

'This is unbearable. *Ple*-ase don't forget I came in here of my own free will to give you information I thought might be helpful to your inquiry.'

'Exactly, Josef,' Kennedy said, 'and the answer to this question will give us a vital piece of information. I need to know the answer, so that when Doctor Taylor is carrying out his autopsy... Well, you know...?'

'No. I did not wear any protection. As I said, it wasn't a planned romantic interlude. It just happened, and that's that,' Josef said. Kennedy half expected him to dust off his hands in a classic Stan Laurel action, as his high-pitched whine continued: 'And now gentlemen, I don't believe I have any more information I have to give you. If that's okay, I'd like to—'

'Why yes, of course, Josef. If you'd like to leave, you've always been free to do so,' Kennedy said, as much for the tape recorder as for Josef.

Josef rose from the table as if to go.

'But,' Kennedy began, 'I do have one final question for you.' Josef flopped despondently back in his chair.

'What did you do after you left Judy Dillon's house?'

'I wandered around Camden Town for a while. It's top you know, Camden Town at night time. Such a blast! I caught the 29 bus and I was home about eleven-thirty or so.'

'Okay, Josef, that'll do for now. We'll see you later if we need to.'

*

'God,' Irvine began, after they'd shown Josef Jones to the front door of North Bridge House. 'He seems to do well with a certain bunch of women who aren't Corrie fans. If you're to believe him, there's a host of women out there waiting for men to drop in on them at seven-thirty every Sunday, Monday, Wednesday or Friday. They're all ready, willing and able to do anything that will spare them from having to watch the telly. And the sad thing is, I haven't met one of them yet.'

Chapter 33

'WELL, THE first obvious thing must be that there's got to be something vital we've missed in Esther's journal,' Kennedy said, enjoying his first cup of tea of the morning.

'But why would Josef Jones be so desperate to get to it? What would he have to lose?' WDC Anne Coles asked, still glowing from her early morning swim.

'Perhaps he was looking on behalf of someone else?' Irvine offered. He'd been up the longest, and by the look of him, was probably the last to bed. That was, of course, assuming Kennedy's chasing the nocturnal butterfly qualified as bedtime.

'Okay, let's go along that route for a moment,' Kennedy said, walking over to his noticeboard and removing Rosslyn St Clair's name card from the list of suspects.

'Is that wise, sir?' Irvine asked, before Kennedy had a chance to bin her name card.

'Well, I think we can accept that the murder of Esther Bluewood and the murder of Judy Dillon are connected. If so...' Kennedy began.

'I'm not so sure we can accept that at this stage, sir.' Irvine added.

Kennedy smiled. He was happy. Irvine was following one of the Detective Inspector's prime rules: Don't make the crime fit the facts.

'Good point, James,' Kennedy began, returning St Clair's name card to the board. 'Let's assume for now that the murders are not connected. Okay? At the very least we can rule her out of the murder of Judy Dillon. Can you accept that?'

'Yes,' Irvine beamed proudly. 'Well, at least any direct involvement.' Kennedy was convinced that his Sean Connery accent was stronger than usual. 'She was in hospital in the Cotswolds at the time of that murder.'

'Do we know how she's doing?' Kennedy asked Coles, as he returned to his desk and his tea.

'Yes. I checked with the hospital this morning. They say she had a comfortable night. She's off the danger list now apparently and she's going to be okay. I'll go up and see her later if you like,' Coles said, removing a wisp of fine blonde hair from the side of her face, and trying to place it back into her very complicated hair arrangement. Eventually she had to settle for tucking the offending strands behind her ear.

'Yes, I would like that. As DS Irvine rightly pointed out, we need more information before we can start eliminating anyone,' Kennedy said. He rested his elbows on his desk and clasped his hands together. He then pulled his hands apart ever so slightly to break the triangle, and clicked his forefingers together, once, twice, three times, before he continued: 'So. Back to Judy Dillon. Whoever murdered her was obviously looking for something. We have to assume it was the journal. She panicked when we took it from her yesterday. Now, Josef Jones, Paul Yeats and Tor Lucas had reasons to want those pages. Although, mind you, it was only a photocopy, so it wasn't as if they were going to be able to completely destroy any evidence. Paul Yeats knew that. He's being trying to get his solicitors to get the original journal back from us. When I read through it, I must say I didn't pick up on anything significant enough for anyone to lose their life over. Okay, Miss Bluewood wasn't at all flattering about the three people I've mentioned. But by now, Yeats must have been well used to the adverse press he'd been getting. Josef seemed extremely proud of his association with Esther, so he could be concerned about what might come out. But as for Tor, I don't know her game at all, only that she's very ambitious and desperate to make a career connection – and it doesn't even have to be her own career. She does have one secret she wants to keep from her brother: the relationship she's been having with a married man, a family friend.'

'God, what an utterly chaotic scene of domestic disharmony,' Coles said, her voice filled with exasperation.

'I couldn't have said it better myself,' Irvine said, smiling at Coles.

'So, are we saying that Jones would have been the only one with a real reason for chasing the journal?' Coles asked, faking a smile back at Irvine.

'But he came in here this morning to admit that he had spent yesterday evening with Judy in her house,' Irvine said.

'Best form of defence is attack,' Kennedy reminded them. 'He knew we'd eventually track him down through DNA testing. Think about it. He was very clever. Evidence of his person is all over Miss Dillon and her flat. He knew clearing it up would have been a near impossibility. So, instead he calmly waltzes in here and says he had sex with Judy Dillon yesterday evening. Completely invalidates in one statement all the work of our team of experts. All he has to say is, "I was there, we had sex. I left her and when I left her she was alive".'

'Then our question would have to be, "Was the murder premeditated?" Did he go there to fetch the journal and stop her telling anyone of his interest? So, he thought, I'll make love to her, that'll take care of the DNA rubbish, cop the journal and then top her.'

'Gross,' Coles said. 'That would mean there had been some sort of relationship going on before. He couldn't have gone there thinking that she would just make love to him at the drop of a hat, would he?'

'Good point,' Kennedy said. 'When we receive Taylor's report, we'll hopefully be able to see if maybe she was raped.'

'No, no,' Irvine complained. 'Jones is too clever for that. And look at him, look at her. Of course she'd have to have been overjoyed to have sex with him.'

'And why's that?' Coles asked, looking down from her very high horse.

'Well, I mean to say, come on... Please, does it need to be spelt out?' Irvine said.

'Moving right along, then,' Kennedy said, cutting into their friendly banter. He, for one, certainly didn't want it to be spelt out. 'I think we need to dig up some more information. There are still too many gaps. Okay, Anne, you're going to catch a train back up to see Miss St Clair?'

Kennedy had taken to addressing Irvine and Coles by their Christian names, but only when the three of them were alone together.

'James, what I'd like you to do is to go and interview the man from the gas company again. Find out from him the exact sequence of events from the minute he arrived at Esther Bluewood's maisonette on Monday morning. Also, take him back to Fitzroy Road and have him empty the gas meter. I want all the coins in the box dusted for fingerprints.

Just then Kennedy's phone rang. It was local solicitor, Leslie Russell.

'Hi, how are you doing?' Kennedy asked, as Coles and Irvine both made pantomime gestures about leaving Kennedy's office. Presumably, Kennedy thought, to get on with their work. He gave them a quick thumbs up, swinging around in his chair when they finally left the room.

'I'm fine, thank you,' said Russell. 'Look, this is a wee bit awkward. I was looking for ann rea. It's very important, official business of course, and she's not in at the paper yet. I wondered, would you have any idea where she is?'

Since when did dinner dates constitute official business? Kennedy thought, but he said: 'Yes, as it happens I do know where she is. Let me give her a call and ask her to ring you straight away.'

The detective thought that was the most discreet way to go about it. There was no point in telling Russell where she was, as it might compromise ann rea with the solicitor, although for the life of him, Kennedy couldn't think why. Yes, Leslie Russell had invited ann rea out twice. On both occasions it was Kennedy's view that Russell thought that they (Kennedy and ann rea) were no longer an item.

'That would be very kind of you. This entire Esther Bluewood thing is a bit of a mess, isn't it? I hear now that the nanny has been killed. Any idea who committed the murders? I assume they're connected,' Russell said.

'I'll get back to you on that, when I know the answer myself,' Kennedy said with a laugh in his voice.

'Sorry, yes, of course, you're still working on it obviously.'

Kennedy suddenly had a thought. 'Tell me, Leslie, do you represent Paul Yeats, by any chance?'

'No. I don't actually. Coincidentally, though, he and his sister have been on to me a few times recently about doing some work for them. Trying to hire me...' Russell said.

'And?'

'I had to decline,' Russell continued, a master in the art of discretion.

'And why would that be?' Kennedy asked, pushing discretion to its limit.

'Oh, there was a possible conflict of interest. You see, I represented Esther Bluewood and I now represent her estate. Anyway, I can't say much more about it now, but I'd really appreciate it if you could get miss ann rea to ring me.' Russell sounded like he couldn't contain a chuckle, and when it burst free, Kennedy spoke:

'What's so funny, Leslie?'

'No, it was just that when I said her name in that form, you know, "miss ann rea", I wondered if the M of Miss is in upper or lower case,' Leslie said, sounding a little embarrassed that he'd had to spell out the reason, for fear the detective might have thought the solicitor was laughing at something else.

Kennedy agreed it was amusing, and said that perhaps Russell should ask the journalist when he spoke to her.

Kennedy clicked the cradle of the phone with his finger and immediately dialled another number, the number to his house in Primrose Hill, in fact. It always felt strange dialling the number to his own house when he wasn't there. How would he feel if a total stranger answered the phone? Kennedy had lived at 16 Rothwell Street for 12 years now. It was just a skip away from the foot of the most beautiful hill in London. This was the first address he'd called home. Up until then, no matter where he lived in London, he'd always referred to 'home' as his parent's home at Portrush in Northern Ireland.

The house was a two minute walk from the Queen's pub and restaurant where Kennedy and ann rea dined frequently. He was thinking about the Queens when ann rea answered the phone. She still sounded sleepy, even though it was nine-thirty. Kennedy had already done what he considered half a day's work by then.

'Hi, lazy bones, don't you have work to go to?' Kennedy said, trying to sound as up-beat as possible.

'Well, hello and good morning to you, too. The paper comes out today, so I don't usually get in until about midday on Thursdays,' ann rea said, adding quickly (maybe, Kennedy thought, a little too quickly): 'I've still a couple of hours to kill if you fancy coming back?'

'Well, now: maybe you have, maybe you haven't,' Kennedy said into his phone. At that moment there was a knock on the door, followed very quickly by the breezy entrance of Superintendent Thomas Castle. Before Kennedy had a chance to welcome his superior in, offer him a seat, say he wouldn't be a moment, or any combination of the above, Castle had plopped himself down on the comfortable leather chair opposite Kennedy's desk. Kennedy mouthed 'Be right with you' at Castle, who nodded in return. Kennedy continued down the phone: 'Look, could you please ring the solicitor, Leslie Russell, as soon as possible. He says it's urgent.'

'Your voice has changed, Kennedy. Has someone come into the office?' the tiny electronic voice in his ear piece said.

'Yes, that's right, he says it urgent.'

'Is it James Irvine?'

'Ah no, that won't be necessary,' Kennedy replied.

'Don't tell me it's that Anne Coles. I keep telling you you're seeing too much of her now that she's out of uniform. She's not out of uniform in your office is she?' ann rea said, not letting Kennedy off the hook.

'No. Sorry, I mean yes. I mean not that way, no. I don't think so. Try higher,' Kennedy said, smiling at Castle, who by now was starting to wriggle in his seat.

'Oh, higher than Coles, but not Irvine, now let me see…' ann rea said. Kennedy knew she was teasing him now. He just wanted to extricate himself without Castle picking up on the fact it was a personal call. Here he was, a grown man in his forties and he was behaving like someone who'd been caught out by a schoolteacher. Mind you, Castle probably acted in exactly the same way when his superior caught him on the phone, and that superior was probably the same with his superior, until you could go no higher, and even then he or she would no doubt behave in a similar way with *someone*, probably their wife or husband, who in turn was probably the same with someone, maybe even a junior bobby on the beat, thereby completing the full circle.

'At a guess, I'd say you were with Superintendent Thomas Castle,' ann rea offered.

'Yes, actually,' Kennedy said, hoping his sign of relief wasn't apparent to his superior. 'That's also correct, but I think you might have more relevant information after speaking with Russell, okay?'

'Sounds very official, Kennedy, but what I'd really like to talk about is what we were doing last night when you were pretending to be asleep,' ann rea said impishly.

'Yes, I'm quite sure that more information will come to light on that at a later time. However, in the meantime I'm just about to start a meeting…'

'Oh come on, Kennedy, you can't get off that easy. You enjoyed it as well, didn't you?'

'Quite definitely. However, I think you'll find the process quite complex.'

'Sorry, Kennedy, what's that code for? You lost me on that one.'

'Well, I could always check out some more details and get back to you later.'

'Kennedy, I don't want us to split up,' ann rea said. Either she was being very careless or else picking her moment very carefully, thought Kennedy.

'Yes, you're right, it is very complicated, but I think for a full explanation we'll need more time, and as I said, I'm just about to start a meeting.'

'Yes, yes, yes. Castle is there staring holes in you, I know, but will you give it a try? I know what I want now, Kennedy, I know what I need. It's you I need. I've been thinking about nothing else for the last day and a half. I'm convinced of it,' ann rea said. The fun had gone out of her voice now and Kennedy could hear the desperation creeping in.

He said nothing.

'Kennedy, you still there?'

'Yes.'

'Will you think about it? I mean, you're not going to rule it out altogether are you?'

'No.'

'What, no you won't think about it or no you won't rule it out altogether?'

'I'd say the latter would be the case, and, as I say, I'd be quite happy to go into this in detail later.'

'Kennedy, please tell me you'll at least consider it, give it a chance, give us a chance. I'd like you to see what I'm like when I don't have any doubts, and believe me, I don't have any doubts any more. None at all.'

'God, that's incredible,' Kennedy said, and Castle ears perked up.

'Is that a maybe, Kennedy?'

'That's a definite maybe. I still think you should ring Mr Russell. He did say it was rather urgent.'

'Okay, Kennedy you can say goodbye now, and I'll talk to you later.'

'Yes, rather. We'll speak later, then,' Kennedy said and breathed a silent sigh of relief as he set the phone down. 'Sorry, sir, I just couldn't get off the phone. I think something important has just come to light.'

'Good. Yes, very good. Now, what about this nanny case? What's that all about?' Castle asked.

'Right. Yes, ahm, Judy Dillon was Esther Bluewood's nanny as you've quite correctly observed. She was found murdered in the early hours of this morning.'

'Yes, yes, I know all of that, buddy, but what's this I hear about someone walking into the station this morning and confessing to the crime?' Castle asked impatiently, straightening his already straight tie.

'It wasn't exactly like that, sir. Someone did come in, but it was to give himself an alibi,' Kennedy offered.

'Yes, yes, of course. I'm sure you're dealing with it. Sorry?' Castle stopped dead in his tracks for a second. 'What did you just say?'

Kennedy then spent several minutes relaying that morning's events.

'So, Josef Jones,' Castle began, following the summary. 'He's our man is he? Is he also in the frame for the Bluewood murder?'

'Much too early to say on any front really – we're still collecting our information, sir,' Kennedy said, trying to sound as non-committal as possible.

'I know you, buddy, always trying to go for the complicated option. In my day, we always used to say, "Don't let the obvious scare you off". It may not be as sexy or as exciting, but sometimes the solutions staring you in the face are the real solutions. Two murders in one week, it's incredible, Christy. Get both these cleared up pretty lively, buddy, and we'll be the toast of the Met. Our figures will look great.'

'Indeed they will, sir. I hadn't thought of it in that way, but now you come to mention it, of course you're right.'

'Good. That's it, then,' Castle said, dragging himself out of Kennedy's extremely comfortable chair. 'Don't forget, buddy, I'm only upstairs if you need me. My expereince and expertise are always available to you, Christy. You've only to ask. My office door is always open, figuratively speaking, of course.'

'Yes, sir, thanks.'

Then, staring at Kennedy from under arched eyebrows, Castle said: 'Was that your young lady you were speaking to when I came in? How are you two getting on? Still stepping out? You've really got to get her to come over and have tea with Mrs Castle and myself, you know.'

'Ahm, well… oh earlier… that was…'

'Right then, I'll be off,' Castle announced, terminating the conversation.

'I'll keep you posted on developments, sir,' Kennedy called after his superior, who was disappearing down the corridor faster than a silver bullet. He started to wonder what this 'buddy' thing was all about. Where had it come from? What had Castle been watching on television recently? And ann rea… Castle had clearly known all along and seen through his charade.

Kennedy was still considering the new 'buddy' angle and the ann rea developments when the phone rang. He let it ring a few times before he picked it up. He found that if he didn't clear one thought out of his head properly, then by the time he'd finished his call it'd be gone. Gone forever, unless he took time to jot down a little prompt note. Now he wrote the word 'alibi' on his pad. Although he'd introduced it flippantly into his conversation with Castle, it had set off another train of thought.

He grabbed the phone.

'Hi, Kennedy here.'

'Hi, Kennedy, it's me,' the voice said.

'Yes, ann rea, and a right little troublemaker you've turned out to be, too.'

'Ah, you have to take your chances where you can find them. Listen can I see you this morning?' ann rea said. Kennedy could hear how excited she was. Perhaps she'd been thinking about their earlier conversation and had daydreamed her way through the next chapter or two of their lives.

'It's kind of awkward,' Kennedy started cumbersomely.

'No, no, Kennedy this is official business. This is your business, perhaps. I've just been told that I'm to be the executor of Esther Bluewood's estate.'

Chapter 34

'YOU'VE JUST made yourself two enemies.' These were Kennedy's first words to ann rea, as he sat down with her in the Delancey Street Café, twenty-seven minutes later.

'Really?'

'Paul Yeats and Victoria Lucas, known as Tor to her friends, but of course you won't be able to count yourself amongst that select band,' Kennedy informed her.

The café was filling up with the *Guardian*, *Telegraph*, *Times* and *Independent* gang, displaying their politics on the masthead of their newspapers. What Kennedy called the 'coffee and cappuccino crowd', who serve to warm up the waiting staff before the lunchtime rush. The café decor suited Kennedy; it was cool but not loud. He liked the Delancey staff, they were efficient, helpful, and never in your face.

Kennedy ordered a tea and ann rea a cappuccino. As an afterthought she then added a breakfast of rosti potatoes with two fried eggs and bacon. Kennedy, throwing caution to the wind, ordered the same, requesting that his bacon be crispy.

'Why should they be my enemies?' ann rea asked innocently.

'You've got the gig they both wanted, and at least one of them thought they'd got it. This is what Leslie Russell wanted you for?' Kennedy said, as their drinks arrived.

'Yes,' ann rea said, scooping up a spoonful of creamy froth and cinnamon from the top of her cappuccino, and popping it into her mouth.

Kennedy stared at that mouth and its perfectly-formed, full and very kissable lips. He found himself returning now to consider ann rea's qualities again. During the period they were apart, it was easier not to focus on her strong points. For Kennedy they were many. She had a very kissable mouth, or as Mr Kipling might say, 'An *exceedingly* kissable mouth'.

'What did he tell you?' Kennedy asked, returning to business, for the time being at least.

'He read the will. Everything is to go to a trust fund set up in the name of her children, to be administered until they are twenty-one. Until that time the trust is to pay for their education and upbringing. The house in the Cotswolds is to be sold and the proceeds also go into the trust. All her future songwriting royalties and record royalties go the same way. My responsibility is to protect her songs... now, what were her exact words? Yes, 'in a manner you feel I would have protected them myself.' She made it perfectly clear that she didn't want any unfinished recordings or demos being released to the public. Leslie Russell told me that Esther felt I would be the best person to protect her songs until such time as Jens and Holmer were old enough to understand. The will says I have the final say until such time as I pass on that decision-making process, in writing, to one or both of the children.'

'Has Yeats been made aware of this yet?'

'Yes, he should have been informed by now. He doesn't get a penny, though. Even the children's payments from the trust are to be overseen, approved and signed off by Leslie Russell, who is co-executor of the will. He's meant to look after all the legal stuff and I'm meant to be "protector of the songs", that's how he put it.'

'He'll be happy enough, it will give him lots of opportunities to have lunches and dinner with you now.'

'Oh, Christy, do I detect a hint of jealously creeping in? Just a little?' ann rea said, teasing Kennedy a little.

The waitress chose that exact moment to deliver their breakfasts. Kennedy could feel himself blush a little. He thought he might be blushing a lot from the way his cheeks were burning.

Kennedy had opted for an Earl Grey tea, which was a bit of a risk for him. Sometimes Earl Grey has a taste of rope or twine about it. Kennedy had never been able to work this out properly: maybe it was the milk. But not the Café DeLancey milk: the tea tasted as refreshing and as invigorating as Kennedy knew it should. He took a large swig in the hope that by the time he completed the ritual the waitress would have served them and left them to their privacy again.

'No. It's just that Russell is an opportunist and there's nothing opportunists like more than the gift of an opportunity.'

'It doesn't matter, Kennedy, not anymore. Not that it ever mattered. I was serious earlier on the phone,' ann rea said, tearing into her bacon.

'After all your doubts and all the trouble you put yourself through, how can you be so sure?' Kennedy replied, making a beeline for his bacon, which was crisped to perfection. He didn't fancy sharing it, no matter how much he liked this woman.

'I don't know. When we split up before I never really thought it was for real. I mean, I was serious and all of that, but I still felt that there was something unresolved between us and that we would come back to it in some way, shape or form. But the other night, it seemed so final. Accepting that I was going to lose you meant I had to seriously consider what I was going to lose. After living with this, even for the shortest of times I decided that I didn't want to be without you; that I just couldn't afford to lose you.'

'But...' Kennedy started. ann rea placed her knife on her plate and raised her palm to Kennedy.

'No. Sorry, Christy, let me continue. It's not just a case of what I didn't want to lose. It's also a case of what I now know I want. You! It might have something to do with Esther dying. I don't know. I really don't. I just know I feel like I've wanted to feel over the last few years. I wanted to have no doubts. What can I tell you, they've gone. I'm totally committed to us. I want it to be the whole nine yards. Everything!'

'Do you think this is wise. As you say, it could be a result of how Esther's death has affected you?'

'No, I didn't say it was because of Esther's death, I said it might have been her death that made me start to think about it. There's a difference there. A big difference,' ann rea said between munches.

'Look, I've been dealing with this for so long in a negative sense...'

'What? Are you saying you need time to think about it?'

'No, I don't need time to think about it. This is what I want. I want it so badly I've spent quite a bit of time conditioning myself to accept that it wasn't going to happen. So I need time to take it all in, to accept that it is going to happen. We've spent so much time going around in circles looking for a door and it looked like we were never going to find it.'

'You sure you want to step through it?' ann rea asked.

'Absolutely!' Kennedy replied immediately, unconditionally.

'Great. So what do you think about the Esther Bluewood trust thing?

'I don't think you can do anything but accept it. She knew what she was doing when she chose you. She knew you would protect her songs,' Kennedy replied enthusiastically.

'I'm glad you feel that way. I think it's an honour,' ann rea said, and set about finishing her food.

'But look, one thing: I'd like you to keep a low profile on this for a while. With first Esther and now Judy Dillon being killed, I think you need to be very careful until we find out who's behind it all,' Kennedy said.

'Yeah. But I think Leslie Russell will have to tell all Esther's living dependants sooner rather than later,' ann rea said.

'In that case, I better get back to my case,' Kennedy said.

'Okay, I'll get this. You go. I'll see you later?'

'Yeah, the end of the day, although I don't know how long it'll be.'

'That's fine. Christy…' ann rea reached out and caught his hand as he was turning to leave the table.

'Yeah?'

'I love you.'

'Wow!' Kennedy said, falling back into his seat.

*

Fifteen minutes later, walking up Delancey Street in the general direction of Parkway and North Bridge House, all Kennedy could think about was that on the third Thursday of the eleventh month at eleven forty-seven in the morning in the Delancey Street Café, ann rea had told him that she loved him.

What expression fitted other than 'Wow!'?

Chapter 35

BY THE time Kennedy returned to North Bridge House, it wasn't that the shock of ann rea's proclamation had worn off, more that his brain had reverted to concentrating one hundred per cent on his two murder investigations. He had an idea.

He went to his office and telephoned Leslie Russell.

After greetings were dispensed with, Kennedy said: 'Look, I was wondering if you'd told anyone that ann rea is an executor of Esther Bluewood's estate?'

'No, Christy, I haven't,' the solicitor replied. 'I had to see if she'd accept the position first. Only then can I disclose the details of the will to Miss Bluewood's dependants and to those mentioned in the will. Paul Yeats, in his capacity as legal guardian of Jens and Holmer, the main beneficiaries of the will; Mrs Violet Bluewood, her mother; and Jill and Jim Beck, who are also mentioned.'

'When will all this happen, Leslie?' Kennedy asked, simultaneously checking through a sheaf of reports that had been left on his desk.

'In precisely fifteen minutes,' Russell answered. Kennedy could hear that something else was going on in Russell's office, aside from their telephone conversation. 'Sorry we're just setting things up now. They've all been asked to come here. I'm expecting them to start arriving any time now.'

'You're not thinking of inviting anyone else along, then?' Kennedy asked.

'No. Are you suggesting I invite you along so you can observe people's reactions as they hear the information?'

'No, I'd never suggest anything like that. But can I assume that in about thirty minutes you will have finished reading the will?' Kennedy kept on his route undistracted.

'Yes. It's a relatively short will, I'll definitely be through in thirty minutes.'

'Good, that's all I needed to know. In thirty minutes time it will be in public domain,' Kennedy said, and without waiting for an answer he continued: 'Thanks for the information, it could be quite crucial to me. I'll talk to you later, Leslie, cheers.'

*

Twenty-five minutes later, at twelve twenty-eight exactly, Kennedy was sitting in his office with Tor Lucas in front of him. Conveniently she was in London as Kennedy had anticipated she would be, eagerly awaiting news of the will. Coles had tracked her down and the three of them sat in the interview room, tape recorder running.

'There are just a few more points we need to clear up today, Miss Lucas,' Kennedy began.

'Oh, yes?' Tor replied, puffing up her mushroom hairstyle. She was badly in need of a return visit to the hairdressers. Kennedy imagined it must be impossible to sleep in such a hairstyle every night without ruining it. The rest of her was as immaculately turned out as ever. She had the style, and the money to pay for the style, but not the pizazz required to carry it off. Today she was dressed in a bottle-green, high roll-neck sweater, a three-piece black pin-striped suit, black stockings and black high-heel leather shoes.

'Have you heard how Miss St Clair is doing?' Kennedy asked, apparently by way of introduction. He checked the clock. The second hand was inching its way towards twelve-thirty.

'Yes, I have as a matter of fact. That brother of mine has a lot to answer for. Believe you me, he's not going to brush this one under the carpet. That poor girl, she nearly died,' Tor said, appearing to Kennedy to voice genuine concerns.

Kennedy thought most people would be disgusted by whatever hand Yeats played in Rosslyn St Clair's abortion. Even if there was nothing malicious involved, Kennedy thought it might be stretching the line of credibility too far in Yeats' favour to excuse him for not being there with Miss St Clair when she was going through such an ordeal. Kennedy felt Tor would certainly not have felt good about the way her brother behaved, to say the least.

Tor's biggest fault, as far as Kennedy could see, was that she still insisted in behaving like as nervous giddy teenager, even though she'd probably said goodbye to her teens twenty or more years earlier. It may have been because she was living in a time warp, waiting for her prince charming, Roger Walker, to see the light and abandon his wife and carry her away on his charger – as she thought he should have done all those years ago. Had she blamed her brother for this, the single biggest disappointment in her life? She always looked like a person who could do with hearing good news. Was this a throwback to the days and nights she'd waited for Roger to call?

'We're trying to track down Paul's movements for last Saturday night,' Kennedy said, half in truth, half as a tester.

'I'm sorry Inspector, I can't help you there,' Tor replied, licking her lips.

'You didn't see him at all on Sunday, then?

No. Well, yes… earlier in the day. I mean, no, I didn't see him. We spoke on the phone.'

'How did he seem?'

'He seemed pretty up-beat to me,' Tor said. Kennedy found himself leaning towards her and nodding in an effort to encourage her to say more. 'But you never can tell with Paul. He's one of those artists who believe that if they can engineer a crisis in their lives, it will act as a creative stimulus. Consequently, you never really know what's real for him and what's not. He said he felt sure everything was going to work out for the best.'

'What do you think he meant by that?' Kennedy asked quietly. Tor leaned towards him as though she was having trouble hearing him.

'I think he meant…' again she hesitated.

'Yes?' Kennedy prompted.

'I think he meant that, we… well, the only think it could have been, the only thing we had talked about was getting Esther's songs and his songs published under the one roof, with me running the operation. There was nothing else he could have been referring to.' She paused before continuing: 'At the same time, he knew that a woman, a woman other than his wife, was carrying his child. How was that going to make Jens and Holmer feel? What about our mother? What about Esther's mother, for heaven's sake? Did he think giving me the publishing rights to look after would content me, make up for all the disappointments he'd caused me? Was that the only kind of baby he could give me? That was his solution you know, when he ran into trouble with his women, he gave them a baby.'

Kennedy thought Tor was doing okay without any prompting, but he decided to play his trump card anyway. You never know what's in the other person's hand, he thought, so you should always play your best cards. That way there are never any regrets. He checked the clock – it was twelve thirty-four.

'Did you know that in her will, Esther Bluewood left control of all her songs and of her records to a journalist friend of hers?'

'Sorry?' Tor said, her head jerking up as if she'd just been woken from a doze.

'Yes she, ahm…' continued Kennedy, 'left all her assets including her songs and record royalties and the house in the Cotswolds, to a trust. The trust will take care of Jens and Holmer until they're old enough to take it over. In the meantime it is to be run by her solicitor and the journalist friend of Esther's.'

'ann rea?'

'Yes,' Kennedy replied, feeling further explanation might only complicate matters.

'That figures. Paul was always saying how well they got on and he was consistently complaining that she never wrote anything good about him.' Tor laughed, thought for a few seconds and continued: 'I asked him if she ever wrote anything bad about him and he said, no she hadn't, and I told him he should count his blessings.' Tor thought for a few seconds and then asked: 'And my brother? What did Esther leave Paul?'

'Nothing.'

'Nothing?' she said in disbelief.

'Nothing,' Kennedy confirmed for the second and final time.

'Well, he's cooked the golden goose, then, hasn't he?' Tor said and started laughing. 'All his plotting and planning, all his clandestine meetings, they've all amounted to sweet eff all.'

'What do you think the objective of all his plotting and planning was?'

'I'm afraid, Inspector Kennedy,' Tor began, regaining her poise, 'I fear he may have done what you yourself suspect him of having done.'

Chapter 36

KENNEDY LEFT the interview room immediately, leaving Coles to conclude the interview. He grabbed Irvine, told him to get a car and meet him at the front of North Bridge House in even less time than it takes the nutrition expert at MacDonald's to do his work.

Using Sergeant Flynn's phone, he telephoned Leslie Russell, insisting the receptionist interrupt the meeting still in progress with Paul Yeats. When he eventually managed to speak to the solicitor, Kennedy asked him to stall Yeats until they had a chance to get there. He knew Russell would be in the client's room, which was on the first floor of the solicitor's office, a three-storey house in Camden Square. The deal was that Russell was to keep Yeats on the premises until such time as Kennedy parked up outside. Kennedy wanted to avoid, if possible, having to pick up Yeats on Russell's property.

Kennedy and Irvine parked illegally, directly outside the solicitor's office, and waited – and waited. Eventually Jim and Jill Beck came out through the front door. The solicitor's door opened for a second time and Kennedy and Irvine, suspecting it was Yeats, prepared to get out of the car.

It was Yeats.

The snag, however, was that their exit from the car was blocked by a traffic warden. A total nutter who ignored Irvine's quiet explanation about them being members of the local constabulary. The warden, proud in his green piped suit retorted, loudly, that if they were in fact members of the local police force, then they should know better than to park illegally.

Paul Yeats witnessed all this and jumped over the adjoining fence and ran through the neighbouring gardens.

Irvine was about to give chase when the warden quoted sub-section D stroke oblique 19c and restrained him.

'You can't leave this car, man. This is my patch, man, and I suggest you do as I say. You do what I say when I say it. You come on to my territory, you have me to answer to. Okay, Scottie? Okay, Paddy?' The traffic warden was now playing to the gallery, an ever-increasing crowd had gathered, interested in the commotion.

Kennedy and Irvine looked at each other in complete disbelief.

'What's wrong, boys, don't you understand the Queen's English? Well, let me spell it out for you. You're getting a ticket and if you try to leave this car here against my orders, you'll be further breaking the laws of the highway and be liable to...'

'Okay that's enough, DS Irvine arrest the stupid tosser. Cuff him, dump him in the back of the car and throw him in the cells when we get back to North Bridge House.'

The warden turned vicious, and began screaming and shouting, but at the same time backing away from Irvine.

'Oh, and DS Irvine,' added Kennedy, 'if he resists arrest, do whatever you need to restrain him.' The crowd were now whooping and cheering just like on the *Jerry Springer Show*.

The hapless warden attempted to turn and make a run for it, but some of the crowd, obviously those with a civil consciousness and not, as later claimed, bigots and haters of the traffic regulators, restrained him until such time as Irvine could handcuff him. Derek, the warden, meekly allowed himself to be put in the back of the car and as the police drove off with prisoner restrained in the rear of the car, the gallery burst into applause.

Irvine and Kennedy turned Derek over to Sergeant Flynn and asked him to book him on a charge of 'impeding the police while in pursuit of their duty'. Kennedy further advised Flynn that because Derek had in effect helped a potential criminal escape, they, the police, were going to have to address the matter of apprehending the said criminal before they would find time to attend to the paperwork associated with Derek.

Derek, realising he was being done up like a kipper, shrugged and fell into an 'if only' mood. Kennedy hoped the main thought was 'if only I'd kept my big mouth shut!'.

In the meantime, Paul Yeats was in the frame but on the loose, so Kennedy had Irvine put out an all-points bulletin on him. Over the course of the next day, Yeats was going to get more publicity than he'd enjoyed in his entire career.

'Well, that was a great bit of fun, wasn't it?' Irvine said, when all the excitement had died down.

'Yeah. It was his own fault, though. I tell you, if these traffic wardens don't cool it, pretty soon we're going to get a call saying one of them's been killed by an irate motorist. They're unbelievable.'

'Come on, sir, with respect, some of them must be okay.'

'Perhaps, but if they had any brains they'd surely be doing something else, don't you think?'

They were back in his office now, enjoying a cup of tea after all the excitement. The phone rang. It was Sergeant Flynn advising Kennedy that a Phil Green from the gas company had turned up in reception asking for either Kennedy or Irvine.

'Good. We'll be out to see him in a second,' Kennedy said. On the way to the front desk Irvine advised Kennedy that he had put out a trace on Phil Green, the first man at the scene of Esther Bluewood's supposed suicide. Irvine had been advised that Green was out on a call. The DS requested Mr Green check in with either himself or Kennedy at North Bridge House as soon as possible.

And here he was in reception chatting with Sergeant Flynn. He apologised to Irvine for being so hard to pin down, but he'd been over in St John's Wood on a call and didn't get the message from Camden CID until about ten minutes ago.

Phil Green was an elongated version of Hannibal Lecter – well, at least of Sir Anthony Hopkin's interpretation of the gourmet serial killer. Perhaps it was the blue boiler suit and blue wellingtons with burgundy toe pieces, that provided Kennedy with the flash. The friendly, yet demonic eyes, and semi-bald head also helped create the illusion.

'I was the first on the scene, my oppo, Packo and myself. We were responding to the call on the gas emergency line from Miss Dillon.' Phil said in his soft Geordie accent. He continuously consulted his notebook as he relayed the information to the police. 'I think she must have dialled and you guys advised us. On the way over to Fitzroy Road I checked the records. We have a little computer in the van. Bugger me, it's great. All mod cons these days. I wanted to see what the installation was. It was a coin-operated meter. A lot of landlords who don't want to be lumbered with former tenants' gas bills make sure meters are fitted so that the tenants have to pay for gas as it's used. When we arrived I turned off the gas in the street as a safety measure, although unless someone had intentionally fed the meter, there was always a good chance that the coins would have been used up. Miss Dillon opened the door for us. She followed us in.'

'Is that usual, surely she could have been danger?'

'I told her to stay behind us, but she wouldn't listen. Bugger me, if she was there beside us all the time, very nosey she was. When we came to the kitchen door, it was closed. I opened it slowly. That was when we saw the body. The next thing I knew, Miss Dillon had collapsed in a heap behind us.'

'You are quite sure that Miss Dillon collapsed before she got near the oven?' Kennedy asked.

'Bugger me, yes, and what a thud. That's a lot of weight to hit the floor. She collapsed just by the door.'

'What happened next?' Irvine asked.

'After we'd made sure she was okay, I checked all the outlets to be sure they'd all been turned off. They were all already off. I remember wondering who'd done it. I assumed Miss Dillon had been in there already and had faked the passing out to make it look like she was seeing the body for the first time. But that's probably just because I watch too many television detective stories.'

'What else did you see?' Kennedy asked

'Well, let me think now, there was a neatly folded lemon coloured towel neatly placed inside the oven and a dark blue towel folded up along the back of the door. I thought about that, sir. Surely if she or anyone else had already been in the house, the towel would have been pushed back to the extreme of the door's opening arc?'

'Did you notice if the towel was back there, in the fully opened position?' Kennedy asked.

'I have to say, I think I was opening the door for the first time,' Phil said. His Geordie roots were obvious by his accent, and he spoke slowly, clearly and confidently. 'I opened the door very slowly. I thought I could feel a little bit of resistance, which would have been the towel. You know all the signs made me think it was a suicide. Like that towel carefully placed inside the oven so that the head doesn't get too uncomfortable as the gas does its evil work. And a towel behind the door to make sure gas didn't escape to the rest of the house.'

'So, to get this totally clear: you definitely did not turn off the gas taps on the cooker?'

'No. They were all turned off already.'

'You're quite sure about that?' Kennedy pushed further on this point, stressing it's importance.

'Bugger me, yes. They were all off. That was when I thought about whether or not Miss Dillon had already been in and turned them off and planted the towel. But I couldn't work out how anyone could plant a towel like that behind the door,' Phil said.

'That part's quite easy,' Kennedy said, offering a possible explanation. 'You close the door to its narrowest position but just enough that you still get out. You lay the towel down carefully along the

back of the door and then you squeeze out through the small opening you have left. When the next person through the door opens it,
they will invariably open it wider than you. So they think they've
pushed the towel back as they opened the door.'

'Only with Miss Dillon, sir... well, bugger me, she'd surely have
needed the door at the fully opened position in order to get out.'

'That's true,' Kennedy said breaking into a warm smile. 'Well
observed. What did you do next?'

'I checked the meter,' the Geordie said. 'The coins had run out.
That was obviously why the gas hadn't continued to escape. I
thought that was quite clever myself. I thought the woman who had
committed suicide had obviously worked out how much gas she
would have needed to kill herself and put the coins in to match the
volume required. She was allowing just enough gas to escape to kill
herself but not enough to hurt the bairns or blow up the house.'

'How would she have done that?' Irvine asked, enthralled by the
information they were receiving.

'Bugger me if I know,' Phil replied honestly. He thought for a
while. 'Well, I suppose you could light the oven and time how long
each 50p piece lasts. I'm sure some doctor or some expert somewhere has written a book about how long it takes to gas yourself
with a domestic appliance, they'd written books about every other
bugger thing.'

'True. If you're desperate enough to kill yourself, or someone
else, there's always somewhere you can find out the expert way to
do it,' Kennedy said, thinking about his next question. 'Any leaks
from anywhere else?'

'No, we checked the rest of the building. It took us a while to get
in down below,' Phil said checking his notebook. 'Mr Higgins was
slightly overcome. The gas from Miss Bluewood's flat had fallen
through the bare floorboards under the sink and cooker. But as you
know he was fine and when we checked the rest of the house it was
okay too. I turned on the house supply from the street again before
we left. And that's pretty much it, sir.'

'You've been very helpful. Thank you very much, Phil, we really
do appreciate your coming in,' Kennedy said. 'DS Irvine here will
see you out.'

When Irvine returned from his chore, he said: 'Well, that was
interesting, sir. Should I have discovered all of that myself?'

'Nah,' Kennedy sighed. 'Just so long as we found it out in time to
fit it to the picture we are building. If indeed it does fit the picture.'

'But you do have some kind of picture forming now, don't you? Is it Yeats?'

'Well, it would certainly be a good idea to have a chat with him, wouldn't it? Let's see how we're getting on with finding him,' Kennedy said, lifting the phone.

Chapter 37

MID-AFTERNOON: nothing new to report, except that Kennedy had put out an all-points bulletin on Josef Jones. It seemed Jones' social conscience had vanished as quickly as it had arrived. Kennedy now had just two names on his noticeboard suspect list:

Paul Yeats

Josef Jones.

Both were missing or in hiding. But where were they? It would be fractionally harder for Yeats to hide out than Jones, as he still had something of a public profile. Could the two of them have been involved in the murder together? Or could it be that Yeats murdered Esther Bluewood, and Jones had murdered Judy Dillon in a totally unrelated incident?

Kennedy didn't feel quite ready to confront either suspect, but Yeats had left him with no alternative following his flight over the gardens of Camden Square. Jones, on the other hand, needed to be in custody, if only for his own safety. Kennedy still had part of the puzzle to work out. It was all a wee bit uncomfortable for him, as he usually liked things to fall into place of their own accord. He decided to spend his time waiting for Jones and/or Yeats to be apprehended by rereading Esther Bluewood's journal. Judy Dillon had possibly lost her life because of something that was in that journal.

Reading it, Kennedy was surprised at how different an atmosphere it created compared to the classic *Axis* album. Kennedy liked her free-flowing style, and was sure he would have enjoyed her work had she ever got round to writing a novel. If, in fact, she hadn't already written one. Deciding what would come out, when it came out, and how it came out, was now ann rea's problem.

An edited version of the journal would make good reading. He wondered whether provisions been made for such an eventuality in her will. On and on he read, searching for something, anything which would give him a clue.

Suddenly he had a thought. What if there were no clues in the journal. What if Paul Yeats was merely desperate to control everything of Esther's, and he'd heard through the fan grapevine about Judy's copy? Perhaps even from Josef Jones. Perhaps Yeats had paid

Jones to retrieve the journal? Perhaps Yeats knew he was out of the will and the copy of Esther's journal was as close as he was going to get to her estate. That certainly would have made him desperate to get hold of it.

Josef Jones could have heard about the journal from Judy. He, in turn, could have dropped the news to Yeats. It certainly wouldn't have come cheap. If Jones was prepared to kill for it, he would most definitely be making Yeats pay through the nose.

But something just didn't fit. Kennedy felt the threads of the case drift away from him. This usually happened when his theories began to veer too far from reality. One minute he was quite happily working his way through the murder, the method and the suspect, and then, all of a sudden, his premise would go down the dumper. This was no bad thing, because it continually made Kennedy reassess his information. Frequently during this rebuilding process, the missing piece of the puzzle would miraculously appear.

So, his own sister had put Yeats firmly in the frame. If Yeats could murder his own wife, then surely that made him capable of murdering Judy Dillon. Hadn't he described her as the 'nanny from hell'? But that was no reason to kill someone, was it? And as for Josef Jones: had he in fact had sex with Judy Dillon because he knew in advance he was going to kill her, and by having sex with her, he was eliminating vital evidence he might have left about her person and apartment?

Was he being very clever? Kennedy, like everyone else, found himself thinking that if Josef Jones had murdered Judy then he'd hardly have raced into a police station first thing the following morning claiming to have been intimate with her the night before. Or would he?

Kennedy made a decision. He decided, for now, to treat both murders separately. Then he would try and find any thread that might tie them together afterwards. He felt happier for making that decision, and he set about his task afresh. He hadn't progressed very far when the telephone rang.

Surprise, surprise: Victoria Lucas had just walked into North Bridge House with her brother, Paul, who was voluntarily surrendered himself to Camden Town CID.

It was turning out to be one of those cases, Kennedy thought. All he had to do was sit behind his desk and every suspect seemed prepared to walk in from the street and offer themselves up.

*

'I'm sorry, Detective Inspector, I have to apologise,' Victoria Lucas announced for the benefit of the tape recorder and for those present in the interview room at the rear of North Bridge House. Those present were: the aforementioned Tor Lucas; her brother, Paul Yeats (aka Paul Lucas); WDC Anne Coles; and Detective Inspector Christy Kennedy.

'And may we know what you want to apologise about?' Kennedy asked quietly.

'Earlier today I may have inadvertently led you to believe that I felt Paul was in some way responsible for Esther's death.'

'Oh,' was all Kennedy could find to say.

'Oh indeed,' Yeats said. He looked more bedraggled than when Kennedy had spotted him outside the offices of Leslie Russell earlier that day. He was dressed in his usual uniform of corduroy brown suit, well worn and threadbare around the elbows and knees. He wore a green high neck sweater identical to his sister's, perhaps even it was his sister's.

'This has all gotten out of hand, Inspector,' Yeats said, directing his voice to the magic eye of the tape recorder. A common mistake, and Kennedy never ceased to be amazed by the number of witnesses who felt the best way to transfer their voice to the tape was by speaking to the recorder and not to the microphone dangling above them like some minute prehistoric exhibit at the Natural History Museum.

'Look, Inspector, I'll admit I was so mad at Paul I'd have been quite happy for him to go to jail, to be honest. But I think that the only thing you'll find him guilty of would be of making me angry. And I'm still livid with him. I still can't believe the Rosslyn story. He assures me he didn't know anything about it, the abortion I mean...'

'I didn't, of course I didn't,' Yeats said, jumping up from his chair. 'I love children. You know that. Rosslyn knew it too. She felt because of Esther's death it would have been bad blood for us to have a child born at that time. She's very spiritual, you know.'

Coles rose from her chair. The threat was enough to make Yeats return to his seat.

'Did Rosslyn feel Esther would have disapproved of the baby?' Kennedy asked.

'I think she would have thought...' Yeats hesitated.

'She would have felt sorry for Rosslyn,' Tor announced, cutting her brother off. 'Esther knew what Rosslyn would have been letting herself in for. Esther probably thought that if Paul couldn't keep it together with her and Jens and Holmer, how on earth would it have worked with anyone else? Esther also knew that if it hadn't been Rosslyn, it would most definitely have been someone else.'

'Hey, sis, don't speak about me as if I'm not here.'

'You...' Tor turned to her left to face Yeats. She found she couldn't finish her sentence and shook her head instead. 'Just keep quiet, Paul, you're in enough trouble already.' She then turned back to Kennedy and Coles on the opposite side of the table. 'I'm a little to blame as well, I suppose. I was pushing Paul to get me involved in Esther's publishing, telling him I wouldn't look after his publishing unless he could get me Esther's as part of the deal. I suppose I've always been trying to punish him for coming between me and an old flame, many years ago.'

'Must we get into all of this now, Tor? How much dirty washing am I going to have to air in public?' Yeats said, holding his hands up in a 'Stop, please!' pose.

'Look, what I'd like to know,' Kennedy began, growing increasingly annoyed by the brother/sister squabbling, 'is why you can't remember exactly what you were doing or where you were on Sunday evening. Asleep after drink is just too vague.'

'If I'd known I was going to need an alibi...' Yeats started.

'Oh stop that television-detective tosh, Paul, and tell the Inspector where you were on Sunday. Tell him exactly where you were on Sunday afternoon and Sunday evening.' Tor was behaving like a schoolmistress now. She was comfortable in this company, a comfort that came from the fact that she knew she had nothing to fear from Kennedy, or perhaps, Kennedy thought, the comfort was coming from the fact that she knew exactly where Yeats was last Sunday. In a strange way she seemed inwardly happier about something than she had in the morning.

'I can't, you know I can't.'

'You don't have a choice, Paul,' Tor said, her impatience growing. It was as if she needed the information released as much as her brother did. 'If you had told the police the truth at the beginning of the week, you'd have saved them and yourself a lot of trouble. So tell them before I do.'

What on earth could this great revelation be, Kennedy wondered? A revelation that Tor obviously felt would get her brother off the hook.

'I... I was with a married woman,' Yeats admitted.

Now there's a surprise, Kennedy thought.

'There's more. Tell them it all Paul. It wasn't just any married woman, was it?'

"I spent the afternoon and evening with Mrs Tracey Walker'

At first the name didn't mean anything to Kennedy. The family name was faintly familiar, and when he saw how much Tor was gloating he suddenly realised why.

'Isn't she the wife of...?' Kennedy started.

'Exactly. You've got it in one. My big brother was committing cardinal sin with his best friend, Roger's, wife.' Tor filled in the details, beaming from ear to ear.

That wasn't exactly what Kennedy had been about to say. He was going to ask if she was the wife of the man Tor had been having an affair with for years. But Tor had beaten him cleverly to the quick, and diverted the focus of attention on to her brother's infidelities and away from her own

'Yes, Inspector,' Tor continued, obviously she'd a way to go yet, Kennedy thought to himself, 'and I'm sure if you'd care to check this alibi with Mrs Tracey Walker, she'd confirm all of this.'

'Oh, I'm sure they won't need to check personally with her, sis. Surely they can take our word?' Paul Yeats said. He was in deep water and sinking fast, and he needed a lifeline of some kind.

'No, no, Paul, in a case this important they'll most definitely need to check it up personally with Tracey,' Tor said, rubbing her hands.

Yeats looked at Kennedy. If it wasn't a lifeline Kennedy threw to him, at least it was a party balloon.

'Well, sir,' Kennedy said rising from the desk and terminating the interview, 'we'll try to be discreet.'

Chapter 38

KENNEDY THOUGHT it was amusing, as in hilarious, that Paul and Victoria Lucas had used two halves of the same couple for both horizontal recreation and alibi purposes. He didn't, however, find it quite so amusing that one of his two prime suspects had removed themselves from his list. That left only Josef Jones, who seemed to have vanished into thin air.

The man with the high-pitched voice was still missing in action, or at least, missing in Camden Town. A big place, full of numerous warehouses, shops, pubs, clubs, railway sidings, areas of parkland, derelict buildings and offices, canals, locks, street trading stalls; not to mention, railway and underground stations.

Kennedy recalled his recent adventures in the basement of the Roundhouse at Chalk Farm and the wealth of potential hiding places he'd found there. But the question was, where would Josef Jones go? He'd a connection with the Jazz Café, but maybe that was too obvious. Even so, thought Kennedy, it'd be a good place to start.

The Detective Inspector sent Coles and Irvine to check the local pubs for any trace. He recalled Jones stating that he and his mates had a fondness for the Landsdowne Pub in Gloucester Place. That would be their starting point, whilst Kennedy headed off to the Jazz Café at the bottom of Parkway.

Due to open at seven, the Jazz Café was a hive of activity, preparing for another busy evening. Eric Bibb was in the middle of a week-long run, and was on stage, putting his extremely tasty band through their paces. Eric's golden voice served to encourage the best from his musicians. The Jazz Café staff tided, cleaned and polished glasses, washed bar tops, restocked shelves, washed and vacuumed floors, creating an ambient noise, that surprisingly fitted in perfectly with Mr Bibb's cool sound. Kennedy was surprised at how clean the club smelt, a scent somewhere between ocean waves and a pine forest. He couldn't identify it exactly, but he did know it came out of a bottle and was far from the fag ash and stale beer aromas he'd been expecting.

Kennedy struck two bits of luck at the Jazz Café: one good; one not so good. The good was that Josef had dated one of the waitresses there for a time. The duty manager informed Kennedy that he thought she, Amanza, was quite struck on young Mr Jones. The bad luck was, sadly, Amanza wasn't on duty that night. The ever-helpful manager gave Kennedy her address: 121 Gloucester Avenue, fifth-floor flat.

Ten minutes later, Kennedy was in her apartment.

'He was obsessive about that singer Bluewood. I got the chills when I heard she'd committed suicide,' Amanza told Kennedy. They were standing on the staircase leading up to her flat, with Kennedy four steps below her. She seemed reluctant to invite him into her rooms, but she didn't mind talking to him. 'He used to make some really wild claims about her.'

'Like what, for instance?' Kennedy asked.

'Oh, at the time we were falling out, he kept claiming he was going to move in with her, which I found quite amusing as he's terrible with children. He's totally awkward around them, just doesn't know what to do. When I asked him about her kids, he seemed convinced the husband would take them.'

Kennedy wondered why this connection hadn't been made before now. This east European, mid-twenties girl didn't seem at all reluctant to talk about Jones. He supposed the team would have got around to her eventually, especially now there was only one name on their suspect list. The main point of the investigation was to ensure that the detective and his team knew as much about the suspect – in this case Josef Jones – as Jones knew about himself. Kennedy thought back to Esther Bluewood and the demons she'd had to wrestle with in her earlier years, and he wondered whether it was possible for someone not to know, or perhaps not want to know, everything about themselves.

'We're looking for Josef at the minute,' Kennedy said, trying to move the direction of his fact-seeking mission.

'Why? Has he done something wrong?' Amanza asked, starting to look nervous. 'He hurt Esther Bluewood, didn't he?'

'We have reason to believe he may be able to help us with our inquiries into the death of Esther Bluewood and...' Kennedy was also going to mention Judy Dillon but at the last second thought better of it. No reason to frighten her too much. By the way she was reacting to him now, she was already in third-degree jitters. 'I was wondering if you'd any idea where he might be hiding? Anyone you know he may be staying with?'

'You've obviously checked out his flat up in Kentish Town?' Amanza said, moving one step down the stairs towards Kennedy.

'Yeah. We've also tried the Jazz Café. They gave us your address.'

'Oh gracious, I've just remembered. He once took me to this really weird place, it's not very far from here. If you go down to the Engineer, take the steps down to the lock and turn left towards Camden Lock. About a bridge or so down there you'll see this large black iron door.'

'What's in there?'

'It's a storage cellar or something. I think it must have something to do with the railway, 'cause it backs on to the track. Josef seemed to think it was a place where they stored stuff they were taking between the railway and the canal. Anyway, I have to admit I wasn't really paying much attention – it was very spooky. I got the impression he considered it to be his own private place. He told me I should have been flattered he'd taken me there. He was trying to take me there for a bonk, but on the way in I saw a couple of rats and I can tell you the last thing on my mind was making love. I ran back to the door and stood and screamed my lungs out until he helped me unlocked the gate and get out. Afterwards I kind of saw the funny side of it, but he didn't ever. It was like it didn't happen. But God, with Esther's death and everything, can you imagine what might have happened if I'd stayed there with him?'

'Don't worry, you're safe now, but I really need to dash off. I'll send someone around to talk to you in the morning,' Kennedy said as he began his exit taking a couple of steps down the stairs.

Kennedy opened the apartment door and stepped out on to the landing. He turned around to say goodbye, but before he'd a chance to blink, she had closed the door. He could hear her securing locks and rattling the safety chain as he made his way down the stairs and out on to the street. He knew it was only a matter of time before she'd be recalling the many intimate moments she and Jones had shared together. Then she'd have a flash of Esther Bluewood, and that was when her real troubles would begin.

He couldn't imagine where along the canal Amanza had been talking about. He knew the route well – it was on one of his regular (recreational) walks around Camden Town, Primrose Hill and Regents Park – but he couldn't for the life of him pinpoint exactly where she was talking about. He radioed North Bridge House to have Irvine and Coles to meet him on the Regents Canal bank, beside the access point for the Engineer.

By the time Kennedy had walked that very short distance, Irvine and Coles were already there and waiting for him. As they hurried down the steps to the canal-side pathway, Kennedy explained to them what the waitress had told him. It took them all of three minutes to reach the black iron door Amanza had described. It was locked with a padlock bar across the six-inch gap to facilitate opening the lock from both sides of the door. Kennedy peered through the gap.

He saw a steep brick corridor, curved at the top and turning to the right about twenty yards away. Somewhere beyond the turn, there seemed to be a light shining. Kennedy could see its reflection glistening on the wet brickwork. Irvine, showing off one of the talents of his teenage years, picked the lock. It took him less than twenty seconds, during which time Kennedy reflected on what might have been Irvine's career if he hadn't chosen the straight and narrow of the police force.

The ever-resourceful Coles had a torch with her, and the three detectives set off down the brick corridor, the sound of their footsteps echoing all around them. Kennedy put a finger to his lips in the classic pantomime 'hush' signal, and they did their best to muffle their footfalls. But there was still sound all around them. The brick-lined tunnel was filled with its own symphony of watery sounds. Similar, Kennedy thought, to those you'll hear in Victorian men's public toilets, where the distant rush of the water working its way through pipes provides a constant soundtrack. Occasionally, these sounds would be interrupted as the fountains in the urinals erupted, jetting forth a fresh flow of water. To Kennedy, it was somewhat like the sound of numerous balloons suffering slow punctures.

In the tunnel, the metallic rhythms of a train passing overhead answered Kennedy's call for hush. It was either on its way to Birmingham or returning home to London. The original line was built for the Euston to Birmingham service. In total contrast to the ferocious sound of the train, there came the gentle 'tug-tugging' from a canal barge engine, as it passed only twenty yards behind them.

Kennedy had prepared his nostrils for the inevitable foul smells, but unusually, none were present. Aside from a damp odour, the predominant smell was that of a strong disinfectant mixed with something sickly sweet Kennedy couldn't quite place.

None of them spoke. Around the first bend of the corridor they spied a second tunnel veering to the left, with a kind of indentation on the right side, just by the bend. By the time they reached that point, Kennedy and his colleagues had worked out that it was a door. Kennedy signed for Irvine and Coles to stay there.

He followed the left-hand turn, which moved up a steep incline. At the end of this corridor was a door. It was identical to the one they'd first come through, with beams of natural daylight spilling through the padlock holes and sharply defining the gaps between the door and its frame. Kennedy approached it cautiously. As he was about to take a peek, he was thrown back by a combination of sheer volume and by the air-flow of a train as it whooshed past within a few feet of the door. His heart missed at least a beat or two. That close, the sound was deafening. In a matter of seconds it was gone, leaving only the whisper of the wind on the railway lines and the drip-drip of water on brick. One of the tunnel's functions was obviously to provide a direct connection between the railway track and the canal.

As he walked back to where Coles and Irvine were waiting, Kennedy felt instinctively that something was not quite right. If his suspicions were correct, Josef Jones had murdered twice and here they were walking unprotected into his... The detective didn't really know what it was they were walking into. Could it be a trap, wired with explosives? Or could he be waiting for them with a knife, a gun or even – Kennedy flashed – a lethal Chunky Kit Kat? He decided not to share this thought with his colleagues.

By the time Kennedy reached them, Irvine had successfully picked the lock to the only internal door in the brick corridor.

The door creaked like it was a prop in one of the old Hammer horror movie sets. Irvine gave the door one energetic tug, hoping to get all the alarm-raising noise over in as quick a time as possible.

The underground chamber they discovered was constructed entirely of nine-inch red brick. Even the curved roof and the four support pillars were red brick. It reminded Kennedy of the original Cavern Club in Liverpool, where the Fab Four had made 292 appearances.

Unlike the entrance corridor – and unlike the Cavern Club, for that matter – the internal walls were incredibly dry. The four columns symmetrically divided the thirty-foot square chamber into nine open-plan units. The central one appeared to be some kind of living area, with two sofas and a couple of easy chairs (all a mix-and-match), arranged in a circle around a long, deep wooden chest that served as a coffee table. Various cups and saucers, sugar bowl, milk carton, and a plate of chocolate biscuits were positioned on top of the chest, as if the inhabitants of the chamber had been disturbed during afternoon tea.

The cups were empty, so another explanation could be that Jones was a lazy sod who just hadn't bothered to clear up. The ceiling was nearly twice the height of the corridor, hence the need for a steep slope down from both the canal and the railway track.

The chamber had obviously been built as a holding area for goods of some kind. They would have arrived by barge and would have been stored here until collected by train, or vice versa. Kennedy was aware that there wasn't much of a crossover between the rail and water routes. The railway system pretty much saw off the barges, relegating them to carrying tourists, in a matter of years.

The unit immediately on the left as they came in, was walled off with hardboard, and the others were pretty much open-plan, although six-foot-high bookshelves did partition off much of the right-hand corner unit. This, Kennedy supposed, was a study area. There were plenty of books on the shelves and about the floor. They were mostly about music and the music business. Also scattered around the floor were piles of magazines: *Q*, *Mojo* and *Music Week* seemed to predominate. In the central area of the study was a rather cheap pine desk and chair and, on the wall, a cork noticeboard.

The noticeboard was crammed with photos, CD jackets, record sleeves, newspaper cuttings, all related to Esther Bluewood. The noticeboard had recently been updated displaying the current press reports on Miss Bluewood's death. Lined up, pride of place and in the centre, were obituaries of the artist.

One of the back shelving units seemed to buckle under the strain of Esther Bluewood memorabilia: posters, photographs, publicity handouts, display units for shops, even a four-foot-high cardboard cut-out of Esther Bluewood holding a copy of her *Resurrection* album jacket. This was a one-off and stood against the unit. Apart from this, the collector – and Kennedy assumed Jones was the collector in question – had several copies of each item, suggesting that he was a dealer, as well as a collector.

The cardboard cut-out of Esther looked quite eerie because, although she was smiling and lively in her pose, she seemed a prisoner in these surroundings. It brought home to Kennedy how such an innocent pose could be the launch pad for someone less innocent's fantasy. In the case of Silly Spice and the mobile she used to launch her career, it just didn't bear thinking about...

The pine chair, which matched the desk, was draped with Jones'

trademark black suit jacket: all four buttons present and neatly
lined up and down one side of the chair. Kennedy was happy to see
the jacket. Although it was very cold outside, the chamber was quite
warm, thanks to several free-standing radiators. Kennedy took a
note to check if they were the same as those used by the Jazz Café.
Jones couldn't be too far away, unless he'd heard them coming and
scampered out via the railway track exit. Kennedy thought not,
they'd surely have spotted him attempting such an escape.

In another of the alcoves, the one in the far right-hand corner
was a makeshift bed. It was made up of a double mattress placed
over two single camp beds, with two bottle-green sleeping bags
lying on top of the blue and (once) white striped mattress.

In this sleeping area there was a armless chair and a couple of
boxes. Kennedy checked the boxes. They had both originally
contained Bushmills Whiskey, but from what Kennedy could
gather, they were now the home for several different bottles: cham-
pagne, red and white wine, some empty, some still sealed. Both
cases had felt-tipped on their sides 'Jazz Café, NW1'. Obviously
Jones had been entertaining at the expense of his employers.

Kennedy tried to figure out what the exact reason was for this
place. Why had Josef Jones set up camp here? It could have been for
any number of overtly devious reasons. He'd tried to bring Amanza
here when she felt he was feeling amorous, so he obviously wasn't
scared of letting his friends know the place existed. Perhaps he'd
planned to bring her back for 'unsanctioned relations' – that was
how Kennedy remembered the Portrush clergy describing it in the
days of his youth, anyway. Whatever… bring her back here for a bit
of the other and murder her as well. Perhaps Jones' plan had been
not to let her live to tell the tale of his secret hiding place. Why had
he, then? Had she kicked up so much of a fuss at the gate he couldn't
risk attracting other people's attention?

Then again, would he really have risked bringing someone down
here, down into this chamber and risked them seeing all the Esther
Bluewood paraphernalia, and then let them live to tell the tale?
Kennedy thought not. Amanza's aversion to mice and rats, not to
mention her aversion to Jones, had probably saved her life.

Kennedy's mind immediately moved on to Jones' other potential
victims. Had he killed anyone down here, behind the doors of his
chamber? There were no obvious deadly implements in view. He
couldn't smell anything in the air other than the mixture of disinfectant and the sickly air refresher.

As Kennedy moved around the chamber as quietly as was possible, he figured the floor plan was like a noughts and crosses skeleton. The central position was the living room. Top right was the bedroom. Bottom right was the study. Centre left was the doorway. Bottom left was a store area, where cardboard boxes, stacks of newspapers, CDs, bottles, Marks and Spencer plastic shopping bags containing rubbish were scattered around. The secrets of the top left-hand unit were hidden behind hardboard walls, solid walls with no visible doors.

Jones had cleverly decided to give himself breathing space by having all of his units adjoining a free space. Or perhaps these units were for future further development? What was it with boys and their secret hiding places, Kennedy wondered? He'd been as guilty as the next in his childhood. He and his mates would always be off exploring secret caves, building huts among the sand dunes or even commandeering local farmers' disused corrugated sheds. But at certain times of the year, the gang would return to the secret place only to find their stash, magazines – *Tit Bits* was as risqué as it got in those days – spare clothes, tins of baked beans (always popular), bows and arrows, lances, etc. smouldering in a fire outside the freshly cleared shed, which by then would be housing hay or something equally seasonal.

Irvine and Kennedy met up at the section walled in by plasterboard. They scanned the entire wall with their hands, trying to find an entrance. None was visible to the eye, but Kennedy gently pushed at each section, hoping he might activate a spring lock. None obliged.

He moved on to the floor on all fours. There was perhaps a quarter of an inch gap at the bottom, but Kennedy could neither see nor hear anything. He checked the plasterboard once more. He was convinced one of the sections would spring open some way and they would find Josef Jones sitting within, grinning like a Glamorganshire cat. He put his ear to the smooth walls, he was sure he could hear sounds on the inside, but he couldn't be convinced that he wasn't hearing the sounds of water in the distance. Every time he thought he was managing to get a focus on a sound, a train would swoosh past, causing a major racket and displacing the air in each and every corner of the chamber. Hence, Kennedy thought, the reason the air in the chamber was so fresh.

Kennedy had an idea.

He signalled for Coles and Irvine to join him near the external door, appearing to be making as much of a racket as possible as he walked. He winked at them and said loudly: 'Okay, we've obviously missed him!' Kennedy winked again. 'Let's head back to the Jazz Café and see if we can pick up his trail again. DS Irvine, radio in to North Bridge House and have them send a couple of people to Jones' flat. He's bound to turn up there sooner or later.'

Kennedy then ushered his two colleagues out of the chamber and made a big deal out of closing the door behind them, while he remained silently inside the chamber. He tiptoed over to the central living area where he quietly lowered himself into the chair that directly faced the plasterboard walls. His plan was to wait and catch Mr Jones returning through his secret door. He was annoyed with himself for not thinking of such a good tactic before.

Forty minutes later, he wasn't quite so sure it had been such a good plan.

He checked his watch, deciding to give it another ten minutes. Josef was doing a neat impression of his namesake, 'No Show Jones'.

Nine minute after he'd positively decided to leave, Kennedy heard a creaking, but just then another train rushed past and he couldn't be sure what he'd heard, or if he'd heard anything at all. But no, there it was again: a creaking. A smaller creak than the door creak, but a creak nonetheless. He tried to eye every single section of plasterboard on the two walls simultaneously to see which of them was going to give way first.

There was more creaking, but still no signs of any movement in the walls. The creaking continued. Just a little at a time, but each appearing to be closer to Kennedy than the walls. He figured it must be a natural echo in the chamber.

Then the strangest thing happened.

The cups and milk carton on the top of the chest coffee table started to levitate. This was just too spooky for Kennedy. Were his eyes deceiving him? He could have sworn the cups and saucers, the plates of biscuits and the milk carton were rising. They were all moving upwards, albeit at an angle, but heavenwards nonetheless. Kennedy shook his head violently. He'd been sitting in the chair for close to an hour. Perhaps he'd started to drift off.

Then the penny dropped. Mr Josef Jones had been hiding in the chest. He'd fixed all the bits and pieces to the top of the wooden chest-cum-coffee table, just like at a mad hatter's tea party, so that no one, such as the members of Camden Town CID for instance, would suspect anyone would be hiding within.

Fortunately for Kennedy, the lid was rising toward him, so Jones was blindsided. Kennedy sat contentedly in his chair, the smile on his face growing in direct proportion to how far the lid was opening. The lid was now raised to its full height and Jones' silhouette began to appear over the edge. He was looking away from Kennedy, in the direction of the door.

"Ah, Mr Jones, I presume?' Kennedy asked loudly, as much for the benefit of Coles and Irvine patiently waiting out in the corridor. 'We've been expecting you.'

Jones made a wild dash for the door, only to be greeted, and apprehended, by Coles and Irvine.

'You shouldn't be so hasty, Josef,' Kennedy said, rather pleased with himself. 'You nearly forgot your classic four-button jacket. You'll catch your death of cold out there without it!'

Chapter 39

BACK IN North Bridge House, Kennedy wasn't quite so pleased with himself. Yes, he had his prime suspect ready for questioning in the interview room, but the majority of the detective's evidence was circumstantial.

Take for instance, the nanny, Judy Dillon. Any forensic evidence they had against Jones was useless the second he'd admitted he'd had sex with her. It was up to Kennedy to prove that he'd done more. Even the motive, the supposed motive, was as flimsy as a Mills and Boon plot. Jones had supposedly murdered the nanny because she didn't have Esther Bluewood's journal. This would have been more believable if he'd killed her because she *had* the journal (and not just a photocopy) and if the journal had been found on Jones' person.

And then there was Esther Bluewood's murder. Jones had gone out of his way to show that Esther was capable of suicide. This was a matter of public record; she'd even confessed it openly on several tracks on *Axis*. Then he'd supposedly murdered her by gassing her and making it appear a suicide.

Kennedy supposed if it hadn't been for Doc Watson, ann rea, Esther's mother and his own niggling doubts – activated by the sight of the two distressed children standing hand in hand, dressed in pyjamas – he too would have accepted Esther Bluewood's death as suicide. Kennedy knew, especially after reading the journal, that Esther Bluewood would never have risked the possibility of her children finding her dead body on the kitchen floor.

Kennedy felt that he was taking on board all of these thoughts and images in much the same way a Roman gladiator would put on his armour to protect him during the battle ahead.

Kennedy had plenty of arrows to shoot, but it was going to be up to Jones himself to show one of the arrows its target. The detective could not delay shooting the first target-seeking arrow any longer. He walked into the interview room.

DC Lundy was already in position by the door, keeping an eye on Josef Jones. Also present was Jones' solicitor, Harry Thomas. Thomas was unshaven and wore a grubby white shirt, opened untidily at the collar, no tie, a pair of denim jeans and blue

Timberland deck shoes with no socks. His hair was brown and dishevelled and he had a faraway look in his eyes. If a stranger had walked into the room with Kennedy and viewed the two characters sharing the accused's side of the table, then he might have been forgiven for confusing the accused with his legal representative.

Looks are often deceptive, but Mr Harry Thomas would not have fooled DI Kennedy for a second. Kennedy knew that Jones had picked his brief very carefully, for there was no one better read on criminal law in Camden Town than Harry Thomas. Few in the legal profession were as shrewd as the scruffy solicitor. He was so committed to his profession that everything else – clothes, looks, personal relationships, socialising and feeding habits – all took second place.

Kennedy immediately removed his dark blue jacket and carefully placed it on the back of the chair directly across from the solicitor, diagonal to the suspect. Irvine, fully togged in his tweeds and brogues, sat beside his superior and directly opposite Josef Jones.

'Okay,' Kennedy began, clearing his throat. 'Let's get started, shall we? This shouldn't take long.'

'I'd prefer,' Harry Thomas said, his accent broad Glaswegian, 'that we put this on record.'

Without further ado, Kennedy hit the record button, announced the date and time and identified those present. He had Irvine read Josef Jones his rights and the show was ready to hit the road.

Kennedy sat opposite the solicitor for good reason: he wanted it to appear to Jones that this was all a formality. That in a way, Jones wasn't so much the suspect as the guilty party and, as such, had little or no role to play in the proceedings.

Jones, on the other hand, wasn't one of those detainees who smirked and gave off an air of 'you'll never make it stick'. Nor did he appear either scared or guilty. You could almost imagine him putting up his hands and saying, 'Okay, hit me with the best you've got.'

'So, Josef,' Kennedy began, stretching out as much as his chair would allow. He swung his hand up towards his head, used one to comb his fingers through his hair, and then clasped both behind his head. 'Let's have a chat about Sunday evening, shall we?'

No response.

'You went over to Esther Bluewood's…'

'I was in my flat.' The evil shrill with which he delivered his reply seemed to shock even his solicitor.

'You told us you were in your flat waiting for Esther, but we both know you were over at her place,' Kennedy continued unabated.

'Actually, for the record, Detective Inspector, my client has stated that on Sunday evening he was in his own flat. Now, let's move on,' Harry Thomas announced, more for the benefit of the tape than for those present.

'Okay, let me rephrase my observation. Let's say we can prove that on Sunday evening, Josef Jones was in Miss Esther Bluewood's maisonette and not in his own flat as he stated.'

This announcement certainly captured the attention of both suspect and solicitor.

'And how, may I ask, can you possibly do that? I was in my flat, as I told you, waiting for her. When she didn't appear, I rang the Jazz Café to see if I could catch a shift so that the night wouldn't be a total waste of time. It so happens there was a shift going and I took it. I was working in the Jazz Café at the time Esther Bluewood committed suicide, Inspector. Everyone else seems to accept that. Why don't you?'

'It's not for us to speculate here and now about how Miss Bluewood died, Mr Jones,' Thomas cautioned his client.

Jones seemed totally taken aback by his own solicitor's reproach. Kennedy felt it was less a reproach and more a case of Thomas wishing to keep the interrogation steadily on the rails.

'Yes. We know you were at the Jazz Café at the precise time of Esther's death. We also know that you provisionally set up your Sunday shift on the previous evening,' Kennedy began.

'Not true. I was just covering myself for the eventuality that Esther might not turn up. With Esther there was always a chance that she mightn't show. Even if she had appeared, she would have been finished with me in a matter of twenty minutes or so. So what was I going to do? Hang around my flat like a spare rooster at a hen party?' Jones said, his high-pitched whine making anything he said difficult to believe. 'If you check, you'll find it normal for people to chase last minute shifts to make up their hours. There's nothing suspicious about that.'

Jones stopped and thought for a few seconds. Kennedy could see the wheels turning behind his eyes. The detective knew that Jones had something further to add. He had a very good feeling about what the fanatic was going to say, so he left him the space to say it.

'You've just admitted,' the squeaky voice began, 'that you knew I was working at the Jazz Café at the time of Esther's death?'

'I said, I knew you were at the Jazz Café at the precise time of her death,' Kennedy confirmed.

'Whatever,' Jones barked impatiently. 'What does it matter? Maybe I didn't use your exact words. But the long and the short of it is surely that I was in the Jazz Café in front of numerous witnesses when she died. So my question to you would have to be, what precisely are we doing right now? By your own admission it doesn't really matter how Esther died. By her own hand or even by someone else's. We have proof it wasn't by my hand. I was somewhere else at the time.'

Jones sat back in his chair. He seemed rather pleased with his deduction. He turned to Thomas and smiled. Thomas didn't return his client's smile. He rubbed his unshaven chin, doing his best country bumpkin impression, perhaps suggesting 'gee, inspector, he just might have something there'.

'Okay, then,' Kennedy said, unclasping his hands from behind his head, swinging forward towards the table and reclasping them in front of him, 'for the benefit of your brief, DS Irvine, and the vital tape recorder, let me explain exactly how it was that you appeared to be in two places at the same time...'

Irvine leaned into the table, copying Kennedy's movement and trying to conceal a little grin, which suggested 'well, this should be interesting'.

'Well, this should be interesting,' Harry Thomas said, as he too leaned over the table.

Kennedy glanced diagonally across the table, only to find Jones ready, willing and able to lock into direct eye contact.

Well, this should be interesting, Kennedy thought as he started to speak: 'Okay. At some time during the early evening on Sunday you visited Esther Bluewood in her maisonette—'

'But...' Jones started, his shriek easily drowning out Kennedy's quiet gentle voice.

'Yes, yes, Josef,' continued Kennedy. 'We've already been around that house a few times so let's try and move forward this time. You were with her in her accommodation. You were with her for whatever reason, her gratification or your fanaticism, it doesn't really matter at this stage. All that matters is that you were there. It would be my opinion that you helped and encouraged Esther with her sleeping tablets. Perhaps she wasn't even aware she was taking them, but they did make her very drowsy.'

Again Jones made signs of protest. This time Kennedy silenced him by merely raising his hand. Kennedy found it as effective as a lollipop man's sign on duty outside the local school.

'Pretty soon she passed out. You then burnt off all the gas left on the meter by lighting all the hobs and the oven on the cooker. When the gas burnt off and the meter was in need of feeding, you were careful to turn all the taps back to the off position.' Kennedy stopped for a moment to take in his audience. Irvine looked intrigued, as did Lundy and Thomas, but Jones' face gave absolutely nothing away.

'The first thing that made me think something was up was that Esther Bluewood fingerprints should have been the last ones on the cooker knobs. That, of course, would have been the case if indeed she had gassed herself.'

Kennedy paused again, and this time shrugged a 'what a silly boy I am?' with help from his shoulders, mouth and chin.

'No! I thought,' Kennedy continued, 'of course not. The last prints on the knobs would of course be those of the person who'd found Esther. They would surely have turned the gas off when they entered the flat and discovered the body. When I checked this, the gasman told me that when he came on to the scene, the knobs had already been turned off. Judy Dillon had not been into the maisonette before raising the alarm, so she couldn't have turned the gas off. She had even fainted from the shock of finding Esther's body when she entered with the gasman.'

Jones looked like he was about to say something. He glanced at Thomas and seemed to think better of it.

'So,' Kennedy went on, 'I wondered how anyone could possibly gas themselves without a supply of gas. Dr Taylor assured me that Miss Bluewood had died from gas poisoning. Yes, he'd also found traces of her sleeping pills in her blood, but not enough to kill her, just enough to send her into a deep sleep. That set me thinking about another supply of gas.'

Irvine appeared lost. Kennedy smiled at him briefly before continuing: 'The whole thing was set up brilliantly to look like a suicide, you know. The towel in the mouth of the oven so Miss Bluewood would feel comfortable. I'm told that the discomfort of a severe crick in the neck can divert would-be suicides from their objective. The other towel was strategically positioned behind the kitchen door, apparently displaying Esther's concern for her children's welfare. A mother as loving as Miss Bluewood would most definitely have ensured her children were protected from escaping gas, had she decided to end her own life…'

'Yes. Yes,' Jones squeaked dismissively. 'That's all very well. She was a wonderful person and a great mother and it would no doubt be a great plot for Miss Marple, but we're all agreed I was elsewhere when all of this was going on.'

'True, true, Josef,' Kennedy said, a smile creeping across his face. He took much comfort from the fact Jones continued to assert that he was absent during the death, rather than saying he hadn't been involved in it. 'I'm getting to that now, and a very ingenious idea it was, too. Two points gave me the clues as to what you were up to. In Miss Bluewood's journal she made reference to how handy you were around the house, always fixing things, soldering this, gluing that, nailing the other, and so on. It seems you're every bit the wee handyman with your tool bag. The second thing was the marks on the oilcloth in Esther's kitchen. You know, Josef, where you pulled the cupboard out from the wall?'

Josef laughed, or tried to laugh. He was quite convincing, Kennedy thought. His whine made the laugh sound more like a wheeze, but he'd made the point.

'What on earth are you on about, Inspector?' Jones said, and then glared at his solicitor as if to say 'do we really have to put up with all of this?'.

Either Harry Thomas didn't pick up the look or he chose to ignore it. Kennedy gave him the benefit of the doubt and decided that the solicitor had decided to ignore his client.

'At first I dismissed the marks on the oilcloth as marks made by someone who had moved the cupboard out from the wall for cleaning purposes. I even thought they might have been caused when the cupboard was originally being positioned against the wall,' Kennedy said quietly.

Everyone at the table related to that for a few seconds before Kennedy continued.

'Then I noticed the pipe from the gas meter and a second pipe parallel to and half an inch below it disappeared along the wall behind the cupboard. The second pipe supplied water to the radiator in the kitchen. When I moved the cupboard out from the wall and saw…' Kennedy paused this time for effect before admitting, 'well, not a lot really. Just two pipes running parallel along the wall about half an inch apart. One, as we said, to carry the gas supply from the gas meter to the cooker and the other, the bottom one, to take the hot water from the electric boiler to the radiator.'

Although he hoped he wasn't showing it, Kennedy was growing perplexed by Jones' apparent indifference to these revelations.

'Under the pipes, however, was a little…' Kennedy resumed his narrative, using his thumb and forefinger to demonstrate how little he meant, 'dirt and amongst the dirt were a couple of tiny specs of candle wax. Initially I thought maybe there'd been a repair, but on closer examination I found that the repair was in fact a piece of gaffer tape wrapped around the pipe. I thought someone had been careless about the repair but I bet you if we went back there now and removed the tape we'd find a hole, probably made with a large nail. My guess would be that you made that hole with the nail and then used candle wax to fill up the nail hole and seal the pipe again. You wouldn't have used hot candle wax but would have allowed it to cool so it would just be malleable enough to fit the hole.

'The rest was simple. You fed the meter with several 50p pieces, just enough to allow sufficient gas through to kill her. Sadly, Esther herself probably supplied enough details of how much gas it would take to kill a human. You set the timer on the central heating to come on at the time you knew you'd be in the Jazz Café.

'At the designated time the central heating system sprang into action, pumping hot water through the pipes in the direction of the cold hungry radiators. The hot water pipe behind the cupboard would have heated up the gas pipe next to it and the combination of the heat and the pressure of the gas would have melted the wax, clearing the hole. The gas would have escaped into the air in the kitchen. I believe when we carry out our investigation more fully, we'll find some deposits of wax inside the pipe, as well.

'As I say, the candle wax melted, the gas escaped, filling the kitchen, where by now you'd placed the comatose Esther Bluewood. The gas does its job and kills her. Then the meter runs out and conveniently stops the supply of gas. You returned briefly in the middle of the night to seal the pipe with the gaffer tape and do any tidying up you felt was necessary. You missed a couple of specs of candle wax though, Josef,' Kennedy said finally.

He'd completed the theory part of his presentation. Only one of the four present seemed unimpressed with his story.

'That's all fine and grand, Inspector,' said Thomas, much to Jones' relief, 'and as good a tale as I've ever heard. However, there is nothing, absolutely nothing, that ties my client into any of it in any way and so… if that is all you have…'

'Oh,' Kennedy said, dissipating the relief totally, 'there's a wee bit more. A wee bit more in fact that ties your client directly to the scene of the crime.'

'And that is?' Jones felt compelled to ask.

'And that is, the 50p pieces in the gas meter. Remember I was telling you about feeding the meter with enough coins to ensure that Esther would be killed? Four of the coins used to feed the meter were found to have Josef's fingerprints on them…'

'But they couldn't possibly! I was wearing gloves…' the words fell out of Jones' mouth in that classic way a suspect traps and convicts himself with his own big mouth. The way it happens, contrary to popular opinion, as much in real life as it does in the movies.

'Thanks for you affirmation of that fact, Josef. Just in case your solicitor has any ideas about trying to have that evidence excluded for whatever reason, can I just advise you both that, yes, you probably did wear gloves when you were doing your dirty work, but you forgot to wipe the coins prior to putting on the gloves, leaving one clear fingerprint, which I'll bet when we check it with your prints, comes from your earlier usage of the coins.'

*

A few minutes later, Josef Jones was charged with the murder of Esther Bluewood and locked in a cell. Kennedy was sure that the ongoing Judy Dillon investigation would be fruitful and that it wouldn't be long before Jones confessed to that murder, too, either out of guilt or – more likely – pride.

'He was a cool customer, sir.' Irvine said, back in Kennedy's office. They were enjoying a cup of tea and starting to sift through the existing evidence on the Judy Dillon case.

'Mmmm, James, I'm not so sure "cool" is quite the adjective. More like shell-shocked, I'd say. I genuinely think he thought he'd committed the perfect crime and that he was going to get away with it. The sad think for me, James, is that he is showing absolutely no remorse.'

'But why did he kill Esther Bluewood, sir?'

'Well, ironically, I'd say it was because he was such a big fan of hers. A fanatic, in other words,' Kennedy said.

'But surely he already had the biggest possible scalp on his belt? He was sleeping with her, wasn't he?' Irvine said, simply and honestly, for he knew no other way.

'Yes, but he also had an ego,' Kennedy began energetically. 'Look how well he dressed. It must be extremely difficult to continuously dress in fine designer clothes on what he earns, but he struggles to do so. Esther said in her journal that she was using him – she never let him get to the point of his own sexual relief. This probably drove him mad. To add insult to injury, she stood him up. Perhaps that was the proverbial straw that broke the camel's back. Perhaps he'd heard she was leaving, perhaps his parents beat him, perhaps a lot of things… whatever… he was cold and calculating about it all. I don't like to dwell on why people commit the crimes they do, or get preoccupied with all that mitigating social circumstances stuff. I don't like feeling sorry for people who have just committed murder. Especially when it leaves behind two motherless children.'

'God, if you hadn't picked up on it, you know his plan of execution… I mean, I've got to hand it to him, sir, that was pretty amazing really – and to yourself as well, sir, for piecing it all together. Incredible, just incredible,' Irvine gasped.

Kennedy had a problem dealing with compliments. Yes, he was a proud man; proud of how he did his work. But when it got down to it, he preferred people to think, rather than voice, their praise.

'Oh, we were in it together, James. I'm just fortunate to be the one who gets the glory of putting it all together,' Kennedy said as modestly as he could, hoping his DS would drop the subject. He'd much rather be discussing the intricacies of the case rather than how clever he was at solving it.

'But with the Dillon murder, sir, didn't you find that surprising? I mean, Jones' involvement, particularly after how clean and tidy he'd been with Bluewood's murder, to then go to the other extreme and be so downright careless.'

'I'm not so sure, James, really,' said Kennedy, replenishing their tea cups. 'Remember, we still don't have anything positive to tie him to her murder,' Kennedy said.

'Yeah. But he did admit he had sex with the nanny on the evening she was brutally murdered,' Irvine protested.

'Aye, true,' Kennedy replied, returning to his seat. 'But don't you see, again he may think he's been very, very clever! I think he believes it was a crime of passion. I don't happen to believe that it was. I think he believed that Judy Dillon had the original copy of journal and he was desperate to get it just in case Esther had written something that might have incriminated him down the line. I believe he was trying to protect himself, to hide anything that might have lead us to the original murder. He wasn't to know that there was nothing incriminating in the journal.'

'Perhaps,' Irvine conceded.

'I think he went to Judy Dillon's flat with the intention of secur-ing the journal and murdering her so that she couldn't spill the beans on him. Let's consider this again, James,' Kennedy said, as he reopened the Judy Dillon file.

Irvine thought, but said nothing.

'He goes around there, has sex with her and kills her. By admit-ting to us that he had sex with her it means that there was no need to wear gloves or to tidy up after himself. His logic works, you see. He knows his sexual involvement with her will have made it very difficult to identify him as her killer. In effect, what he's saying to us is, 'Yes, I had sex with her. But prove I killed her.' No one saw them. He didn't knife her and leave a chance of us finding the knife. He didn't shoot her with a gun. He didn't bludgeon her over the head with a blunt object leaving fingerprints and the chance that specks of blood might turn up on his clothes or body.'

'So how do we prove he killed her, sir?' Irvine asked.

'Well, number one, we don't really need to. He's going to be going away for quite some time for the murder of Esther Bluewood. Number two, I wouldn't mind betting you a few bob that his ego will encourage him to sing in the end. There are only two reasons to commit the perfect crime. The first is so you can get away with it, scot-free. The second is so others will admire your handiwork. He's been caught for a different crime, but that stops him getting clean away with the murder. So really, there's no reason for him to deny the nanny's homicide. He can stand back and bask in the glory he no doubt believes he deserves.'

'And if he doesn't, sir?'

'And if he doesn't, James,' Kennedy replied, passing half the files on the Judy Dillon case to his colleague on the other side of the desk, 'then, I'm afraid that's where you and I will have to step in. You see, the perfect crime only exists in theory. In practice, there's always going to be something, some little thing left behind or something said, something that will eventually catch the perpetrator out. I bet you if we look closely at these files, James, we'll find that little some-thing that will prove that Mr Josef Jones isn't quite as clever as he thought he was. So, if you get stuck in, I'll get another brew started.'

Chapter 40

SATURDAY MORNING: the first Saturday morning of the rest of their lives, and Kennedy and ann rea were woken up before daylight by the dawn chorus. Kennedy was convinced that a bat led the Primrose Hill chorus. The logic being that it seemed to matter not a lot that darkness still covered the area, the birds were up before daylight and causing a racket every single morning of the year. In spring and summer it was good to be woken up, so as to experience the breathtaking sunrises. But these cold, dark and wet wintry mornings were different.

The truce between Kennedy and ann rea had got off to a great start. Kennedy was slightly (but only slightly) worried that they'd been in conflict for so long now that maybe without that edge, their relationship would lose its focus. It would be just great, he thought, to be allowed to melt away into the relationship and enjoy it.

ann rea interrupted the racket outside their window: 'This is good.'

Kennedy couldn't argue with that. He had what he'd been looking for. She, for her part, had lost the doubts that had clouded both their lives for so long. He responded with, 'Yeah, this is good.'

Sorry? he thought, This is *good*?

He thought back to the first time he'd met ann rea, at Heathrow Airport. He recalled how attracted he was to her, how she literally left him breathless. He thought of the very slow start to their relationship. Her discouragement. The (what seemed to him, at least) ages it took to get their relationship off the ground and then the numerous seas of stormy waters they'd had to sail through.

Now here they were, survivors of all that fate had thrown at them and he thought of the lyrics of a Jackson Browne song:

> *See – I always figured there was going to be someone here*

He mentally fast-forwarded to another part of the same lyric:

> *Anyway…*
> *I guess you wouldn't know unless I told you*
> *But…*
> *I love you*

Well just look at yourself –
What else would I do?

Kennedy did look at ann rea and in that moment he agreed, why on earth wouldn't he love her?

And then they wound themselves around each other and fell asleep again.

Could this be true happiness? Enjoying a Saturday morning lie-in? It had been such a long hard climb and then such little respite.

An hour later the phone beside the bed rang.

Kennedy came round slowly and managed to answer on the seventh ring.

'Sorry to disturb you, sir.'

It was Detective Sergeant Irvine, as apologetic as it was possible to be.

'Yes, James?'

'I'm at the Free House near the Royal Hospital. You'd better get over here quick. We've just found the body of a young girl.'

'Yeah?'

'She's a nurse, sir.'

'Yeah?'

'We found a photograph in her wallet, sir.'

'Yeah?'

'It's a photograph of the same nurse and Dr Ranjesus, sir.'

'I'll be right over, James.'

AND FINALLY...

For the music, I thank Mary Margaret O'Hara for her ground-breaking work, *Miss America*, which I used as a template for Esther Bluewood's *Axis*. Other albums which helped put the leaves on the trees were Jackson Browne's *I'm Alive*, Blue Nile's *Peace At Last*, and last, but by no means least, Nick Lowe's evergreen *Dig My Mood*.

The lyrics quoted on the final page are from Jackson Browne's 'Hold On Hold Out'. The song was written by Jackson Browne and Craig Doerge and appears on the *Hold Out* album, and a very fine work it is too. The lyrics are reproduced by kind permission of Swallow Turn Music and Fair Star music – thanks a million to Buddha and Clee.

It's important to note that this is a work of fiction and I thank you for reading it.

Paul Charles
Camden Town
August, 2001

The Do-Not Press
Fiercely Independent Publishing

Keep in touch with what's happening at the cutting edge of independent British publishing.

Simply send your name and address to:
The Do-Not Press (Dept. HISS)
16 The Woodlands, London SE13 6TY (UK)

or email us: hissing@thedonotpress.co.uk

There is no obligation to purchase
(although we'd certainly like you to!)
and no salesman will call.

Visit our regularly-updated web site:
http://www.thedonotpress.co.uk

Mail Order

All our titles are available from good bookshops, or (in case of difficulty) direct from The Do-Not Press at the address above. There is no charge for post and packing for orders to the UK and EU.

(NB: A post-person may call.)